BRADL

and the Cu

To: Ruby

Best wishes

DAVID LAWRENCE JONES

BRADLEY BAKER

and the Curse of Pathylon

Amazing Adventures of Bradley Baker

THE PATHYLON TRILOGY – BOOK ONE

Cover illustrated by Abie Greyvenstein

Author's Official Website: bradley-baker.com
Become a fan of Bradley Baker: facebook.com/thebradleybaker

ISBN 978-0-9561499-3-0

5

First published in the UK 2011
Avocado Publishing - Devon United Kingdom
www.avocadopublishing.co.uk

This book is dedicated to

Lindsey, Samuel, Benjamin & Harriette

…and to Tracey who read it first!

. . . .

HYLON

FREYTOR

Volcano

City of Cor

City of Frey

The Red Ocean

N

W   E

S

Wolf Cowl

Hooked Point

REKAB

Yeldarb Forest

The Satorc Sea

Crystal City

Pyramids of Blood

Emerald Caves

1

The Long Journey

A huge iceberg has drifted slowly across the Red Ocean from the arctic region of Freytor. The journey's end is near and it moves effortlessly towards the shores of Devonia, one of the five regions that make up the medieval world of Pathylon.

Warm waters and strong currents have honed what shipbuilders would consider a streamlined hull out of a once shapeless lump of ice. The rear of the structure towers above what could almost be described as a ship's deck and has now taken on the appearance of a gigantic sail. Smaller blocks of ice have accompanied it during the long journey and they continue to sail close by like a fleet of naval frigates in support of their mother ship.

A strange species called Freytorians are working on board the arctic craft. They are an intelligent crew of polar bear creatures that walk upright and move briskly within the iceberg structure in order to keep warm. Their costumes are made from stitched animal pelts to protect them from the wintry conditions inside the vessel and their harpoon weapons are used to great effect, as they scavenge like pirates across the continents. They are a forceful species who struggle to trade with other lands and their leaders are keen to clean up their ruthless image.

Their frozen homeland of Freytor has grown barren and they are running out of food. This particular journey has been planned with careful precision and endorsed as a mission of peace. They have travelled to seek out new opportunities and to barter their valuable *grobite* currency in exchange for much needed provisions.

Pathylon is known throughout the ancient world as a reliable resource for quality food produce and minerals. Representatives from Freytor's remote continent have continuously failed with bids to secure a recognised trading agreement. Members of the Pathylian Royal Congress have always denied the Freytorians access to their shores because they were viewed untrustworthy. This particular voyage must prove fruitful and the crew has worked efficiently throughout the long journey to transform the drifting block of ice into a fully functional sea-worthy craft.

The iceberg has been adapted to incorporate all the latest nautical computer technology. Its incredible speed is generated from both the wind powered ice-sail and a water propelled turbine located deep below sea level within the structure. A series of tunnels have been mined with great precision to connect the engine room to a vast number of living chambers and administration quarters inside the ship.

The transformation and conversion of the vessel has been overseen by a veteran General called Eidar. The muscular creature stands over seven feet tall and appears very concerned, as he looks seaward from the ice-carved command bridge. The grey-bearded giant snarled an aggressive command, as he focused the lens of his extended telescope to magnify the enormous rock that appeared in the distance. "Two degrees West!"

"Aye-Aye General Eidar," replied the first mate, as he entered the new co-ordinates into the iceberg's mainframe computer.

The General placed a large paw over the lens and closed the telescope with an assertive stroke, as he turned to address the command bridge. "We have travelled far my friends and all that stands before us is that rock directly ahead… soon we will launch the landing crafts and deliver our message of peace to this world they call Pathylon!"

Eidar was not supposed to have taken on this particular mission. He was an Army General and head of the Freytorian ground forces. His knowledge of the open seas was limited to the training room, however his aggressive leadership was necessary to ensure the journey was a success. His younger twin brother Admiral Norsk was supposed to have commanded the voyage to Pathylon but he was too busy developing a new underwater craft that would transform the Freytorian Navy into an elite force. So Admiral Norsk remained back in Freytor, whilst Eidar held the responsibility of securing their ice-bound homeland's future.

The General turned to face the sea again and extended the telescope once more to view the silhouette of the rock projecting out of the water against the crimson seascape. It simulated the upturned bow of a shipwreck, as the reflection from the red skies above covered its jagged edge with a warm glow. The first rays of sunlight now descended upon the calm shimmering sea and the whole sky was ablaze with the dawn of a new day.

The great iceberg sailed closer towards the rock and the crew made their final preparations to enter the mainland's estuary. The icy command bridge was still a hive of activity and the Freytorian General continued to deliver his instructions.

The bright neon lights emanated from the ship's computers and illuminated the control desks. The navigators were engaged with their compasses making precise calculations on their nautical charts to avoid a possible collision with the large rock.

Before embarking on this long journey, General Eidar had researched the archives and discovered that the rock obstructing the ships safe passage was a small deserted island, known throughout the ancient world as the mystical *Island of Restak*. "Have you entered the new co-ordinates into the ship's computer?" he roared and took his place in the ice-carved command chair.

"All readings look okay, Sir," replied one of the ship's navigators, as a nervous tension spread across the bridge.

"Readings look... okay?" confirmed Eidar, as the huge vessel started to negotiate the needle-like rocks that surrounded the small island. "Looks okay... is not good enough you idiot - I need a more definite reading than okay you fool!"

"What I meant to say was, err... I meant to say, Sir..." stuttered the terrified navigator.

"Stop mumbling, you imbecile!" growled the General, as he rose from his seat. "And give me a straight answer... now!"

The General marched over to the navigator and struck him around the head with his huge white paw. The crewman cowered, as Eidar took hold of his collar and tossed him across the bridge like a heavy piece of navigational equipment. "Get out of my way and let me do it... you incompetent moron!" he roared and started to type in the correct co-ordinates into the computer.

The angry Freytorian successfully navigated the ice-vessel around the rock and his controlled maneuver was greeted with a mass celebration and a huge sense of relief. A chorus of cheers and applause began to echo across the command bridge, as the petrified navigator got back to his feet. Still nursing his wounds, the crewman returned to his control desk and announced the General's success through the intercom system.

News of the action soon spread throughout the vessel and the ship's polar explorers began a unified chant of triumphant congratulations. The iceberg began to sway slightly in the shallow waters, as an abundance of stamping snow-boots shook the frozen craft. The bottom of the ship scraped across the shingle sea bed, as the excited activity of the thousand or more crewmembers became more intense. Eventually, a claxon sounded out from every amplifier and the celebrations finally came to an end.

The tide created by the rocking ship continued to crash against the extended hull and the waves eventually began to subside, as the glacier steadied its balance. The ship was now sturdy and this enabled the injured navigator to build up enough courage to take back control of the colossal ship. He steered the great vessel under the large metal expansion of the Satorc Bridge, which linked two of the five main regions that made up the incredible world of *Pathylon*.

The waves were still choppy and the tip of the ship's icy sail scraped the bottom of the bridge. A deathly silence fell across the decks of the iceberg, as the expanse of iron above swayed and creaked. Eventually the snowy vessel slowed to a safe berth in one of the rock-laden bays, known to visitors of Pathylon as the *Mouth of Sand.*

General Eidar calmly commended the disheveled navigator. "That's much better crewman... now let's berth this great lump of snow." He then pressed a number of illuminated buttons on the arm of his command chair and placed an order through the intercom to the engine room. "Lower the main anchor."

"With pleasure... Sir!" replied the chief engineer, as the great iron weight plunged into the water and a small tsunami resulted by crashing the warm waters against the icy hull.

General Eidar summoned his first mate and expressed a concern. "Our vessel may have sustained some damage during the arduous journey across the Red Ocean!" he snarled. "Take twenty *Rakers* and examine the sides of this thing to check for any damage – this block of ice has to take us back to Freytor... and we haven't much time!"

The first-mate summoned the Rakers, who specialized in all aspects of assault work. They were sort of like the SAS of the Freytorian Army and the General had enlisted them on the voyage to add strength in depth to the regular naval crew. The fearless beasts began to abseil down the side of the iceberg's hull and started their systematic inspection of the huge glacier.

The brilliant white structure stretched across the bay creating a barrier between the rocky cliffs of the *Satorc Estuary.* A multitude of portholes shone like jewels in parallel lines along the side of the vessel, twinkling like stars as each of the ship's inhabitants ferried through the tunnels preparing for the next stage of their expedition.

The iceberg had been anchored for some time and arrangements were being made for a scouting party to leave the ship. The clinking of chains could be heard, as a small wedge-shaped landing craft was lowered from the upper deck into the water that led into the rocky cove. Eight Freytorians emerged from a large porthole and clambered down from the ship to board the smaller boat. Seven of the scouting party struggled to maneuver an extremely heavy object into the landing craft.

The eighth member of the group roared his instructions to his fellow ice-bears. "Be careful with that thing... the contents are very precious – the General would be most annoyed if anything were to happen to it!" instructed the intimidating figure, who appeared to be directing the off-loading of a round wooden cask.

"Yes Sir!" chorused the other seven workers, as a deep grey mist surrounded the iceberg and the sound of the waves crashing against its sides produced a chilling rendition.

The team of eight Freytorians worked with great effort and precision, as they placed the container and its valuable contents at the front of the wedge-shaped landing craft. The group leader picked up one of the heavy oars and used it to push the small boat away from the icy platform. He joined the rest of the exhausted group to take a seating position and with oars at the ready they all began to row in unison towards the mainland of Pathylon.

General Eidar stood tall and watched over proceedings from the command bridge, as he muttered a concerned retort. "I hope they are successful in delivering our message of peace to the populous of Pathylon!" He groaned, as the scouting party slowly floated out of view and finally disappeared into the sea mist that lay thick around the shores of the bay. "I can't afford for anything to go wrong... if I fail to secure the trading agreement – I will suffer the consequences upon my return to Freytor!" ranted the General and waited till the mist had enveloped the landing craft before moving away from the viewing gallery.

A quivering crewmember on the command bridge approached the great white bear and saluted, as he asked tentatively. "Did the launch go as planned, Sir?"

The General ignored the trembling private and pushed his large paw against the top of the cowering sailor's head, as he strode across the control bridge. The nonchalant commander made his way towards the exit. "I will be in my quarters!" He roared and turned to the bridge supervisor to demand an update. "Call me as soon as you hear anything!"

"Aye-Aye Sir!" replied the red-faced supervisor, as the doors of the pod swished open.

General Eidar stepped into the transporter pod and turned to face his saluting command crew, as the doors swished effortlessly back together. A single electronic beep sounded and the lights above the doors flashed, as the pod elevated the muscular ice-bear direct to his penthouse suite.

2

The Evil Curse

The General was still absent from the command bridge and no communication from the launch party had been received by the crew on the ice-ship. The eight scouts had been gone for over two hours and the supervisor was growing very concerned regarding the whereabouts of his Freytorian crewmembers. A message was sent to his quarters and the order was eventually given for the deployment of more search parties to seek out the missing scouts. More landing crafts were launched, but all the searches proved futile. The thick sea mist was making the operational search very difficult so the order was given to abandon the Freytorians futile efforts.

General Eidar appeared back on the command Bridge and marched over to the viewing gallery. "Pathylon will pay for this!" he growled and tilted his head backwards to display a pristine set of razor sharp yellow fangs, as the saliva streamed from his mouth. "Get all the landing crafts back inside the ship... and let's move this lump of ice away from this blasted place!"

As ordered, all the landing crafts were hoisted back into the gigantic vessel and the anchor was raised. The iceberg was then guided gracefully back under the Satorc Bridge and out of the bay towards the Red Ocean through a haze of thick fog.

The Freytorians had travelled to Pathylon on a mission of hope to trade and make peace, but the search had failed to produce the missing landing craft. The General had done everything he could to try and locate his missing crewmembers and he now felt there could be only one possible reason why the eight scouts had disappeared – they must have been taken as prisoners. He was furious at the loss of his scouting party and even more frustrated at the loss of the sacred cask, which was on board the missing landing craft. The container was full of valuable *grobite* currency and he feared the wrath from his superiors back in Freytor for losing such a precious cargo.

A meeting was hurriedly convened between the ship's hierarchy and they all agreed it was important to seek retribution for the disappearance of the missing scouts. Although there was no actual proof of any wrong-doing, retaliation would be inflicted upon the Pathylian population immediately in the usual Freytorian manner by the casting of an evil curse over the five regions. As well as being a ruthless pirate, the General also held the necessary powers to inflict evil magic – it was his main weapon in battle.

The sea fog was getting even thicker, as the great ice-ship sailed back towards the Island of Restak. The General ordered the huge anchor to be lowered once more and his entourage followed him in regimental formation. He made his way down from the command bridge along the smooth icy passageways to another waiting landing craft. He then ordered his command group to stay behind whilst he clambered aboard the small boat to embark upon a solitary journey across to the deserted island.

The commander carefully guided the landing craft across the choppy water and once on dry land the wrathful Freytorian made its way up the side of the sacred rock to stand before the towering Kaikane Idol. The great stone carved monument stood proud some twenty metres high majestically representing the ancient god of the Red Ocean. The idol contained great mystical powers and by summoning the dark side of his thoughts, General Eidar was able to extract a rich vein of evil from the ancient statue.

The revenge-seeking Freytorian threw up his arms and launched a violent threat of terror via beams of flashing bright red lights, which sparked from within his cloak and enshrouded the Kaikane Idol. Bolts of crimson lightning flashed from the tip of the monument and roles of thunder clapped through the shifting stratus above, as the electrical storm spread across the low horizontal layer of purple clouds.

The exhausted commander exhaled a venomous vocabulary of hate towards the twisting dark clouds above. He held out his arms and pointed his white paws upwards in a final display of strength, as more bolts of red light emitted from his sharp black claws. "The evil spell is now cast and the curse has descended upon the Pathylian population!" he recited, as the lightning strikes tore into the surrounding landscape.

The dark spell was effectively engaged and the Kaikane Idol finally stopped glowing, as the exhausted General

19

slumped to the ground. He had done everything to ensure the curse could only be lifted upon the safe return of the eight missing scouts.

Over an hour had passed and General Eidar still lay motionless on the ground. With the exception of the waves crashing against the rocks below, there was a deathly silence on the Island of Restak. The sunlight had now been replaced with dense clouds and there was a faint drizzle of rain falling from the darkened skies. At last the weary Freytorian regained consciousness and found enough strength to sit upright in the damp foliage. He looked up at the Kaikane Idol and recalled his merciless act. The thought of revenge encouraged a fierce roar of evil laughter, which echoed across the island.

The General stood up and looked out to sea at the waving crewmembers that were standing on the upper decks of the motionless iceberg. He flipped his cloak over his shoulder to reveal a set of bulging muscles that flexed beneath a covering of pure white fur. He walked confidently away from the ritual site and quickly descended the rock with little effort. He maintained a majestic stroll then started to jog, as he approached the landing craft. The huge bear launched his muscular frame into the air and the small boat lurched forward, as the craft scraped along the shingles of the shoreline. Eidar landed firmly in the seat of the craft with no pause in his action, he picked up the two oars and then set off effortlessly across the water in the direction of the frozen mother ship.

The evil curse was gaining momentum and it was too dangerous for the Freytorian vessel to stay within the Pathylian waters for much longer. All the smaller blocks of ice had now disappeared and the main glacial structure had significantly reduced in size. Earlier the great ice-sail had cleared the Satorc Bridge with ease and it was now some ten metres shorter because of the thaw. Time was running out and the arctic creatures had to start making their journey back home.

General Eidar was now safely on board, but there was one last task for the ship's crew to undertake before heading back to Freytor. In order for the curse to mature properly, they had to seek out a disciple to maintain the shroud of darkness now cast over Pathylon. An experienced member of the ships navigational team knew of an evil Hartopian called Varuna, who was presently employed in the capacity of High Priest for Pathylon's northern most region; the Blacklands.

Varuna had a merciless reputation and in the past he had made numerous unsuccessful attempts to discredit the royal family. It was well documented that he had a proven desire to attain full control of all five regions following many unsuccessful military coups against the King.

General Eidar felt the Hartopian's selfish acts would make an ideal platform from which to represent the Freytorians, as their new ambassador to Pathylon and so he conveyed an order across the control deck. "Seek out the one they call Varuna and let's complete this task!"

"What about the missing scout party?" asked the first-mate. "We can't just leave them here... they will never survive the effects of the curse!"

"They are probably dead already!" replied General Eidar, as he pushed more buttons on his command chair. "Anyway, unless the curse is lifted no-one in Pathylon will survive... so they have to release our lost crewmembers." He raised his voice. "Now stop arguing and let's head for the Blacklands!"

Instructions were communicated to the engine room from the command bridge and the huge turbines inside the vessel began to groan under the weight of the vast glacial structure. The giant chain links were drawn out of the water again and the clanking of heavy metal against solid ice echoed through the ship's passageways, as the enormous anchor scraped against the hull of the great iceberg. The giant vessel strained and creaked as it moved away slowly and headed along the coastline of Pathylon towards the Blacklands region in search of the demented Hartopian; Varuna.

3

A Message in the Mirror

Meanwhile, in a world far away from the strange polar bear creatures, the children of Ravenswood Primary School had finished their final term for the year. Secondary education beckoned Bradley Baker after the six week holiday break. He intended to make the most of the time before he rejoined a select group of his friends in the autumn at Maulby Grammar School for Boys.

Bradley's mum had arranged for the two of them to stay with her older sister in Devon. The first two weeks of the summer holidays would be spent with Aunt Vera in Sandmouth and Margaret was making the final preparations for their journey down South. Bradley was in the upstairs bathroom and he had just climbed out of the bath tub following a hot shower.

Whilst drying himself with a towel, he celebrated the heroic victory over Emperor Thorag. The confrontation with the make-believe evil ruler of Trog had just taken place behind the shower curtain. Like most eleven-year-old boys, Bradley's vivid imagination was a constant hive of activity. Quite often, his thoughts would stretch beyond the most bizarre fantasies, which took place in the strangest of magical worlds. The fictitious Emperor was just one of many characters that he would combat with during his morning wash-time routines.

The young adventurer's concentration was suddenly interrupted by a stern female voice that emanated from downstairs. "Bradley... have you got out of that shower yet?" shouted Margaret. "Water costs money you know!" she continued, as he wrapped the towel around his head to muffle his mother's predictable tones.

Bradley removed the towel and replied. "Yes Mum... I'm just getting dried off!" The disgruntled boy resumed his bathroom routine and used the towel to wipe the condensation from the mirror above the wash hand basin. Having no more use for the towel, he turned to hang it on the radiator and then reached down to retrieve his underwear.

As he turned back to pick up his toothbrush, he noticed that the mirror had steamed over again. Bradley picked up a flannel but before he had chance to wipe the mirror some letters started to appear in the condensation. The boy stared in amazement, as the letters became clearer. He looked away briefly and reached down to pull up his underpants. He then focused his attention back on the mirror and without thinking read the words out loud. *"Pathylon is in danger!"*

The door opened suddenly and his mother entered the bathroom carrying freshly laundered towels. "What did you say dear?" asked Margaret, as she noticed the puzzled look on her son's face.

Bradley shook his head repeatedly from side to side in an attempt to dispel the trance. He looked at the mirror again, but the writing had disappeared and the condensation began to obscure his reflection. He wiped the mirror clean again. "Mum... I could have sworn there was a message on the mirror."

"Oh yes... and what did it say?" asked Margaret, in a disbelieving tone and placed the towels neatly on a shelf above the bath.

"Don't make fun, Mum... I'm being serious – the message said something about *Pathylon* being in danger!" exclaimed the excited boy.

"You and your fairytale adventures... I can't think what your mates think of your vivid imagination," replied Margaret, as she plucked the discarded towel from the radiator and then attempted to dry her disgruntled son's hair.

Bradley reluctantly squirmed away. "Give over Mum... I'm not a kid anymore – I'm nearly twelve... I'll do that!" he insisted, as he snatched the towel from his startled mother.

"Hey... don't get too big for your boots – it's a few months yet till your birthday!" replied Margaret. "Anyhow, that's no way to treat your Mum... now hurry up and get dried - I want to clean this bathroom," she continued and then disappeared into a nearby bedroom.

The condensation had now evaporated from the mirror and Bradley's vision was also much clearer, as he stared at his reflection. His soft brown hair was still disheveled from his mother's unwelcome intervention and he remained motionless. He still wasn't sure if he had been imagining things and his mind started to wander again, as he spoke softly. "Have all the conflicts with Emperor Thorag finally pushed my sense of reality over the edge?" He wondered, as he shook his head to dispel the imaginative thoughts. The puzzled boy then looked down and could not believe he had allowed his mother to enter the bathroom whilst he wore just his underpants. The fact that he was wearing them back to front and inside out did not help his case for juvenile embassment.

Meanwhile back in the Blacklands, General Eidar's meeting with Varuna proved to be a great success and the Hartopian agreed to become the Freytorians newly appointed Ambassador. Varuna's agreement came easy for he had other ulterior motives to attain the necessary power and his intentions were very much focused on the Pathylian crown.

The evil curse had now taken on a timely and more effective medium, in the form of a strategic plot to dethrone King Luccese, the present ruler of Pathylon. Varuna could not believe his luck and welcomed the Freytorian curse. He was reveling in the chance to act as their disciple and rule Pathylon under a dark evil cloud.

The General returned to the frozen vessel and the order was given from the command bridge to set sail. With the anchor raised for the final time, the iceberg set off again on its long journey back to Freytor. Eidar wanted to stay behind to help Varuna but his thoughts of colder climates were enough to coax him away. The Freytorian felt confident that the Hartopian would instill total anarchy in his absence.

Following the ice-bear's departure, Varuna was quick to amass a great army made up of his fellow Hartopians from the Blacklands and the ferocious giant lizard-like warriors of Krogonia. He was eager to oversee and carry out the invasion of the Royal capital region of Devonia.

Many hard fought battles took place under the darkened skies and a number of the King's bravest battalions and loyal noblemen lost their lives in defence of the Pathylian throne. With Luccese army now heavily depleted a final assault on the Devonian capital ensued. A surprise attack at nightfall resulted in an uncontested and enforced abdication of the true King. Even the heralded armies from the Galetis Empire could not save him from the evil clutches of Varuna.

It did not take long for the Hartopian to stake his unlawful claim to the throne. There was no resistance because he was protected by a ruthless army of followers and he also had the endorsement of the Freytorians to support his campaign of terror. The power of the dark curse grew stronger so a hurried coronation followed and Varuna was successfully crowned the new King of Pathylon.

He soon made use of the Shallock Tower, which was situated on the outskirts of the Royal City of Trad, to imprison Luccese and his beautiful Queen Vash. They now had to endure an embarrassing and torturous existence inside the cold cells of the tall needle-shaped monument.

Unbeknown to Varuna and prior to his wrongful entrapment, Luccese had managed to advise an ally to act on his behalf and represent the people during his unlawful imprisonment. The Good Samaritan had been given the responsibility to venture out of Pathylon to visit a new world to seek help. One of his tasks would be to lay down the clues that were necessary to recruit a group of true modern day heroes from the outside world. The twelve *chosen ones* would be employed to create a firm foundation for a successful bid to lift the evil curse. Their mission would be to restore peace and light to the magical regions of Pathylon and would contain a multitude of arduous tasks that gave no assurance to their own personal sacrifices.

During the months that followed, Luccese kept in regular contact with the Good Samaritan by deploying a trained falcon to relay coded messages through the iron bars of the window, which encaged the royal couple at the top of the Shallock Tower. However, the great bird of prey grew weary, as its continued efforts to maintain the vital link between Luccese and his loyal servant became more frequent. A final effort to maintain communications had failed. The exhausted bird was struck by a stray arrow, as it perched on the tower window ledge. Time was now running out and Luccese had potentially lost all contact with his faithful ally on the outside.

The deposed King had used the deadly sliver of wood embedded in the falcon's midriff to good effect. He had removed the arrow from the stricken bird and attached one last message to it. By utilizing the elasticized cord that secured his robe, Luccese had made a makeshift bow by tying it to the bars of the window. The arrow was launched and carried far by the strong winds that blew around the tower. It travelled across the River Klomus and eventually came to rest within the great Forest of Haldon.

A Devonian nobleman happened to be riding by and tracked the course of the arrow. He rode his trusty mount at great speed and gave chase to retrieve the arrow. He eventually found it, with the message still attached, pinned to a great cretyre tree deep inside the forest. He realized the importance of the message and he continued southward through the forest and into the region of *The Galetis Empire*.

The precious note was eventually passed to the Good Samaritan and it read;

"My Trusted Ally,

I hope you find this message … for I call on thee one last time my loyal friend. You must seek out the Chosen Ones and rekindle the powers of Restak. Now please hurry, Varuna must not seize control of all five regions of Pathylon, he already controls Devonia, Krogonia, the Forest of Haldon and the Blacklands … he must not succeed with your region. The Galetis Empire must not fall into the evil clutches of this traitor. All of Pathylon is dependent upon your success my friend. Good Luck in your quest to find the Chosen Ones!

Your dear friend, Luccese"

The Good Samaritan was in fact Meltor, a High Priest who still held a crucial position as leader of the Galetis Empire. Luccese knew that Varuna would need to unite all five regions of Pathylon and he urged Meltor to embark on a hasty recruitment of the chosen ones before it was too late. In his note, the true King had called for one last attempt to release Varuna's evil grip on Pathylon. Support for the brutal Hartopian was growing stronger and only the security of Meltor's allegiance prevented the antagonist from controlling all five regional High Priesthoods.

King Luccese knew full well that the only way to dispel Varuna and lift the curse would be for his trusted friend to find the chosen ones. The Kaikane Idol on the Island of Restak was the key to unlock this terrible situation and it would take someone with great courage to orchestrate the extraction of its powers and thus release the forces necessary to eradicate the dark curse.

Dispelling the evil would depend upon the discovery of the contents of the round sacred cask, which had been lost in the misty waters when the Freytorian landing craft set out from its mother ship. It would take great cunning by the Good Samaritan in his plans to guide the necessary help to the resting place of the valuable grobite treasure. There was no margin for failure, this difficult task would determine who became the chosen ones and King Luccese knew Meltor was his only chance to complete the quest.

Unbeknown to Varuna and the vengeful Freytorians, the winds of terror that blew strong over the world of Pathylon were about to take a dramatic change in direction. The Good Samaritan's efforts to entice the necessary help from the outside world and liberate Pathylon from the evil curse were soon to be rewarded.

A young boy seeking adventure from another world and a different time dimension was about to embark on an incredible journey. Bradley Baker's daring enthusiasm alone would be infectious enough to herald a new hope to the condemned regions of Pathylon.

4

The Gladiator

Bradley was still coming to terms with the strange message in the bathroom mirror. He was having doubts as to whether he actually saw it or if it was his imagination playing tricks. The frustrated boy so wanted to believe it had just happened but was too busy helping to lift the heavy suitcases onto the driveway. His mother was loading the luggage into the boot of the family estate car and she was deep in thought, as she spoke out loud. "It's a shame your Dad's working away at the moment... and with Frannie staying with Grandma - it's just you and me Son!"

Bradley was totally oblivious to what his mum was saying and just nodded. He had abandoned his chores and was now engrossed in his games console. He switched on the portable appliance and simultaneously opened the rear passenger door of the car. With full concentration still on the screen, he climbed into the vehicle, as the electronic device gave out a loud introductory chorus. With one hand still clutching the game console, he pulled at the seatbelt with the other and secured the shiny clip into the belt housing beneath the centre rear armrest.

Margaret finished loading the car and watched in amazement, as her son journeyed deeper into the world of electronic gaming. Then she turned and walked back towards the house leaving him with his hand held battle zone, as the sound of gunfire emanated from the small device. Margaret disappeared into the house to make her final inspection, as Bradley pounded his thumbs on the control buttons.

About ten minutes later Bradley's mum reappeared and proceeded to lock the front door of the family home. She re-approached the car and the driver's door was soon slammed shut, as she settled into the driver's seat and pulled at the seat belt. "Right then, my precious little man... it's time to go," she said, whilst securing eye contact with her son through the rear-view mirror. "Oh by the way... did you use the bathroom?"

Bradley cringed and lowered his head out of view from the mirror. He hated it when his mother spoke like that, however he *had* forgotten and understood fully what his mother was saying. As soon as they had reached the first motorway services, he would have to request the usual toilet stop. The crimson-faced eleven-year-old pitched his head back into view and witnessed a look of rage from his mother. "You've forgotten... haven't you?" She flung open the driver's door. "I don't believe it... he does it every time!" she ranted and raised her eyes towards the heavens.

Bradley immediately switched off the gaming console and unclipped the seat belt. He scampered out of the car and met his frustrated mother at the front of the house. Margaret ushered him under her outstretched arm and ordered him upstairs in readiness for the long drive ahead.

The four and a half hour journey to Devon was nearing a satisfactory conclusion. Margaret had left the M5 motorway well behind at junction thirty one and she was now enjoying the peaceful rural surroundings as she drove the family estate car along the winding tree lined country roads. She took one hand off the steering wheel and reached over to press the button on the centre console that operated the front driver's door window. A rapid inrush of air filled the inside of the car with the fresh smell of the Devon countryside. She was keen to replace the stale air that had been created by her sleeping son following the burger and chips stop at a motorway service station midway through the journey. The window was returned to its closed position and Bradley remained asleep. She was keen to maintain a feeling of calm to the final part of the journey, which had been secured so far by the handsome boy's slumbering.

Bradley's mum began to recognize certain landmarks. She slowed the car down and glanced over at a farmyard entrance that had a sign displaying the sale of *Devon Clotted Cream* and *Freshly Laid Eggs.* As the car passed the farm, the road inclined to a steep brow and over the other side the road twisted and turned like a grass snake and headed down towards the sunlit bay. Only a few more hedge lined corners for the weary travellers and the small seaside town of Sandmouth would finally be in to view through the insect splattered windscreen. Margaret had safely arrived in good time, and the journey had taken just over five hours and was fully inclusive of only one toilet and burger break for Bradley.

The weary driver climbed out of the car and made her way round to the boot and released the lock. Margaret lifted a heavy suitcase from the car and placed it gently on the ground next to her son's surf emblazoned travel hold-all. She was feeling dehydrated and was in need of some liquid refreshment. A cup of freshly brewed tea accompanied by one of Vera's homemade baked scones and strawberry jam would do nicely. The farm sign she passed earlier had reminded her that Devon clotted cream could only compliment the regional dish. Her sister always had plenty of cream in stock and although the calories would pile on, the thought of the first bite encouraged Margaret to temporarily abandon the luggage and seek out Bradley.

Margaret opened the rear passenger door to find her son still sound asleep. The seatbelt, which had protected him throughout the two hundred and eighty seven mile journey, was covering the lower part of his face. The position of the belt was causing Bradley's upper left cheek to make an awkward acquaintance with his eyelid. "Bradley dear," she whispered, whilst gently touching his shoulder. "Wake up… we're here."

The boy stirred and started to mutter words inherited from his semi-consciousness. His long eyelashes flickered in response to the brilliant sunshine piercing through the temporary window blind, which was strategically positioned to aid his comfort during the long journey. His mother's voice was soft and reassuring. "It's alright Bradley, it's only me… I'm sorry if I startled you - it's been a long journey and you've been sleeping for some time." she said, as she stroked his hair. "Try to open your eyes now."

Bradley woke from his slumber and started to gain consciousness. He was so pleased to see his mother and it took a short while for his eyes to readjust to the brightness of the sunlight reflecting from the metal trim, which surrounded the car door. He noticed her head was in silhouette with the clear blue sky and the tree branches behind her simulated antlers. The boy refocused his eyes and smiled at the thought of his mother looking like a proud stag reindeer. "Hello Mum... are we there yet?" he asked and stretched out his arms, whilst yawning loudly. "Are we in Sandmouth?"

"Yes dear," she replied and then looked over to the front door of her sister's cottage. "And I think your Aunt Vera has just spotted us... so come on, let's get you inside and we'll get a brew on."

Bradley loathed visiting his aunt but absolutely loved where she lived. The quaint thatched cottage was built in the early eighteen hundreds and overlooked the bay. His memories of the coastal town, still called the *Mouth of Sand* by some locals, were happy and carefree. There was always lots of exciting places to explore and he had particularly enjoyed playing in the rock pools at Amley's Cove during previous visits with his parents and younger sister.

They had made the journey down south without Frannie because she was suffering from a really bad cold. She was staying with Grandma Penworthy back in Ravenswood because Patrick was working long hours away. It was thought best to let her stay with Margaret's mother on this occasion, especially as Aunt Vera would no doubt complain at the slightest sound of a sniffle. Grandma was also sitting the family pets; a Burnese Mountain Dog called K2 and a grey Persian cat called Sky. Both animals would have to endure a few weeks of supermarket-canned food and dry biscuits, whilst their usual diet of fresh meat and pasta dishes remained resident in the fridge freezer. Bradley only had his mother to keep a close eye on him this time round, so he felt this particular visit would be quite stressful. She was a very protective mum and this could pose an unwelcome obstacle when faced with a perfect opportunity to explore the rock pools at Amley's Cove.

Aunt Vera energetically emerged from the cottage holding out her welcoming arms. "Hello my darlings!" she shrieked and homed in on the weary travellers, whilst peering over her dark rimmed spectacles. Her short grey haircut stayed in shape as the aging woman steadied her awkward gallop to a cumbersome waddle. She appeared alongside the car and fulfilled her objective by awarding Margaret two glancing kisses on each cheek. "Oh it's so good to see you, my darling!" she exclaimed, in a manufactured tone of affection.

Bradley was now in immediate danger. The initial greeting ritual was at a crucial point and he knew full well that his aunt would now attempt to place sloppy wet kisses onto his already seat belt marked face. As his aunt prepared to pounce for the inevitable slobbering, he compared the situation with that of the brave Roman Gladiator, who had appeared chained to the coliseum arena in the DVD movie he had watched just days before. In the movie there was a dramatic fight-scene in the arena, where a ferocious tiger had approached a slave. Just like the chains that bound the ankles of the gladiator, the seat belt tightened around Bradley's waist as he struggled to stay clear of Aunt Vera's slobbering jaws.

With the Gladiator still clear in his mind, Bradley thought of a plan to defend himself. In the movie, the final leap of the tiger had prompted the Gladiator to reach for a metal stake, which was used by the slave to great effect. He remembered the mid-journey stop at the burger bar and quickly looked to his right hand. He then reached for the empty coke cup lying on the back seat of the car complete with sealed plastic lid and well-chewed straw.

As Aunt Vera closed in for the kill, Bradley placed the cup in front of his face and accidentally pushed the end of the straw up her left nostril. "Ouch!" she yelped, lifting her head sharply.

"Sorry!" apologized Bradley, as his eyes opened wider in amusement.

"What did you do that for Bradley?" shouted Margaret, as she looked on in complete shock and disbelief.

Bradley calmly explained his way out of the situation. "I was thirsty and I just remembered... I hadn't finished my drink from the services and well I... err - didn't want to waste it!" he concluded with a cheeky smile, as Vera jolted her head backwards. She hit her head on the under-roof of the car and was now rubbing her head, whilst checking the ends of her fingers for a nose bleed.

The bedraggled fifty seven-year-old produced another one of her false smiles. "It was an accident... don't fuss Margaret," she uttered. "Now... let's get this little chap out of this hot car and inside for a nice refreshing drink," continued Aunt Vera, as she finally collected herself and waddled off back towards the cottage.

Bradley watched her shuffle her short stout figure away and could not help but focus his attention on her large bottom, as it wobbled inside her brightly coloured nylon dress. This prompted him to launch into some negative comments about his aunt. "Mum... I find it hard to believe that you have such an annoying sister – she's so full of herself."

Margaret reacted sharply. "Hey, that's enough... your Aunt Vera will hear you."

"Well she never makes any effort to visit us in Ravenswood and we always have to travel down to Devon... not that I'm complaining - I love it in Sandmouth," he replied.

"Yes Bradley, I agree... your Aunt Vera has a very annoying way of making lots of fuss when we arrive - and then about half an hour later followed by the usual cup of tea and homemade scones, she tends to give the impression that the presence of an eleven-year-old boy in search of adventure is going to cause a great deal of inconvenience to her weekly schedule... now come on let's get inside before she bursts a blood vessel."

His mother's witty comments confirmed his thoughts. It was obvious that Aunt Vera felt uncomfortable around him, especially when the old battle-axe would feel the need to conveniently make herself scarce every time Margaret mentioned the tubby little woman's participation in any planned family outings.

It was going to be an uphill challenge for adventure this week and Bradley's thoughts returned to the gladiator movie. The chains in the form of the lap belt were off temporarily, released following the brief encounter with the tigress, but how would he escape to seek the treasures that were beholden to him at Amley's Cove.

The rest of the afternoon was spent unpacking the suitcases and settling in to the new surroundings of Aunt Vera's cottage. It was now seven o'clock in the evening. "It's getting late," said Margaret, awarding Bradley an informative look as her neatly trimmed eyebrows lowered towards the top of her nose. She had promised her sister that Bradley would be in bed early so they could catch up on the latest family gossip. So the reluctant boy was ushered upstairs to the bathroom, where he was subjected to a quick wash and teeth cleaning exercise. With the seat belt marks long gone from his face, he settled down for the night and was left to ponder the days ahead.

Bradley was feeling very tired and the long journey had finally taken its toll on the young adventurer. The message on the mirror was still clear in his mind and the words *'Pathylon is in danger'* faded into his imagination, as he drifted off to sleep.

5

A New Friend

The first light of the following morning had presented Ravenswood with a dull outlook and the skies above the Yorkshire village were slightly overcast. However, the air was quite warm and the early formed dew had started to evaporate from the pretty flowerbeds in Grandma Penworthy's front garden.

The frail old woman made her way slowly to the front door and she attempted to turn the handle with her arthritic aching hand. "Damn locks!" she moaned and struggled to operate the door latch. "That husband of our Margaret promised he'd fix this blooming thing!" she muttered to herself.

Finally she managed to turn the latch and open the door. Grandma bent down and collected the two pints of milk, which had been left on her doorstep by the local milkman. She carefully gathered the milk cartons into her arms and closed the front door.

As she made her way back down the hallway, a dog's bellowing cry could be heard in the kitchen. The barking was quickly followed by a loud thud. Grandma peered around the door and noticed her granddaughter's legs sticking out of a cloths pile on the floor.

Frannie had stumbled and collided with the great Burnese Mountain Dog and she had landed on top of Grandma Penworthy's ironing pile. K2 had given out a loud yelp and had sought sanctuary in the pantry. What great luck for the terrified hound, the residue of breakfast cereal that Frannie had spilt onto the pantry floor was a welcome reward for the throbbing pain he was now feeling in his giant front paw.

As K2 lapped up the last few corn flakes, Grandma bent down to examine the contents of the ironing pile. "Frannie Baker… where are you?" she shouted, as she clung on tightly to the two semi-skimmed milk containers.

"Under here Gran!" yelled Frannie, as she fought with her guardian's enormous knickers. The little four-year-old lifted her head from the ironing pile and offered a puzzled look to Grandma. A pair of brown surgical stockings lay across the top of Frannie's head giving the impression of a sweet little mountain maid.

Grandma struggled to lift her out of the ironing pile and then applied the necessary tender loving care to reassure her granddaughter that life would go on, no matter how many knocks and grazes she would have to encounter. "What have you been up to you silly thing?" asked Grandma. "Come on Pumpkin… let's get you upstairs for a wash and dressing," she added and finally laid the milk cartons to rest on the kitchen work surface.

At that moment the telephone rang. Grandma made her way slowly across the hall in the direction of the lively telephone, in readiness to answer the call. Frannie noticed the snail like speed of Grandma's reaction and nipped in front to lift the receiver, just as the old lady reached out to pick it up. It was Frannie's father enquiring after the health of his young daughter and to ask whether Grandma had heard from Margaret and Bradley.

Frannie wiped the simulated candle wax that was streaming from her nose onto her sleeve and then handed the telephone handset to her frustrated grandmother.

"No Patrick... they haven't phoned yet – give me your number and I'll get our Margaret to call you after I hear from her!" shouted Grandma. "It's only five past eight... I expect they are still sleeping after their long journey to our Vera's!"

Patrick pulled his mobile phone away from his ear and shook his head to dispel the echoes of his mother-in-law's loud tones. He returned the handset to his mouth and recited his telephone number to Grandma as she took 'what seemed like an hour, to write it down. Finally, he thanked his wife's mother for bringing him up to date and agreed to wait for her to call him later.

He placed the phone on the workbench and continued with the electrical installation work at the Chelby site. He paused for a moment and then connected the delicate wires onto the terminals of the electronic sensor, which monitored any overheating within the giant motor. He then looked around and up into the enormous winding engine house where he was working.

Patrick was missing his family very much and could not wait for this particular contract work to finish, so he could be reunited with them again. He wasn't happy about Margaret and Bradley making the long journey to the south coast alone. The trip was originally planned as a family holiday, but the urgency for completion of the winder motor commission with E.M.M.C.O. had taken priority. He would not be able to settle until he had heard from Grandma Penworthy and he checked his mobile phone again to make sure it had a good signal. The number of bars on the display flickered between four and five, now he was satisfied that he would be able to take the call when it arrived.

Grandma Penworthy's comments could not have been further from the truth. Bradley was watching the portable television in Aunt Vera's parlour and his mother was out on the patio eating freshly prepared toast and homemade apricot jam. The sun was burning bright in the blue cloudless Devon sky and the weather forecast bore further good news from the radio playing beside Margaret's chair.

"Oh my goodness… I've forgotten to call mother to let her know we arrived safely!" exclaimed Margaret.

"She'll be pulling her hair out by now," said Vera. "You know what she's like!"

"Can I use your phone Vera?"

"My dearest Margaret… you have been visiting this house for the past twenty three years - you don't need to keep asking permission to use my telephone," she replied smugly with an encouraging open-handed gesture. "Please feel free my dear!"

Margaret acknowledged her sister's response and proceeded to make the call to their mother. She fulfilled her obligation and gave the adoring pensioner all the assurances that were needed in relation to their safe arrival. She then offered Bradley the opportunity to speak with Frannie. He gave his mother a scowling glare and flatly refused to take advantage of her offer to communicate with his little sister.

Instead he made an immediate exit into Aunt Vera's back garden to check out the Sandmouth wildlife. Margaret was left to reassure her daughter that Bradley still loved her and he may talk to her later. She then persuaded Frannie to hand the phone back to Grandma and concluded her conversation with the usual talk about the weather and so on.

Bradley strolled around the garden kicking at the daisy heads, which peeped tentatively above the unmown lawn. The tips of the grass were very dry and as he pitched his right foot into the moist roots, he collected the rich Devon red soil onto the toe of his white sports shoe. He mimicked a famous free-kick by one of his footballing heroes and pretended to *bend the flower heads like Beckham.*

He soon grew tired of his re-enactment of England's World Cup quarterfinal football match with Argentina and proceeded to look around for something else to occupy his boredom. Bradley's attention was drawn to the white picket fence at the bottom of Aunt Vera's garden, so he approached the fence and leant over. There was a public footpath at the other side that was about six feet away from a slight incline leading down to a limestone wall with railings, which edged the cliff side. He saw his first opportunity to escape from the confines of the garden and explore. He was fully aware that the footpath led down to Amley's Cove.

Bradley stared at the path and thought for a few seconds about the inevitable consequences that would result should he wander off without permission from his mother or aunt. He lifted his head, stared out to the glistening sea and continued to ponder his great escape. Bradley was just about to make his decision when he heard a voice calling him. He trained his eyes towards the sound of the voice and looked over towards the fruit trees in the far corner of the garden. He noticed a boy, who was frantically waving his hands and standing precariously on a wooden bench, which was located along the footpath.

"Hello!" shouted the boy, noticing that Bradley had spotted him at last.

The loud call had startled Bradley because he was still half focused on his planned assault of Amley's Cove. This stranger had suddenly ruined his concentration. "Hello there!" repeated the boy, still shouting. "You look like you're in some sort of trance... what are you thinking about?"

Bradley couldn't believe how rude he was and that he was still trying to attract his attention. He tried to ignore him and turned around to head back towards Aunt Vera's cottage. However, the boy did not give up and he continued to introduce himself, as Bradley walked with his back to the fence and headed up the garden path. "Don't be alarmed mate... hey wait up - my name is Musgrove Chilcott!"

The tall fourteen-year-old was a local boy, who lived with his mother in a cottage just a few doors down from Aunt Vera's house. He had a brother of eighteen called Simon, a royal marine recruit, based at the nearby Lympstone military training camp. Musgrove missed having his brother around and he was always out and about playing in the bay, pretending to be a soldier. One day he too hoped to join the elite naval regiment and follow in his brother's footsteps. "Why are you ignoring me... I don't mean you any harm?"

Bradley finally gave in and turned around to acknowledge Musgrove. As well as being very tall, he was slender with blonde hair and he looked a bit scruffy in appearance. He was wearing dark tinted sunglasses, a loose fitting white T-shirt with some kind of surfing motif emblazoned across the chest and baggy blue knee length board shorts.

Bradley approached the fence and then responded to the boy's persistent line of questioning. "My mum told me never to speak to strangers... especially ones with names like Musgrove."

"Ah... you can talk then?" Musgrove replied confidently. "And you've got a sense of humour!"

"Eh?" replied Bradley.

"Seriously mate... I only wanted to know if you could come out and do a bit of exploring?" added Musgrove, as he pointed to the edge of the cliff.

Bradley dismissed the boy's sarcastic reply and completed his regimental inspection by assessing the boy's feet. Musgrove wasn't wearing any shoes or socks and his knees were scuffed and covered in dirty seaweed. "What happened to your shoes?" he asked. "...And why are your legs so dirty?"

"Oh yeah... err right - well I was exploring the cove and lost them whilst..."

Bradley interrupted, excitedly. "Do you mean Amley's Cove?"

"Yeah... err, *Amley's Cove* – it's located at the foot of these here cliffs!" continued Musgrove.

"I know where Amley's Cove is!" exclaimed Bradley, in a confident tone.

"Hey, calm down mate... wind your neck in - all I want to do is explain what has happened?"

Bradley walked red-faced towards the fence and then apologized for his abrupt manner by offering his hand to help Musgrove over the picket fence.

Up close the boy wasn't actually as tall as he first thought, however he did tower over Bradley somewhat. This was not that unusual because Bradley was quite small for his age and received constant torment from his classmates at Ravenswood Primary School. Playground taunts such as *titch* and *shorty* were all too familiar to him, but he had learned to cope with each situation and just ignored any petty comments made by his peers. His father had encouraged him to be much stronger in defence of his height, especially as he would be moving up to Maulby Grammar School after the summer break.

Bradley justified his mood to Musgrove with the excuse that he was bored and frustrated at not being able to go down to the cove. He finally decided to communicate in a friendly manner with Musgrove and he confidently introduced himself formerly to the persistent teenager. "Hi... my name is Bradley Baker - but you can call me *Brad* if you like." He jumped on every opportunity to convince others that his preferred name was really Brad. He had watched many bare-fisted action movies with a film star of the same name and looked upon the hunky star as a bit of a cult hero.

"Nice to meet you Brad Baker.... oh and err - *thanks* for helping me over the fence."

"That's okay," replied Bradley. "Anyhow... what were you doing down in Amley's Cove - and how on earth did you manage to lose your shoes?"

Musgrove told his new friend that he had noticed a small round shiny object glistening in one of the rock pools. He had taken off his shoes and socks so as not get them wet. When he returned to the place where he had left them, they had disappeared.

"Did you see anyone else down there?" asked Bradley.

"No," replied Musgrove. "It spooked me a little though... and I cut my knees as a scrambled up the rocks to get away."

Bradley suggested some first aid treatment and rushed inside to ask his mother for some sticking plasters. She followed her energetic son back into Aunt Vera's garden to meet his new friend.

"Hello young man... I'm Bradley's mum," said Margaret.

"Oh, err...hello – I'm Musgrove Chilcott."

"What a splendid name you have – how did you come about a name like that?" asked Margaret.

"*Muuummmm!*" interrupted her embarrassed looking son. "Don't be rude!"

"Oh... it's okay - I get quizzed about my name quite a lot," said Musgrove. "After all... it is quite an unusual one - I blame my Gran...she's dead now - but she used to read the local *Devon Life* magazine every month and she apparently picked the name out of an editorial about a man called *Musgrove Buckthorpe*... he was an antique dealer from Totnes or something!"

"Well I think it's a wonderful name," said Margaret. "I hope you're proud of it."

"*Yeah*, well... my mother certainly liked it – she must have done, because she took gran's advice about the old antique dealer," laughed Musgrove. "I've sought of grown to like it... anyhow - most of my friends just call me Muzzy."

"Can *I* call you Muzzy?" asked Bradley.

"Yeah - if you like," replied Musgrove.

"No Bradley... I think you should address your new friend by his proper name - anyhow I wouldn't like it if someone shortened your name to Brad!" exclaimed Margaret.

Bradley and Musgrove looked at each other and smiled. "I think your mum is right *Bradley*... you'd best call me *Musgrove*."

Following the A & E procedures from Bradley's mum, she asked Musgrove to explain his predicament. Bradley could see a perfect opportunity for a legitimate and early exploration of Amley's Cove and immediately popped the question. "Mum?" he asked. "Can I go with Musgrove to find...?"

"No!" interrupted his mother sternly. "I know what you are going to ask... and as you see from Musgrove's knees - it is very dangerous down there on those rocks."

"But Mum!" Bradley pleaded. "Musgrove has lost his socks and shoes... and he will get into trouble if we don't go and find them!"

Aunt Vera appeared from the cottage. She had overheard the conversation and offered a lifeline to Bradley and his new pal. "I have already arranged to see Old Mac the fisherman today... to collect my fresh halibut." She announced. "His boat will be moored down in the lower end of the cove later today... you can both come down with me later if you like - and we will see if we can locate the missing items that your new forgetful friend has lost."

Bradley afforded his aunt a rare smile and then pulled on Musgrove's arm. The excited boys huddled together and made the necessary arrangements to meet up around noon that day.

6

An Unusual Discovery

K2 left the sanctuary of the pantry, having licked up all the spilt cereal and was now barking at the petrified postman at the front garden gate. Grandma Penworthy had not closed the front door properly and the dog had taken full advantage of the situation.

Charlie Dabbs had risked life and limb in an attempt to post the mail through the letterbox. He still had the un-posted letters in his trembling right hand and was contemplating risking the short distance to the letterbox again or whether to wait for assistance. During the chase, K2 had bitten a chunk of material from the postman's trousers and the dog continued to bark whilst standing his ground.

Charlie did not have to wait too long. Frannie released herself from Grandma's embrace and ran towards the front door. The cute redhead stood and stared at the fracas that was taking place at the cottage gate.

Frannie chuckled to herself and then let out a high-pitched plea for help. "Grandma… K2 is scaring *Postman Pat!*"

Unaware of her innocent sarcasm, the little girl pointed at the quivering man, as the old lady arrived by her side. Grandma Penworthy apologized to the postman and excused her young granddaughter; however she was more concerned about her free subscription to *Pensioners Weekly*.

"Have you got my magazine in your hand Mr. Dabbs?" she enquired, failing to notice the exasperated look on the postman's face. "It should be here by now… its way overdue - it should have been here three days ago," continued Grandma.

"I think I have it here Mrs. Penworthy," replied Charlie, desperately fumbling through the mail. "Yes… here it is!" he exclaimed, hoping the elderly lady would now call off the huge dog.

Frannie intervened. "Come on boy!" she yelled, as the postman waved the cellophane wrapped magazine in the air. "Go and find Sky!"

That was all the encouragement K2 needed. He loathed the grey Persian cat and leapt back into the house to seek out his prey. The postman grabbed the opportunity and finally completed his mission. Grandma was happy at last to receive her subscription, as she watched the postman pull at the threads on the seat of his pants.

"Sorry about your trousers Mr. Dabbs!" shouted Grandma, as she clutched the mail close to her pinafore. "Are you alright my dear?"

"Oh… I'll be okay Mrs. Penworthy – my trousers might be torn but my underpants are still intact." the postman chuckled, as he disappeared into the next door neighbour's garden.

Meanwhile, back in Sandmouth, Musgrove and Bradley bounced about on the back seat of Aunt Vera's Morris Minor. The old car wound its way down the narrow dirt track, which was very steep with passing-points for vehicles along the way. On a number of occasions the wheels came very close to the edge of the sandy verge. Bradley tried to ignore the imminent danger and his mind wandered again as he stared out of the side window.

"Look at the sheer drop down to the rocks!" exclaimed Musgrove, as he grabbed his friend's arm and whispered. "I hope your aunt's driving skills are up to scratch!"

"Yeah... it looks pretty dangerous!" replied Bradley nervously, hoping that Aunt Vera was wearing the correct spectacles to secure a safe passage to the bottom of Amley's Cove.

They eventually reached the lower end of the track and the white coastal landscape opened out and its reflection gleamed proudly in the midday sun. Old Mac's boat was bobbing around in the water and occasionally the small ripples of water forced the craft to touch the side of its temporary wooden berth. The fisherman's pride and joy was a small vessel with the name *Galetis* emblazoned in red painted italics against its black and yellow hull.

Aunt Vera and the two boys got out of the car. They then made their way over to where the fishing boat was berthed. The smell of freshly caught mackerel from the crates in the back of the boat wafted in the clean sea breeze.

Musgrove turned to Bradley. "Hey Brad, do you think Old Mac would take us out to sea in his boat?"

"Maybe," replied Bradley, as he looked up at the fisherman who had overheard them discussing a possible voyage across the seas.

The athletic old man jumped from the boat onto the jetty and Bradley gave him one of those cute-little-boy looks so as to invite a positive response to Musgrove's question. "Let's get on with it then... Vera – my old love!" insisted Old Mac, rubbing his black beard that was starting to show signs of ageing with its grey tips.

Bradley presumed by Old Mac's total blanking of his little puppy dog impression, he and his friend would not be exploring the great oceans of the world at this stage of their careers. So both boys turned away simultaneously and looked out over Amley's Cove, trying desperately to spot Musgrove's missing items of clothing.

Aunt Vera's face was turning a shade of red to match the colour of the name on Old Mac's boat, as the ageing fisherman offered subtle compliments relating to his customers' hairstyle.

Bradley turned his head back with mouth open ready to ask his aunt whether he and Musgrove could go ahead and look for the shoes and socks. Vera was totally oblivious to her nephew and was too busy enjoying Old Mac's chat up lines. Bradley pulled a disapproving face in reaction to Aunt Vera's frivolous behaviour and shrugged his shoulders at Musgrove.

"Get a load of this!" commented Bradley. "Mushy, *or* what..?"

"Don't knock it... Brad," replied Musgrove. "You're never too old for love... or so my mum says!"

"Yeah... right!" replied Bradley. "Well... let's leave these two love birds alone shall we...?"

Vera proceeded to return Old Mac's compliments and as she rabbited on the fisherman shifted his eyes to catch Bradley's attention. Old Mac winked at Bradley as if to award a gesture to indicate that it was now safe for them to go off and explore the cove.

Bradley thought this gesture was very strange and unusual, but at the same time grasped the opportunity created by the fisherman's time-wasting tactics.

"Nice one... old man - I guess this is our chance Muzzy," said Bradley.

"I think you're right," replied Musgrove, excitedly. "Let's go mate!"

The two boys turned their backs on the adults and carefully started to negotiate the jagged mollusk laden rocks, avoiding the slippery seaweed that lay limp beside the glistening rock pools. Bradley looked back to see if his aunt was still engaged in conversation with Old Mac. Vera continued to flirt with the fisherman, so the boys moved further away towards the spot where Musgrove had last seen his footwear.

"Arrgh!" shouted Musgrove, as the instep of his barefoot met with a sharp mollusk on one of the rocks.

Bradley held his hand out to his friend. "You okay, Muzzy?"

"Yeah... I'm fine Brad,' replied Musgrove, as he checked the graze on his foot. "It's just a scratch... let's keep moving - before your aunt runs out of chat up lines!"

"I do feel sorry for that fishing bloke - he's got his hands full there!" laughed Bradley.

"Yeah... your aunt certainly has a large personality," agreed Musgrove, as he made reference the Vera's rear. He chuckled, then changed the subject and continued. "Hey... Brad - did you notice the name of his boat?"

"Mmmm... *Galetis*," replied Bradley. "Never heard of that before... what do you suppose it means?"

"Don't know… let's ask the old fella when we get back – we'd better hurry," reiterated Musgrove, as he pressed forward.

Bradley followed his friend's directions and they soon reached the area where Musgrove had earlier spotted the shiny object. There was still no sign of his missing footwear, so the two adventurers began to search the shallow water pools for the gold-coloured object that Musgrove spoke of earlier.

Meanwhile in Chelby, Patrick Baker had been working for the past three days with a firm of electrical engineering contractors. The international company was called E.M.M.C.O, which manufactured industrial motor switchgear and currently employed Bradley's dad as a specialist electrician.

Patrick joined the company about ten years ago following his unfortunate redundancy from the National Coal Board. Silvermoor was a colliery that had to close down during the 1990's and he used to work as a surface electrician at the mine. He found it quite amusing that he and his wife Margaret had just bought a new detached house on the site of his old workplace. A developer had purchased the Silvermoor Colliery site and had built over forty dwellings on and around where the old shaft winders and surrounding power plants used to stand. Bradley would often be teased by his classmates at school about the fact that his house was built directly above the East Pit Shaft that was sunk a thousand of metres and more into the ground. Patrick would spend many hours reassuring his son that there was no chance that the house would disappear into the abyss. The top of the shaft had been capped with at least fifty metres of reinforced concrete when the underground workings were finally abandoned.

Patrick abandoned the thoughts of his son's fears about the classroom scare mongering. He was feeling tired and had managed to complete the automated winder installation, at the North Yorkshire site, five days prior to the company's scheduled completion deadline. He was keen to get back home to Ravenswood so he decided he would catch an early train and travel back from Chelby via Sheffield.

Back in Devon, Margaret had decided to take a trip to the nearby city of Plymouth. A new shopping centre had opened since her last visit to the area and this had attracted her interest. She was constantly being branded a fashion conscious yummy-mummy, so Patrick's wife had decided to live up to her reputation and participate in a bit of retail therapy.

Margaret was a very attractive woman and many adoring glances passed her way as she elegantly ascended the escalators into the shopping mall. She made her way over to an information board and proceeded to check the list for the whereabouts of her favourite ladies fashion outlets. She headed off towards her preferred clothes retailer and happened to walk passed a *Waterstones* book shop. The aroma of freshly roasted beans emanated from the franchised *Costa Coffee* outlet inside the store and this drew the caffeine loving shopaholic inside.

Margaret made her way passed the latest bestselling novels and ordered her usual *Gingerbread Latte* with *Almond Croissant* from Nigel the barista, then made her way over to a quiet allocated corner of the shop. She chose one of the comfortable sofas and stretched out her shapely legs, as she studied the shopping centre information leaflet.

The minutes drifted into hours and the trip to Plymouth was a well-deserved break from Vera and the children. Bradley's mum was keen to take full advantage of her childfree day and she intended to utilize it well inside the enticing designer shops.

Meanwhile in Yorkshire, it was two minutes to two o'clock on the Wednesday afternoon. Patrick was standing in readiness to alight, as the express train arrived at Sheffield station. Bradley's father had decided to check on Frannie and her grandma because his wife and son were not due back from Devon until Sunday week. He had come up with an idea and hopefully a pleasant surprise for his four-year-old daughter.

The train finally stopped, as Patrick stepped down from the carriage and then made his way down the platform, as he headed out of the station. He immediately summoned a taxi, which was waiting outside on the rank. As he climbed in the vehicle, he instructed the driver. "Please take me to 14 Silvermoor Close, Ravenswood – thank you!"

"Did you say Ravenswood… mate?" asked the taxi driver and pressed a button on the digital meter.

Patrick perched his bottom on the edge of the seat and acknowledged the driver by nodding in the rear view mirror, as the taxi set off. The sudden acceleration forced him back into his seat and he quickly secured his lap belt. The bright red L.E.D's on the meter burst into life to indicate the starting cost of the journey, as the driver attempted to conduct a conversation with his tired passenger. "Nice village… that Ravenswood," commented the driver, as he reached for a leaver on the steering column. The taxi's indicators clicked loudly, as it pulled out of the station taxi rank and onto the main road. "My cousin used to work at the old colliery you know."

"Really… I used to work there myself," replied Patrick, in an uninteresting tone.

"Mickey Davies was his name… he used to be a banks man," continued the taxi driver. "Did you know him?"

"Can't say I did…," replied Patrick, who just was not in the mood for conversation and before the driver had a chance to continue, he pressed a button on his mobile phone and pretended to have a conversation with someone.

The taxi driver obliged and stopped talking, as Patrick referred to his mobile phone directory. He attempted to make a quick telephone call to Vera's home, to see if Bradley was coping okay with his favourite aunt. There was no answer. "They must be out," he said out loud, as he put his phone back in his pocket.

The driver caught site of his passenger in the rear view mirror. "What was that mate?" he asked, hoping to resurrect the conversation.

"Oh… nothing - just making a few calls," replied Patrick, as he frantically reached into his pocket to retrieve his phone again.

Patrick need not have worried. There was no time to start the conversation again, as the taxi pulled up outside Grandma's house. Patrick quickly lent forward to check the meter reading and subsequently paid his fare. He collected his hold all and thanked the driver by giving him a small tip.

The taxi sped off and Patrick made his way over to Grandma Penworthy's front gate. He stood for a few moments to catch his breath in readiness for the onslaught of an over-excited daughter and slobbering hound.

Patrick knocked courteously then entered Grandma Penworthy's house and he was greeted with a coordinated leap and hug from Frannie. Once inside the hallway K2 came bounding up and knocked both of them to the floor. The dog proceeded to apply an ample supply of saliva over Patrick's face, as his big pink tongue searched for every crevice. The clumsy hound then turned his attention to his master's clothing and tugged on his trouser leg to gain more attention. The cat seized her opportunity and jumped out of the open window in the kitchen. It was a welcome escape for Sky, after being penned in the corner for about half an hour by the muscular mountain dog; thanks to Frannie and the postman episode.

"How are you feeling now, Frannie?" asked Patrick, as he cuddled his daughter. "You seem to have stopped your coughing... have you taken all your medicine?"

Frannie snuggled inside her father's jacket. Her face reappeared complete with horizontal bogey smears across her flushed cheeks and she wiped the remainder of her nasal fluids on his coat, as she nestled back into his warm embrace. She reappeared again and looked up at Patrick's unshaven chin. "Yes Daddy... Grandma has taken good care of me - I'm feeling a lot better now thank you."

Whilst drinking one of his mother-in-law's special brews, Patrick sat and admired his daughter play time with the doll's house that grandpa had made for Margaret when she was about Frannie's age. Grandpa had died only last year so Grandma was still getting used to life on her own. There was little chance of increasing the Penworthy clan on Vera's side. Grandma's eldest daughter had never married and was never likely to ever since she had been two-timed by a local *'Sheffield Casanova'*. Following his mishandling of her affections, Vera fled the area and was now living a quiet life of solitude in Sandmouth. She moved down South to Devon about thirty-five years ago and had no intention of ever returning to her birthplace, in the tiny Yorkshire village.

Patrick lifted his coat and inspected the extent of the snot stains on his jacket lining. Grandma interpreted what her son-in-law's next request would be and she reappeared from the kitchen with a damp cloth to remove Frannie's homecoming welcome. "You don't have to do that Ma... really it can wait till I get home," insisted Patrick, as he pulled a funny face at Frannie.

"Now you shush, my dear... I'll soon have it cleaned up," replied the persistent old lady, as she made the smearing worse by spreading it over a much wider area of his coat lining.

"Thanks Ma... that's very kind of you," said Patrick. "Now you don't have to bother with that... let me do it."

Frannie giggled amusingly, as Patrick finally wrestled the tatty cloth out of her grandma's obstinate grip and the determined old lady finally relented. He then recomposed himself and attempted to play down the unnecessary attention that was clearly entertaining his daughter.

7

The Disappearing Halibut

Back in Amley's Cove, Bradley and Musgrove were still searching for the teenager's lost belongings. Aunt Vera was still busy talking to Old Mac and this had afforded the boys the chance they had been looking for to go onto the rocks and spend quality time searching for the missing items.

"Over here, Muzzy!" shouted Bradley, as he pointed down at one of the rock pools.

"What can you see, Brad?" replied Musgrove.

Bradley had a great big grin on his face, not because he had found Musgrove's shoes, but because he was calling him Brad all the time. He liked this very much and felt quite rebellious by opting to call his friend Muzzy against his mother's wishes.

"Look down here... in this rock pool!" shouted Bradley. "There's something glistening between two large stones!"

Musgrove quickly clambered across to his friend and knocked a small pebble into the water with his barefoot. He waited patiently for the ripples to subside then peered down into the rock pool and spotted a small crab. The little sea creature scurried sideways along the sandy bedrock and stopped next to the small round object that Bradley had spied. The bright round shape looked very much like the metal coin he had seen earlier. It appeared to be wedged between the two stones and it was too far down under the water to reach by hand. The two boys avoided the risk of falling into the pool and instead marked the spot.

Bradley and Musgrove searched around the cove to see if they could find any long thin pieces of driftwood that could be used to dislodge the coin.

Aunt Vera concluded her conversation and handed Old Mac some money in exchange for the fish. She turned towards the car clutching her prize halibut, which was neatly wrapped in the sports pages of yesterday's edition of the *Herald Express*.

Vera noticed the boys on the rocks and shouted for them to come back to the car. "Come on you two... it's time to go!"

"Aunt Vera... we've found something really good!" replied Bradley, as he waved his hands above his head.

"Never mind that... get your little legs back over here young man - I shall tell your mother you've been misbehaving!" retorted Bradley's aunt, as she pointed her finger and waving her hand frantically. "It will be an early bath and bed for you tonight if you continue to mess me around!"

"There she goes again... going on and on," muttered Bradley.

"Doesn't your aunt realize that you're not a kid anymore and you don't like that sought of thing being said about you?" said Musgrove, as he offered some moral support to his friend.

"Obviously not!" exclaimed Bradley.

Bradley was very annoyed with his aunt this time; especially as his new best friend was standing right next to him. He displayed an act of playful ignorance and made out that he hadn't understood her request. He pretended he was stuck on top of the rocks and the plan worked perfectly, as the doddery middle-aged woman struggled over the slippery rocks towards the two boys.

Bradley waved his hand and led her straight to the spot where the sparkling coin-shape object lay. Aunt Vera peered into the rock pool and noticed the gold-coloured disc, as it shimmered in the shallow water. "Pass me that stick... please - err, what's your name?"

"It's Musgrove... Mrs. Penworthy!" replied Muzzy and instinctively held out his arm to offer help to Bradley's aunt. She subsequently ignored his act of chivalry and he cast the unsteady woman a polite grin, as she continued to balance her large frame whilst hanging on for dear life to the wrapped fish.

"Ah... yes, err - Musgrove," she repeated and took hold of the long piece of drift wood. "I don't need your help thank you very much... now, I'll see if I can dislodge it."

Aunt Vera used the stick to support her rotund frame and placed the newspaper-wrapped fish on top of the rock, as she bent down. In an awkward attempt to retrieve the metal object, her left foot accidentally caught the halibut and it plopped into an adjacent rock pool. Bradley looked on in horror, as he watched his aunt try to salvage the mystical gold coin from its watery haven. She had now put all her concentration into retrieving the small shiny disk and she was completely oblivious to her prize fish that had disappeared.

"Here we are!" exclaimed Aunt Vera, as she held the gold coin aloft.

"Can I have a look... please?" asked Musgrove, as he held out his hand.

Aunt Vera reluctantly handed over the prize. It was in perfect condition, about three centimetres in diameter and it had a small hole in the centre.

"Look... there is an inscription of some kind on one side and an unusual star-shaped pattern on the reverse side," exclaimed Musgrove, as he held the coin up towards the blue cloudless sky.

"What do you think it is Muzzy?" enquired Bradley, as he peered at the object whilst his friend examined it.

"Well Brad... I think it might be an ancient coin of some kind," replied Musgrove.

Aunt Vera looked solemnly at Bradley and asked Musgrove to stop calling her nephew Brad.

"This awful slang must stop... I shall not tell you both again – now please use the names you were christened with!" she snapped.

Musgrove looked at her in astonishment and did not know quite what to say. After all this was a time for celebrating a great discovery, not trying to explain away the natural boyhood name-shortening of your new best friend.

Aunt Vera turned and started to make her way back to the car, calling for the two boys to follow as she steadied her balance on the uneven surface of the rocks. Suddenly she stopped and looked back towards Bradley. "Oh... and please don't forget to pick my lovely fresh halibut that Old Mac gave me!"

Bradley cringed and turned to Musgrove. "She's not going to be very happy."

Musgrove sniggered as Bradley shouted back to his aunt. "Err… its gone – it's not here anymore Aunt Vera!"

"What do mean it's not there? - I left it on the rock!" she screeched.

Aunt Vera made her way back to the boys and witnessed Musgrove attempting to retrieve the sunken fish from the depths of its watery grave. "My lovely fish… this is all your fault Bradley Baker - you and that blooming coin of yours!"

"But Aunt Vera, I…"

"Don't speak boy… just you and your friend get your bodies over to that car!" she growled.

"I think we'd better get a move on Brad … err - I mean Bradley," said Musgrove.

Aunt Vera turned away again mumbling to herself, as she headed off fuming back in the direction of the car. Bradley was amused and scratched his head, as he watched his aunt in disbelief.

Musgrove called out. "Look Brad… my shoes!"

Bradley looked over his shoulder and noticed that his friend's shoes and socks were positioned on the rock just where he had left them above the pool where they had found the coin object. "How did they get there?"

"I don't know," replied Musgrove, as he picked up his footwear. "Maybe Old Mac saw something."

Musgrove looked over to where the fisherman had been standing. Old Mac had since boarded his boat *Galetis* and was now sailing out of the cove. "Well… we will have to wait for another opportunity to ask him - it looks like Old Mac's has gone off to catch some more fish."

"Yeah and I never got a chance to ask him about the name on his boat… come on Muzzy – we had best be off," insisted Bradley. "My aunt doesn't look too happy."

The boys followed Aunt Vera back to the car. Bradley could now expect even more changes to his plans for that evening. An early bath and bed would no doubt be preceded by an in-depth interrogation seeing as Vera's fresh halibut had slipped into the rock pool, whilst she had attempted to retrieve the coin. Anyone exploring that particular rock in future would be able to witness Sandmouth's local pub football scores wrapped around a tasty bit of fish laying like a wreck at the bottom of the pool.

A hasty journey along the bumpy lane leading out of Amley's Cove ensued. The tired car came to a halt on the hard stand next to Vera's cottage. Bradley's aunt climbed out of the car and she was still fuming. She slammed the car door and headed empty-handed along the pathway that led to her cottage.

As per Aunt Vera's stern instructions, Bradley and his new friend said their quick farewells. Musgrove started to head back to his house just three doors down from Aunt Vera's cottage and Bradley followed his aunt through the gate.

"See you tomorrow!" shouted Musgrove, as he reached the front of his house.

Bradley waved and then assessed the look on Aunt Vera's crimson face. He quickly returned his attention to his new friend. "Err…maybe!" yelled Bradley, as he disappeared into Vera's front porch.

Meanwhile back in Yorkshire, Frannie continued to play with the old dolls house and she looked up at her father and smiled. Patrick looked like he was about to announce something and she stared at him offering him the opportunity to reveal all. "Frannie… would you and K2 like go on a long journey?"

"Oooh… yes please Daddy – but what about Sky?"

Patrick suggested that it might be a nice surprise if they travelled by train to Sandmouth to meet up with her mother and Bradley. "Unfortunately Aunt Vera doesn't like cats so Sky will have stay with Grandma."

Frannie loved the idea but was quite saddened about leaving her pet behind. However, she leapt up off the floor and threw her tiny arms around her father's neck and gave him a big kiss on the end of his nose. "I can't wait Daddy - can we go now?" she demanded and brushed the backs of her tiny fingers over Patrick's stubble. "…and can you have a shave please, Daddy?"

"Yes sweet pea - I'll have a shave when we get home," replied Patrick, as he picked up his daughter and swung her around. "I'll take that as a definite yes then…we'll set off for your Aunt Vera's first thing tomorrow."

"Daddy… I asked if we could go right now!"

"No darling… we can't go right this minute - I'll need to make a quick call to the ticket office and arrange for us to pick up the tickets at the railway station in the morning."

Patrick collected his daughter's belongings together and they both said their goodbyes to Grandma Penworthy. Frannie insisted on finding her pet cat so she could get one last cuddle before she left. Sky was sat on the front lawn licking her paws and cleaning the backs of her ears. The girl approached the cat to offer her farewells and Patrick struggled with K2, as he pulled on the lead. The dog barked aggressively at Sky and cat scampered under the hedgerow, Frannie scolded the clumsy hound. "K2… you are a very naughty boy!" she shouted.

"Come on princess… you'll see Sky again when we get back home from your Aunt Vera's," said Patrick, as he struggled to hold on to the powerful dog and balance Frannie's backpack over his shoulder. He managed to pick up his hold-all and they finally set off down the front path.

Frannie was eventually persuaded by her father to leave the confines of Grandma's garden and they walked K2 the few hundred metres down the hill to the new housing estate, which was built on the old Silvermoor Colliery site. She was very excited at the prospect of seeing her mummy again so soon and she was also looking forward to seeing Aunt Vera, as well as tormenting her older brother.

Back inside the cottage Bradley looked bemused, as his aunt continued with her soap-box ranting in the middle of the lounge. The shell-shocked boy sat on the settee next to his mother and let his mind wander whilst Aunt Vera rattled on about the loss of her prized Halibut. "Stupid old coin thing!" she shouted, sarcastically. "The boy isn't even a relative of mine… and his mother has the audacity to ignore me in the street – and to make it worse she only lives a few doors down the lane!" bawled the grumpy spinster, referring to the Chilcott family at number sixteen.

Bradley's attention was resumed at the mention of his friend. "I wonder why…" he mumbled, as Margaret nudged his ribcage.

"What are you going on about Vera?" asked Margaret, as she struggled to keep a straight face after overhearing Bradley's quip. "You're not making any sense… please calm down - you'll give yourself a heart attack!"

"Oh never mind," replied Aunt Vera in a lowering tone. "What do I care… you'll both have to settle for bread and jam for tea tonight!"

"Can I have chocolate spread instead?" asked Bradley, cheekily.

"Bradley!" warned Margaret, as she stood between her cheeky son and volatile sister. "Please don't wind your aunt up any more than she already is!"

"Right that's it... I'm getting fed up with all this - I'm off to see Selwyn the butcher!" said Vera. "Maybe he can ensure the safe delivery of his pork sausages and best cut rashers of bacon into my frying pan for tomorrow's breakfast!"

Margaret looked at Bradley and smiled. The look on his mum's face assured him that his aunt was simply having one of her funny turns and for him not to get too concerned. Vera noticed the way her sister had looked at him and she responded by snatching her car keys from the coffee table. She stormed out of the cottage with her nose aloft, and clutched her shopping bag to her chest. They both cringed as the door slammed so hard it lifted the lounge curtains. "Oops!" they exclaimed simultaneously and huddled together on the sofa.

The few relaxing hours that Margaret had spent in the Drake Circus Shopping Centre earlier that day had now drifted into insignificance. The reality of family squabbles dominated the present moment, but she was glad to be holding her adventurous son. Bradley cuddled into his mother and indulged in a packet of prawn cocktail flavoured crisps.

Mother and son took advantage of Vera's absence and enjoyed their time together on the sofa, whilst the familiar theme tune from *'The Weakest Link'* sounded out from the television set.

8

A Perfect Fit

With Aunt Vera out of the way, Bradley was able to tell his mother all about his adventure at Amley's Cove and how Musgrove had found the gold coin. Margaret was very impressed with the way her sister had helped the boys retrieve the coin and not in the least bit surprised to hear that her kind intentions were so short lived. "It all sounds very interesting... but it's time for your bath now... Bradley," she suggested, after listening to the excited tones of her adventurous son.

"Do I really have to Mum?" pleaded Bradley, as he dropped his shoulders and hung his arms by his side like a depressed orangutan.

"Yes... son!" said Margaret. "You have been playing in salt water today and I don't think your Aunt Vera will appreciate dirty footprints on her nice clean sheets... do you?"

"Oh, all right!" replied Bradley, reluctantly.

Bradley's display simulated the repellence of a slug near salt, as Margaret escorted him upstairs to the bathroom. He made sure the bathroom door was secure before getting undressed and scattered his clothes on the floor, as the water flowed from the taps.

It did not take long for the bathtub to fill with hot soapy water and the playful boy picked out his favourite toy soldiers from the toilet bag that Margaret had placed beside the wash hand basin. The military personnel were thrown at random into the water and floated helplessly on the surface. Bradley turned off the water supply and climbed on to the sides of the bathtub on all fours. The agile youngster spanned the tub like a great suspension bridge, as he tentatively tested the temperature by lowering his left big toe into the water.

"Ouch!" screamed Bradley, as he straddled the bath tub. "The water is too hot!" Bradley's outburst attracted the unwanted attention of his protective mother.

"Are you alright in there Bradley?" shouted Margaret.

"Yesssss!" replied Bradley, as he readjusted his balance. "Stop whittling Mum!"

"I'll whittle you in a minute you cheeky devil!" replied Margaret, reciprocating the use of the Yorkshire lingo, which her son had put to a defiant use.

"Sorry Mum… it's just that the water you've ran – it's a bit too hot for me and I can't get in it!"

"Well run some more cold then!" replied his mother.

"Right Mum… I'll do that then!" yelled a grinning Bradley, with an element of sarcasm in his tone.

"Just wait till you get out of that bathroom!" threatened Margaret. "It's times like this when I think your Aunt Vera is right about your back-chatting!"

"You need to chill out more, Mum!" laughed Bradley. "Just like this water!"

Margaret smiled in acknowledgement of her son's witty remark, as she pressed her ear against the bathroom door. "I'll be downstairs… please make sure you wash your hair!"

Bradley chose to ignore his mother's last request, he was too busy concentrating on maintaining his balance, as he spanned across the tub. Now using only three limbs, he reached for the cold-water tap and increased the water level by about a third. Bradley also made use of his hand as a paddle and proceeded to scoop up the cold water and deliver it to the far end of the bathtub. Whilst directing the water back through his legs, he attempted to reveal some of the toy soldiers that had disappeared inside the foam created from Aunt Vera's aromatherapy bubble bath.

Distribution of the cold water supply was now complete. A further test with his big toe and in the bath he jumped creating a tidal wave of water that travelled the full length of the bath and over the end onto the varnished pine floorboards. The energetic scuba diving expert started to explore the soapy depths and splashed around unaware of the bright glow that emanated from one of the pockets in his crumpled trousers, which had been strewn in the corner of the bathroom.

At that moment the bathroom light flickered and Bradley looked up from the tub. The soapy bubbles dripped from his chin as he held onto the edge of the bath and he popped his head over the side. He noticed the gold coin had appeared in the middle of the bathroom floor.

"Where did that come from?" he muttered to himself. "Muzzy must have slipped the coin into my pocket when we said our farewells."

The inquisitive boy reached out of the bath leaving watermarks on the toweling bathmat. He picked up the coin and examined it more thoroughly this time. Bradley submerged the coin in the clean bath water and this revealed a message around its outer edge.

Bradley hadn't noticed this when they first discovered the mysterious object in Amley's Cove. The inscription around the edge of the coin read;

'Thee, who hath taken this to thy belonging, seal it again to bring forth magic powers!'

"What could this mean... seal it where?" he thought.

Bradley gave the coin a nice soapy lather and cleaned out the hole in the centre with one of Aunt Vera's cotton buds. He put the coin on the side of the bath whilst he continued to play for a while. His toy soldiers took precedence over the new discovery, they were much more fun and besides he liked to line up the figures and pretend to make them dive into the rapids below the waterfall, which was simulated by the running water from the cold tap. The chrome bath utensil holder that straddled the width of the tub acted as a makeshift bridge and Bradley positioned some of his soldiers in strategic positions across its span in readiness for battle with the infantry below.

Bradley removed the long handled back-brush from the utensil holder and pretended to use it as a surface to air missile launcher and multi-purpose enemy submarine. He proceeded to air bomb the back-brush from the chrome bridge with some of Aunt Vera's coloured bath balls that looked just like clear marbles. He was a little anxious when they started to melt in the warm water and he started to panic at the thought of his aunt's anger in response to his irresponsible waste of the perfumed bath oils.

The sides of the bathtub were now very slippery and Bradley continued his bath time play by creating as much lather as possible and started to apply the soapsuds to his face. He imagined himself to be Old Mac the fisherman and imitated the bearded man by pretending to sell some fish to an imaginary Aunt Vera. Bradley soon grew tired of the beard and reached for his toothbrush and utilized it as a disposable razor blade and subsequently styled the full beard down to a *goatee* design. He continued to sculpture the bubbles and create other predictably differing types of moustaches. Bradley concluded his fashionable look with the addition of sideburns. The bubbles started to disintegrate before he had chance to finish his facial artwork.

"Have you finished in there yet, Bradley?" enquired Margaret, as she knocked on the door.

Bradley was startled by the sound of his mother's voice and quickly rinsed the remainder of the soapy lather from his face. "Nearly!" he replied remembering his mother's final request, as he reached for the shampoo bottle and accidentally knocked the gold coin back in to the water. "I'm just washing my hair!"

Bradley poured a liberal amount of shampoo into the palm of his hand and applied it moderately to his wet hair. He quickly rinsed it off again and decided it was time to pull out the plug. He reached for the chain that attached the rubber bung to the bathtub. As he started to tug on the chain, the gold coin vibrated and started to glow again. He could hear strange murmuring noises emanating from the water as he continued to drag the plug out of the plughole.

The plug finally released from its vacuum and shot to the surface of the water. A parallel line of bubbles followed and this prompted the coin to mysteriously rise out of the water into the air. Bradley stared in amazement, as the coin hovered and rotated with great speed over the bathtub. Then the coin suddenly stopped spinning and it plummeted back into the depths of the bath's soapy water.

Bradley was both frightened and intrigued at the sight of the airborne object falling into the bath again. An eerie sound echoed around the tub, as the coin clinked on the bottom. He began to feel nervous and shouted out for his mother, but his screams for help could not be heard. He watched in disbelief, as a gap appeared in the bubbles on the surface of the water. He peered below the surface to witness the coin tilt upright onto its edge and roll towards the plughole.

An array of sparkling yellow stars filled the room and then Bradley's clothes lifted up from the bathroom floor. They hovered over his head for a moment then the garments started to fall at random, as he dived backwards into the water. They landed above him on the surface and he came back up for air, as the white sports shoes hit him on the head. They then rebounded onto the side of the bath and eventually landed in the soapy bubbles. His white t-shirt began to sink beneath the surface and his blue checked top and trousers fell around his shoulders. He pulled them free and was dragged back under the water again, as bubbles of air chased to the surface.

Meanwhile back in Ravenswood, Patrick had prepared a light supper then packed their cases ready for the morning. After the meal Frannie was ushered upstairs to bed. By the time K2 had bound up the stairs in hot pursuit, the little girl had climbed under her covers.

The big dog darted into Frannie's bedroom and jumped onto her duvet. He then proceeded to lick the four-year-old's face followed by a ritual of nine continuous circles on the same spot before settling his arched frame into the back of the little red-head's knees. The sheer weight of the dog squashed her against the bedroom wall but she managed to force him back by pushing her legs against the wall. The dog groaned, as she gently elbowed him and they eventually settled down for the night.

Patrick had packed the suitcases and completed the final preparations in readiness for their train journey to Devon. He was now relaxing in front of the television and he placed a mug of hot tea on the coffee table, as he settled back into the sofa.

The familiar sound of *Big Ben* echoed out between the dramatic headlines that introduced the ten o'clock news. The night cap remained untouched and it was not long before his head slumped sideways into the cushion, as he fell asleep.

Back in Aunt Vera's bathtub, the gold coin had finally reached its destination. *A perfect fit.* The disk sat snuggly in the plughole and immediately upon engagement the water in the bathtub changed to a bright green colour. The seal was complete and the hole in the centre of the coin started to open wider and wider. Bradley felt himself being drawn towards the green hole and the current quickened, as the rapids became taller and faster.

Bradley emerged above the surface of the water again but struggled to keep his balance, especially with a plastic soldier still clasped in one hand. The sides of the bathtub were coated in oil, which made it difficult for him to stay upright. The water lashed up against his stomach and he fell sideways, hitting his head on the edge of the chrome handgrips. Momentarily he lost consciousness and his head crashed into the water, as his lungs started to fill with the soapy liquid. He quickly opened his eyes in a panic and searched for the light shining at the surface. He emerged yet again gasping for breath and he could feel the bathroom taking on a different dimension.

"Was the bathtub increasing in size or was he shrinking?" Bradley thought out loud, as he was pulled towards the plughole.

His thoughts of the latter were confirmed, as he swirled round and round with the army of toy soldiers that followed the same path within the parallel vortex. His clothes twisted with him and he grabbed each piece one by one and dressed himself, as he turned and spun in different directions. It was an amazing achievement, he had never got dressed so quickly but a sense of survival hastened his actions.

The water continued to splurge around him and the inevitable happened, as he was eventually sucked through the centre of the gold coin. The adventure through the plughole and down the drainpipe had begun. Bradley's wish for excitement and exploration during his stay at Aunt Vera's was now being realized.

At the family home in Ravenswood, Frannie woke suddenly. K2's snoring sounded like the gurgling of water being sucked down a plughole. Now she couldn't get back to sleep. The weight of the heavy dog, against the back of her legs, was very uncomfortable so she pushed as hard as she could in a vain attempt to move the great hound further down the bed. K2 could not be moved so she lay awake staring at the assortment of fish printed on the border that ran around the top of the walls below the coving in her bedroom. She felt alarmed for some reason but at the same time felt excited at the thought of visiting Aunt Vera in Devon.

Frannie's concentration was interrupted and she sensed something wasn't quite right with her brother. She lay awake for some time thinking about what he might be up to. She was distracted by the sound of rushing water behind the wall next to her bed. Her father must have just used the bathroom, which neighboured the little girl's bedroom. "I hope you're okay Bradley," muttered Frannie, as her eyes grew heavy again. She could not stay awake any longer and she drifted back to sleep again.

Meanwhile, Bradley was still being carried along by the torrent of oily scented bath water and he continued his frightful journey down the drainpipe. He twisted and turned, falling deeper and deeper into the darkness below. As he fell, he looked up at the green light that emanated through the centre of the coin which was getting further and further away, as he spiraled around the u-bend and onwards infinitely along the smelly waste system.

A successful navigation ensued along and around more curves in the pipe and finally to the abyss in the form of a vertical pipe linking the first floor bathroom to the ground floor level of Aunt Vera's cottage. The petrified boy plummeted deeper and deeper into the unknown.

Suddenly there was a loud fanfare of mystical sounds and an aura of flashing multi-coloured lights filled the drainpipe. The inside of the pipe became a vortex of spiraling images and the falling water gushed around Bradley's helpless body.

The astonished adventurer managed to look down towards his feet, he could just make out the ground getting nearer and nearer. At last the impact with the soft floor was imminent and Bradley braced himself, as he landed feet first into a soggy bed of putrid waste. The toy soldier that had accompanied him throughout the ordeal was knocked out of his hand and sent hurtling across the chamber.

The smell inside the chamber was disgusting and he fought to free himself from the stale foliage, which was up to his waist. Bradley struggled free and rolled over to more solid ground. He got to his feet and started to remove the brownie-green slime that had built up inside the waste system for centuries.

Suddenly he flicked his head slightly to strain his ear at the sound of running water. He looked around the dark chamber in search of the noise and soon his eyes became accustomed to the grey light. In the corner of the chamber he could just make out a cluster of fungi. Bradley made his way over to the toadstools and noticed that water was running down the sides of the wall behind them.

Bradley carefully climbed up the stalk and onto the top of one of the toadstools. He gained his balance and then reached out to the water. To his astonishment, it was clean and fresh so he proceeded to shower beneath and wash the putrid slime from his clothes.

His eyes became more accustomed to the darkness he noticed something familiar. Bradley jumped down from the toadstool and reached down to pick up the green object. He held the toy soldier and stared at it for a little while.

"Well... what did you think of the ride commander?" asked Bradley, as he made conversation with the green plastic paratrooper in his hand. He slipped the toy soldier into his pocket and looked around the chamber in search of a way out. The sides of the cave-like room were covered with sewage stains and the smell of stale water was overpowering.

Bradley pinched the end of his nose and turned towards the stalks of the giant toadstools. He noticed an opening at the base of one of the stalks and walked slowly towards it.

"This is just like one of the internet games I play at home on Dad's computer," he thought. Bradley was absolutely amazed at what was happening to him, it was unbelievable. He thought back to the inscription around the edge of the gold coin.

'Thee who hath taken this to thy belonging, seal it again to bring forth magic powers!'

Bradley began to summarize to himself out loud. "The seal was obviously made when the coin landed in the plughole... it must have created the magic powers to send me down the plughole and through the drainage system below Aunt Vera's cottage – but how will I get back up?"

He placed his hands on his hips and peered up at the opening above his head. The inside of the pipe, which had just delivered him to the smelly chamber, towered infinitely above him and the green light was now hidden from view. He had travelled through the main drainage system and was stranded deep below the cliff-side town of Sandmouth. It would appear the only way out of the chamber was back up the pipe, but it would be impossible for him to reach the opening without the aid of a ladder or rope. Even if he was fortunate enough to reach the opening of the pipe he would not be able to climb up it – it was too far back to the surface.

Bradley did not feel frightened any more. The young adventurer was determined to find out more about the magic power's emitted by the gold coin. He became more curious of the gap in the stem of the toadstool and the inquisitive boy walked towards the opening. He reached out his hand to feel inside and then bravely ventured forward into the unknown.

9

The Blueberry Queen

Once inside the giant toadstool it took a few seconds for Bradley to adjust to the dimly lit surroundings, as he refocused his eyes at the tiny round lights that were set into the walls of the inner stalk. The strange twinkling objects created a wonderful haze within the fungi and gave the appearance of small multi-coloured gems, which omitted beams of soft light all around. Although the walls of the toadstool's stem were round on the outside, the inside of the stalk appeared to be a gigantic square-shaped room. The circumference outside could not have measured more than four metres, yet the room inside was about the size of a school gymnasium.

Bradley took a few tentative steps forward and he closely followed his shadow, as it passed eerily over the smooth surfaces of the inner stalk. His eyesight was now fairly well focused and he continued to look from left to right, as he took each careful step.

81

Bradley's attention was drawn to the shiny surfaces of the walls and he monitored his distorted reflection on both walls either side of him. As he neared the far end of the room, he became more aware of his reflections coming closer together. He now realized that the room wasn't square at all - the room was actually tapered. By the time he had reached the far end of the long room, he was able to reach out and touch both walls either side of him with his out-stretched arms.

Bradley stopped suddenly and looked down in amazement, the surface of the floor in front of him now felt different and it appeared to be made of something metallic. The composition of the soft padded floor of the inner stalk had now changed to a steel-like hardness.

The inquisitive boy knelt down to touch the metal and was astonished to find he was standing on the top step of a great iron staircase. He stared downwards and followed the line of the steps, which spiraled downwards like a raging tornado to what seemed infinity.

Bradley continued to inspect the structure of the strange staircase and he noticed it did not appear to have anything to support it. Even the unusual handrail hung in limbo and the steps just swirled down and around into the eerie blackness of the abyss.

"This is absolutely amazing!" Bradley exclaimed out load, as the echo of his voice tapered back into the odd-shaped room.

Bradley leaned over further to see if he could make out how far down he would have to descend, in order to reach the bottom of the metal staircase. The boy's curiosity got the better of him and he quickly got back to his feet. "Well... here goes," he whispered to himself and used the handrail to steady his balance.

Bradley quickly pulled back his hand, as the dampness of the handrail sent a shiver down his spine. It appeared to be made of some kind of moist plant vine, as it extended in a twisted fashion parallel with the staircase with nothing to support and connect the two together. He plucked up enough courage and he started to descend the staircase. It seemed to go on and on, as he continued around and downwards further into the darkness. Down he went, deeper and deeper into the abyss until the tired boy finally reached the last step of the staircase.

The long descent had exhausted Bradley and he bent over to place his hands on his knees, whilst he took in heavy breathes of air. How he needed a drink of some kind right now, as he lifted his head to look around his new surroundings. Again it took a short while to refocus his eyes and he found himself in a very large stone-clad room.

Bradley was now in a round chamber, which was adorned with many ancient-looking arched shaped doorframes spread evenly apart all the way around the circumference of the cobweb covered walls.

The exhausted boy took a little more time to catch his breath and then proceeded to count the number of doors within the weird looking archways. There were eight in all, each having a silver plaque fixed in the centre with some sort of inscription written in bright green paint. Above each door, Bradley noticed that the lintels were actually carved images made from a granite-type stone. Each image was shaped like a mysterious-looking head with a bear-like snout exposed beneath hoods that draped over and around the top of each arched doorframe.

The inquisitive adventurer moved closer to one of the doors to check the spelling on the silver plaque.

The plaque read;

'BARREK - an intruder from the land of Freytor.'

Bradley decided to walk round the room to check the inscriptions on the front of each door. He assumed that the names on all the doors must be associated with the hooded heads that adorned the top of each doorframe.

Unbeknown to Bradley, the inscriptions on each plaque were the names of the eight Freytorian traders that had made up the scouting party, which was separated from the great ice-berg mother ship. The Pathylian extremists, who had captured the intruders from Freytor, had sentenced them to an eternal incarnation into the stone frames that now surrounded the sacred doors. The names of each prisoner appeared in alphabetical order and they read as follows;

BARREK, ERRIHAN, FESTANU, GOMMERRA, LETOCH, MOKO, NEBACKOO and TOUMON.

Bradley reached out and touched the door marked LETOCH. The door felt cold and wet and the startled boy quickly pulled his hand away. The crimson slime clung to the ends of his fingers creating parallel threads of syrup that hung down like telegraph lines. He looked at his fingers and they were covered in bloodlike red juice. Innocently and without any hesitation he put his sticky fingers to his mouth. The glistening syrup tasted like wild fruit berries and Bradley quickly spat out the sour sample in fear of being poisoned. He recalled what his mother used to say when he was younger, about not eating wild fruits when out playing in Silvermoor woods.

Bradley's attention was suddenly taken away from the foul tasting session and he cocked his head to listen out for the loud noise, which sounded like metal grinding against metal.

He didn't have to wait long and his concentration was disturbed by a thunderous banging sound.

The loud noise sounded like some sought of industrial turbine, just like the ones that his father installed and maintained as part of his contract work for E.M.M.C.O. He likened the sound to the heavy electrical machinery because last year his mother had persuaded his father to arrange a day visit for Ravenswood Primary School.

During a guided tour of the workshops, Bradley had been amazed at the size of the turbines and had enjoyed the lectures presented during the tour. The guide had explained how using different sources of energy generated electricity and how the turbines transformed the energy into electricity, which powered homes, hospitals and factories etc.

Bradley's thoughts of the school trip faded and he turned around and looked up to see the spiral staircase, which he had just descended upon, corkscrewing into the air. It was the ascending metal staircase that was creating the strange grinding noise and as it disappeared upwards he now had no way out of the room except via one of the hooded doors.

The puzzled boy looked around for help. He was becoming rather worried and shouted out in a panic-stricken voice. "Mum… Aunt Vera – can anyone hear me?"

There was no reply from the roofless space towering above the chamber. Bradley was very frightened and rushed around the room frantically trying to open all the doors but they were all locked. Then he noticed something sticking out from under the door marked *MOKO*. He bent down to inspect what looked like the corner of a piece of paper.

Bradley took hold of the paper and pulled out what appeared to be a scroll with a red seal that had been broken sometime before. He picked up the scroll, which had now recoiled into a tubular shape.

With the scroll re-opened, he read out loud the words written on the ancient paper. *"We from Freytor ask you to think deeply!"*

Bradley paused for a moment and looked around his surroundings. "What could this mean?" he whispered to himself.

It was as if reading the message had sent Bradley into a trance and he started to do what the message had instructed him to do. He started to think deeply and resurrected memories from his past.

Bradley loved Grandma Penworthy's tasty blueberry muffins. Every Sunday he and Frannie would visit Grandma whilst their mum and dad played for the local pub team in the area boules league. At around four o'clock in the afternoon Grandma would always present a tea tray for the children with a cake selection to befit a King. Frannie used to call her '*The Blueberry Queen'*.

In his thoughts, Bradley could see Frannie in the front room of Grandma's house. The little red-head was asking her a question. *"How do you make your cakes so fluffy Grandma?"*

"Plenty of air bubbles in the mixture and 190 degrees in the middle of the oven… my dear," she replied, as Bradley pictured his Grandma cupping her frail hand beneath Frannie's chin.

Bradley's hypnotic state faded and he focused back on the situation and the problem now facing him. He had remembered thinking about blueberry muffins so he looked for a silver plaque with a name that began with the letter *B*. He focused on the one marked *BARREK* and after about ten seconds the door opened of its own accord. Bradley leapt forward and following an athletic forward role, he landed awkwardly against the wall on the other side. The confused boy now found himself in a torch lit passageway that had been carved within the solid rock. "Phew!" he exclaimed. "At last I'm through... that was wicked!"

Bradley walked ahead and made his way along a series of winding passageways that led to another dark chamber. He entered the tall cave-like room and heard a familiar voice calling out to him from the far end.

"Brad, is that you?"

"Who's there?" replied Bradley, tentatively.

A tall slender figure appeared out of a dark corner and ran towards the frightened boy and startled him. "Muzzy!" exclaimed Bradley, in a gleeful voice. "How did you get here?"

"Through the door marked *MOKO*," he replied, comically. "I remember thinking of my late grandfather's old Morris Marina car and – *hey presto* - the door swung open!"

Musgrove had also made his way into the large chamber through one of the eight hooded doors, which in fact all led to the same place. Bradley gave a loud sigh of relief and laughed, as they continued with their friendly meeting ritual.

A few minutes had passed and they began to survey the chamber in more detail. The flames from the burning torches that hung from the walls flickered and danced in the gentle breeze that blew through the passageways. The light from the fire caused their shadows to dance on the rough stone sides of the cave and the boys followed the length of their silhouettes upwards into ceiling void, which towered above them some fifty metres and more.

"How long have you been here?" asked Bradley.

"Not long… about five minutes," replied Musgrove.

Bradley explained how he had been playing in Aunt Vera's bathtub and how he was then sucked through the centre of the coin and sent hurtling down the drainpipe. Musgrove was able to clarify his friend's story by confirming that the same had happened to him whilst he was taking a bath.

"But I had the gold coin that we found," insisted Bradley. "So how did you manage to get sucked through the plug hole too?"

Musgrove put his arm around his friend's shoulder and started to explain what had happened. "After your Aunt Vera dropped me off outside her cottage, I took the opportunity to slip the gold coin into your pocket."

"So how come you were able to get down here now without the coin?" insisted Bradley.

"Simple… I already had another gold coin," replied Musgrove, excitedly. "I had found it in the rock pools at Amley's Cove about three weeks before you arrived to stay with your Aunt Vera."

Musgrove revealed to Bradley that this wasn't the first time he had adventured through the drainage system below Sandmouth. On this occasion he had travelled down the drainpipe in good time to wait to see if his new friend would join him. He had discovered the magic power of the first gold coin about two weeks ago in the bath tub, which was a rare occurrence for him. He would normally take a shower, which was much quicker and more convenient.

Musgrove had tried desperately to explain his epic adventures to his mother, but she wouldn't believe him and he reminded Bradley of their first meeting in Aunt Vera's back garden. "Do you remember when we first met?"

"Yes I do, but…" replied Bradley.

"…And do you remember asking your mum to take a look at the cuts on my knees?"

"Yes, but …"

"…And then later you offered to help me find my shoes and socks?"

"Yes… yes… So what's your point...?" asked Bradley, looking very puzzled.

"Well, I sensed you were looking for adventure… and you seemed like a really nice kid," said Musgrove.

"Please don't call me a kid!" snorted Bradley. "It's bad enough with Aunt Vera being so condescending without you starting!"

"Don't be offended Brad," replied Musgrove. "I didn't mean anything by it."

Musgrove was forgiven, for he had called his friend by that muscle bulging, semi-automatic machine gun wielding, film star name again. "I deliberately planted the coin in your pocket… so there was every chance the same would happen to you as it did to me - at least then someone would believe my adventure stories."

"I see…" replied Bradley.

Musgrove paused for a moment. "Have I offended you?"

"What do you mean?" asked Bradley.

"I mean… by the way I tricked you into going down to Amley's Cove with me to find my shoes and socks," explained Musgrove, as he placed hand on his friend's arm.

"Naaahh," responded Bradley shrugging his shoulders. "It was great to go down to the cove so soon… anyway we wouldn't be here now having this great adventure if it wasn't for you."

"Thanks Brad… I'm so glad you're not angry with me!"

"So what happens now, Muzzy?" asked Bradley. "How do we get out of here?"

"I don't know!" replied Musgrove, as he shrugged his wide boney shoulders.

"What do you mean, you don't know!" exclaimed Bradley. "Stop trying to frighten me!"

"I'm not trying to frighten you, Brad," said Musgrove. "I honestly don't know where we go from here… each journey is always a new adventure!"

This was Musgrove's fourth visit to this strange and mysterious world via the plughole. The initial part of the journey was always the same up to the sacred hooded doors. Each time the scroll appeared he had to think different thoughts. Up to and including this journey, he had entered the chamber through the hooded doorways named; *'LETOCH', 'NEBACKOO', 'TOUMON'* and now *'MOKO'.*

Musgrove explained. "I would always remember my incredible journeys up to this point… but I can't remember how I get back home."

Bradley looked down at the floor and said nothing, as Musgrove tapped him on the shoulder again. He regained eye contact with the forlorn looking boy, which prompted Bradley to look over to where his friend was pointing.

"Come with me… wait till you see these," said Musgrove, as he pulled on Bradley's shirtsleeve.

The two boys walked to the far end of the chamber, which at first was hidden from view behind a large boulder. "Look Brad… do you see those wooden doors over there – what do you think of those?"

"Oh my goodness… Muzzy - they're enormous!" exclaimed Bradley, as he looked up at the huge doorway. He could hardly miss the large oak paneled doors with the black iron studs riveted at strategic points along their construction. The hinges alone were bigger than the family estate car. He stood opened mouthed in awe of the breath taking monuments that stood before him. "I wonder what's behind them."

The great wooden doors stood about twenty metres high. Burning torches were held secure in medieval-style iron brackets on the walls at either side of the doors and the word *Pathylon* was scorched into the broad wooden lintel. The word was scribed in some kind of medieval-style writing and the light from the flickering torch flames made it appear to move within the oak beam.

The letters seemed to dance as the fire from the lanterns reflected against the granite walls that surrounded the immense doorway. "Now *that's* what I call a pair of doors!" said Bradley. "But where do they lead and look Muzzy… that word - *Pathylon*!"

"What about it, Brad?"

"That's the word I saw in the mirror in my bathroom back home!" he exclaimed. "The message read… *Pathylon is in danger!*"

"I don't know anything about that!" replied his friend. "Maybe it was a sign… calling you for help!"

Bradley insisted that they should find out and pulled on his friend's arm. "Come on Muzzy!"

The two boys ran across the chamber and stopped in front of the oak doors and stared up at the massive entrance in front of them. Bradley noticed an unusual stone slab to the left of the doors and he rushed over to investigate. "Look

Muzzy… over here!" he shouted and pointed to the floor. "There's a large star set in the ground with markings etched into it!"

"Let's see," said Musgrove, as he made his way over. "Oh yeah, a five cornered star… and look at the size of that red jewel in the middle - it looks like a giant ruby!" he exclaimed. "Wow… that's some gem isn't it?"

Bradley brushed away the dust to reveal an emblem etched into each corner of the star. The large gemstone was now sparkling vibrantly and it cast a red glow around the chamber. They both knelt down to examine the carved granite in more detail. The five etched markings displayed on the star represented; a strange-looking tree, a tower, a snow-capped mountain, a burning sun and some sought of frog-like creature.

"What could these pictures mean?" asked Bradley.

"I'm not sure," replied Musgrove. "They do seem familiar… I have a faint recollection of them!"

Musgrove noticed that by disturbing the dirt the ruby now had an obvious gap all the way around it. He stood up and placed his foot on the gemstone and stepped back from the star. The large oak doors suddenly began to move simultaneously with a spine-chilling creek and a loud grating of wood against rock emanated around the chamber as the doors opened.

"Whatever happens from this point forward mate, we might never remember!" exclaimed Musgrove, as Bradley looked up at him with trusting eyes. He had great faith in his new found friend and his ability to get them back home. With that single thought in his mind he ventured forward very tentatively and clutched Musgrove's arm again, as they walked through the entrance and into the next chamber.

The next room was even bigger than the last and was full of strangely carved statues depicting amphibian creatures and weasel-like animals. The cavern was very *'Aztec'* in appearance and there were lots of bright multi-coloured lights shooting all around the chamber. A large whirling light, which emitted a kaleidoscopic affect took centre stage and drew the boys towards it like a magnet.

With one last look at each other they continued forward and began to run towards the light. Just like two athletes competing in the triple jump, they strode in tandem and took off together into the air, landing in the centre of the twirling spiral.

Round and round they travelled as the flashing lights darted like lasers in different directions. The optical illusion created by the twisting lines made the boys appear smaller and smaller as they travelled towards the middle of the spiral, eventually disappearing into the centre and into the unknown.

The mysterious journey down the drainpipe had now moved to a crucial stage. The swirling vortex was transporting Bradley and Musgrove to a strange place where unusual creatures dwelled. The evil curse was growing stronger and the boys continued on their journey deeper into the spiraling abyss. Soon they would be hurled into a dangerous world of chaos and confusion, a world known as *Pathylon!*

10

Mr. Tangerine Man

The evil curse orchestrated by General Eidar had already attained some devastating results. The populous were living in great fear and the Kingdom of Pathylon was now in complete turmoil. The throne had been claimed by Varuna and he had unlawfully elected himself the new King of Pathylon.

The heavy skies and continuing rolls of thunder did not concern the weasel like creature. He had planned his rebellion well and the support of the Freytorians had made his rewarding journey to the Royal City of Trad very easy.

Following his raid on the Royal Palace, Varuna sentenced Luccese and his Queen to imprisonment within the Shallock Tower for eternity. The true King and his wife Vash would be left to perish hidden away from the wicked tyranny that was to rule over the darkened land.

Varuna had now taken up residence in the Royal Palace, which was located in *Devonia*, high on a hillside overlooking the city of Trad. The new self-appointed King chose to keep Trad as the capital of Pathylon because of its central location in relation to the other four regions.

Whilst taking a tour of the Royal Palace, Varuna surveyed the extent of his new empire on a map that adorned one of the palace reception walls. He revelled in the realization that he now ruled over the great expanse of land that was evidently detailed before him.

To the North beyond the Mountains of Hartopia, the *Blacklands*; to the West across the River Klomus, the *Forest of Haldon*; to the East across the Satorc Bridge, *Krogonia;* and to the South beyond the Forest of Haldon and adjacent the Mouth of Sand, the *Galetis Empire.* To the south of the Galetis Empire stood the mountainous region of the Peronto Alps and beyond these mountains lay an uncharted area called the *Unknown Land.* It was revered throughout the land that this part of Pathylon was cursed and no one dared to venture into it. Anyone who had attempted to travel into the Unknown Land had never returned to tell the tail.

The Hartopian sniggered to himself, as he walked away from the map and towards the great flight of stairs that led to the great ballroom. "My world may be dark... but it's all mine – ha ha ha!" He roared, as his vicious laughter echoed around the hallway.

Deep within the Forest of Haldon, Sereny Ugbrooke was lost. The young girl was another victim of the mystical powers that had been emitted from one of the gold coins whilst she had bathed at home, back in her own world. She had been sucked through the plughole, through the Sandmouth drainage system and into Pathylon via the vortex hidden behind the great oak doors. Sereny had journeyed through the spiral, which had transported her into the Forbidden Caves on the outskirts of the forest.

Sereny had been walking for some time and she sat down to catch her breath. She peered up at the tall trees, which disappeared into the dark clouds that hung low above the forest. The nervous twelve-year-old refocused her attention to a winding path, which cut through the tall cretyre trees like a theme park maze. In the distance she could make out a broad figure moving slowly in her direction. As it moved nearer, she could just make out the giant orange hulk-like figure plodding towards her. She looked to her right and darted into the foliage to hide.

She peeped through the blades of pamper grass at the eight foot monster, as it passed by. She could not believe the immense size and ugliness of the strange being. The sheer bulk of the creature caused a rush of adrenaline to pass through her slender frame and she fainted. Her limp body fell to the ground and she landed softly in the crisp undergrowth that covered the forest floor.

The lizard-like ogre heard the snapping of twigs and he turned around immediately. He then drew his sword from its sheath with great agility and assessed the surroundings. He moved towards the opening in the undergrowth and looked down to where Sereny had fallen. She was laid on her back with her slim figure crumpled within the long grass. The pretty girl was wearing a white and red T-shirt with the words 'New York' embroidered over the printed number 'seventy two.' Her dark blue mid-shin length hipsters and white sporty footwear complimented her fashionable top.

The slimy amphibian had not seen this type of clothing before and he was curious, as he stared at the young being. From the length of Sereny's hair, he assumed she was a female. She was obviously still in a state of shock, as her body continued to tremble. Her arms and legs twitched in the long grass that grew against the tall poplar-shaped cretyre trees.

The large creature was fascinated by the red lights in the heels of the white shoes that flashed every time the girl moved her feet. The orange warrior steadied the girl's movements and picked her up in his strong muscle bound forelimbs. He carried her effortlessly through the woods for miles and eventually to the safety of his lodge at the edge of the Forest of Haldon, next to the banks of the River Klomus.

The views across the river were breathtaking, in the distance you could just make out the silhouettes of the Royal Palace and the Shallock Tower against the Devonian landscape. On a fine day, you could make out the Mountains of Hartopia on the horizon, which bordered Devonia with the evil Blacklands.

Although the skies were full of dark heavy clouds, it still felt quite humid. The large armour-clad frog-like amphibian decided to light a fire just a short distance away from the lodge. Soon the flames were established and he laid Sereny on the ground near to the fire so she would keep warm. After a while he poked the tip of his sword into the embers of the campfire in an attempt to resurrect the dying flames. He looked to his left and admired the pretty young girl as she lay asleep in the lush green clover, wrapped warmly in a large cretyre leaf, which he had cut down earlier.

The obese giant was called Grog and he was an ugly looking brute. His slimy webbed fingers clasped the jewel-headed sword handle as he prodded the embers once more.

Apart from a short spell in the Blacklands, he had lived in the Forest of Haldon all his adult life, since leaving the spawning grounds at Flaclom in the land of Krogonia. The forest was named after an ancient Pathylian King who occupied the throne during the time when the Kaikane God inhabited the Island of Restak.

Grog was unsettled by rumours being spread by the Tree Elves that inhabited the great forest. They spoke of an evil curse laid down by the Freytorians coinciding with Varuna's recent enforced uprising against King Luccese. The speculation of both events was causing widespread unrest throughout all the Pathylian regions. The restless Krogon was also concerned about the constant presence of dark clouds above Pathylon ever since the dethronement of Luccese.

He turned his attention back to the female laying on the ground in front of him. He had no idea who the girl was and he sat on an overturned tree stump patiently, waiting for her to wake. He had not seen anything like her species before and was intrigued by her head of hair with long blonde ringlets held in two bunches by thin blue bows.

Grog was a Krogon outcast. He had never qualified as a true warrior, due to his very gentle and caring attitude. He wasn't the brightest of species, but what he lacked in common sense, he made up for with his tremendous strength and bravery. However, this was questioned a year before reaching full adulthood when a rival challenged him just three days before the annual Krogon ritual. The event was staged for those destined to leave the spawning grounds on the Flaclom Straits. All students had to take part in various challenges to prove their worth.

Zule was the rival Krogon that had challenged Grog to a dual. This was to be a battle to the death; only one of them would be allowed to survive. The victor would earn the right to sit at the side of the High Priest of Krogonia and learn the ways of the Priesthood. The ultimate reward would be to achieve regional status and attain the mystical powers that the Priesthood represented. The ultimate honour would be to become a candidate for the Pathylian throne.

The battle was due to take place during the ritual ceremony, but Grog did not want to fight. It wasn't because he was afraid of Zule - on the contrary he just did not want to kill, or be killed by his fellow Krogon and childhood friend. The battle never took place and he was banished to the Blacklands to spend the rest of his days of adulthood in the company of the Hartopians. He had managed to escape their evil clutches and soon fled from the dark Blacklands through Devonia to the Western region of the Forest of Haldon. The Tree Elves had adopted the gentle Krogon and afforded him a small homestead next to the banks of the River Klomus on the edge of the forest. One day he hoped to return to his homeland in the East and to meet his childhood rival again and wish him peace.

The girl awoke and interrupted his memories of a reminiscent past. Sereny pushed the cretyre leaf away and sat upright. She stretched her arms into to the air and yawned, as she stared at Grog. "Gosh err, *slight over-use of the self-tanning lotion…* I assume you're not going to hurt or eat me - *Mr. Tangerine Man*?"

Grog grunted, then smiled and assured the girl that no harm would come to her. "Who are you and from where have you travelled?"

"My name is Sereny Ugbrooke… I'm from Sandmouth in Devon," she answered confidently. "Who are you?"

"My name is Grog... I am a Krogon warrior," he replied. "It is an honour to make your acquaintance... Sereny Ugbrooke."

"You don't have to use the Ugbrooke bit... that's just my surname," explained Sereny.

"Surname?" he quizzed. "What does that mean?"

"Oh never mind," replied Sereny, sarcastically. "So you consider yourself a warrior eh... so where's your army then and what's with all the body armour?"

"This is my battledress... but I no longer belong to an army," replied Grog, as he held his head in shame. "I am an outcast!" He went on to explain his situation and how he had ended up in the Forest of Haldon. Sereny listened intently as he told her about the new evil King Varuna and all about the world of Pathylon.

"Pathylon!" she exclaimed. "That's the name above those big oak doors inside the caves."

"Oak doors?" asked Grog. "What is this *oak* you speak of?"

Sereny explained about the great oak trees that grow near her house back home. She then told the Krogon about her journey into Pathylon and the power distributed by the gold coin.

Grog was intrigued to find out more about the entrance to Pathylon that led from the girl's world. "So... you say that you travelled through a brightly coloured spiral from your Sandmouth place and entered Pathylon via the *Forbidden Caves?*"

"Didn't know what they were called... but yes that's correct," replied Sereny. "Go to the top of the class."

The puzzled Krogon continued. "Well, as far as I am aware, no one has ever entered those caves in recent times!"

"Well you're wrong…. because I'm here!" giggled Sereny.

"It is written in the ancient Kaikane Scrolls that no living creature should attempt to go beyond the entrance and into the Forbidden Caves. If they did, and they were caught, they would be sentenced to an eternal existence in the Unknown Land to the south of the Galetis Empire," recited Grog, as if he were reading from an ancient scroll.

"Gosh… you really know how to charm a girl – don't you?" she replied sarcastically. "Well… I'm not bothered what your ancient scrolls state - I'm telling you that I entered into these woods from a massive cave and I don't care whether it's forbidden or not… that's what happened!"

Grog was taken aback by the strength of the girls reply and felt he needed to justify his stance by a further informative display of local knowledge. "I've heard the Forbidden Caves are inhabited by some rogue Hartopian slaves who have joined up with a band of renegade death troops," explained the Krogon. "They have taken some Freytorian intruders prisoner and have encapsulated them in stone somewhere deep inside the caves."

Sereny looked on bemused and totally forlorn as Grog continued with his epic description of recent events. "If the extremists hadn't imprisoned the Freytorians for their own gain, this blessed curse wouldn't have been cast over our lands in the first place!"

"Yeah… well, I did think it was a bit dark when I got here – the clouds are rather grey," explained Sereny. "I thought it was getting near night time."

"The curse has cast a grim darkness over Pathylon!" exclaimed Grog, as he pointed to the skies. "I fear the light will never shine down on these lands again."

Sereny did not have a clue what the frog-creature was ranting on about. All this talk of ancient scrolls, death troops, Pathylian extremists and evil curses was a bit daunting for her to comprehend. She just wanted to go back home. "I must ignore these dangers you keep waffling on about," insisted Sereny. "I have to go back to these forbidden caves you talk about... I must return to my family - they will be worried sick about me!"

At that moment Sereny's brave words were interrupted, as Grog heard a noise. It sounded like the cracking of more twigs under foot. "Quick... Sereny Ugbrooke - hide," he whispered. "I think I hear someone coming this way!"

"It's just *Sereny*!" she insisted. "You don't to use the Ugbrooke bit...eeerrkk!" she croaked, as the Krogon cut short her chatting and pulled her to one side.

They hid behind the upturned tree trunk that had been occupied by the grotesque amphibian's posterior for the past three hours. Sereny kept her head low as Grog peered around the side of the bark. He spotted two figures in the distance, they looked like very similar beings to the girl he was protecting within the gentle grip of his strong arms.

The two figures approached the campfire and one of them looked over to the tree stump. He spotted an orange leg with a webbed foot and a dull metal armour plate leading up to the knee. Grog pulled his leg back in, hoping they had not seen him.

"Who goes there?" said one of the strangers. "Come out and let us see you!"

Grog's mind flashed back to the aborted fight with Zule and he was not prepared to show the same unwillingness to fight the trespassers. He pushed back the girl's ringlets and whispered in Sereny's ear. "Do not be afraid my fair maiden… I will fight to the death to protect you."

"Be careful," uttered the terrified girl.

The giant ogre leapt from his defensive position and challenged the petrified looking mortals. He held his sword aloft in his webbed hand and uttered a battle cry that when translated into Krogon meant fight to the death. *"Ovilazim Zen du Joradim!"* he shouted and propelled him forward with his muscular hind legs over the tree stump. The ground trembled, as he maneuvered his great frame and landed in front of the two quivering wrecks. Grog pulled back his arm with sword aloft and was about to wield his blade across the heads of both intruders with one foul swing.

Sereny suddenly interjected, as she appeared from behind the tree stump and shouted at her chivalrous guardian. "Grog… stoppppp!" she screamed. "Don't hurt them!"

The Krogon warrior reacted instinctively to the girl's pleading tones and heeded her request, as he discontinued the death action of his weapon. "I told you to stay hidden!" He commanded and the Lizardman looked around to witness Sereny rushing towards him with her hands waving frantically in the air.

"Never mind… that's Muzzy Chilcott - he lives in the same town as me!" she explained, as Grog stood down and returned his sword to the crisscross patterned leather sheath attached to his belt. Sereny ran up to the two boys and threw her arms around Musgrove. "Muzzy… I'm so glad to see you!"

Musgrove was pleased to see his school friend too and welcomed the warm embrace from the pretty girl. "Fancy meeting you here!" he exclaimed.

Sereny released her affectionate hold on the lanky teenager and looked over to Bradley. She was very taken by the young boy's good looks. "Who's your friend, Muzzy?"

"Oh sorry… this is err - Bradley Baker," replied Musgrove.

"Nice to meet you… *Bradley!*" admired Sereny.

Bradley's face turned a little red, as he accepted Sereny's friendly gesture by shaking her delicate hand. Musgrove couldn't help but notice an instant attraction between the two and he felt uncomfortable about it. He really liked Sereny but had never mustered enough courage to tell her. So he quickly interrupted the brief liaison and took the girl's hand to guide her away from the young contender.

Grog was feeling very uncomfortable about the presence of the two new male visitors. He did not like the way Sereny had flung her arms around her fellow human and the way she had stared at the younger male. He shied away and turned to head towards the path that led to his lodge.

"Wait…Grog!" shouted Sereny. "Where are you going?"

Grog turned around and lifted his head and Sereny ran over to the sulking Krogon and held out her arms. She looked up at his sad round tangerine-pitted face and could not help but imagine the deep pores of his complexion simulated that of orange peel. She wrapped her tiny arms around the podgy belly of the bashful pond creature. "Don't be jealous… you are my real hero - thank you for defending me so honorably *Mr. Tangerine Man.*"

Grog patted her head and creased his leathery face with a smile. He asked Sereny if she and her friends would like to join him for a meal at his lodge by the river. They all agreed and he pointed the way. Bradley, Musgrove and Sereny followed in single file along the forest path until they reached the primitive-built wooden hut. They approached the arched wooden entrance, which was covered with a green-leaved shrub that twisted around the rickety porch.

The Krogon invited them inside the lodge and was keen to make them feel welcome, as he made his way over to the large stone fireplace. The three children looked on inquisitively, as Grog stacked up a mound of pre-sawn cretyre logs on top of some dry grass. He then struck two pieces of flint together and the grass burst into flames. The children settled down into the comfy hand-carved armchairs in front of the roaring fire, whilst their host busied himself in the small kitchen.

It was not long before Grog reappeared with piping hot bowls of homemade cretyre leaf soup. The weary group of travellers sat around in front of the dancing flames and chatted excitedly to the Krogon about their adventures to date. He was desperate for a full account as to why the three strangers had entered his world of solitude in such bizarre circumstances. The evening closed in and he wasn't disappointed to hear the descriptive way the three friends explained how they had all chartered their entry into the world of Pathylon through the hooded doorways inside the Forbidden Caves.

Their account of the journey into the caves had substantiated the story Sereny had told Grog earlier. He looked into the pretty girl's eyes and smiled. The Krogon then turned to Bradley and Musgrove. "I think it might be a good time to retire... I have a spare-room upstairs for you two - please feel free to make yourselves comfortable."

Whilst Grog went outside to fetch more logs for the fire, the boy's made their way up the basic wooden stairs. They were quickly followed by Sereny. "Wait up you two... don't leave me alone with him," she whispered. "Did you see the way he was looking at me?"

"Don't worry," replied Bradley. "We'll protect you... won't we Muzzy?"

Musgrove gave Bradley a frowned look. He felt it was his duty and only his to protect Sereny. "No... I'll make sure you stay safe!" he exclaimed and held out his hand to welcome her up the stairs. "Bradley's a little too young to ensure your safety... but don't worry - I'm here for you."

Bradley noticed the affectionate glance that the girl had cast him so he reacted to Musgrove's comment. "Muzzy... I'm more than capable of protecting Sereny – thank you very much!" He insisted, as Sereny afforded him a pleasant smile whilst deliberately avoiding Musgrove's invitation of chivalry.

Grog re-entered the lodge and the Krogon was surprised to see the lounge empty. He looked up to the top of the staircase and noticed his three guests leaning over the rail on the landing, as they called down simultaneously to their host. "Goodnight Grog!"

Bradley, Musgrove and Sereny did not wait for an answer and quickly disappeared into their respective bedrooms before the Krogon could question their abrupt exit. The disappointed Lizardman dropped the logs onto the hearth and rested his large bottom into his favourite fireside chair. The flames of the fire soon died and the embers continued to glow for a while. It was not long before the bellowing of Grog's snoring could be heard echoing through the lodge, as all the guests settled down for the night.

Bradley lay awake on his bunk, as he stared up at the straw-lined ceiling and soon fell asleep to dream of the dangers that lay ahead for his two friends and their new Krogon ally.

11

Unfinished Business

Varuna had arranged to visit the Pathylian region of the Galetis Empire, where he planned to meet with the long serving High Priest called Meltor. He needed the highly respected Galetian to join with the other regional High Priests and offer his allegiance to the new government. Meltor was a model servant to the true King Luccese and it would take some persuasive tactics on his part to convince the highly respected aristocrat to switch his loyalties.

Varuna had cast his powers of persuasion under the darkened grey clouds that hung over Pathylon and he had already ensured the support of the others. However, he knew Meltor would be reluctant to follow his regime, but he was feeling very confident about securing the recruitment of the stubborn old Galetian.

Under the previous rule, a High Priest called Pavsik had governed the region of Devonia. After only two days into

Varuna's enforced reign, Pavsik was dispelled by the Hartopian because of his devoted loyalty to Luccese. The nobleman had refused to conform to his demands and the new ruler of Pathylon condemned the traitor to join his mentor and spend the rest of his time in the Shallock Tower.

The evil Hartopian needed to replace Pavsik and he could not risk appointing another Devonian ally. So he took the advice from an old Krogon campaigner Harg, the High Priest of Krogonia. The leader of the Lizardmen recommended a young and inexperienced Krogon warrior called Zule. Varuna heeded this advice and appointed the young champion as his trusted aide to watch over the royal capital and protect his back from would-be assassins. The appointment of Zule did not prove popular with the Devonians for they had traditionally held one of their own kind as High Priest. They were powerless to resist Varuna's decision and the threat of more destructive tyranny from the Hartopian was enough to convince the lower Devonian noblemen that Zule would make a worthy High Priest for their region.

Zule relished the opportunity to inherit the mystical powers that betroth the High Priesthood. Someday, he hoped to succeed Harg as High Priest for Krogonia. The very thought of ruling in his fellow Krogons in his own region was an ambition born from his early years training on the Flaclom Straits. However, his appointment to the Devonian High Priesthood was a good start to his career and even triggered thoughts of a possible succession to Varuna's throne in years to come.

Zule was a muscular triple horned lizard-like warrior, standing nearly ten feet in height. His shear strength and athletic agility stood him in good physical stead. He felt he could take advantage of the mystical powers that his rookie Priesthood afforded him and Zule relished the chance to put this into practice. One of his first tasks would be to seek out and challenge an old friend, Grog. Zule still felt bitter about the battle that never took place with his fellow Krogon many years ago. He was determined to locate his bitter rival and complete the unfinished business that should have taken place on the Flaclom Straits.

Harg, an overweight dictator, was nearing his last years and the hooked battle tooth at the end of his upper jaw was showing signs of decay. The old Krogon walked with a hunched appearance, the weight of his crescent head of horns made his inability to move comfortably more apparent. He accepted the new King with open arms. The Krogons had been at war with the Devonians for centuries and he welcomed the new alliance with Varuna. Even the Satorc Bridge, the only way into and out of the regions Krogonia and Devonia, was now open and the armed guard that patrolled the Krogon side had been disbanded on the orders of Harg.

Flaglan was the beautiful and curvaceous High Priestess for the Forest of Haldon. The scantily clad sorceress had served under several rulers and had no real allegiance to anyone but her own self-ego. She was just satisfied that Varuna had allowed her Priestess role to continue under his new regime. Unbeknown to her, Varuna had eyes for the radiant temptress and viewed Flaglan as a future queen. The Hartopian had ulterior intentions to seek courtship once he had secured the allegiance of all five regional High Priesthoods.

Varuna also needed a High Priest replacement for the Blacklands. The Hartopians that populated the mountainous region had gained a King of the same species but lost a regional leader when Varuna vacated the Priesthood and stole the throne from Luccese.

So Varuna decided to appoint a weak controllable half-breed called Basjoo Ma-otz, a small armour-clad rat-type creature with two large razor sharp teeth that hung from the front of his upper jaw. He had the usual red-eyed Hartopian squat weasel-like features, which were enhanced by that of a common wild mammal called flax. His disgraced father had unlawfully taken a female flax and forced wedlock resulting in the birth of a crossbreed.

Basjoo Ma-otz lacked any good sense, inherited from his mother and he always carried his *Staff of Evil* around wherever he went, to protect him from those of quick wit. The staff could wield strange dark forces upon its attackers and was crowned with the skull of a Galetian child, slaughtered during a Hartopian ritual. The ceremony had followed a failed bid to invade the Galetis Empire some years ago and the murdered child was the granddaughter of Meltor.

Prior to his promotion under Varuna, Basjoo Ma-otz had always managed to avoid the Galetian High Priest. However, his rise to the position of equal status would force an inevitable encounter with the aging swordsman.

Basjoo Ma-otz was always very keen to impress his Hartopian master. For most of his adult life he had served as an apprentice under Varuna within the evil government of the Blacklands. Even though Varuna had taken the throne of Pathylon, darkness and slavery would still be one of the main key policies under the regime of Basjoo Ma-otz.

Meltor had already arranged to attend a flax hunt within the Forest of Haldon and had set off from the City of Kasol two days ago. He knew full well that he would avoid Varuna and thus postpone the inevitable subsistent demands of the evil Hartopian. Hunting the wild foxlike creatures always summoned memories of his granddaughter's murder, due to the fact that Basjoo Ma-otz was indeed half flax. Meltor's deep-set hatred of Basjoo Ma-otz encouraged and incensed him to seek out the small scrawny creatures given any opportunity.

Unaware of Meltor's deliberate absence, Varuna and his entourage had now arrived in the capital City of Kasol as the sun was at its highest. The new King had travelled from Devonia, by Hoffen-drawn chariot and had suffered an exhausting journey through the barren desserts of the Galetis Empire region.

The evil dictator was wearing his usual black outfit made up of draping robes and the horned-skull headdress that had instilled fear into all those that had taken sight of the evil red-eyed Hartopian. He lifted his head and looked up at the rooftops of Kasol. The piercing red slits that were excuses for eyes in his long narrow saber toothed snout, assessed the surrounding buildings as he rode through the centre of the city on the Royal Chariot.

The roofs of the many buildings were shaped like domes and covered in dust. In the early hours of that morning, a ferocious southern wind had blown in sand from the nearby Peronto Dessert and the airborne particles had settled and caused the roof tiles on each dome to sparkle like glitter in the mid-day sun.

Varuna dispatched a messenger and waited patiently for the council member to return. He had sent the royal servant into the regional parliamentary chambers to inform Meltor of his arrival. The messenger was embarrassed and re-appeared on the marble steps that fronted the ornate building and shrugged his shoulders.

"My lord... no-one inside the chambers has seen or heard of the High Priest Meltor - apparently he has failed to chair the parliamentary session today," explained the quivering royal servant.

Upon learning of Meltor's absence, the evil King was overcome with rage. Varuna reacted angrily by flinging his cape around his shoulders and raised his hairy arms in the air. "How dare he avoid me!" he roared, as he signalled for his entourage. "Meltor will pay for his obstinacy!"

Lieutenant Dergan ran over to his master's chariot and waited nervously for the irate Hartopian to issue his orders. Varuna's facial expression changed and he began to speak in a calm and assertive manner. "Deploy a small unit to seek out Meltor and destroy him... bring back his Galetian head on a platter!" he ordered, as he turned to his plump little lieutenant. "We must eradicate all · non-conformists... mustn't we Dergan?"

"Yes my lord... you can rely on me to bring back your prize - oh great one!" replied the lieutenant. "The flax hunters will now become the hunted."

"Oh, just get on with it you bloated Wartpig!" growled Varuna.

Dergan was startled by the sudden change of Varuna's tone. The frightened Wartpig took a step back and immediately ceased his creepy behaviour and began to summon his squad of crack troops. The grovelling officer cowered away from the royal chariot and focused his attention on the task ahead.

Following a brief inspection of his troops, Lieutenant Dergan set about his mission to seek out and destroy Meltor.

With his unit of sixteen elite soldiers marching behind him, he headed off on foot in the direction of the Forest of Haldon. The edge of the forest was only a few hours walk from the City of Kasol and the thought of confronting Meltor sent a cold shiver down his spine.

The gentle sound of the water rippling up against the banks of the River Klomus could be heard inside Grog's lodge. The aquatic echoes, together with harmonious sound of the exotic birds that inhabited the Forest of Haldon, woke Bradley. As the feathered wildlife warbled out their chorus of morning song, the tired boy squirmed and wriggled beneath his fur bed covers. The dancing sunbeams, which pierced through the grey clouds above the tall cretyre trees, streamed onto Bradley's eyelids through a small gap in the torn canvas blinds that adorned the small guestroom window.

Bradley leant over towards the twin bed adjacent to his, which was made of neatly sawn cretyre logs secured by hemp, and nudged his friend who was still sound asleep. Musgrove did not move and Bradley jumped out of his temporary bunk and placed his hands on the boy's shoulders.

Bradley began to push his friend up and down into the soft feathered mattress until he fluttered his eyelashes and let out a disgruntled gasp of morning breath followed by an unconscious sentence made up of four moans and three snorts. "Wake up Muzzy!" he shouted and then stepped back from the bed. Bradley began to draw back the tatty window blinds. "Come on... get your lanky lazy bones out of that bunk!"

Whilst Musgrove Chilcott had slept like a log all through the night, Bradley had laid awake thinking of what to do next. He was still unsure about Grog and whether he should trust his Krogon host. Musgrove finally lifted his head from the stained pillowcase and then cast his friend a disgruntled look, as sun beams attacked his squinting eyes.

"I hate mornings!" exclaimed Musgrove, as he pulled the pillowcase over his face.

"Get up Muzzy... I'm hungry," replied Bradley, as his friend removed the pillowcase and proceeded to pick out bits of fluff from his mouth.

Bradley could feel his stomach churning and he began to feel very hungry indeed. He cast his mind back to the breakfast routine in Ravenswood and pictured the kitchen breakfast bar at number 127 Braithwaite Road. He visualized lashings of ice-cold milk and a selection of cereals complete with free gifts inside each box of *Choco Pops* and *Golden Nuggets*. His early morning daydream was interrupted by Musgrove's exclamations of inquisitiveness.

"Hey Brad... look at these weird clothes," remarked Musgrove, as he pulled back his matching stained bed sheets and shuffled along the edge of the mattress.

Musgrove had also noticed two scruffy-looking uniforms with matching headscarves, which lay draped over the end of the makeshift wooden beds. Bradley picked up a small piece of torn notepaper that had fallen on the floor.

He read out the scribbled message;

> *'Put these on and I will explain later!*
> *Regards Grog'*

Bradley and Musgrove looked at each other and scrunched their shoulders simultaneously. "What do you suppose this is all about?" asked Musgrove, as he picked up one of the headscarves and wrapped it around his head.

"Not sure, but you look rather daft with that thing on your head!" replied Bradley, as he handed Musgrove the fragile piece of paper.

As the young teenager studied the note, Bradley heard Sereny shouting Grog's name and he made his way to the window. He pulled back the blind further and looked out towards the river in the direction of Sereny's soft voice. She was sat on the end of the jetty; her blonde hair no longer in bunches, but moving freely in the soft breeze.

Bradley stared at the pretty girl for a short while and then noticed a small rowing boat in the water below the jetty. Grog was sitting precariously in the boat, his enormous behind spanning the width of the small craft and perched on the cross beam with oars at the ready.

Bradley moved away from the window and persuaded Musgrove to get ready. Both boys quickly washed and reluctantly changed into their Pathylian costumes. "I'm not wearing this stupid headscarf," said Musgrove. "I'll look like a right prat!"

"Take it with you," replied Bradley. "I'll leave mine off as well... we'll see what Grog has to say about it."

They both rushed downstairs and out through the front door of the lodge. Still running, they made their way down to the banks of the River Klomus to meet with their female companion and the obese Krogon. Sereny spotted the boys running down the path and looked down from the jetty at Grog who was still waiting patiently in his boat. Bradley and Musgrove made their way to the end of the jetty and both boys crouched down to talk to Sereny and the overweight amphibian.

"Hi Sereny," said Bradley, in a bashful tone.

"Hello Bradley," replied Sereny. "How are you feeling this morning... did you sleep okay?"

"I'm fine thanks... but I didn't sleep very well at all," replied Bradley. "I lay awake quite a bit... I couldn't stop thinking about my parents and how we are all going to get back home to Sandmouth!"

Sereny put her hand on Bradley's arm and tried to reassure him that everything would turn out all right. Bradley smiled at her and noticed she had also changed into her period costume earlier. She was wearing her new clothes well and Bradley was impressed by the way the girl's slender figure fitted neatly into the tan coloured suede waistcoat. All three children had the same cream long sleeved shirts tied with a cord at the neckline, and different shades of grey baggy pantaloons tucked into the tops of their weathered black boots.

Musgrove questioned Grog as to why he had asked them all to wear such ridiculous looking uniforms. "I feel like *Sinbad the Sailor* in this lot!"

"Sorry if you don't like the outfits... I found them last winter in an abandoned chest that had been washed up onto the riverbank - I thought it might be a good idea for all three of you to wear costumes that were more appropriate and so you didn't stand out too much," Grog replied.

"Who would wear this type of clothing?" asked Bradley.

"Young Devonians from the City of Aedis," explained Grog. "You should be accepted as Aedisian servants, so long as you two boys wear the headscarves I gave you."

"Why do Bradley and me have to wear these stupid scarves and *not* Sereny?" asked Musgrove.

Grog laughed. "Well... for one simple reason - *all* Devonian males have two small horns sticking out of their

116

heads!" explained the amused Krogon. "So if you two can grow a couple between you within the next few minutes... you won't have to wear the scarves!"

"I guess that's a good enough reason!" replied Bradley, as he turned to Musgrove. "I told you Grog would..."

"Okay, okay, leave it Bradley... stop going on - I'll put the damn scarf on, all right!" agreed Musgrove.

Grog continued to laugh at Musgrove's expense, but also looked a little puzzled and offered a question to the tetchy teenager to ease the tension. "Anyway... who is *Sinbad the Sailor*?" asked the Krogon.

Sereny interrupted. "Where we come from, *Sinbad* was portrayed in story books as a heroic adventurer who fought evil monsters and things... he was only a mythological character - I don't think he really existed."

Grog rocked around in his rowing boat, as he readjusted his seating position. "I see... well, we may need someone like your *Sinbad* chap to protect us from Varuna – after all, he's a bit of a monster as well you know!" he joked and reached for a small leather pouch that was fastened to the belt around his fat belly.

"What's in there?" enquired Bradley.

"Grobites," replied Grog.

"What are Grobites?" asked Bradley.

Sereny interjected again before he could answer Bradley's question. "Maybe the answer to our problem," she said, with a smug look on her pretty face. "Show him Grog!"

The Krogon had shown Sereny the contents of the pouch earlier that morning, whilst Bradley and Musgrove had been sleeping. He held out the pouch and Bradley leant down from the jetty and cupped his hand to receive the contents of the bag. As Grog twisted his webbed hand to release the

117

contents, Bradley could see four small gold coins falling into his palm.

"Look Muzzy... more gold coins with holes in the middle!" cried Bradley.

"Where did you get those from Grog?" Musgrove asked with excitement.

"As I said, they are called grobites and for many centuries now they have been adopted as the Pathylian currency... they originate from a faraway land called Freytor," explained Grog. "The ferocious Freytorians have tried to invade Pathylon many times... but on one occasion they attempted to trade their grobite currency for minerals - since then we have traded with grobites at city markets throughout the five regions for all our food and provisions."

"That all sounds very interesting... but what about these with the holes in the middle?" reiterated Bradley.

"Those are quite rare," replied Grog. "It is said the ones with the centre missing are worth quite a lot more."

"But these are exactly the same type of coins we found in Amley's Cove," said Musgrove, as he examined the pieces of treasure.

"Well according to the inscription on the coins we found, they are supposed to bring forth magic powers," explained Bradley. "But there doesn't appear to be any inscription around the edges of those particular coins."

Grog explained. "I have heard a rumour that has spread throughout the forest... apparently the Freytorians recently made another visit to our world and eight of them disappeared somewhere around the Mouth of Sand." He continued. "The strangers were supposedly carrying a cask full of these *grobites*... it is said that the evil curse that now shrouds our land, was cast because the Freytorians believe that their crewmembers had been imprisoned in the Forbidden Caves. The Tree Elves that live within the Forest of Haldon inform me, that prior to Varuna's recent uprising against King Luccese... the missing cask contained *twelve* sacred grobite coins - I guess those are the coins that hold the mystical powers you talk of."

"You mentioned the Mouth of Sand," said Sereny. "Muzzy and *me*... we both come from a coastal town in our world called Sandmouth!"

"Because the names sound so similar... maybe there is some connection between our world and Pathylon," suggested Bradley. "Maybe Sandmouth and the Mouth of Sand are the same place... but separated by some kind of time-barrier or something - maybe the giant spiral thing, that we travelled through, is some kind of *time machine*!"

Musgrove nodded to acknowledge his approval of Bradley's theory. He then turned to Grog and directed another question at the Krogon, who was still bobbing from side to side in the little rowing boat. "Do you suppose the twelve coins lost by the eight visitors from Freytor were purposely dropped and left in the rock pools for someone like us to find them... so we could enter Pathylon?"

"I can't answer that," replied Grog. "The rumours suggest that a dense sea mist engulfed the bay and no-one knows what happened to the cask... but the Tree Elves can confirm that the eight Freytorians were indeed imprisoned inside the Forbidden Caves and have been immortalized in the stone door frames that guard the entrance into Pathylon."

"We've seen the hooded doors you speak of," enthused Bradley, as he explained further about the names of the intruders on the door plaques.

Sereny asked. "If the coins were dropped into the rock pools and if they are the same coins that we found, do you suppose the coins acted as keys to transport us from one time span to another?"

All three youngsters spoke simultaneously and kept firing questions at Grog. This whole mystery was getting too in-depth for the orange creature and he could not verify all of their questions. All he could tell them was of the stories told to him by the Tree Elves.

Grog recognized that the children were getting frustrated and the large amphibian was keen to help the trio find their way back to their own world. He suggested that they travel in his boat. "By following the water's flowing torrent… it will lead you down river to the Satorc Estuary and round to the Mouth of Sand - which may hold the clues as to how you can get back to your own world."

"Oh I do hope you're right… I'm really missing home," said Sereny, as she stroked Grog's arm.

"It's obvious, from what you have told me… the Forbidden Caves contain the entrance to Pathylon - maybe the secluded underwater caves at the Mouth of Sand is your way out?" he suggested. "Failing that… I would recommend you visit the wise old High Priest – Meltor, who may have other ideas that may assist you all."

"Meltor?" quizzed Bradley.

"He is a kind wise Galetian… and the High Priest for the Galetis Empire - he lives in the City of Kasol," said Grog. "He could spread a little light on the answers to your questions… apart from Harg, Meltor is the oldest and wisest of all the High Priests in Pathylon - if anyone knows what's really going on, he will!"

"Anything is worth a try," said Musgrove. "Let's head for the Mouth of Sand and try the underwater caves first."

"Sounds like we have a plan!" confirmed Bradley. "Let's go!" He exclaimed and they all agreed to travel with Grog down the River Klomus, as they climbed aboard the little rowing boat.

The gentle Krogon started to maneuver the small dingy away from the jetty as he worked the oars into the wake.

The Lizardman soon settled into a steady rowing pace and he started to sing a Krogon song, as they journeyed along the river in the direction of the Satorc Estuary.

12

The Eternal Chosen One

Lieutenant Dergan and his troops had reached the edge of the Forest of Haldon. The weary foot soldiers had been travelling non-stop and were in need of water, as they sought time to rest their aching legs for a while.

The Lieutenant deployed a scout to retrieve fresh water from the nearby River Klomus. Upon reaching the banks of the river, the young soldier looked out across the swirling rapids. He spotted the small rowing boat carrying Grog and the three children. The over-laden craft was carried along by the strong rapids. It was heading down-river and the soldier immediately drew his horn from his cloth side-carry, as he blew a warning signal to his squadron. The noise from the wind instrument alerted Dergan and the other troops, who had just started to make camp inside the great forest.

The warning signal could also be heard deep inside the Forest of Haldon and the petrified flax, which was being chased by Meltor and his hunting party, was spared in pursuit. The lucky creature fled into the undergrowth, as the heard of Hoffen kicked up dry dirt from the cracked forest floor.

Meltor raised his hand to halt the chase and he slung his white hooded cloak onto his broad shoulders. He pulled at the reigns and turned around the head of his horse-like mount. The Hoffen's long black main left a trail of flowing hair as it galloped with its rider's heals digging into the saddle straps. Meltor abandoned the hunting party and headed off in the direction of the horn blower.

Meltor reached the edge of the forest and rode towards the banks of the river. In the distance he could make out the foot soldier with the signal horn in silhouette still pressed against his lips.

The High Priest neared the startled horn blower and his Hoffen reared up into the air, as it threw its rider to the floor. Meltor got to his feet immediately and the lieutenant's messenger lunged forward with his horn in one hand and a dagger in the other. The agile Galetian drew his trusty sword from its sheath and swung a fatal solitary slice through the neck of the trooper. A gush of blood streamed from the open wound, as the horn blower's head fell onto the hard ground then rolled down the bank and splashed into the water. The limp lifeless body fell awkwardly and it followed the detached head down the bankside, as the two parts became entangled in the reeds.

Meltor heard more footsteps and turned around suddenly to face four more strangers on the edge of the riverbank. It was Grog and the three children. They knew the horn blower had spotted them and as soon they had seen Meltor, they had decided to head for shore to aid the High Priest.

"Please don't kill us... don't hurt us!" screamed Sereny, as she sought refuge behind the giant Krogon.

Grog instantly revealed the terrified girl by slumping to his knees to praise the great High Priest. "Meltor... your highness - oh great Meltor!" he exclaimed. "We are humbled by your presence!"

"Get to your feet, Krogon... and explain yourself!" demanded Meltor, in an immediate display of mercy towards the three youngsters and their respectful guardian.

Musgrove assisted the Krogon and intervened. "The horn blower spotted us on the river and the rest is self-explanatory by the look of it... that poor so-and-so in the reeds looks like he got bit ahead of himself!" He laughed.

Meltor was not amused by the young human's wit and instead he turned his attention to Bradley, who was oblivious to his friends humour and stared intriguingly at the strong tall figure. Bradley felt there was something familiar about Meltor's face and the Galetian High Priest reciprocated by smiling, as if to acknowledge the boy's curiosity. Their brief exchange of glances was interrupted by the sound of dragging wood, as Grog pulled his boat out of the water and pushed it into the reeds to cover the dead soldier. The Krogon proceeded to camouflage it with some cretyre leafs before joining Bradley and his friends, as they gathered around the High Priest to explain who they all were.

Meltor listened briefly to what Musgrove, Sereny and Bradley had to say. He then suggested they waste little more time as more troops were bound to follow the warning sounds. Meltor then looked around for his Hoffen mount, but it had fled the scene. The High Priest suggested they all make their way on foot back up the river to the rope bridge, which crossed over the River Klomus and into Devonia.

The small band of fugitives had met Meltor sooner than expected and under very extreme circumstances. Bradley looked forward to hearing more of what the High Priest had to say. He hoped that Meltor would confirm Grog's story as to whether or not there was a link between the Mouth of Sand and his Aunt Vera's home town.

Meltor knew more than they thought and soon they were all going to find out the truth about the gold coins and why they had journeyed into Pathylon during this time of the evil Varuna's dark and sadistic reign.

It did not take long for the newly formed allied quintet to arrive at the bridge that spanned across the still expanse of water. The rapids had long disappeared and Bradley looked across to the banks of the calm water that bordered the other side of the river. The sunbeams powered their way through the branches of the tall trees that lined the northern banks of the River Klomus, as the dark clouds shifted eerily above.

Meltor informed Grog and the young adventurers. "I have every reason to believe that Varuna will pursue us relentlessly... the new evil King will not tolerate my rebellious behavior!"

Bradley stared at Meltor and wondered what lay ahead in Devonia. He was worried just how far back the ensuing Varuna and his troops were. "What have I got myself in to?" he muttered to himself.

Meltor led the way over the ancient rope bridge and one by one the others followed, as they trod carefully along the fragile crossing. A gentle breeze developed and quickly intensified into a strong headwind causing the expanse of water below to rush hurriedly towards the Satorc Estuary. Each member of the group held on tightly to the ropes either side of the narrow bridge with only a single woven platform to steady their feet.

Grog was the last to step onto the Devonian side of the river and the exhausted Krogon made his way over to where the others had gathered. Bradley, Musgrove and Sereny were sat on a rocky mound and were listening intently, as the wise old priest strode backwards and forwards with his worn hands clasped behind his back.

Meltor broke his silence and began to expand on the ancient story, as told by Grog's forefathers. "The eight Freytorians that had supposedly disappeared into the sea mist off the Mouth of Sand were actually taken prisoner by a rogue squad of Devonian Death Troops and charged with trespassing by renegade noblemen from the City of Castan," he explained. "The eight imposters were then questioned inside the Forbidden Caves and sentenced to serve an eternal existence encapsulated inside solid granite," continued the Galetian High Priest. "I can confirm that the eight arctic bear-like visitors from Freytor were indeed submitted to painful torture by a band of Hartopian slaves inside the caves, which are located on the eastern side of the Forest of Haldon."

"There were some strange hooded doorways with faces like bears that we passed through on our journey to Pathylon," explained Bradley. "Isn't that right Muzzy?"

"Yeah…that's right," agreed Musgrove.

Bradley continued his line of questioning. "Are the Freytorians trapped inside the hooded doorways, which we passed through?"

Meltor responded to the boy's interrogation. "Yes… the magical power expelled by a now-deceased ex-High Priest called *Borella* was used to transform their mortal bodies into arched stone frames with doors that tasted of wild fruit berries!"

Bradley explained to Meltor about the names that adorned the eight strange doorways, which had eventually led into the chamber containing the great torch lit oak doors with the heading *Pathylon* above them.

"So, you have also seen the great entrance that leads into Pathylon, have you, young sir?" asked Meltor.

"Of course we did!" interrupted Sereny. "How do you think we all ended up here," she added, sarcastically.

Meltor stared at Sereny to afford her a disapproving look. Sereny's response to his glare resulted in her face blushing to a shade of pink and the embarrassed girl gave a wry smile, as if to offer an apology to the great Galetian High Priest. He accepted the girl's silent apology by nodding and then he turned back to face Bradley.

"Actually, this is Muzzy's fourth visit to Pathylon!" stated Bradley, picking up the conversation from where he left it, before Sereny's untimely intervention.

"Then surely he must know the way back to your own world!" exclaimed Meltor.

"Well it's not as simple as that," replied Musgrove. "As I explained to Brad before we jumped into the spiral... I knew the way in but - not how to get out. I can't even remember ever being here in Pathylon, before!"

"That is very interesting my young friend... err, Muzzy... is that your name?" asked Meltor, as he stroked his grey beard.

"Oh, err... it's okay Sir – some call me Muzzy... but if you prefer - please call me Musgrove." replied the nervous teenager.

"So how do you explain *your* presence within our world again, Musgrove?" asked Meltor.

"Well, I obviously returned safely to my own world on the three previous occasions because I am here to tell the tale," said Musgrove. "But I don't remember anything about how I got out of Pathylon or anything that happened during each visit... it's as if all knowledge I had of this place has been erased from my memory - each time I returned back home."

Meltor was intrigued to here that Musgrove had experienced so many incredible journeys into his mystical world. The High Priest was still unsure why Musgrove had made three previous visits, but he was certain that his fourth visit to Pathylon, accompanied by his friends, would prove to be the most dangerous and testing of all. "It was written in the ancient scrolls that should the Pathylian throne fall into evil hands, a Good Samaritan would hail a message to attract a saviour from a world beyond the realm of Pathylon," continued the wise old priest. "An incentive has recently been awarded to the true King Luccese, by the band of Hartopian slaves, currently assisting the renegade Devonian Death Troops, guarding the Forbidden Caves... they are prepared to assist in lifting the curse that currently holds Pathylon in darkness in return for payment of great wealth upon Luccese successful return to the throne."

"So how can you lift the curse?" asked Bradley.

Meltor began to explain to the group about the twelve sacred grobite coins. "The twelve clues left by the Good Samaritan must be found and acted upon... those who find the sacred coins can then assist in the release of King Luccese from the Shallock Tower." He continued. "The true King of Pathylon would then be able to recite the scriptures from the ancient scrolls whilst the *Chosen Ones* make the vital link around the Kaikane Idol... this would reverse Borella's spell and thus release the eight prisoners and ultimately lift the evil curse over Pathylon that was originally put in place by a Freytorian General called Eidar."

"Who is General Eidar?" asked Bradley.

Sereny interrupted. "Grog told me about him... he's the mad commander of the Freytorian ice-ship that carried the crew of polar bears from Freytor!"

"Very good my dear," applauded Meltor, as he clapped his hands together. "The Krogon has taught you well... not so sure about the *polar bears* though!"

Bradley looked at Musgrove and Sereny and then turned to the High Priest. "I guess we must be three of the twelve chosen ones... after all we found the clues and picked up the message via the sacred gold coins?"

"Indeed you are, my dear Bradley... indeed you are!" agreed Meltor.

"Well here we are then!" added Musgrove. "So what do you want us to do now?"

Sereny interrupted again. "Not so fast Muzzy, you speak for yourself... how on earth can *we* possibly help Meltor and his people - we're just children!"

Bradley and Musgrove scowled at their female companion. What a stupid thing to say, they both thought. "Children!" blasted Bradley, as he glared at the spoilt girl. "Children she says... saints preserve us!"

"Calm down Brad," said Musgrove, amused at the way Bradley had reacted against Sereny.

"Sorry Muzzy... but how can she stand there and be so negative," exclaimed Bradley. "We must help King Luccese escape from the Shallock Tower and return him and Queen

Vash to the throne... I feel it is our duty to help reinstate peace and good will to the land of Pathylon!"

Musgrove was very pleased that Bradley had poured scorn on Sereny. "Here... here!" agreed the smug teenager, as he punched the air with his right arm.

Unaware of Musgrove's jealous retort, Meltor continued. "I think you boys have a good understanding of the situation," he laughed, as he held out his strong hands and then proceeded to pat Bradley and Musgrove simultaneously on their backs.

"Pathetic!" muttered Sereny, as she scowled at the boys then turned away to seek support from her tangerine friend.

Grog lifted his head. The Krogon had kept quiet during the deep conversation, but upon hearing Meltor's explanation, he decided to add to the debate. "Err...ermm!" He cleared his throat and continued. "I was told by Zule, that there would be a challenge to the throne of King Luccese.... and I did not doubt his word because he had close links with Harg the High Priest of Krogonia - my childhood friend repeated the stories on many occasions whilst we trained on the Spawning Grounds."

"You look annoyed and frustrated!" declared Bradley in a concerned tone. "What's wrong?"

Grog replied. "Well you see... I never really took Zule seriously at the time - the plan to dethrone Luccese must have been conspired between him and Harg in a pact to harmonize the Krogon and Devonian regions."

Sereny approached Grog. "Isn't Zule the one you spoke of before... the one you were supposed to fight?"

"Yes," replied Grog, as he bowed his head again. The mention of his arch rivals name made him pause and think. "Now that Zule has inherited the High Priesthood of

Devonia... he can wield his inherited mystical powers in an attempt to seek me!"

"What would happen if he found you?" asked Bradley.

Grog replied. "It is inevitable that a battle to the death would take place between us at some time in the very near future... but the odds are heavily in favour of Zule – for he is a strong warrior and the current champion of Krogonia!"

Meltor sympathized with Grog and thanked him for his input. The Galetian then concluded his interpretation of the whole situation. He suggested that the Good Samaritan had purposely dropped the twelve gold coins into the waters off the Mouth of Sand. The coins had acted as beacons of hope to summon a team of individuals, who were capable of orchestrating an uprising against the evil Varuna, and thus free the prisoners and lift the curse laid down by General Eidar.

"You said that there were twelve coins marked with the sacred inscription," commented Sereny, as she returned to the fold. "Three have been recovered, which means we must locate either the rest of the coins or the individuals that found them... in order to fulfill our quest to release Luccese and the Freytorian prisoners."

"Glad to see you are taking a more positive role in our discussions Sereny... you are correct in your calculations - and your evaluation," replied Meltor. "Indeed... your summing up was first class my dear!"

Sereny smiled and moved to one side as Bradley stood up and declared his allegiance to King Luccese. "So... we are all agreed then!" said Bradley. "Meltor will lead us to seek out the other nine chosen ones."

The small group of renegades all acknowledged Bradley by nodding. Meltor also approached him to offer his thanks for his loyal support. The boy's adopted leadership impressed him, even though he was the youngest of the friends. He was intrigued by the eleven-year-old's qualities and had a strong feeling that Bradley could well be *the eternal chosen one* that the Kaikane Gods described in the ancient scrolls.

"We must act quickly if we are to stand any chance of releasing King Luccese and his beautiful Queen from the Shallock Tower!" exclaimed Meltor, as he ushered his weary band of rebels. "It's time to move from here with our heads held high… and onwards to the Royal City of Trad!"

13

The Ignorant Kalmog

Varuna's Wartpig lieutenant and his troops were not far behind Meltor and his band of juvenile rebels. A member of Lieutenant Dergan's scouting party had discovered Grog's camouflaged rowing boat, hidden in the reeds. The lifeless body of the horn blower was found beneath the upturned boat by the side of the River Klomus.

"Over here Sir!" shouted the foot soldier.

The lieutenant walked over to where the stunned soldier was standing. The dead horn blower appeared to be lying face down in the water and the lieutenant bent down to lift up the messenger's head. As he took hold of the horn blower's straggled hair, the neatly severed head parted company with its lifeless body. He pulled back quickly and dropped the blood-stained head back into the water. "This looks like the work of a Galetian sword!" he exclaimed, as he looked around for footprints. "Meltor will pay for this!"

The angry Wartpig quickly rounded up his troops and they followed the tracks along the river. It did not take them long to reach the rope bridge where Meltor and his rebels had crossed.

"They must have crossed the river at this point... Sir," uttered a foot soldier. "Their tracks stop here at the bridge Lieutenant."

Dergan looked over to the other side river and then turned to his troops. "They can't be too far away... I will take ten of you and seek them out - the rest of you go back to the City of Kasol and inform his Royal Highness King Varuna of what has happened!" continued the shocked Wartpig. "Tell our new ruler we will camp at the far side of the bridge and await his orders... now, don't just stand there - *go!*"

"Yes, Lieutenant!" replied the soldier, as he turned and ran.

Dergan was becoming distressed and knew he must find the fugitives or face the wrath of his evil ruler. With this in mind, he set out to cross the bridge with his ten-foot soldiers following behind like a row of sheep. One by one they crossed the flimsy structure, as it swayed from side to side, the group having to stop occasionally to steady the pendulum effect of the bridge. They finally regrouped on the solid ground of the Devonian territory and he ordered his troops to make camp. "We will stay here for the night and await Varuna's instructions...when the wild flax calls at first light - we will then seek out our new enemies."

The scouts arrived back in the City of Kasol and broke the news of the horn blower's death at the hands of Meltor. The new king was furious at the way Meltor had deliberately opposed his regime and ordered his entourage to head north immediately to join up with Lieutenant Dergan. "Prepare the royal chariot and saddle up the Hoffen… there is no time to lose - we must return to Devonia!" roared Varuna. "Meltor will regret his actions and I'll make sure he pays for his mutiny!"

Varuna was left frustrated and angry that the unification of the regional High Priests had not been achieved. His evil plans for an uncontested dictatorship had taken a slight knock-back. Meltor had managed to upstage Varuna's cunning plan to complete the Freytorian curse and bring total darkness over the Pathylian population. Varuna was determined to crush the renegade priest's rebellious acts and he felt a personal vendetta fermenting inside his twisted mind. Meltor's obstinacy was becoming a huge thorn in his side and he must act quickly to dispel the Galetian leader's disruptive influence.

The Hartopian climbed onto his chariot once more and headed out of the Galetian capital of Kasol for a rendezvous with Lieutenant Dergan.

Meltor and his young group of assailants continued to move quickly. They had covered a lot of ground and were now about two miles from the royal capital. It was getting dark and nightfall was closing in, a rare brown and white coloured flax ran across the path in front of Musgrove, which made Bradley think about his Burnese Mountain Dog back home in Ravenswood.

"I wonder what K2 is up to," said Bradley.

"Who is K2?" asked Meltor.

"He's my dog," replied Bradley.

"What is a dog?" interrupted Grog, as he rubbed his leathery palms together. "Do you eat this… err – dog thing?"

Grog's huge belly was empty and he needed to eat something pretty quick, he pictured a dog as a juicy joint of meat being turned on a spit over a roaring fire.

"No… you flipping well can't eat my dog - he's my pet back home!" Bradley replied, appalled at Grog's comment. "Anyway he's built like a Hoffen and he'll make *minced-Krogon-meat* out of you!"

"Now, now… you two, I think it's time we all settled down for the night," said Meltor calmly. "Let's re-focus on the task in hand… Bradley - you and Musgrove go out and collect some firewood so we can set up camp?"

"Okay… yes Sir," acknowledged Bradley. "Come on Muzzy… let's do as Meltor says!"

"We need to build up our strengths if we are to find the other chosen ones and embark on our rescue mission to free King Luccese and Queen Vash from the Shallock Tower," reiterated Meltor.

Meltor turned to Grog and asked him to utilize his Krogon hunting skills and find food for the hungry party to prepare them for their heroic assault to rid Pathylon of the evil Varuna. He felt honoured to have been awarded the opportunity to serve with Meltor, especially as their mission was to save the true King of Pathylon.

Sereny volunteered to join Grog in a quest to find food and the brave warrior accepted with pleasure. "Stay very close to me at all times." He insisted.

"Okee-dokee… *Groggy babe*," replied Sereny. "…and please stop fretting – I'm quite capable of looking after myself!"

Grog smiled at the pretty girl and the two companions set out to find the nourishment that they all needed to continue with their mission.

At last Meltor was alone and able to contemplate his own future. He felt very vulnerable and knew the scout he had slain by the river would have been found by now. Varuna's anger flowed through the curse that hung over the ancient land and Meltor could feel it.

Meltor knew that Varuna did not accept failure and his decision to defy him in favour of Luccese would infuriate the evil ruler. The Galetian High Priest's decision to befriend three very young and inexperienced children, plus an overweight Krogon, may not have been the most wise and logical decision he had ever made. However, Meltor felt in his heart that he had made an honorable and bold move towards securing a slim chance to defend Pathylon against the evil Hartopian from the Blacklands.

Meltor had listened to the three children from the outside world very intently. He was holding back an important secret and he was beginning to feel very guilty about not confiding in Bradley, Musgrove and Sereny. He knew a way out of Pathylon, but had failed to tell the children.

The High Priest was sure that Bradley and the others would insist on travelling to the secret location to escape the tormented world of Pathylon. However, Meltor feared for the fate of the arcane kingdom and its democratic future lay in the hands of the three young visitors. He had to stay faithful to King Luccese and follow the incentive provided by the renegades that guarded the Forbidden Caves. It was important that he held back from telling the truth and that the other nine coin holders were found before it was too late.

Varuna arrived at the campsite where he discovered Lieutenant Dergan and his troops enjoying a feast of freshly cooked flax with boiled Hoffen milk. The sight of such a relaxed gathering infuriated the raging Hartopian and he approached stealthily.

"Dergan... what do you think you are doing?" roared Varuna.

The startled Lieutenant immediately leapt to his feet, completely taken by surprise at Varuna's quiet arrival at the campsite. "My Lord... I didn't see you there - this is a pleasant surprise!" he started to explain.

"Be quiet you insolent and incompetent Hoffen-faced fool!" growled the furious evil King, as he kicked soil onto the flames of the fire.

Dergan replied. "But, your greatness... I was just preparing my troops in readiness for your command and..."

"Be quiet you ignorant Kalmog, get yourself dressed for battle and round up your squadron... we will set out immediately to destroy Meltor and his cronies once and for all!" warned Varuna.

Lieutenant Dergan bowed his head to acknowledge the King's request and then scampered away to relay the order to his troops. "How dare he call me a Kalmog!" muttered the trembling Wartpig.

The disgruntled lieutenant was entitled to be offended by Varuna's cruel comments. Kalmogs are very stupid vermin-type beings that dwell in the sewers of Castan, a city to the west of the Royal City of Trad. Dergan was not amused by Varuna's insults, but he dared not verbally defend himself against such a powerful and evil Hartopian.

Whilst Dergan organized his soldiers, Varuna reveled in his own self-importance. The Hartopian ordered his entourage to erect the Royal Pathylian Standard above a temporary canvass that he had seized from his incompetent lieutenant. The evil King waited inside the tent whilst the Wartpig regrouped and inspected the foot soldiers.

Unbeknown to Dergan, Varuna had also requested more support to seek out the band of rebels and the arrival of ten Devonian Death Troops, clad in bright red body armour with the traditional Satorc Sea Urchin 'black skull emblems' emblazoned on each arm, would provide the necessary back up they needed. The elite troops had been drafted in from the nearby town of Aedis, which was the base for the fearless Pathylian special-forces unit and their training complex.

Varuna was confident he would track down and exterminate the fugitives very quickly with the help of his new reinforcements. He was now quite relaxed about Meltor's non-conformity, as he knew he had the most hostile and merciless brigade of warriors that Pathylon could produce at his disposal. With the exception of the mutinous extremists guarding the Forbidden Caves, the Death Troops allegiance was always to their ruler, whoever he was, and they would be prepared to lay down their lives for their King.

At last Lieutenant Dergan had completed his inspection and ordered the whole group to prepare for their impending search. The temporary canvasses were dismantled and the campfires doused. The dark skies above offered a brief indication of morning, as the beams of daylight pierced through a broken cloud and shone through the tree branches that bordered the banks of the River Klomus. The ten death troops, together with Varuna's entourage made up of twenty-five palace workers, foot soldiers and confidants, took position in readiness for their grueling march through Devonia to seek out the five royal traitors.

A fanfare of horns sounded and the group moved forward with Royal Standard aloft. Varuna stood high and proud inside the Royal Chariot and gave out a loud roar of relief. He then settled back and muttered to himself in an evil tone. "You and your fledglings will pay dearly for your betrayal… my dear Meltor."

Back in the outside world, Margaret was becoming very concerned about the length of time Bradley was taking to get washed. She knocked on the door of Aunt Vera's bathroom to encourage her son to hurry up and get out of the bathtub.

"Come on Bradley… hurry up!" she shouted, as she pressed her ear to the door. "That water will be cold by now – you will catch pneumonia!"

There was no reply and Margaret was starting to get very agitated. She shouted again and knocked harder on the door. "Bradley, I won't tell you again… out of there – now!"

There was still no reply from inside the bathroom. Margaret was now livid and she banged even harder on the door. "Am I wasting my breath?" she cried. "Bradley, this is not funny anymore… if you don't answer me I'll get your Aunt Vera to open this door when she gets back!" she threatened. "I'm sure you won't want her to see you with nothing on but your smile!"

Still no answer came from Bradley. But then unbeknown to Margaret, there was never any likelihood of a reply from the young adventurer. She finally lost her patience and the bathroom door was successfully unlocked from the outside using one of Aunt Vera's nail files. She was joined by her sister who had just returned and heard the ranting and raving from downstairs. "What on earth is going on Margaret?"

"Bradley is up to his usual tricks and spending far too long in the bath," replied a now very red-faced Margaret.

"It's blooming marvelous… you spend hours trying to get them in the dammed water and you have to spend days getting them out again," said Vera, in an exaggerated tone and pushed the door open.

The sisters tentatively peered into the steam filled room, as they both shuffled nearer to the edge of the bathtub. They feared the worst and both expected to see Bradley floating on the surface of the soapy water.

Margaret reached over and lifted the plug chain. "He's wrapped it around the taps and all the water's gone!" she exclaimed. "Where is he?"

"I don't know," replied her confused sister. "Maybe he got out and went into the bedroom."

"He couldn't have... the door was locked from the inside," stated Margaret. "I unlocked it using your nail file… *and* I broke it - sorry Vera!"

"Don't worry about that my dear… I'll go and check the bedroom anyway," said Vera.

"Well… there is no water left in the bathtub - so he must have got out," said Margaret, as Vera brushed past her and headed into Bradley's bedroom. She searched inside the wardrobe, behind the curtains and under the bed. "The little monkey's not in here!"

Margaret shouted to her sister to come back into the bathroom. She had noticed the gold coin in the plughole. Vera shuttled back across the hall and into the clammy washroom. She then stared down, through her steamed up spectacles, into the bathtub and focused on the gold coin.

"That looks like the shiny object that Bradley and his new friend found when we were down in Amley's Cove earlier," explained Vera, as she removed her spectacles to polish away the water vapour that clouded the lenses. "Fancy taking that thing in the bath with him… and I hope he's not scratched my nice bath tub!"

As Vera knelt down to inspect the surface of the bath, Margaret pushed her sister aside and leant down to successfully dislodge the coin from the plughole. She was fascinated by its appearance and read the inscription around the edge.

"I wonder what it means," said Margaret, as Vera gathered her balance.

"You didn't have to push me like that!" she exclaimed, as the coin began to glow and vibrate in her sister's hand.

Margaret ignored Vera's niggling rant. She was too startled to concentrate on her sister's irrelevant complaint and without hesitation she dropped the coin back into the bath. The gold disk rattled against the metal tub and then span on its edge for a short while. The two women watched intently, as the coin then rolled back towards the plughole. The bemused sisters looked at each other in astonishment, as the coin fell neatly back into the round hole and sealed itself.

The middle of the coin began to open, as beams of green light emanated through the centre and burst out like lasers striking through the steam filled bathroom. The parallel shards of luminosity moved about like flashing sabres, as they started to swirl faster and faster. "What's going on, Margaret?" asked Vera, in a trembling voice.

"Where is my Bradley?" shouted Margaret, as she clung onto her sister's blouse.

"I don't know my dear!" replied Vera. "But I'd hazard a guess that all this palaver has something to do with his disappearance!"

The two women let out a simultaneous scream and a loud clap of thunder reverberated around the small bathroom, as a green flash of lightning struck the coin. The taps twisted and turned of their own accord and water started to cascade into the bathtub. More steam filled the room and they felt their feet lifting off the ground, as they grabbed a tighter hold of each other. As they were raised into the dense smog filled air, they started to travel around in circles and felt themselves shrinking in size before plummeting into the bath water. Both women screamed again as they were drawn towards the plughole.

With a final clasp of thunder echoing in their ears, they were sucked through the centre of the coin and into the bathtub's waste trap. Like two wooden logs being tossed over the edge of a cascading waterfall, they were then sent hurtling down the vertical drainpipe in a torrent of rushing water that carried them along on their incredible journey.

14

The Search Party

It was 9.35am and the train from Sheffield arrived twenty-five minutes late at Sandmouth station. Patrick and Frannie made their way along the carriage to collect their suitcases from the luggage racks adjacent the sliding doors. K2 tugged at his lead in a premature attempt to escape from the *Virgin* inter-city express.

Frannie pulled back at the leash and scolded the great hound. "K2... will you stop pulling me?" The sudden jerk on the leash resulted in the big clumsy dog gasping for breath, as the collar tightened around his twenty-inch neck.

Patrick looked down at his four-year-old daughter and smiled, as K2 continued to choke. He loved the way she tried unsuccessfully to master the Burnese Mountain Dog and offered some encouragement and advice on how to stop the excited canine from creating such a fuss.

They disembarked from the train and gathered their luggage together on the platform. Patrick looked over to an advertisement hoarding and noticed the telephone number of a local mini-cab company. He took out his mobile phone and rang for a taxi to take the weary trio to Aunt Vera's cottage.

The taxi arrived within the four minutes waiting time, as promised by the mini-cab coordinator. It subsequently sped them into the village and down to the thatched cottage on the coastal road. Patrick was hoping to catch Frannie's mum, brother and aunt by surprise.

Patrick paid the driver and unloaded their luggage from the taxi's boot. Frannie and K2 ran towards the front gate of Aunt Vera's cottage. The great hound sprung open the picket gate and by the time the dog had reached the front door he was dragging poor Frannie behind him. The bounding animal had caused the gate to spring back shut, so Patrick re-opened it and ran down the cobbled path to assist his bedraggled daughter. "Are you okay, Princess?" he shouted, as he witnessed Frannie pointing to a small graze on her knee.

Frannie lifted her face out of the marigolds that grew in the border that edged the cobbled path. She looked up forlornly at her father and pointed to her leg. "Daddy... look what K2 has done - I think I'm going to need a plaster putting on it!"

Just like any normal four-year-old, Frannie was always looking for an excuse to apply a band-aid to any visible part of her anatomy.

Patrick helped his daughter to her feet and then rang the doorbell. There was no answer, but he could hear a vacuum cleaner being used inside the cottage. He waited for the noise to cease and then depressed his finger on the doorbell again. A figure appeared behind the frosted glass window and the door was unlocked. The door was opened fully and Patrick looked very surprised. A pretty teenage girl stood tall in the doorway and greeted them.

"Oh... err - *hello*!" said Patrick. "Who are you?"

"I think I'd better ask you the same question!" replied the girl, sternly.

"Oh... *sorry* - I'm err... Patrick and this is my daughter Frannie," he answered. "I'm Margaret's husband... err - Vera's brother in law."

"Hello Sir... I'm sorry to sound so abrupt - it's just that I wasn't expecting anyone so early," replied the girl. "Please come inside!"

Patrick and Frannie stepped into the porch and removed their shoes, while the girl disappeared into the kitchen. She returned with a cloth in her hand and approached K2 to make a fuss of the big hound by shaking his head with her palm. "What a beautiful dog and what big paws he's got... I'd better wipe his feet - you know what Vera is like about dirt on her carpets!" she explained and knelt down. "What breed is he?"

"He's a Burnese Mountain Dog!" replied Frannie, proudly. "He's called K2... you know - after that big mountain in the Karakorum Range on the Pakistan and China border!"

"Oh... err, right!" replied the girl. "Wasn't expecting that... you're a very confident little girl – aren't you?"

"Mmmm... K2 is the second highest mountain in the world you know – not this K2, the big pointy K2 with the snow on the top!" declared Frannie, as she stroked the top of the dog's huge head and giggled.

"Ermm, well, okay... thank you Frannie – you certainly *are* very clever," confirmed the girl affectionately, as she turned her attention to the slobbering hound. "Hello big fella... and you are *soooooooooo* gorgeous – now give me a paw."

K2 welcomed the attention by lifting a paw and simultaneously licked the girls face, as she attempted to clean one of his huge pads.

Patrick watched in amusement as the friendly teenager brushed off the dog's affections. He thought about what Vera's likes and dislikes were and looked forward to antagonizing her with K2's antics during his visit. "Where is everyone?" he asked. "Oh... and what's your name?"

"What a lot of questions," replied the girl cheekily, as she rose to her feet and watched K2 bound off through the house to explore the cottage garden. "My name is Julie... but everyone calls me Jules - my mother is Vera's housekeeper but she's not feeling too well today, so I'm filling in for her."

Jules was quite tall for a seventeen-year-old and her straight shoulder-length brown hair complimented her pretty face. She was wearing a pair of white denim hipsters and a lilac V-necked top with the word *'ELVIS'* across it in silver sequins. "I don't know where Vera has gone!" she exclaimed and chewed frantically on her gum. "The house was empty when I arrived here this morning."

"Daddy... maybe Aunt Vera and Mummy have gone down to the beach with Bradley," suggested Frannie, as she removed a rather large green bogey from her left nostril and stood there with it perched on the end of her finger.

"Maybe you're right, Frannie," replied Patrick, handing her his handkerchief. "But it seems a bit early in the day for that... now - please blow your nose Princess, that's a good little girl."

Patrick retrieved his saturated handkerchief and made his way into the lounge. Jules offered to make them drinks and disappeared back into the kitchen. She returned shortly afterwards holding a silver tray. She placed the tray down onto the coffee table and began to pour Patrick a cup of tea. Frannie received a glass of cold orange squash, but K2 had to make do with a bowl of cold water for now.

"Would you like me to find a dressing for that graze on your knee, Frannie?" asked Jules.

"Mmmm… yes please," replied Frannie, as she followed Jules into the kitchen again.

They both reappeared and Jules excused herself so she could continue with her housekeeping duties. She then hurriedly finished off the last few bits of ironing. Jules was itching to get away to spend the afternoon down on beach with her boyfriend, Simon Chilcott. The love-struck girl was taking advantage of his leave from the Royal Marines training camp. She always tried to spend quality time with him during his home visits and resented the fact that her mother wasn't feeling too well. Jules was a little annoyed that she had been lumbered with Aunt Vera's housework on such a beautiful sunny day. She felt frustrated at not being able to spend more time with Simon.

Musgrove Chilcott's older brother was due to call for Jules at around one o'clock, after she had finished her chores. It wouldn't be long now and the love-struck girl was continually looking up at the station clock on the kitchen wall, counting down the minutes as she pressed the last few duvet covers.

There was a loud knock on the front door and the doorbell rang. K2 barked aggressively and Jules rushed to greet the visitor. She opened the door expecting to see Simon's handsome face, but instead discovered a serious looking police officer.

The policeman stood under the porch canopy and removed his helmet. He looked up and down at the attractive brunette, as Jules stared at the officer's balding head. She stood back to let him into the cottage, as he placed his helmet back on his head. "Could I speak with your mother or father?"

"This is not my house - but please come in and I will ask the owner's brother-in-law if he can help you," replied Jules.

The policeman followed her into the lounge where Patrick was sat perusing the local newspaper. He looked up and peered over his reading glasses at the uniformed man and reacted in a surprised manner by dropping the Sandmouth Herald onto the floor. Frannie's father quickly rose to his feet. "My goodness... a policeman!" he exclaimed. "What can we do for you officer?"

"I believe the owner of the house is not *here*?" asked the policeman.

"Well... my daughter and I only arrived a short while ago and there was no one in when we got here - except Jules that is," explained Patrick. "Our visit to Sandmouth wasn't planned and we were hoping to present my sister-in-law with a pleasant surprise... but she isn't here at the moment - I think she may have nipped out somewhere with my wife and my son... they should be back soon - I hope."

The policeman removed his helmet again and tucked it under his arm. K2 was sniffing at his trouser legs and gave out an approving bark. "Allow me to introduce myself... I am P.C. Sharp from the Sandmouth Constabulary - I'm sorry to have bothered you, but we are undertaking a search of the area for a missing boy." The concerned policeman continued. "He was reported missing this morning by his mother... we don't normally react so soon - but this particular boy is my nephew and I would be grateful if you could look out for him!"

The well-built police officer was clearly upset and he reached into his top pocket for his note pad and pulled out a photograph. "Here is a picture of him, his name is Musgrove... his school friends call him Muzzy – he's fourteen-years-old."

Patrick took the photograph from the officer's trembling hand and Jules leant over to look at the picture. "That's Musgrove Chilcott!" she screamed. "My boyfriend's Brother!"

The girl's exclamation was interrupted by a loud knock on the front door. The door was pushed open and Simon Chilcott came rushing into the house closely followed by three fellow royal marine recruits. All four strapping young men were meticulously dressed in khaki uniforms with their black boots and brass belt buckles gleaming immaculately, from hours of intense polishing.

"Simon!" cried Jules, as the excited girl ran over to her boyfriend and flung her arms around his broad neck. "What's happened to Muzzy?" she asked desperately.

"Hi babes... we are all out looking for him," replied the handsome blonde haired soldier. "The little toad went A.W.O.L. last night... this is the fourth time it's happened apparently - according to mum!"

"What's all the fuss about?" asked Frannie, as she picked at the dressing to reveal the newly-formed scabs on her knee. "...and what does *hay woll* mean?"

Simon looked down at the cheeky-faced inquisitor, as Frannie gave him a glaring once-over and stared at him from top to toe. Then the little girl insisted in a frustrated tone. "I asked what all the fuss is about!"

Simon stared at Jules and then at P.C. Sharp. Not even his commanding officer back at the training camp had spoken to him so sternly. The little girl was certainly making a lasting impression on the new recruit who was only thirteen weeks into his training at Lympstone Barracks.

"Frannie... don't be rude," said Patrick to his confident offspring. "Simon and the nice policeman are very worried about Musgrove... otherwise they wouldn't be out looking for him!"

"I wasn't being rude Daddy... I just want an answer to my question – anyhow... Musgrove's a silly name for a boy."

Patrick produced a raw smile and finally satisfied his daughter's curiosity. "A.W.O.L. means *'absent with-out leave'*, sweet pea... and you shouldn't make fun of people's names – it's not very nice."

Frannie looked a bit put-out by her father's comments, so she screwed up her freckled nose and tried to look none the wiser. She turned away to summon K2 to heel. The two then disappeared into the kitchen and out of the back door and into the garden to continue with the delectable task of picking the scabs on her knee again.

"Sorry about my daughter," said Patrick, as he turned to Simon. "She can be a bit forward for her age... I blame her mother," he added jokingly.

The joke did not break the intense atmosphere that had developed in Aunt Vera's lounge. Simon and his elite squad of three gathered around the police officer to devise a plan to search the Sandmouth area more affectively. Aunt Vera's cottage was the last home they had visited, so the most likely place to find Musgrove now would be down in Amley's Cove.

The police officer turned to Patrick, who was a little red-faced following his failed attempt to lift the morale of the worried relatives. "Would you like to help us look for young Musgrove?"

"Of course I would!" replied Patrick. "Just tell me what you want me to do officer!"

"We need to form a search party!" exclaimed P.C. Sharp. "I suggest some of us make our way down to Amley's Cove to carry out a systematic search of the caves and pools... before the tide comes back in!"

"*Jules*... I'd be very grateful if you'd be so kind and look after Frannie and K2 for me – I'll go down to the cove with Simon and his uncle?" asked Patrick. "It's safer for you here and I am sure Vera, Margaret and Bradley will be back very soon."

Jules nodded and called out to Frannie, as Simon reassured her that they would be back soon. The marine looked upset and suggested to his girlfriend that a phone call to his mum would be a good idea. He thought it best to let her know that they were all going down to Amley's Cove and for her not to worry.

One of Simon's marine colleagues approached him. Chris placed his large hand on his friends shoulder. "We'll find your brother... don't worry mate!"

The third marine recruit was a Scotsman from Glasgow called Tank. He had inherited his name from of his huge size. He was extremely tall and built like an armoured patrol vehicle. The last of the marine recruits was called Bomber, a brown-skinned Cockney from the East End of London and he offered further support to his fellow soldier's girlfriend. "Jules... please tell Simon's Mum we'll bring back Muzzy safe and sound!"

Jules reluctantly agreed to look after Frannie and K2, as Patrick wrote a small piece of note paper for Margaret and

Bradley. He explained where he was going then left it on the coffee table. He felt the discovery of the Chilcott boy's whereabouts had become more important than surprising his wife and son.

Bradley's father followed the police officer and the marines out of the cottage. P.C. Sharp had parked a police-marked transit van outside Vera's front gate. All six men hurriedly boarded the vehicle with the officer electing to drive. Patrick sat between Tank and Bomber and he looked down at the size of the marines' thighs. His knees fell short of theirs by about a shoe's length and he felt like a sardine squashed in a tin.

The police officer started the transit's engine and slipped the van into gear. Each member of the search party bounced around and held on to the police van's safety handles as P.C. Sharp steered the noisy wagon down the bumpy road, which led to the cove. Patrick crooked his neck and looked back out of the rearview window of the vehicle. Vera's house disappeared from view and he thought to himself about Frannie and just how long it would take his daughter to annoy her new babysitter. He began to think deeply about Margaret and Bradley and he could not wait to see them again. "I do hope they are both okay... wherever they are," he muttered to himself.

Tank overheard Patrick's mumbling and reassured the worried parent that everything would be okay by grabbing his thigh. Bradley's father winced under the pressure of the Scotsman's huge hand on his limb. He mustered a smile for the burly Glaswegian and thanked him for his concern, as the van continued along the bumpy road that led down to Amley's Cove.

15

A Secret Cave

Following their dramatic plunge into the abyss, Margaret and Vera had negotiated a safe passage through the gap at the base of the toadstool stem and had followed the trail down the infinite staircase to the chamber that housed the eight hooded doorways.

The women had found the scroll under one of the doors and read the message. They had thought long and hard about *garlic* of all things and this had enabled the sisters to make their way through the hooded door adorned with the name *GOMMERRO*.

Once inside the torch lit corridors, they had made their way into the next chamber that housed the tall oak doors. The gigantic monuments that towered above now confronted the two terrified women.

Margaret read aloud the inscription that appeared high above the doors on the lintel that supported them. "Pathylon!" she pronounced, in a nervous tone.

"Excuse me... excuse me," repeated Vera, as she readied herself to offer one of her annoying and unwanted opinions. "Can I make a suggestion...?"

"Well our Vera... you always do anyway - so why should I stop you from making a suggestion now!" exclaimed Margaret. "Especially, dear sister... as it's such a critical and stressful time in our lives!"

"Oh well... if you are going to be like that - I won't bother then," said Vera, as she put her hands on her broad hips and turned away.

Margaret pleaded with her sister not be so touchy and get on and explain what it was she was going to suggest. "Come on then Vera... I can see you're eager to tap into your supply of scintillating advice!"

"Well, can I suggest we go back and get some help?"

"Nice one... our Vera," replied Margaret. "You certainly know how to encourage a sister in need," she said, sarcastically. "You can't expect us to get help... when we can't even go back the same way as we came in - the staircase we climbed down disappeared back up into the air, you great noggin!"

"Don't be like that... our Margaret - I was only trying to help," said Vera, as she turned her head away again and started to sulk. Margaret went over to her older sister and put her arm around the small rounded lady in an effort to comfort her. Vera looked round at her sister and started to cry. "I'm so scared," sobbed Vera, emotionally. "Where on earth are we and where can poor Bradley have gotten to?"

"Come on Vera, don't cry... it should be me that's crying not you – everything's going to be okay," Margaret reassured her sister. "We'll find our way out of here and don't worry about Bradley... he may only be eleven but he's got the strength and mind of someone twice his age!"

Vera gathered her composure and walked towards the doors. "Maybe these great things will lead us out of this smelly sewer."

Margaret's sister took a step backwards, as the oaks doors started to open slowly. Vera had stood on the red gemstone that centered the five-cornered star. Both women gasped with amazement, as the doors opened wider and wider. They peered through and witnessed the flashing multi-coloured lights that spiraled symmetrically. The vortex swirled with a hypnotic motion and drew the two women nearer.

"Come on, our Vera... it's my turn to make a suggestion!" exclaimed Margaret. "I suggest we go this way!"

Margaret took hold of Vera's hand and they both ran awkwardly towards the brilliant white light at the centre of the vortex. They both jumped into the light. *Whoooosshhh...* round and round they travelled, deeper and deeper into the multi-coloured display. Smaller and smaller they appeared, as they reached the centre of the spiral and then they vanished out of sight.

Meanwhile back in Sandmouth, P.C. Sharp's search party had already scoured most of Amley's Cove. Patrick and Tank were looking in and around all the rock pools, whilst Simon and his uncle checked out the caves along the cliff sides.

As Simon stepped over a large piece of driftwood, he lost his balance and fell awkwardly. His left leg was caught between a piece of seaweed-covered driftwood and a protruding rock.

"Are you okay?" enquired P.C. Sharp.

"Give me a hand to shift this will you, uncle?" Simon asked the policeman, embarrassingly.

The well-built police officer lifted the lump of mollusk-covered debris with ease and released Simon's foothold. As the driftwood was discarded, the sand scurried back into the void as the seawater flowed and swirled in the rock pool. The driftwood had hidden a round shaped object, which was now sticking out of the sand. Simon made P.C. Sharp aware of his discovery, which appeared to be a wooden cask with green stained brass corners, held together with raised iron studs.

The police officer helped Simon to clear the loose sand that was preserving the old crate. They tugged on the container and it started to move, as the corner piece broke away. More water and sand filled the space where the crate had laid, as Simon noticed a group of shiny objects inside the container. "Look!" he exclaimed. "It's full of gold coins!"

"Well whadda you know... it looks like we've found some pirate treasure!" exclaimed P.C. Sharp, as he reached down to pick up one of the coins.

The two men proceeded to extract all the coins from their watery haven and then placed them on top of a nearby flat-topped rock.

"How many coins are there?" asked P.C. Sharp.

"Hang on... let me count," replied Simon, excitedly. "One... two... three... four..." The marine continued to count. "...twenty five!" he concluded and placed his hand back inside the cask to check for more coins, as he pulled out the final piece of treasure. "Look at this one, Uncle." He cried and rubbed his thumb around the edge. "This one has some sort of inscription etched into it."

"Oh yes... so it has," agreed P.C. Sharp, as he picked up another coin with writing engraved around the circumference. "So has this one... but it's a bit dirty - can you see what it says?"

Simon looked at the coin between his uncle's fingers, as P.C. Sharp held the inscribed coin up to the sunlight to allow his nephew to read out the message. *"Thee who hath taken this to thy belonging, seal it again to bring forth magic powers!"*

Simon began to sort through all twenty-six coins and counted out the ones with the inscriptions around the edges. "There are nine of them marked with the same inscription!" he declared.

"Och... nine what?" interrupted Tank, as he made his way over to see what all the fuss was about. The Scottish marine recruit had heard Simon's voice reverberate against the cliffs and had noticed his fellow marine and the police officer had stopped to look at something. Tank had noticed that they were standing over one of the rock pools and the Highlander had overheard Simon's exclamation. He was intrigued to know what they had discovered and started to make his way over to them.

Simon and P.C. Sharp had completely forgotten for a slight moment about why they were in the cove. Finding and counting the gold coins had suddenly distracted them from the real priority, which was finding Musgrove. "Nine gold coins... with some kind of inscription engraved around the edge of them!" shouted Simon, as he looked across to his colleague stumbling over the rocks.

Tank finally made it over to where Simon and P.C. Sharp had found the contents of the cask. "Blooming marvelous!" said Tank. "You get to go treasure hunting during your leave... whilst we all spend our free time searching for your missing wee boy!"

Simon acknowledged Tank's frustration and put all twenty-six coins in his combat trouser pockets for safekeeping. The weight of the treasure caused his clothing to hang heavy. He turned to P.C. Sharp and suggested they carry on with the search for his brother and check out the coins in more detail later, once they had found Musgrove safe and sound. P.C Sharp agreed and they both gave Tank an assured look that their attention was fully back on the job at hand.

Following their thrilling journey through the spiral, Pathylon had now welcomed two more strangers into its mystical Kingdom. Margaret and Vera were now wandering through the dark passageways within the forbidden caves.

Just then they heard the sound of marching feet. They quickly hid behind a large rock whilst a group of red uniformed soldiers passed them by. Unbeknown to Margaret and Vera, the soldiers were a group of renegade Devonian Death Troops who had imprisoned the eight missing Freytorians inside the Forbidden Caves.

Once the soldiers had gone, the two frightened women reappeared from behind the rock and then made their way through the winding passageways that led out of the caves. They suddenly found themselves standing in a small opening within the great Forest of Haldon.

The two ladies looked shaken and worried. Vera brushed the stone dust from her cloths and looked around and up into the tall cretyre trees. Strange winged squirrel-like animals leapt from branch to branch, their bushy tails acting as buoyancy devices as they darted back and forth between the high treetops.

"The skies are really dark and so miserable... and this place feels spooky!" exclaimed Margaret, as she scanned the thunderous clouds above the tall tree tops.

"Hey Margaret... look at those,' said Vera, as she pointed out a pair of squirrel-like creatures in the branches of a nearby cretyre tree. "They are so cute and elegant... don't you think?"

"Yes Vera... aren't they just - I am sure those little rodents are very happy jumping around in their cosy surroundings!" exclaimed Margaret. "However, we have more important things to think about... for a start - I would like to know where those soldiers in the red suits came from and I'd also like to know where we are!"

"Well, it's obvious where we are..." said Vera. "We're in Pathylon... well that's what it said above those big doors before you dragged me into those silly twirling lights."

"Yes, yes... alright clever clogs - I am fully aware this must be Pathylon," said Margaret, sarcastically. "What I meant was... where in Pathylon are we - and where do we go from here to find our poor little Bradley?" she added, as she walked over to where a beaten path had been made in the forest undergrowth.

"It looks like you've answered your own question, Margaret," said Vera. "Why don't we follow that path and see where it leads us?" suggested the oldest sister.

Just then Margaret let out a scream of delight as she bent down to pick up a small green plastic object that was lying in the long grass. She held the little toy soldier aloft and started to jump up and down. Margaret had found one of her son's bath toys. "Look, our Vera... this confirms my Bradley is here!" she exclaimed.

The discovery of the plastic toy gave fresh impetus to the two sister's quest to find Bradley. The women decided to follow the path and headed off into the Forest of Haldon to search for him. Vera looked upwards into the tall cretyre trees and glanced further at the dark grey skies above. "Where in hell's name are we?"

"Hell is quite an appropriate description!" replied Margaret. "Let's move on quickly Vera… look - there's another path that leads deeper into the woods."

"Are you sure we ought to go in there, Margaret?"

"Come on Vera… there's no going back now!"

The two sisters followed the path and headed off into the dark forest in search of Bradley. Both women were spurred on by the discovery of the toy soldier and hoped for a way out of the strange grey world that they had found themselves in.

Meanwhile in Amley's Cove, Bomber was climbing further up the cliffside to ensure that Musgrove was not lying on any of the numerous hidden cliff ledges that adorned the rocky heights. He had spotted a small opening in the rocks, about twenty metres up the cliff-side and he had decided to ascend further to check it out. As he neared the opening, he was startled by the sudden appearance of an adult seagull that had been nesting nearby. The gull was instinctively protecting its young and began to dive at the marine in a desperate bid to defend its territory.

Patrick heard the commotion above and looked up to where Bomber was shouting and waving his arms at the large bird. "I think Bomber's in trouble!" he exclaimed. "Come on Tank… he needs help!"

Tank followed Patrick over and around the rocky pools and they both headed for the base of the cliffs where Bomber was desperately hanging on for dear life. Simon and P.C. Sharp had also noticed the mayhem that ensued and started to make their way over to help Tank and Patrick.

The police officer had an idea and returned to the police van. He opened the boot compartment and pulled out a heavy bundle of hemp rope. Chris asked if they needed his help and was told categorically to stay put near the radio, just in case Musgrove's mum tried to contact them. P.C. Sharp had left a walkie-talkie with his sister so that they were able to communicate with her from the onboard radio in the van. Chris was to stay in the vehicle to man the radio in case any news broke, in relation to the missing boy's whereabouts.

By the time P.C. Sharp had returned to the base of the cliff, Tank had already started to climb up to help his fellow marine. The police officer handed Patrick the rope and he shouted up to attract his attention, as he prepared the coils of hemp for launch. Tank immediately stopped ascending the cliffside and looked back down towards Patrick and P.C. Sharp. "Throw it up then!" he ordered, holding out his arm. Patrick propelled the rope into the air, but it fell well short of his position.

Further up the cliff, Bomber was receiving continual aerial bombardment from the aggressive seagull, as Patrick attempted three more throws without success. P.C. Sharp could see that his efforts were futile and took back control of the rope and used all his strength and height to rocket the twined hemp above Tank's head. The rope settled around the eighteen-inch neckline of the Scotsman.

Tank then called to Bomber who was about fifteen feet further up the cliffside. "Och aye mate... get a load of this!"

Bomber turned his attention away from the frantic maneuvers of the annoying bird for a few moments and looked down to where tank was positioned. "Come on then... fling it up here!" he replied, in a very broad East End accent.

Tank thrust the rope towards Bomber. He caught hold first time and extended the rope to enable sufficient length to tie a knot in the end. He then proceeded to use the knotted end of the rope as a weapon to fend off the onslaught of the irate seagull. After a few more vicious bombardments from above, the bird finally gave up on its vain attempts to knock the marine off the side of the cliff. It hovered above for a while and then returned to its nest to attend to the young chicks, which were now squawking frantically.

Bomber edged his way towards the small opening in the cliffside and secured the rope around a thick branch that was growing out of the rock face. Tank continued his climb towards Bomber with the aid of the rope, quickly followed by P.C. Sharp, Simon and Patrick. All five men congratulated each other and crouched on the ledge next to the small opening in the rocks. Patrick peered through the gap in the cliffside, which Bomber had painstakingly discovered. "I can't see much," he announced and strained his eyes to focus into the dark opening. "I'm going inside to take a closer look."

"Here... take this flash light," said Simon, as he unclipped the small metal torch from the key ring that was attached to his belt.

Patrick accepted the offering and proceeded to squeeze his upper body through the small gap in the rocks. He flicked the switch on the flashlight and shone the torch in front and surveyed what looked like the inside of a small cave. He focused the torch beam ahead towards the back of the eerie chamber to discover another opening that appeared to lead further into the cliffside.

"Can you see anything?" asked P.C. Sharp, in a hopeful tone. "Can you see any sign of our Musgrove?"

Patrick prized himself back out of the tight crack and reappeared onto the ledge, covering his eyes until they readjusted to the strong sunlight that reflected off the white cliff face. "The opening leads into a small cave... but there's no sign of Musgrove in there fellas," he assumed. "However, there does appear to be another opening at the far end of the cave... it's quite possible, if the young boy went in there - he could have ventured further into the cliffside."

"Let's go in and take a look," suggested Bomber.

The other four members of the search party agreed and prepared to squeeze through the entrance to the cave by discarding any items of clothing that they felt were too cumbersome.

Simon shouted down to Chris, who was still sitting in the police van. "Use the radio and contact my mother to tell her we are going into the cliffside to look for Musgrove!"

Chris appeared from the van and stretched his arms aloft in an attempt to relieve the cramp in his shoulders. He looked over to the group and gave the thumbs up to acknowledge receipt of Simon's instructions. He then got back in the police van to radio the message along to Mrs. Chilcott. He reappeared from the van and watched on tentatively as, one by one, the five men squeezed through the gap in the cliffside and disappeared into the cave.

16

A Hostile Transformation

Margaret and Vera had managed to negotiate their way through the great forest and had found themselves at the edge of the river. The continued darkening of the heavy sky was causing concern and they quickened their steps in search for some temporary shelter.

They only had to travel a short distance along the riverbank, when they came across Grog's lodge. The small cabin was nestled in a tight group of trees about twenty metres from the water's edge.

"That looks like a sensible place to rest for a while," said Margaret. "I'll walk over to see if anyone is at home."

"Be careful, our Margaret… you don't know what might be lurking in there!" warned Vera, as she followed tentatively behind her sister.

Margaret ignored her over-protective sister and proceeded to knock on the front door. She placed her ear to the door and listened for any movement inside the log cabin. She could not hear any noise, so she knocked again to make sure and then waited. "It would appear there's no-one home." She concluded.

"Try the door handle then," suggested Vera. "It might be unlocked."

Margaret turned the heavy iron latch and pushed the door. "It's open!" she exclaimed. "Come on Vera - let's look inside."

The two ladies moved slowly through the doorway and entered Grog's lounge. Vera held out her arms and fumbled around the tops of the primitive wooden furniture. She touched something metal and took hold of what appeared to be a lantern of some kind. It felt very similar to a miner's gas lamp that Grandma Penworthy was given as a memento of her husband's thirty years of service down Silvermoor Colliery. Vera pulled back the striking clip and forced it back into the lamp quickly, causing the flint inside to spark and ignite the fuel on the wick.

The warm glow from the lamp illuminated the lodge and the women continued their search of the strange looking cabin. They crept up the creaky wooden stairs and looked around inside the upper rooms.

"There's definitely no-one here," said Margaret.

Vera seemed to ignore her sister's comment and walked over to the bunks in one of the bedrooms.

"Vera, did you hear what I just said?" demanded Margaret.

"Yes dear," replied Vera. "Never mind that... look at these Margaret - they look like Bradley's trousers!"

Margaret rushed over to where the abandoned cloths lay. She picked up the blue-checkered shirt and sniffed the soft cotton fabric. "It's definitely Bradley's shirt... he's been here Vera – my boy is alive!" screamed Margaret. "We've got to find him... he may be in danger!"

"Calm down love... I'm sure there is a simple explanation for all of this," replied Vera, as she placed the lantern on the small cupboard next to the bunk.

"But *why* has he left his clothes *here*?" exclaimed Margaret, as her sister rested the lamp on the bedside cabinet. Then she noticed a crumpled up piece of paper on the floor. She picked it up and unraveled the note. "The writing's a bit scruffy... but I'll try to read it without my glasses," she said. *"Put these on and I will explain later... regards Grog* – that's all it says."

"Bradley must have changed into some other clothes," said Vera. "But who's *Grog*?"

"Don't know... but I think you're right Vera," replied Margaret. "And look... there are some other garments on the bed opposite - I wonder who they belong too?"

Vera picked up the shirt with the surfing motif emblazoned across the front. She held the shirt close to the lantern to get a better look at the garment. "I recognize this!" she exclaimed. "This belongs to that Musgrove Chilcott... the boy I took down to Amley's Cove with Bradley."

"You mean *both* Bradley and his new friend have been in here," said Margaret. "Come on Vera... we've got to find them before that *Grog* creature harms them."

"Hang on Margaret... this Grog may be a good person - who is trying to help the boys," explained Vera. "Let's not jump to any conclusions... we've got to be sensible about this and think positively - anyhow, its pitch black out there and we don't stand a chance of finding them tonight – we don't even know where *we* are, let alone *them*!"

Margaret slumped onto one of the bunks and cupped her hands into her face. She started to weep uncontrollably. Vera sat down beside her sister. It was now her turn to offer the reassurance and she placed her arms around her sister's neck in an attempt to award the comfort she needed. Margaret's head was pulled towards her older sister's chest and her hair was stroked gently. Vera spoke softly and reassuringly. "Come on love... don't get upset - everything will be okay."

"Oh Vera," sniffed Margaret. "I couldn't bear it if something horrible has happened to Bradley and his friend."

"Don't worry... I'm sure they're fine," said Vera. "That Chilcott boy looked like he could look after himself... and our Bradley's not behind the door you know!"

"But..." replied Margaret.

"...there's no buts about it," interrupted Vera. "At least we know Bradley isn't alone in this god forsaken place."

Vera was displaying a remarkable calmness and she managed to stem the flow of Margaret's tears. The older and wiser sister then suggested that they stay the night in the lodge. Margaret reluctantly agreed. She lay back on the bed and grabbed a hold of the scruffy looking pillow. Margaret could smell the scent of her son on the cushion and she scrunched the soft pillow tightly against her chest.

The two women finally settled down on the same bunks that Bradley and Musgrove had slept in the night before.

Bradley Baker focused his attention on a shooting star that appeared through a gap in the thick grey clouds. He could not sleep and the restless boy sat upright and looked around at his slumbering comrades who had formed a neat circle around the low flames of the campfire.

Meltor was snoring loudly and he held his trusty blade close to his chest as he slept. The dying embers of the fire flickered and reflected in the jewels that adorned the handle of the Galatian's sword. Bradley turned his attention to

Musgrove, who was making high pitched whining noises and fidgeting beneath the large cretyre leaf that acted as protection against the cold of the night.

Bradley likened his dreaming-friend to K2, who acted in the same way when he yelped out loud during his dognapping. It was also apparent that Sereny and Grog had managed to settle comfortably and they both lay very still. He laid back into the soft grass and continued to stare up at the dark skies. With the exception of the shooting star, which had now disappeared from sight, the lack of shining heavenly objects made him feel uncomfortable.

The campfire was now a bed of white ash and the pitch-blackness haunted Bradley as the thick clouds moved slowly over Pathylon. Although he felt a deep fear inside, the nightfall seemed to bring some kind of peace. The tired boy could no longer fight his consciousness and he closed his heavy eyelids. He fell into a deep sleep filled with images of his mum and dad, which took precedence over the thoughts of his present uncertain situation.

A new morning broke and the dark dawn sky cast a grey shadow over Pathylon. The cheery bird songs that usually emanated from the native Wartula were silenced by the evil spell, which was growing stronger as each day past. The bright yellow feathers that adorned the wings of the heron-like creatures could no longer be seen soaring above the forests. The Wartula birds had abandoned their nests high in the branches of the cretyre trees and they had now flown south to the land of the great lakes. Many other forms of wildlife had also taken leave and deserted the miserable damp environment, which had been affected by the deadly curse.

The world of Pathylon was transforming into a hostile land that smelt of death. It was supposed to be the height of the summer, yet the silhouettes from the trees cast a mid-winter image along the horizon, as their broad green leaves began to wilt in the absence of sunlight. The River Klomus ran blood red as the fish and other water creatures suffocated through lack of light and oxygen. The wrath of the Freytorians had struck a devastating blow to all living matter throughout the five regions and time was running out for the inhabitants of Pathylon.

Meltor had woken early and he was busy ushering his band of rebels into some sort of order. He had already enlisted the help of Bradley and Musgrove, who were busy lighting a small fire, made out of the logs and branches, which they had collected from a nearby wood. Grog and Sereny had just returned to the campsite, with armfuls of nourishing provisions made up of Pathylian vegetables, clear spring water and freshly culled flax.

All the food preparations were complete and the group could now enjoy a healthy and wholesome breakfast, which would provide them all with the strength they needed in readiness for their daily tasks. Grog skinned and prepared the young flax that he had stalked and slain using his trusty blade. He then proceeded to skewer it, in readiness for roasting over the established flames of the campfire. The Krogon joined Meltor, Bradley, Sereny and Musgrove and they all sat around the fire and consumed the tasty meal made up of baked kelf plant seeds, wanjol beans and roast legs of flax. The food was delicious and the mealtime served as an excellent opportunity for Meltor to chair the meeting, which would determine the group's plans for the day ahead.

After about an hour, the meal had settled in their bellies and, following much talking between the group, Meltor announced their imminent departure. Bradley helped Grog to douse the fire and the brave band of freedom fighters collected their loose belongings. They headed off in the direction of Trad and the Shallock Tower.

Bradley and his friend's had now been walking at a steady pace for over three hours, but Sereny was showing signs of fatigue. She fell further behind and shouted ahead to ask the group to slow down. "Wait for me... I can't go on any more!"

They all stopped and Bradley made sure he would be the first to her rescue. With no hesitation, he ran back to help his weary friend. As he approached, Sereny smiled at him and offered out her hand. "Thanks Bradley... I owe you one," she said, as he took hold of her slender fingers and pulled her up from the ground.

Bradley put the girls arm around his neck and walked with her towards the others, who were standing impatiently with their hands on their hips. Bradley ignored them and instead offered some sincere words of encouragement. "Come on... Sereny – it can't be too far now," assured Bradley, as he held tightly to the girl's slim waist. "It's too dangerous to stop here... Varuna and his army will be following us – we can't give up now."

Meltor began to walk at a quick pace and Sereny turned her attention to the old Galetian. She afforded him a disapproving glare and the High Priest responded by offering some stern words of support. "Come along my dear... Varuna and his entourage will be closing in on us soon – we must move faster!"

"I'm going as fast as I can!" insisted Sereny.

Meltor stopped again and turned around, as he walked towards Sereny. The High Priest then lowered his tone and spoke softly in her ear. "I know it's hard for you Sereny... but please try harder – we must make our way quickly to the Royal City," he explained and threw one half of his great cloak back over his right shoulder. "Maybe we will find the other nine chosen ones there."

"What if we don't find them?" replied Sereny.

"Then we will have to conjure up a plan to save King Luccese on our own,' replied Meltor. "Even more reason for us to hurry... now come on Sereny – that's the spirit!"

Sereny moved forward and quickened her pace. Bradley looked round at Musgrove... Grog looked straight at Bradley... Musgrove smiled at Sereny... and then they all turned their heads to the front in the direction of Meltor, who had now made his way ahead of the group.

"Okay!" replied Musgrove. "You're the boss!"

"That's the spirit everyone," said Meltor, as he walked backwards facing his troop of brave hearts. Then turning to face forward, he shouted. "Now let's move on with haste my young friends!"

Grog had volunteered to take up the responsibility of rear guard to the precession. He proceeded to clean the flax blood from his sword and returned it to the sheath at his side. He then looked ahead as Meltor and the others marched onwards in the direction of Trad. He cast his mind back again to his childhood confrontation with Zule. He felt sure he was bound to cross paths with the new High Priest of Devonia and he drew a deep breath and tried to put Zule out of his thoughts, for the time being, at least.

Meanwhile back in Sandmouth, Chris was still asleep in the police van, but the rest of the search party was now wide-awake. They had decided to use the cliffside cave, which they had discovered in Amley's Cove, as a temporary shelter for the night.

"Let's take a look over here then," suggested Simon, as he and Tank approached the back of the cave. Bomber and P.C. Sharp followed close behind and Patrick handed Simon the torch so the tall marine could inspect the opening at the back of the cave. It was arched in shape and looked like it had been hand crafted using some kind of primitive tooling.

The five men passed under the arch and into another part of the cave. As they walked towards the centre of the next chamber, they were careful not to catch their heads on the low roofline. The cave heightened as they approached the far end and the light from the torch revealed paintings of strange creatures, which adorned the walls. The paintings portrayed lizard-like men with triple horned heads wielding swords, weasel-like creatures dressed in dark cloaks, humans with horns and laurel leafs on their heads, pictures of strange lands and maps with rivers, forests and cities.

"Wow!" shouted P.C. Sharp. "Just take a look at that lot... I can't quite make out the writing – it's really primitive!"

"Some landmarks on the map look really familiar... the shadows from the torch make it difficult to see but I can just make out a few words – Forest of Haldon?" stated Tank, as he struggled to focus on the cave wall.

"I think you're right mate – and I agree the map does look a bit familiar," agreed Simon. "See that bit jutting in there... it looks like the coastline around Amley's Cove but the words on the map say Satorc Estuary," continued the inquisitive marine, as he turned to look at his uncle whose mouth was still wide open in response to the sight of such a historic find.

Patrick joined the *gob-smacked* policeman and spent a few minutes analyzing the paintings and the map. "They appear to be some sort of prehistoric cave paintings... but they don't look that old – they look too modern to be from that period in time." He explained. "As for the map... it looks like someone has taken a great deal of effort to produce such a detailed drawing – the coastline may look familiar but the names certainly don't."

P.C. Sharp agreed. "You're right Patrick... I've never heard of Devonia or Krogonia - and look there's even a mountain range called the Peronto Alps!"

Simon turned his attention away from the strange wall etchings and started to look around the large cave for another means of exit. He scanned the full circumference of the chamber and returned his attention to the wall paintings. Just then he noticed a staircase depicted in one of the etchings on the far right of the cave. Simon shone his torch and followed the long painted staircase along the roofline of the chamber. At the end of the map painting where the mountain range ended - the image took on a more realistic state. He began to move the torch from side to side, and noticed that shadows were appearing against the wall. The steps were indeed real and they led up towards a large rock in the far corner of the cave and then seemed to disappear into the roof of the chamber.

"Hey fellas... look!" shouted Simon, as he pointed to the ancient staircase. "I think I've found a way out of here!"

The others looked over to where Simon was pointing the torch and applauded his find. They all hurried over to check out his discovery and watched intently, as Musgrove's older brother moved away some loose stones at the base of the ancient staircase. "Where do you think they lead to?" asked Tank, with a puzzled look on his face.

"Not sure mate," replied Simon, as he glanced at P.C. Sharp. "But I think we should find out… don't you uncle?"

"I concur with that lad," replied the police officer. "I'm sure if our Musgrove did find his way into this cave… his curiosity would have led him that way."

"Then let's go!" insisted Bomber, as he pointed ahead. "You lead the way Simon!"

Simon acknowledged his fellow marine and began to ascend the stairwell. The steps were very worn and crumbled beneath his polished boots, as he carefully held on to the cave wall for support. He positioned his feet into two crevices in the rock face at the top of the large stairwell.

One by one the rescue team climbed up to the base of the stone steps. Patrick gazed up at Simon at the top of the staircase. "Is it safe?"

"Watch those two steps just in front of you… they have deteriorated quite badly," replied Simon, as he re-positioned his feet and held out his hand. "Come on… I'll grab each of you as you pass me and pull you round on to the top step of the staircase."

Patrick led the rest of the group and they started to ascend the steps like a row of ants following each other in single file. The search party reached what they all believed to be the top of the staircase and Simon successfully guided each of them to the safety of the ledge. All they had reached was a small landing and Simon pointed the torch up into the void ahead. The stone staircase seemed to go on infinitely and the group caught their breath as they readied themselves for the next part of the ascent.

17

The Gatekeeper

Bomber counted each step, as he climbed higher and deeper into the cliffside. By the time he and the others had reached the seventy-fifth step, the staircase had widened and the incline grew shallower. As the floor leveled out they noticed a small arch-shaped wooden door carved into the rocky passageway, about ten metres ahead. The door appeared to be about a metre in height and was secured with a large iron padlock.

Patrick approached the thick vertical iron bars, which were set in a square opening in the centre of the door. He peered into the opening and stared into the blackness. Suddenly, a strange imp-like face appeared on the other side of the door and startled him. "Aaarrrghhh!" screamed Patrick, as he jolted backwards and stumbled over a raised stone. "What the eck was that?"

"What was it Patrick... what did you see?" asked Simon, as he and the others rushed to help Bradley's father to his feet.

"I don't know," replied Patrick. "But it was an ugly looking thing!" he exclaimed, as he positioned his hand over his lower back to ease the pain derived from his unceremonious fall.

Tank approached the door and shouted through the opening. "Who goes there?"

A short silence followed and then a squeaky yet croaky voice responded to Tanks question. "I am the Gatekeeper," replied the strange figure behind the bars. "Now go back to where you came from - you do not belong here."

"Open this door at once... in the name of her majesty's constabulary!" ordered P.C. Sharp.

"*Her* Majesty?" replied the Gatekeeper. "I only answer to *His* Majesty."

"Just open this door... you cretin – we are wasting valuable time!" replied the police officer.

"Time... time... time - I have so much precious time!" replied the Gatekeeper.

"Why are you guarding this doorway?" enquired Patrick, as he approached the door and put his face to the iron bars again.

There was no reply from the Gatekeeper and this time Bradley's father did not flinch, as the grey-faced goblin-like creature met Patrick's eyes with an intimidating glare. With only the metal rods separating their stare, they glared at each other for a few seconds as if their eyes were locked in combat.

The pointy-eared creature broke the silence. "Do you really believe I will let you pass... you pathetic mortal?" recited the Gatekeeper in a threatening tone.

"It is important you let us through," replied Patrick, calmly. "Why do you hide behind this door and insult me?' he asked.

"My friends and I just want to pass through so we can find a missing boy from the village above."

"Only the *Chosen One's* can pass through this gate from your side... that's what is written in the ancient scrolls of Restak!" exclaimed the fiendish dwarf.

Patrick was totally fazed by the goblin's comments and turned to the others for moral support. None was forthcoming so he moved away from the door and rejoined the group. "I can't seem to get through to him... we have to find a way to distract this creature."

"You're right," said Simon. "The cocky little chap needs to be taught a lesson... fancy a bit of rough stuff – Bomber?" He looked over to his fellow marine and intimated to him by nodding and lowering his eyebrows. Simon then flicked his head in the direction of the door.

Bomber knew what Simon had in mind and the Londoner was sure he wanted him to use his cheeky Cockney vocabulary to confuse the creature. He stepped forward and approached the door to meet the Gatekeeper face to face. "Hey... ugly mug?" he shouted. "Get your shriveled little backside over here ... I want to talk to you!"

The Gatekeeper looked very confident and its wrinkled face appeared at the other side of the bars. Suddenly, its facial expression changed to that of astonishment as Bomber cupped the fingers on his hand in a gesture to summon the goblin creature closer to the bars. As the Gatekeeper moved forward, Bomber could see the blue hairs that grew around the goblin's chin and upper lip. The dwarf-like being's broad mouth opened slightly to expose needle-like pointed teeth that were a yellowish black in colour and its breath reeked of stale seafood.

Bomber quickly uttered a bit of *cockney-slang* and whilst the goblin attempted to decipher the unusual vocabulary, the marine had forced his clenched fist through the bars and floored the poor creature with one accurate and ferocious punch on its crooked nose.

"Och... nice one Bomber!" shouted Tank, excitedly. "Right on the snippety-snout!"

"Think nothing of it... darling," replied Bomber, feeling very proud with the accuracy of his sharp jab.

P.C. Sharp approached the door and looked down through the bars at the felled dwarf on the other side. He noticed a silver key attached to a piece of thin rope tied around the Gatekeeper's waist, which was holding the creature's robe in place. The police officer turned to the others and asked them to look around for a long stick or something, so he could attempt to hook the key from the dwarfs clothing.

They all looked around, but could not find anything suitable for the purpose. At that moment a groaning sound emanated from behind the door. A hairy hand with long-nailed fingers forced its way through the bars. The silver key was clasped tightly in the dwarf's hand as he felt for the iron padlock that secured the door.

Everyone stepped back in amazement as they watched the Gatekeeper attempt to locate the keyhole on the padlock. Patrick approached the door and reached out to help the dwarf insert the key into the lock. With a quick turn the rusty padlock clicked open and fell to the stone floor making a clinking sound that echoed down the steps to the wall painted chamber below.

The small creature pulled its arm back through the bars and slowly opened the door. The timber creaked as the door pivoted on its ancient hinges. The Gatekeeper looked up at

Bomber and scowled at the six-foot marine. "You didn't have to do that," croaked the dwarf, as he held the bridge of his rough and wrinkled nose. "I was going to let you through anyway."

The strange little figure sat on the floor and rubbed his face. He was feeling very sorry for himself and was approached by Bradley's father. "Why were you so rude and nasty to me?" asked Patrick, as he picked up the heavy padlock from the floor.

"I've been waiting centuries to meet someone from your world at this exit, but no one had ever turned up... until now that is," replied the dwarf. "Give me some credit... I had to show some resistance - at least."

"You said exit!" queried P.C. Sharp. "Don't you mean entrance?"

"No... this is an exit - from my world," stated the wounded dwarf.

"What world?" asked Tank. "And anyway...why are you called the Gatekeeper?"

"Pathylon!" replied the dwarf. "My world is called Pathylon and I am employed to guard this door with my life!"

"Does this Pathylon have anything to do with that map on the wall at the bottom of the staircase?" enquired Bomber. "And have you ever heard of Devonia or Krogonia... and a mountain range called the Peronto Alps?"

"Yes... the names of the places you speak of are indeed in my world!" he exclaimed and introduced himself as the Gatekeeper of Pathylon.

The dwarf informed the group that his real name was *Turpol*. He continued to explain that he had been appointed by the Pathylian High Priesthood to guard the exit and as far

180

as he was aware, the gate was the only way out of his strange and mystical world. He spoke in great detail about how Pathylon was split into the five regions and was currently under the evil rule of Varuna, a heartless Hartopian from the Blacklands. He also told them of Luccese, the true King of Pathylon, who was imprisoned in the Shallock Tower together with Queen Vash and Pavsik, the deposed High Priest of Devonia.

Simon stopped the grey-coloured creature before he became more embroiled in the story of the strange world. "Please stop talking and listen to me!" he ordered. "Now, what did you say your name was... *Turtle* – are you winding me up?"

Turpol looked up at the young marine and offered him a puzzled look. "My name is Turpol... not *Turtle* and I only wind up Galetian clocks from time to time!" he replied. "You should get a Galetian clock!" ranted the bemused troll-like figure. "They keep excellent time you know!"

"No, I don't want a *gleeshan* clock... or whatever you said - I meant are you real or what?" he asked sarcastically. "I don't believe all this rubbish you're coming out with... now where is my brother?" demanded Simon, as he started to lose patience and quickly reached out his hand.

Simon placed it against the dwarf's throat and lifted the little creature up against the passage wall. Turpol kicked his legs frantically has the marine pinned him against the hard stone. Tank and Bomber rushed over to aid the dwarf and proceeded to pull Simon away. They held the marine steady until he had calmed down.

"That's not going to help matters!" shouted P.C. Sharp. "Now, just control yourself lad!"

"Och aye… cool it matey," said Tank, as he consoled Simon. "I know you are worried about your brother Muzzy… but that's no excuse for you to go around picking on wee Turpol here - now is it?"

Turpol readjusted the robe around his neck area and regained his balance and composure. The poor little goblin-like creature could not believe how much aggravation he was receiving from this band of human bullies and he was beginning to feel very nervous. His voice trembled as he made another attempt to explain himself. "I have not seen anyone from your world at this side of the door for the past five centuries," said Turpol. "And you can see by the state of the rusty hinges on my door, that it not been opened for such a long time," he added. "So this Muzzy person you speak of could not possibly have passed by me… nor could he have attempted to speak to me."

Simon turned to P.C. Sharp. "What do you make of all this stuff uncle… do you think he's telling the truth?"

"If we are to believe Turpol here… I'm afraid my dear nephew that you're little brother has eluded us, yet again - and I am getting very concerned for his safety," stated the police officer, as he lifted his peaked helmet and scratched his balding headline.

The inquisitive Gatekeeper watched as the group of men gathered around the blue uniformed human, talking with very serious tones and with grim expressions on their faces. The dwarf approached the group and spoke. "I am kept informed about events that may affect the security of Pathylon… it is very important that the High Priesthood do this so I am able to protect the exit from any foreign intruders."

"Do you have any news that may be relevant to us finding my brother?" asked Simon.

The Gatekeeper replied. "Recently I received an update about a renegade High Priest called Meltor... there are rumours of an uprising against Varuna." The dwarf then cleared his throat. "Now... if I may make a suggestion!" he shouted, as all five members of the rescue party finally paid Turpol the attention he felt he deserved.

"Well... go on then – get on with it!" insisted Bomber.

The dwarf composed himself and spoke. "I keep in regular contact with my employers in the Royal Capital and I'm sure I'll be able to help you find this boy you call Muzzy."

"His real name is Musgrove," said P.C. Sharp.

"How can you help us?" asked Patrick impatiently.

"Well... since the true King Luccese was so cruelly overthrown by Varuna - I have being feeling very saddened by the way Pathylon has been transformed into a dark and evil world," explained Turpol. "Now, I normally keep *myself to myself...* although I swore an allegiance to guard Pathylon from intruders - I feel very strongly about the way Varuna has stolen the crown from Luccese and...."

"What are you trying to say, my wee friend?" interrupted Tank, as the burly marine put his shovel-sized hand on the little creatures shoulder.

Turpol looked up at Tank nervously. He was glad that the Scotsman was displaying a more pleasant approach than Bomber, who had floored him only minutes before. He felt pleased that the human was now showing some sign of friendliness, which the little creature had craved for so long. "I can't let the vows I took all those centuries ago overrule my conscience," said the dwarf, as he held his arm aloft with fist clenched. "I feel your arrival at my door at this time of unrest is an important sign and it has given me the confidence to act!"

"Are you trying to tell us that you think you know where my little brother may be?" asked Simon.

"I have to be honest with you... the renegade High Priest that I speak of has visited me on many occasions," declared Turpol. "I chose to keep Meltor's identity a secret from you at first because I felt quite sympathetic towards his cause... his attempt to remove the evil curse that shrouds our world is very admirable." Turpol paused for a moment. "Meltor has not passed my way for some time and I was recently informed that he has teamed up with a small band of rebels and that Varuna is growing increasingly angry at the amount of time it is taking to secure their capture," explained the Gatekeeper, as he strode back towards the small doorway. "I am also informed that three small human-like species, together with a disgraced Krogon, are helping Meltor to evade the wrath of Varuna."

"*So* you think that Muzzy might be one of the rebels helping this Meltor bloke?" suggested Bomber, as he scratched the stubble on his rugged chin.

"He might be... I can't be certain," explained Turpol. "It's all rumours... the communications relayed to me have been very patchy - to say the least."

"Never mind... go on Turpol – please tell us more," insisted P.C. Sharp, in an encouraging tone. "The information you have is important... no matter how sketchy."

The group gathered around Turpol and crouched down to the dwarf's level, as they waited in anticipation for the nervous creature to continue. There was still plenty to tell and the Gatekeeper was enthralled at the attention he was receiving. He continued with his theory about the possibility of Musgrove playing an important part in Meltor's rebellion.

18

The Shallock Tower

Bradley held out his hand as Musgrove stood above him. He had managed somehow to land upside down in a bed of brambles and could not move an inch. Musgrove reached down, locked his strong grip around his friend's hand and pulled him clear of the ditch that he had fallen into whilst unsuccessfully attempting to jump over it. Grog was laughing uncontrollably and had to be calmed by Sereny.

"It's not funny you great big orange oaf!" shouted Bradley. "I could have hurt myself!"

"I'm sorry Bradley!" croaked Grog, as he finally controlled his laughter. "It's just the way your little legs were stuck up in the air... you looked like a stranded koezard - that had fallen head first into the Peronto Dessert quick sand."

Bradley finally saw the funny side of Grog's interest in his embarrassing accident and conjured a smile. He then asked politely for an explanation in relation to the koezard and what sort of a creature it was. Grog obliged and explained to him in more detail about the large lizard-type mount reared and employed by the Krogons. "I used to own a stunning example of a koezard when I was growing up on the Flaclom Straits…he had a large black patch around his left eye." The sullen Krogon lowered his head in remembrance of his trusty mount. "I called him *Shatar* - he was taken away from me when I was expelled for not fighting Zule."

"Don't be sad," said Bradley. "Maybe one day you will be reunited with Shatar," he added, as he brushed the dust from his Devonian outfit and made his way over to Grog to comfort him.

The ditch where Bradley had encountered his test of resilience was just a few hundred metres from the base of the Shallock Tower and Meltor called a meeting to discuss the group's next move. Everyone gathered around and kept low as the aging High Priest told of his limited knowledge of the tower and the group listened intently to his plan of attack. Meltor knew of an ancient tunnel that ran beneath the Shallock Tower, which led out to a secret opening about twenty metres from where they were crouched. Musgrove and Bradley volunteered to check out the immediate area for any unusual objects that may be covering any holes in the ground. The two boys made their way through the long grass, crouching and crawling as they avoided being spotted by the armed guard that patrolled the base of the Shallock Tower.

"Hey Brad… isn't this exciting?" exclaimed Musgrove, as they searched the undergrowth.

"Well, it certainly beats crab fishing in the rock pools at Amley's Cove," replied Bradley, as he tried to keep up with Musgrove.

Bradley and his friend searched on all fours for quite a while, but with no success. Musgrove popped his head out of

186

the long grass and attracted Meltor's attention by simulating the sound of a cuckoo. The Galetian looked over to where the boys were positioned and acknowledged them by waving his arm.

Sereny alerted Meltor to an unusual looking rock about fifteen metres directly ahead of them. It stood very prominent just to the right of the boys. The shape of the rock appeared to be like a giant egg and it seemed completely out of place with the surrounding landscape.

The old Galetian caught Musgrove's attention and initiated the rock's position by pointing towards the structure. The boy instinctively nudged his elbow into Bradley's side and the two boys started to crawl through the long grass. Within seconds the commando-like adventurers had reached the base of the large stone. Bradley and Musgrove stood upright in the sandy ground and positioned their backs against the rocky boulder.

"Can you see what I see, Brad?" asked Musgrove, as he noticed a small metal rod sticking out at the base of the rock.

"Yes, it looks like a lever of some sort," said Bradley, as he brushed the undergrowth to one side and glanced down at the rusty mechanism supporting the giant stone.

Before Musgrove had a chance to signal to Meltor that they may have found the entrance to the tunnel, Bradley pulled the lever towards his chest. Nothing happened because the rock had not been moved for such a long period. It was obvious that the mechanism that controlled the movement of the heavy stone had jammed.

Grog appeared next to the two boys. "What's happening?" he asked. "And what's that groaning noise I can hear?"

There was a dull grinding sound emanating from beneath the big rock. The startled trio crawled away from the huge boulder, as it started to move to one side exposing the rails that had enabled it to move so effortlessly.

Grog signalled to Meltor and Sereny by cupping his webbed hand and raising his arm above the long grass, waving it up and down so as to invite them across in the direction of the rock.

In return, Meltor offered a strong hand to Sereny and she reciprocated by placing her petite fingers into his powerful grip. They quickly joined the others by the side of the rock, which had now stopped moving to reveal an opening in the ground.

Grog peered into the hole and relayed to the others that there was a deep shaft, which sank for a quite a way down. There was a wooden ladder attached to the sides of the shaft and the Krogon revealed. "This must be it, Meltor… shall we make our way down?"

"Yes, but not all of us," replied Meltor. "At least one of us must stay here to ensure the entrance to the tunnel is secured and to guard it to make sure no-one follows the rest of us."

"Who should stay?" asked Bradley in a brave tone and in the hope that Meltor would not choose him to stay behind.

Meltor suggested that Grog should guard the entrance beneath the rock. He felt it had to be the Krogon warrior, as he was the strongest of the group.

Grog agreed and he watched in admiration, as the others started to descend the rickety ladder. As they disappeared from view, the strong lizard man pulled the lever and the rock began to move back over the hole in the ground. He looked across the open land that separated the egg-shaped rock and the tall structure of the Shallock Tower. He could just make out six armed guards patrolling the perimeter fence at the base of the tower.

Meltor and the others made their way deeper into the shaft, as Grog settled down into the tall grass and kept a watchful eye over the surrounding plains.

Deep within the cliffside and huddled together beside the Gatekeeper's doorway, the members of the search party were all keen to find out more about Turpol's revelations. They were waiting to glean information from the dwarf about the possible whereabouts of Musgrove and the others.

They had listened to the Gatekeeper for a short while and now started to question the little creature in more detail, as the police officer spoke calmly. "If Musgrove is helping this Meltor fella, how did he manage to get into your strange world without passing you?" he queried.

"As I said to you earlier... I guard the exit from Pathylon - not the entrance into it," reasserted Turpol and produced a broad grin that spread across his wrinkled face.

"So where is the entrance to this so-called Pathylon place that you speak of?" demanded Simon. "And wipe that stupid grin off your ugly mug!"

Turpol was enjoying the banter with the five strangers. He had waited quite some time to see and talk to anyone other than the odd messenger sent by the High Priesthood. He did not like Simon's attitude but understood the young marine's anguish and delayed his answer no longer. He could sense that the group of humans were getting agitated and restless. "The entrance to my world can be found in the forbidden caves... situated on the outskirts of the great Forest of Haldon," said the dwarf. "But you can only enter Pathylon if you possess a *Sacred Grobite*... these were lost by the Freytorian travellers that came to our land - via the Red Ocean."

"Freytorians... Red Ocean – what are you going on about?" insisted Simon, as his face reddened with anger.

The dwarf ignored the marine's wrathful tone, as he turned to the others and replied. "The eight arctic bear creatures... known as Freytorians - disembarked their mother ship, which was anchored in the Mouth of Sand just below these caves." Turpol continued to describe how the outsiders, who had visited his strange world from far across the oceans, introduced the grobites to trade for Pathylian goods. He told of the cask of treasure that was dropped into the waters of the bay and of the prisoners from Freytor. The dwarf then explained how they had been encapsulated in granite around sacred doorways, located somewhere within the forbidden caves.

Simon was furious at the dwarf's dismissive gesture towards him and was becoming increasingly impatient with all the talk about Pathylon and its history. "Stop all this gibberish about polar bears, forbidden caves and sacred coins... just tell us how we get into this god forsaken world of yours!"

Turpol looked straight at Simon, as he glared and raised his croaky voice. "I'm trying to help you and I'm putting my life at risk by disobeying the Pathylian High Priesthood... I don't know why I should be bothered to help you ungrateful humans!" Insisted the dwarf, as he waved his short arms frantically above his pointed-ears and continued to scorn the young marine.

Tank interrupted the Gatekeeper's scolding of Simon and turned to Patrick and P.C. Sharp. The huge marine pointed at the pockets on Patrick's trousers. "Get 'em out mate!" he declared. "Show little Turpol here... the coins that you and P.C. Plod found in the cove."

The police officer did not look very impressed with Tank's remark and waved a pointed finger back at him. "You can cut that out... you cheeky young soldier!" he retorted. "You're not too big for a clip round the ear!"

Patrick smiled, as the police officer dressed down the marine and acknowledged Tank's request by emptying his pockets onto the rocky floor at the top of the steps.

Turpol's deep black eyes seemed to light up as the coins glistened in the torch-lit surroundings of the passageway. "Ooooh... lots of shiny grobites!" he exclaimed. "And look... some are inscribed around the edges - they must be the sacred grobites, which were left behind by the Freytorian prisoners!"

Patrick handed one of the gold coins to the excited dwarf. Turpol held it close to his face and examined the grobites, as he read out the inscription to the others. *"Thee who hath taken this to thy belonging, seal it again to bring forth magic powers!"* he quoted. "What an honour this is... to actually hold a sacred grobite - it is a very special experience. Only the *chosen ones* have these," he added, as he reluctantly handed it back to Patrick.

"The chosen ones?" questioned P.C. Sharp, with a puzzled look on his face.

"Yes... now you have the sacred grobites - you must all be chosen ones!" exclaimed Turpol. "It was written in the ancient Kaikane Scrolls that a Good Samaritan would send out twelve distress beacons in the form of gold coins to attract twelve brave warriors," explained the dwarf.

Turpol continued to explain to the humans about the Freytorian prisoners and the promise of re-mortality and a return to their mother ship should the chosen ones accomplish their mission successfully; thus ridding Pathylon of the dreaded curse.

"What mission?" asked Bomber, as he scratched the top of his head.

"A mission to repel the evil, that General Eidar and Varuna employed throughout the five regions... and by freeing Luccese the true King of Pathylon - thus restoring the good back to the to the land!" exclaimed Turpol. "Oh... and before you ask – General Eidar was the commander of a Freytorian ice-ship, which... by the way - was an actual iceberg that had broken away from the southern ice shelf of..."

"Stop right there Turpol... enough talking!" demanded Simon, as he stepped forward and turned to face the others with his hands clasped firmly behind his back. The solemn look on Simon's face was evidence of a turn in his belief and understanding of the mystical world of Pathylon. He looked at Turpol with a more respectful stare. "I think the time has come to influence the little rebellion that this Meltor bloke has instigated... let's go and find my brother!" he declared, as he dipped his upper body awkwardly so as to pass through the Gatekeeper's door.

The dwarf called Simon back and explained to the tall marine that he could not enter Pathylon in that direction unless he held a sacred grobite in his left palm.

Patrick interpreted the Gatekeeper's statement and proceeded to search through the twenty-six gold coins to find the sacred grobites. He picked out the coins with the inscriptions around the edges. "There are only nine in total," he countered and then held out the coins.

"That means that there are three sacred grobites missing," said Turpol. "Did you check to see if you had recovered all the coins from the cask?"

P.C. Sharp nodded his head and told the dwarf that Patrick had double-checked inside the ancient container that they had found in the rock pool.

"The other coins must have fallen out of the crate when it was dropped and must have been discovered by someone else," surmised the Gatekeeper.

Turpol requested the coins be handed over to him and Patrick reluctantly passed the coins to Tank who in turn confidently placed them in the dwarf's dry and wrinkled hands. The Gatekeeper then took the nine sacred coins and placed one in each of the left hand of the five members of the search party. A sixth he took into his own left palm and gave the three remaining coins back to Patrick for safekeeping.

"What are you doing Turpol?" asked Simon. "Why have you taken a coin for yourself?"

"I have decided to stand with you and fight against the evil regime of Varuna and join you in the quest to free Pathylon of its torment!" stated the little grey creature. "I too feel it is my destiny to be a chosen one!" declared Turpol, as he attempted to straighten his cruelly hunched-back, then stood on his tiptoes to make himself appear taller.

Simon chuckled to himself. He thought it was very amusing that the little creature's head still fell short of his waistline even though the Gatekeeper had extended his height to its absolute maximum.

"Who said anything about fighting against evil?" asked the policeman. "All we want to do is enter this Pathylon world and find our Musgrove… then get the hell back out of there – we don't want to take part in any trouble!"

The police officer was an endearing uncle and although he had never married and had no children of his own, he loved Musgrove as if he were his own son. All he wanted to do was to retrieve the young Chilcott boy and return him safely to his mother. Fighting against evil and freeing a true Pathylian King was not on P.C. Sharps agenda, however he was prepared to move mountains to find his nephew.

Bomber interrupted and disagreed with P.C. Sharp. "Well I think we should get ourselves in there and kick some butt!"

Tank agreed, he also wanted some of the action and Simon was certainly not going to refuse a fight, all three being royal marine officers in the making. Patrick was a little skeptical but did not want to be perceived as a coward, so he too agreed to follow the Lympstone training camp trio into battle. Being a serving police officer and a relative of Simon, P.C. Sharp was left with no choice. He could not afford to let his sister's oldest son wander off as well, especially when he had a direct influence on the situation. Should Simon disappear in front of him or there would be hell to pay. He was determined to return back up the cliffside with both his nephews.

The five were now united in their decision, as they locked their outstretched hands. Simon announced. "It's agreed then... we will help Turpol to seek out Meltor then we will attempt to release King Luccese and Queen Vash from the Shallock Tower."

P.C Sharp confirmed. "Very well... and in return we will seek help from the Pathylian population, in our quest to find Musgrove, and hopefully secure a hasty return back to Sandmouth once the task was complete."

19

The Vortex of Souls

Ten Devonian Death Troops, led by Lieutenant Dergan, marched ahead of Varuna and his entourage. They had now reached the makeshift campsite that had been occupied by Meltor. The Death Troops searched the surrounding area but found no sign of the renegades.

By the time King Varuna had arrived, Dergan and the Death Troops had already reassembled and were stood to attention as the weasel-like Hartopian sped in front of them, perched high in the Royal Chariot.

The two hoffen that pulled the chariot fought with the reigns that controlled them and snorted heavily. The animals perspired heavily, as the hot streams of sweat rose from their muscular frames and filled the air with the smell of oiled leather saddles.

Varuna looked down at the Devonian Death Troops and then turned to his Lieutenant. "Well, Dergan... have you found any trace of the rebel scum?" he asked, in a demanding tone.

"No your royal excellence," quivered Dergan. "They have already fled this campsite," concluded the cowering Wartpig.

"So how long ago do you suppose they left this place?" asked the evil King.

"Not long, sire… about two hours - maybe three," replied Lieutenant Dergan.

This comment ignited more rage in the belly of Varuna and he tilted his head backwards. His magnificent skulled headdress tilted slightly, as the red-eyed dictator stared upwards and roared his disapproval into the dark Pathylian skies. "Meltor has outwitted us yet again!" He growled and declared. "There will be no rest for any of you till the Galetian traitor is found!" he continued to rant, as the royal chariot began to negotiate an about turn in readiness for a hasty departure. "We will move on immediately… we must find the rebels and destroy them!"

Lieutenant Dergan raised his hand and signalled to his troops to prepare their armory and move on. He wasn't going to challenge Varuna's decision this time, even though he knew that his soldiers needed rest in order to recuperate from their long march.

At that moment, a horn blew to signal the approach of several scurrying koezard mounted with an entourage of important guests. The large salamander-like creatures powered their long hind legs, as they carried their riders over the distant hillside towards the royal group.

Varuna ordered his leading coachman to stop the chariot, as he watched the ten koezard descend the incline that led down to Meltor's deserted campsite. As the mounted creatures drew nearer, the Hartopian recognized the two leading riders. "Harg… and Zule!" he exclaimed. "What a pleasant surprise to see my two finest High Priests in such immaculate battle armour," stated the evil King, as he complimented the two Krogon warriors.

As Varuna completed his appraisal of Harg and Zule, he had not noticed the beautiful slender figure that was mounted on the pure white albino koezard, grazing behind Harg's mount. Flaglan, the High Priestess that represented the Forest of Haldon, had also travelled to meet up with her new King and was not very impressed with the way Varuna had just described Harg and Zule as his two finest High Priests.

"Then I must be your finest High Priestess!" boasted the exotic sorceress in a captivating and sultry voice. Her perfect female form oozed from her skimpy clothing, as she dismounted from her nervous koezard.

Varuna's three hearts began to beat violently in tandem, his red eyes widened and shone as the sorceress from the great forest climbed up into the Royal Chariot and moved towards him and pushed herself up against the Hartopian's robes. Flaglan then proceeded to stroke Varuna's weasel like snout with her slender fingers and fluttered her eyelashes at the evil King.

"My dear Fla...Fla...Flaglan," stuttered Varuna. "It is always a pleasure to see you, and of course you are a fine sorceress and a loyal patron to my dark Kingdom."

Varuna's self-composure returned as he encouraged more attention from his attractive attention-seeker. His plans for a courtship with Flaglan still ran passionately through his yellow blood. However, he knew Flaglan's attention was not sincere and he would have to force the High Priestess from the Forest of Haldon to yield her resistance. Although, Flaglan did have a weakness and Varuna was fully aware that it was her inability to control her yearning for materialistic objects. The evil King would tempt her with exotic cloths, priceless jewels and more mystical powers that would befit a future Queen of Pathylon.

He finally turned his attention away from Flaglan's flaunting and looked up at the heavy clouds that darkened the land. He demanded to know why three members of the Pathylian High Priesthood had ventured far to meet him under such dangerous conditions. He was very concerned that a high percentage of the Pathylian hierarchy was away from the royal city of Trad and very little experienced leadership was left in place to guard the Shallock Tower.

Harg explained. "We are here to help you capture Meltor!"

Zule interrupted the aging Krogon leader and provided further assurance to Varuna. "We heard of the old Galetian's unwillingness to co-operate with you and felt you may need some assistance!" Harg's mature apprentice then dismounted from his koezard. Zule assured the evil King that he had nothing to fear about the temporary control of the royal city. "We have left Basjoo Ma-otz in Trad, just in case Meltor and his small band of rebels turn up there... he has travelled down from the Blacklands to oversee the security measures we put in place around the Shallock Tower - before our departure."

Zule had an ulterior motive for making the journey to join Varuna. His intentions were not just to help the evil King secure Meltor's capture. The Krogon warrior had also heard that Meltor was being supported by a small band of fugitives. He had been reliably informed that his old rival was part of the rebel pack and he relished the chance to destroy Grog once and for all.

Varuna looked embarrassed, as he released Flaglan's grip on him and then he pushed her away. The sorceress lost her footing and stumbled off the Royal Chariot and fell to the ground.

"What's wrong with you Varuna... how dare you treat me that way?" demanded Flaglan, as she picked herself up and scrutinized her clothing for any marks and tears. "Now look what you've done!" she shouted, as the High Priestess examined the torn sleeve attached to her flowing transparent garment.

"Silence!" roared the evil King.

Varuna felt that Meltor had made him look like a fool. After all, he had deployed ten of the best Devonian Death Troops in Pathylon and still he had failed to capture the rebellious High Priest. The last thing he needed right now was for three of his elite council to see him defeated in this way so he decided to play down Meltor's evasion and invited the two Krogon warriors and the still-fuming Flaglan to join him for a royal supper. "I am so sorry my dear... I did not mean for you to slip like that," said Varuna, as he climbed down and put his black-cloaked arms around the slim frame of the beautiful sorceress. "Let me make it up to you."

"You can start by replacing this dress!" demanded Flaglan, as she continued to pull at the tattered threads of fabric that hung from her sleeve.

"Once we have captured Meltor I'll order the finest seamstresses in Pathylon to make you a thousand dresses my dear... for now, let's put this little incident behind us and enjoy the evening," said Varuna in a creepy voice, as he again enrobed Flaglan's slender frame and escorted her away from the royal chariot. "Dergan, we will make camp here for the night," ordered Varuna, changing his mind about not allowing any rest for the weary foot soldiers and the other members of his royal entourage.

Lieutenant Dergan looked relieved and immediately ordered his death troops to make camp. Instructions were given to the rest of the entourage to go out and search for the necessary food source in readiness for the royal supper.

The deployment of personnel to find food and firewood was prioritized and the preparations got underway for the erection of various multi-coloured canvass awnings to be assembled in the shadow and protection of some nearby cretyre trees. The Royal Standard was to be raised above Varuna's tent, much to the jealousy of Flaglan. Varuna was sure Meltor's capture would be a formality now that the uninvited reinforcements had arrived and he felt more relaxed about delaying his pursuit of the obstinate Galetian till the morning. Varuna would use the evenings dining and hospitality to get closer to Flaglan. The opportunity was also ripe to further unite the allegiance of Devonia and Krogonia by practicing more of his evil and manipulative tricks on Harg and his rookie High Priest Zule.

Deep within the cliffside, the Gatekeeper lifted the flamed torch from the wall and led the way through the small door he had been guarding for what had seemed an eternity. Simon followed close behind the dwarf, with the other members of the search party in immediate pursuit.

Turpol was embarking upon a brave journey. The dwarf was taking a huge risk by guiding his newfound acquaintances through the winding and dipping tunnels that led to the *Vortex of Souls*. The search party's desire to find Musgrove was intense and he hoped the vortex would carry them all safely into the mystical world of Pathylon.

A constant flow of salty water seeped through the tunnel roofs and flowed down the walls like small rivers. Whilst negotiating the damp passageways, Turpol took some time to inform the group about the magical powers that the vortex held. "If each of you were to enter the vortex with a sacred grobite clenched in your left palm... the direction of travel inside the vortex would be reversed," he explained, as a droplet of water bounced off his hooked nose. "This would then propel you back through the swirling currents and into the world of Pathylon."

It was a very dangerous process and the success of transportation, without complications or loss of life, could not be guaranteed. The group listened intently and then continued to travel through the narrow passageways, which was made more difficult by the hundreds of stalactites that hung low from the tunnel roofs.

The search party managed to negotiate past the sharp obstacles, which had formed from the salty water filtering passing through the cliffside over thousands of years. The only injury was to P.C. Sharp's shoulder, which was badly gashed as he misjudged the last hazardous rock formation. The police officers uniform was torn and his jacket sleeve was covered in blood. Simon called ahead to Turpol. "Hang on... my uncle is hurt pretty bad!"

Turpol turned around and made his way back to where the policeman had stopped. "How bad is it?" asked the concerned Gatekeeper.

"Oh... it doesn't seem too deep," replied the marine, as he ripped the lower part of his uncle's shirtsleeve to make a bandage. "I think this should stem the bleeding."

"Stop fussing," said P.C. Sharp, as he took the makeshift cotton swab from Simon. "It's only a flesh wound... look - the bleeding has stopped already!"

"How much longer till we reach the vortex?" asked Patrick, as he tapped Turpol's arm.

"It's not far now," said the dwarf. "The Vortex of Souls is about fifty metres ahead of us, just around the next bend... but be very careful, an unfriendly group of Skeloyds guard it - we may not receive a hospitable welcome."

"Hey Turps... tell us - what exactly are these Skeloyds you're harping on about?" enquired Bomber.

"They are half-dead creatures that are employed by the ancient High Priesthood as tunnel workers," replied the dwarf. "Back in the *Second Century B.K...* and before they became Skeloyds - their original form was that of Devonian labourers who had been punished because a small section of the workers had attempted to travel out of Pathylon, whilst the vortex was being installed."

"So what happened to them?" asked Tank.

"Because they did not have the necessary authorization from the High Priesthood to make the journey, the vortex ripped out their souls whilst being transported and only their half-dead skeletal bodies reached the other side," continued Turpol. "Instead of facing an instant execution, the Skeloyds were entrusted with just enough life to enable them to guard the vortex against any intruders that may stumble across it from the outside world – they say that...."

Before the Gatekeeper could conclude, a loud rumble shook through the rocky tunnels, which suddenly interrupted his explanation. The ground tremored beneath their feet and Tank held onto the side of the tunnel for support. "What was that?" he shouted, as his fingertips tightened around a chalky ledge that jutted out of the solid rock.

"It felt like an earthquake," said Patrick, steadying himself against the tunnel wall.

Turpol turned his attention to Patrick and Tank. The dwarf explained that the ground only shook in that way when the Vortex of Souls was being used for transportation. "Someone must have travelled through the vortex... there can't be any other explanation!"

"Listen... did you hear that?" asked Bomber. "It sounds like a scraping noise," he surmised, as he stepped forward and put his ear to the side of the tunnel. "I can hear it through the sides of the rock!"

"That will be the Skeloyds," said Turpol. "They are probably excavating more fallen rocks from around the opening of the vortex... every time the *Vortex of Souls* is used, the edge of the tunnel around the portal collapses - the amount of stress that is put on the tunnel walls is dependent upon how many pass through the vortex at any one time."

Simon moved forward towards the bend in the tunnel. The rest followed in a single file and ushered behind him as they all crouched behind a large curved boulder that jutted out of the tunnel wall. The marine slowly moved his head and peered around the edge of the rock that shielded them from the empty eye sockets of the busy tunnel workers, who were busy moving rubble away from the entrance to the vortex.

The group of Skeloyds was now some twenty metres ahead and Simon began to count them. "Sixteen..." he whispered. "...and there appears to be two other figures surrounded by another small group of them."

The Skeloyds pushed the two petrified vortex-travellers towards an arched opening to the left of the damaged exit point. They then disappeared through the arch and left just seven workers to guard the vortex portal. Four of the remaining creatures continued to clear the debris and the other three stood in front with their large sabre-type weapons attached to their boney waists. One of them looked over towards where Simon and his friends were hiding. "I think it's spotted us," whispered Simon, as he pulled his head back from view.

"What do we do now?" asked P.C. Sharp.

"Wait here," insisted Turpol, as the dwarf stood up and walked away from the rock. "I'll distract them," he whispered, as he moved forward to meet the weird looking skeleton creature.

The Gatekeeper was instantly recognized because he had made regular visits to see the flesh-eaten creatures, whilst guarding the entrance door to the tunnels. The Skeloyds had also acted as Pathylian messengers, relaying information, delivering food and supplying provisions to Turpol, which had been sent through the vortex from Pathylon. "Hello, my old friend!" snarled the Skeloyd. "What brings you down here Gatekeeper … shouldn't you be guarding the sacred door?"

Turpol replied in a nervous tone. "Yes but I decided to take a relaxing stroll to stretch my legs and I thought to myself… why not pay a visit to my Skeloyd friends down at the Vortex of Souls." He continued to distract the Skeloyd, which allowed Simon and the others to sneak past.

The group made their way towards the arched opening where the two figures had been ushered away. In the meantime, two other guards joined their compatriot to check out why Turpol has wandered from his post. Lots of hollow laughter and shouting ensued and it was obvious that the little dwarf was doing enough to keep them amused.

Tank whispered to his colleagues. "It looks like the other creatures are preoccupied with rebuilding the vortex portal," as the noise from the swirling turbine echoed down the passageway.

The vortex intrigued Patrick and the sight of the enormous turbine triggered his electrical engineering mind, which prompted a quiet comment. "I would love to find out about the source of energy that makes it work."

"Never mind all that," said P.C. Sharp, overhearing Bradley's father. "Let's get out of here before these creepy skeletons spot us."

Simon led the way through the arch and into what appeared to be a workshop of some kind. The room was full of mining equipment and industrial tooling. The walls were carved from the rock and the roof had some kind of winching device hanging down from a horizontal girder. Patrick felt quite at home, apart from the unusual cutting implements and weird looking machinery, it reminded him of the electrical workshop he used to work in at Silvermoor Colliery.

A red light emanated from behind a half closed door that was situated at the far corner of the workshop. "Listen," whispered Simon. "Can you hear the muffled sound of voices?" he asked, as he turned to Bomber.

"Yes," replied the puzzled soldier quietly, as he pointed at two moving shadows that cast human-like silhouettes against the wall. "The noise is coming from behind that door... there's someone or something inside that room."

Simon moved slowly towards the red light and cautiously pressed his back tightly against the door. He positioned his hands down by his sides and placed his shaking fingers against the metal surface. The marine then shuffled sideways and hooked his head around the edge of the door to investigate the contents of the room.

20

Skeloyd Encounter

Simon peered into the small room to witness the backs of two familiar figures seated with their female forms illuminated by the strange red light. The fidgeting women were each tied to a wooden chair by their hands and feet. The relieved marine scanned the rest of the room's interior and smiled, as he called over to the others. "There no sign of any Skeloyds in here but I think Bradley Baker's father might like to come over and take a look first!"

Patrick raced across the workshop and entered the room, as he let out a loud scream of delight. "Margaret!" he exclaimed. "Is that really you?" He could hardly believe his eyes and immediately started to untie his terrified wife.

Aunt Vera reacted angrily. "Get these blasted ropes off me!" She shouted and continued to vent her disgust at the way the Skeloyds had treated the two sisters. Tank quickly moved over to the ranting woman and untied the ropes that bound her ankles to the chair.

Patrick finally released his wife and she flung her arms around his neck, as he enquired as to the whereabouts of their son. "What's happened to Bradley?"

"I don't know, my darling!" replied Margaret, as she stood up out of the chair. "But he's got to be around here somewhere... we found his cloths in a lodge by a river."

"What lodge... which river – where have you been?" demanded Patrick. "What in heaven's sake are you talking about?"

Margaret prepared her husband for her explanation. "Well you're probably going to find this hard to believe... but Vera and I were swept away by the bath water – we were sent hurtling through the centre of a gold coin and down into the drainpipe below Vera's cottage!"

Patrick afforded his wife with a confused look. "Drainpipe, bath water... gold coin - you mean one of these things?" he declared and pulled one of the sacred grobites from his pocket.

Vera exclaimed. "Yes that's it... that's just like the coin in the plughole!"

"Please keep your voices down," whispered P.C. Sharp, in a calming manner. "Otherwise you'll attract the unwanted attention of those blasted skelewob things again."

Margaret heeded the police officer's advice and lowered her voice, as she continued to explain to Patrick. "The last time I saw Bradley was before he went into Vera's bathroom after his visit to Amley's Cove... the bathroom door was locked from the inside and it was if he'd just disappeared - it wasn't long after that we embarked upon our own incredible journey that sent us both down the drainpipe to a giant mushroom thingy!"

Vera interrupted her sister. "Once inside the *toadstool* we went down a spiral staircase that led to a chamber full of weird hooded doorways – once we'd passed through these we eventually ended up in front of some really big oak doors…"

"Then what happened?" asked Patrick.

"Well, these led us into yet another chamber that had some kind of swirling lights in it… Margaret and I jumped into the lights and they transported us to some caves," replied Vera excitedly. "As it turned out we'd been sent to Pathylon… anyhow our Margaret found one of Bradley's toy soldiers and then…"

"This sounds absolutely fascinating," said Patrick, as he tried to stop Aunt Vera talking.

Vera was determined to finish and she launched straight back into her account of amazing events. "…we then walked through a great forest and followed a river which led to the lodge our Margaret was telling you about – we stayed there for the night and…"

"Thank you Mrs. Penworthy… I'm sorry to interrupt but I think we've got the just of it all," said P.C. Sharp.

"No you haven't… you rude man – don't interrupt me while I'm trying to explain about me and our Margaret's arduous journey," scolded Aunt Vera, as the police officer's face turned a rosy shade of pink. "Now where was I… oh yes – after our overnight stay in the lodge, we followed the river until we found an abandoned rowing boat," she continued, as everyone looked on worriedly in case the Skeloyds reappeared. "We used the boat to travel down river to the estuary…"

P.C. Sharp plucked up the courage to stop Aunt Vera again. "Mrs. Penworthy… I'm so sorry to interrupt you, but I must stop you there… we've got to move on from here – we are in immediate danger!"

Vera crossed her arms in annoyance and continued undeterred. Whilst they all regrouped, she followed everyone around concluding her appraisal of their remarkable journey by explaining how they had lost control of the rowing boat and found themselves being pulled by underwater currents towards some caves located at the base of the cliffs that towered above the cove. She explained how they were then swept deep inside the caves and eventually caught up in a giant whirlpool, which ultimately transported them through the vortex into the clutches of the Skeloyds.

Tank broke the unyielding silence within the group. "Wow... that was hell of a journey – Mrs. Penworthy."

"Yeah amazing... and you have just described some of the things that Turpol told us back in the tunnel," confirmed Simon, in an assuring tone.

Patrick supported his sister-in-law by joining the conversation again and exclaimed. "...except the bit about the bathroom and the drainpipe - that bit is really bizarre."

Margaret afforded Vera an assuring smile and commended her sister on her dogged attempt to describe their encounters. She then looked over and starred at the strange looking creature in the corner of the work shop. "Anyway, enough about how we got here - what about you lot... and who are you?

The dwarf stepped forward and bowed his head. "I am Turpol." He then disappeared out of the workshop.

"He's the Gatekeeper... we came across him whilst searching for young Musgrove Chilcott – it's a long story," said Patrick, in an attempt to divert his wife's attention away from the strange-looking dwarf. "Oh... and this here is Simon - young Muzzy's brother."

Vera interrupted with a smug look on her face. "So you are the infamous dashing royal marine recruit, Simon Chilcott... your girlfriend's mum comes round to clean my house you know!"

Patrick ignored his sister-in-law's petty remark, as he told Margaret about their search for Simon's brother. He explained how the group had entered the Sandmouth cliffs and discovered a cave full of wall paintings. He then continued to explain how the search party had met Turpol guarding a small door at the top of the steps that led up from the cave. "The dwarf guided us through a series of dark tunnels and we ended up here... at the entrance to the Vortex of Souls," he explained and then realized the amount of time being wasted. "P.C. Sharp is right... I think we had better get out here before those Skeloyds find us," insisted Patrick, as he put the sacred grobite back in his pocket. "I'll talk to you later about the treasure we found in Amley's Cove."

Aunt Vera overheard Patrick talking to Margaret and told him that Bradley and his new friend had found a similar coin in the rock pools when they had visited Old Mac the fisherman.

"I think our Bradley must still be with Musgrove here in Pathylon?" asked Margaret.

"It certainly looks that way," replied Patrick. "Especially as you found one of his toy soldiers and a set of his clothes... it looks to me like you and your Vera followed him down the drainpipe - however, I still find that part of your story absolutely incredible!"

Whilst Patrick, Margaret and Vera had been discussing Bradley's whereabouts, Simon had been searching for a safe way out of the workshop. "Let's go through here," he suggested and opened another metal door.

Everyone ushered through the exit that eventually led through into a massive cavern, with its roof towering above a hundred feet and more. The whole group was startled by a swarm of bats, which appeared from crevices inside the cave walls. The creatures flew around their heads for a short while, darting in different directions before disappearing out of sight, as their screeching sounds faded up into the tall roof of the chamber.

A fenced walkway prevented anyone from falling into the abyss below and the ledge swept all the way around the perimeter of the cavern. There was a single narrow walkway that led to a central island in the middle of the cavern. Standing tall was a large piece of hi-tech industrial machinery positioned on the island, which looked very much like another industrial turbine. The machine was creating a loud buzzing sound that intrigued Patrick. "This must be the power source that feeds the Vortex of Souls."

At that moment a loud siren erupted and filled the cavern with high-pitched tones. Everyone covered their ears to protect them from the piercing sounds that emanated from numerous audio speakers positioned around the cavern. Turpol reappeared and was accompanied by a group of Skeloyds who followed the dwarf through the entrance to the chamber.

The sirens finally stopped sounding and the Skeloyd leader stepped forward. "Allow me to introduce myself… my name is Dreel and I have spoken with Turpol about your quest to find the missing Chilcott boy - I find your predicament quite amusing and feel you are wasting your time."

"You can't stop us from entering the vortex!" shouted Simon. "We have to find my brother and his friend… Bradley Baker!"

211

Dreel sighed and shook his skeletal head. "I care nothing for the one you call Bradley Baker... the vortex of souls is dying and those two females have weakened it even more because they decided to travel through it together," claimed the Skeloyd, as he pointed to Margaret and Vera.

Tank and Bomber moved quickly towards Dreel, their huge fists clenched at the ready. As they neared the Skeloyd leader, three other Skeloyds moved across to defend him. With their battle-sabres drawn, they stood ready to protect him from the impending onslaught of the muscular marines.

The creatures out-numbered the soldiers and it was useless to fight without weapons so P.C. Sharp shouted out to advise the two men to stop. "Stand down fellas... we did not come here to fight with them!" shouted the police officer, as he turned his attention to Dreel. "We just want to find my nephew... his Mother is very worried about him back in Sandmouth!"

Tank and Bomber stood back and abandoned their assault. They moved aside to allow Margaret to step forward and plead with the gloating Skeloyd. "Please, Mr. Dreel... sir... we also want to find our son Bradley - we think he is with his friend at the other side of the vortex."

Turpol moved away from the Skeloyd leader to re-join his friends. He looked at Margaret and awarded her a comforting smile. Then the dwarf scowled at Dreel to show his disapproval of his actions against the humans. He knew how frustrated they were feeling because their souls had been confiscated and their bodies were made up of shredded flesh on brittle bones. All that held them together was their sheer will to survive to seek revenge on the High Priesthood regime that had condemned them to this horrible existence.

"Stop feeling so bitter, Dreel!" exclaimed Turpol. "You of all beings should want to rebel against the evil Varuna and his dictatorship - help these people to find their two lost boys and they will do all they can to release Luccese from the Shallock Tower!"

Dreel scowled and thrust his battle-sabre into the air, as a show of defiance. The Skeloyd did not like being spoken to in this way, especially by a dwarfish Gatekeeper.

Turpol continued to appraise their pitiful predicament. "Didn't King Luccese promise you, that one of his policies would be to find a way to heal the vortex during his reign of Pathylon? - Help us to defeat Varuna and I promise you... I will relay your efforts back to Luccese."

"What difference would it make?" asked Dreel.

"It will surely encourage him to accelerate the vortex's healing process and enable the hasty return of your souls... you will then be able to return to Pathylon as heroes and enjoy a mortal life again," replied Turpol.

The good health of the vortex was vital if the Skeloyds souls were to be saved. Their souls were actually inside the vortex and if it were to die their souls would be lost forever.

Patrick stepped forward. "Maybe I can help you... I am a qualified electrical engineer - let me look at the mechanism that operates the vortex and I'll see if I can do anything to repair it."

Dreel was impressed with Turpol's statement and the comment made by the human engineer. He summoned his fellow Skeloyds around him, as they entered into a heated debate on whether to trust the Gatekeeper and his new found friends. Following a brief discussion, Dreel reappeared from the group and offered his decision. "We agree to help you!" he stated. "But only if you can meet three conditions."

"What three conditions are those?" asked Turpol, anxiously.

Every one waited for his response. Vera was holding tightly onto Margaret's arm, as they watched Dreel pace up and down. Patrick, P.C. Sharp and Simon and the other two marines hoped that the conditions could be met. At last Dreel spoke out and made his demands. "*One* - that your friend Patrick here examines the vortex to see if he can repair it … *two* – if he fails to heal the vortex then Luccese must authorize a contract to heal the vortex and carry out his promise to attach the souls to our lifeless bodies… and *three* - once Luccese is returned to the throne… I am awarded a regional High Priesthood, together with the powers that it represents!"

The dwarf looked at Patrick and then at the others. Simon rushed towards Turpol and pleaded with him to accept the conditions that had been laid down by Dreel. Then the Gatekeeper whispered something in the marine's ear and advised him to tell the others. The informed soldier stepped back and did what the dwarf had requested.

"Well, Turpol… can you ensure that my three conditions are met?" asked Dreel, as a shred of decayed skin moved in unison with his jaw.

Turpol approached the Skeloyd and stared at him for a moment. The dwarf focused on the loose piece of flesh hanging from his boney chin and then invited him to come closer. The Skeloyd bent down and the Gatekeeper started to whisper in Dreel's flesh-eaten ear, "I have the answer to your demands and it's…"

There was a brief silence before he concluded his answer. Turpol then shouted in a loud piercing voice. "Nooooooooooooooooooooooo!"

The Skeloyd pulled his head away from the dwarf, with the sound of his reply still reverberating in his head. At the same moment, Turpol drew a hidden sword from beneath his cloak and with one accurate swing sliced into Dreel's skinny waist and severed his decaying body in half. The upper body part of the Skeloyd leader tried to crawl away and its severed legs flinched, as the last drop of life faded away. The severed creature's fraught attempt to escape the Gatekeeper was swiftly halted, as Turpol swung his sword once more and crashed the blade down onto Dreel's head with a fatal blow.

Simon punched his clenched fist in the air and cheered, as he ran forward to join the fight. Tank picked up the battle-sabre and launched himself at the other Skeloyds. Turpol threw his sword to Simon and quickly made his way over to assist Tank in his crusade, as one by one the Skeloyd creatures fell to the ground.

The two marines cut down the Skeloyds like a hot knife through butter, as Bomber joined in with the fighting. He wasn't prepared to let his two colleagues have all the fun. Without a weapon, he used only his bare fists to plough his way through the battle scene. He pulled back his arm in readiness for another thundering blow and then felt a cold sensation rush through his body. He looked down at his mid region and witnessed the blade of a battle-sabre pierce through his stomach.

Bomber had been stabbed in his back and the weapon had penetrated straight through his tough body and split the buttons on the front of his khaki uniform. He fell sideways and hit the ground hard with a thud and two more Skeloyds pounced on top of him. A cascade of stabbing blades entered his helpless body and he stood little chance against the ruthless onslaught of the zombie-like creatures.

P.C. Sharp reached into his pocket and pulled out a can of deterrent spray. He waded in to where Bomber was struggling to fend off the Skeloyds and the policeman aimed the jet of fluid into their eye sockets. The creatures dropped their weapons and screamed, as the fluid penetrated their skulls. Patrick noticed what the police officer was doing and went over to retrieve the two discarded battle-sabres. With a blade in each hand he thrust them into the two Skeloyds and they both slumped to the floor in a deathly heap.

At last all the Skeloyds were defeated. There was an eerie stillness around the cavern until Simon broke the silence and shouted. "Is everyone okay?"

"Bomber is hurt pretty badly!" replied P.C. Sharp and Simon immediately rushed over to where his friend was lying.

Patrick explained. "He's been stabbed through his back and has multiple stab wounds to his chest and stomach... the Skeloyd's blade went straight through him - he didn't stand a chance!"

Simon bent down to assist the police officer and Patrick, as they helped the injured soldier to sit upright. Blood continued to gush out of the marine's upper body, as Bomber spat more blood out of his mouth and started to choke violently. "This doesn't look good... does it, mate?" he spluttered, in a cockney accent and looked up at Simon. "I don't feel right inside, me old darling!"

Bomber offered a faint smile at Simon and held out his blood stained hand to Tank, who was now by his side. The Londoner's eyes slowly closed and his head slumped forward onto his chest, as he passed his last breath. Simon immediately burst into tears and he threw himself onto the marine's limp body.

Tank put his arms round Simon to comfort him and he immediately shrugged off his friend's affections in a defiant show of frustration. The distraught marine lifted himself up from his dead colleague and allowed an emotional outburst to fill the cavern void. "Whyyyyyyyyyyyyyyyyyyyyyy!" he shouted, as his voice faded away into the darkness of the rocky surroundings. "Why Bomber?" he repeated, with a deflated and heartbroken voice.

The sound of the screeching bats could be heard in the distance, as Simon's haunted tones echoed through the cavern and his uncle approached. "Come on, lad," said P.C. Sharp, as he put his arm round his nephew to comfort him.

The rest of the group rushed over and everyone rallied together to witness Patrick and Tank lift Bomber's motionless body from the spot where he had fallen. They proceeded to carry him back out of the cavern and lay him on one of the slab benches inside the Skeloyds workshop. The marine's warm blood continued to seep from his lifeless body and created a syrup-like pool on the top of the worktable before ebbing over the side of the bench and onto the dusty workshop floor.

The Gatekeeper watched in horror as Bomber's precious blood soaked in to the porous rock. "This wasn't supposed to happen," he declared and dropped his head forward. "Simon... I'm so sorry - so very, very sorry!"

A deathly silence pervaded the workshop and Turpol stepped to one side, as the distraught marine brushed past him. The sombre atmosphere inside the room was accompanied by a faint drone of the turbine that was struggling to turn the vortex, as it idled intermittently in readiness for another journey into Pathylon.

21

A Few Home Truths

Grog was still waiting patiently next to the egg-shaped rock. He suddenly heard the sound of galloping creatures approaching and lowered his fat amber belly further into the long grass. Through the strands of the undergrowth he could make out three koezard and one of them had a mark on its head. There was only one koezard in the whole of Krogonia that had a large black patch around its left eye and it was called Shatar. The unique koezard was Grog's mount, who had been taken away from him when he was dispelled from his native homeland and to make things even worse, the Krogon warrior that sat upon Shatar was Zule.

Grog struggled to contain his anger, as it rushed through his amphibian body like pure adrenalin. He was not prepared to let Zule get away with this and the thought of revenge struck him like a bolt of lightning. Without thinking he stood up and made himself known to his bitter rival. This was a reckless thing for him to do because not only had he put his

218

own life in danger; he had also made the egg-shape rock a potential target of curiosity. Grog stared at the Krogon Champion and his rival finally caught his eye.

"Well, well… if it isn't the coward of Krogonia himself - the disgraced village idiot known as Grog!" shouted Zule, as he turned to Harg and sniggered at the sight of his old spawning chum. Grog retained his composure and gave no reply, as Zule continued to ridicule him. "So you've stopped hiding away in the depths of the great forest have you?"

Grog refused to be intimidated by the warrior's aggressive taunts and he continued to stand deathly still avoiding eye contact with his fellow Krogon.

Harg was surprised to see Grog give himself up so easily and began to laugh in husky tone. "Zule… bring the disgraced Krogon over to me."

The young warrior obeyed his leader's request, as he confidently dismounted the koezard and walked over to where Grog was standing in an assertive manner. Shatar followed Zule's steps and then passed him by to nudge his old keeper, as he offered a gentle greeting by lowering his head.

Grog whispered in Shatar's ear and stroked the steed's long neck. "Hello… old boy - I've missed you my old friend."

"Take your filthy webbed claws off my koezard!" shouted Zule, as he stood tall over his bitter rival.

Grog glared upwards. "Your koezard?" he challenged. "This is Shatar and he belongs to me… you stole him from me, Zule!"

Harg was still perched high on his lizard mount and could hear Grog's pitiful display of defiance. The Krogon leader scratched the end of his disfigured nose horn and gave out a loud growl, as he shouted to his apprentice. "This might be a good time to settle an old score!"

Zule turned to Harg and acknowledged his wishes by nodding his triple-horned head. The champion warrior then turned to Grog and offered a gesture by laying his hand on the sword that adorned his leg armour. "I offer you the chance to redeem your honour and fight with me here today."

"It is not a question of honour and you know it!" replied Grog. "Back on the spawning grounds of Flaclom, we were supposed to have been friends... I did not wish to fight you then and for the same reason I do not wish to fight you now."

"You haven't altered one little bit, Grog... you are still a gutless coward and you haven't changed your pathetic ways – you are fat and ugly," provoked Zule. "If you insist on our so called friendship preventing you from combat... then let the ownership of the koezard you call Shatar be the trophy!"

Grog knew he could not reason with Zule. The newly appointed High Priest of Devonia was intent on revenge and the presence of his mentor Harg was not helping the situation. He knew he had to fight his old rival, but first he must draw his enemies away from the entrance to the secret tunnel, which led to the Shallock Tower. Meltor's efforts to release King Luccese was of paramount importance and Grog could see this as the perfect opportunity to buy some precious time. Bradley Baker and the others would know nothing of this act of bravery but he was intent on diverting Harg and Zule's attention away, even though it may result in his own death at the hands of his Krogon rival.

"Very well... I will fight with you, Zule!" challenged Grog. "But not here!"

Harg intervened and asked. "Where is it that you wish to fight my champion warrior?"

"I wish to battle with Zule on the Flaclom Straits in my homeland of Krogonia!" demanded Grog. "I feel it is only fair to carry out such a dual in the area where the original contest was to take place... all those years ago – then we will see who the *real* champion is!"

"That is a brave and splendid suggestion!" acknowledged Harg. "But remember, Grog... Krogonia is not your homeland any more - you must earn your right to call it that again by defeating Zule!"

Harg continued to remind Grog that he had been banished from his birthplace because he had dishonoured himself and indeed his fellow Krogons by not accepting the ceremonial combat with Zule during their proof of adulthood.

At that moment the third koezard edged in front of Harg. The pure white albino mount was ordered to halt by its beautiful rider. Flaglan the High Priestess from the Forest of Haldon was growing impatient and informed Harg of Varuna's plans. The aging Krogon was reminded that his priority was to find Meltor and the band of young humans. "King Varuna's orders were very clear," she stated. "We are to find the rebels before they attempt to free Luccese."

Flaglan and Harg raised their voices and began to argue, as the royal chariot carrying Varuna approached. It was led by Lieutenant Dergan and followed by the loyal Devonian Death Troops, as the remainder of the King's entourage remained in close formation. The other seven remaining Krogon warriors, mounted on their koezard, galloped along the right flank and gathered around the quarreling High Priests.

Varuna's chariot came to a halt alongside Harg's koezard. "What is going on here?" he demanded. "Harg... why do you raise your voice to the beautiful sorceress that covets the great forest?"

"I can assure you Varuna… Flaglan and I were merely discussing your immediate plans to capture Meltor," explained Harg, as he mellowed his tone.

"Then why were you both shouting at each other?" asked the inquisitive Hartopian.

"Because of that ugly thing!" scathed Flaglan, as she pointed to the Krogon prisoner.

"Ahhhhh!" exclaimed Varuna. "You must be the one they call Grug!"

"My name is not Grug," corrected the stubborn amphibian. "I am Grog and I am a Krogon warrior!"

"Krogon warrior… eh?" replied Varuna and continued to provoke. "You don't look like much of a warrior to me… *tell me Grug* - do *you* know the whereabouts of Meltor and the three human children?"

"I don't know what you are talking about," replied Grog calmly. "I was just wandering through Devonia looking for food and shelter."

"Don't lie to us Krogon… we are well aware that you have been enlisted by that rebellious old Galetian - Meltor!" accused Lieutenant Dergan. "And it must be an amazing coincidence that you happen to be near the Shallock Tower, which holds Luccese prisoner?" quizzed the over-zealous Wartpig.

Varuna glared ferociously at Dergan. The piercing red eyes of the evil ruler conveyed a clear message to the petrified soldier for him not interrupt his interrogation of the Krogon rebel again. Dergan immediately stepped back and cowered against the royal chariot.

Grog stuck to his story and persuaded Varuna that he had split up from Meltor and the three human children, back in the Forest of Haldon. He explained that he knew nothing of their whereabouts and continued to inform his intrigued audience that his only intent now was to fight with Zule to settle an old score.

Varuna listened to Harg's explanation about the importance of the dual between the two old rivals and how the old Krogon felt it was a splendid idea for them to travel back to the Flaclom Straits in Krogonia to cement the ritual.

"What about Meltor?" exclaimed Varuna. "His capture is our prime objective... this battle between your Krogon pair can surely wait!"

Zule approached Varuna and Harg then begged for the fight to go ahead immediately. The immaculately dressed Krogon warrior spoke to Varuna with much reasoning and persuasion. "My great King... surely Lieutenant Dergan and his crack force of Devonian Death Troops can guard the Shallock Tower in our absence," pleaded Zule, as he readjusted his brightly coloured chest-plate. "No one... not even Meltor would be able to penetrate such a formidable defensive position, my lord!"

Varuna pondered over the request, delivered so emotionally by his newly appointed High Priest. "Very well," agreed the sympathetic Hartopian. "It is against my better judgment, but you will have your moment of revenge and glory – however, we will return back here immediately, as soon as you have devoured this pitiful lizard creature!" concluded Varuna, as he pointed to a nervous looking Grog.

Zule brushed past Shatar, causing the koezard's left eye to blink within the smooth black patch of skin that surrounded it. The rookie High Priest of Devonia approached Grog and looked down on the plump and overweight Krogon. Zule snarled and his sharp blood stained teeth glistened with the saliva that oozed from his yellow and pink mouth. "At last... I have the opportunity to crush your fat bloated body into the ground!" he scorned and lowered his head, then pushed his glistening upper jaw against Grog's reddened face.

About an hour later Varuna, Harg, Flaglan, Zule and the rest of the royal entourage left for Krogonia. Lieutenant Dergan was left with instructions to reinforce the tower guard and form a defensive ring around the base of the Shallock Tower. The Wartpig was to utilize the Devonian Death Troops and the rest of his ground force battalion.

Zule joined King Varuna on the Royal Chariot whilst Grog was gagged and tied to the saddle of his trusty mount, Shatar. The journey across the Satorc Bridge and on to the Flaclom Straits now beckoned for Grog, in readiness for his dual of destiny. Unbeknown to Varuna, his plan to buy time for Meltor had worked. He hoped and prayed it would be worth the pain he was to endure at the hands of old rival.

Meanwhile in the underground tunnel leading to the tower, Bradley and Musgrove followed close behind Meltor, as Sereny tried her best to avoid the cobwebs that spanned the thin passageway. They passed under the metal arches that supported the roof of the tunnel, which finally led them to the base of the Shallock Tower. Meltor turned to check on his three young helpers and encouraged them to move faster.

The Galetian had spotted another ladder that was attached to the sidewall of the tunnel and he was keen to ascend as quickly as possible, to check whether it led into the tower. Meltor swept his cloak over his right shoulder then began his ascent, as the three children gathered at the base of the ladder and looked up to see the old Galetian's boots disappear into the void.

It did not take Meltor long to reach the top and he extended his strong arm upwards with force to open the rusty bolts that secured the wooden trap door. With little effort, the final bolt was dislodged, as the High Priest started to lever the door open using the base of his neck and shoulders. Following a short period of huffing and grunting and much heaving and groaning, the trap door finally gave way and the exhausted Galetian was able to start lifting the heavy door away from the opening.

A dust-filled stream of grey light beams cast a faint shadow behind the children at the base of the ladder. "What can you see?" whispered Bradley, as he stared up at the blackness beyond the trap door.

"Nothing... it's too dark and dusty," replied Meltor, as he finally maneuvered the door away to reveal the opening, enabling him to finally climb off the ladder and onto the floor above. The dust started to settle and Meltor called down to Bradley and his friends. "Okay you three... it's safe for you to climb up!"

The three children did not hesitate and ascended the ladder. They squeezed through the narrow trap door opening and found themselves in a very dimly lit, cold and wet chamber. As they adjusted their focus to compensate for the lack of light, shapes started to emerge in the form of chains and shackles that adorned the chamber walls.

"I presume this must be some sort of dungeon or torture room... by the look of all this stuff," presumed Sereny as she held onto Musgrove's hand. "Look at all those heavy chains!"

Sereny continued to assess the chamber and her eyes gradually became more accustomed to the eerie darkness. The only element of light being emitted into the room was from a small cobweb covered window at the top of one of the chamber walls. As her eyes focused more, she let out a loud scream. Musgrove instantly felt for her mouth and covered it with his hand. Sereny's muffled cries continued, as she stared at a disfigured skeleton hanging in the chains that were fastened to the wall beneath the small window.

"Try to be a little quieter," whispered Meltor. "Please try not to be frightened... it's only a bunch of old Wartpig bones."

Bradley looked up at Meltor with a frightened stare and grabbed his cloak. The old Galetian pulled him towards his muscular frame and gave him a reassuring hug. "Don't you worry either my little friend... we'll protect you - won't we Muzzy?"

"Err... yes, Meltor... no - pr... problem," replied Musgrove, as his voice trembled whilst responding to the High Priest's reassurances.

Meltor reached down and replaced the trap door. He then walked over to the far end of the chamber towards a closed wooden door. "This must be the way out and into the corridors that lead to the Shallock Tower stairwells."

The others followed close behind their rebel leader and watched as he tried the heavy iron door handle. It turned slowly and Bradley whispered to his friend. "This is a proper fine mess you've got us into Musgrove Chilcott."

"Leave it out, Brad... you told me you wanted adventure and you can't get better than this - can you?" replied Musgrove.

"I suppose not... but it is rather scary," said Bradley.

"Oh come on you little wuss!" exclaimed Sereny, in an unfamiliar retort. "It's not that scary."

Musgrove and Bradley looked at her and then at each other and both exclaimed simultaneously. "Says she!"

Meltor laughed quietly, for he knew the boys were right to be condescending towards the young girl. Sereny had certainly showed little sign of calmness when the Wartpig skeleton had come into focus.

The High Priest felt the need to calm the situation. "Come on you three… stop tormenting each other," said Meltor, as he controlled his amusement. "We have some serious business to attend to."

Sereny acknowledged the old man's calming words and asked. "Do you think we should go back for more help?"

Meltor still had a firm hold on the door handle and replied in a puzzled tone. "Grog is best placed guarding the entrance to the tunnel… I'm afraid we are very much on our own my dear – we'll have to make the best of what we've got."

Bradley intervened. "I don't think Sereny was referring to Grog."

Sereny nodded. "Bradley's right I…"

Bradley touched Sereny on the shoulder and she cast him a gentle smile. He looked for her approval and then carried on. "I think what Sereny is trying to say is… well - when you explained to us before, about the prisoners from Freytor, you mentioned there would be twelve chosen ones that would be called upon to help save Pathylon from the clutches of the evil King Varuna."

Musgrove felt inclined to offer further comment and added. "Yeah… we are only three of the magic coin holders - shouldn't we go back and find the other nine?"

Meltor asked the three children to be calm for he was confident that the other nine coin holders would materialize in due course. He continued to explain that good would overcome evil and they just had to have more confidence in their own ability. "You must continue to trust my judgment… I know it is difficult for you all - but the future of Pathylon is in your hands," he explained. "Whatever lies behind this door will no doubt test your resolve… but we must stick together and pray that the help you have mentioned will guide its way to us."

"How can you be so sure?" asked Bradley.

Meltor paused for a moment and then decided to inform the three children of some important information. "There is something that I failed to tell you about when we first embarked on our journey through the tunnel to the Shallock Tower… about halfway through I felt a violent shuddering through the rocks."

"Now you mention it… I felt it too," admitted Musgrove, as he awarded Sereny an inquisitive look.

"Yes… so did I," said Sereny and looked at Bradley. "What about you… did you feel anything?"

Bradley acknowledged that he too had felt the tremors, but asked Meltor what significance the rumblings had. The High Priest proceeded to tell the three children about the Vortex of Souls and that it was a way out of Pathylon and back to their own world.

Musgrove reacted angrily. "Why didn't you tell us about this before?" he exclaimed. "We could be on our way back home now… safe and sound!"

Meltor acknowledged Musgrove's frustration and apologized. He took his hand off the door handle and insisted that they all sit down while he explained why he had not told them earlier about the Vortex of Souls. He had some serious explaining to do and the astonishment on the children's faces after hearing his devastating comments, gave the Galetian an indication that he had to fully justify his reasons for not informing them about the vortex earlier.

Meltor paused and bit softly on his bottom lip. He felt the time was right to explain his role in this whole situation. As the children looked on intently, the rebel High Priest of the Galetis Empire proceeded to expand upon his knowledge of the outside world. "I have travelled many times to Sandmouth via the whirlpool... and through the vortex."

Bradley looked closely at Meltor. The dust had finally settled inside the chamber and the dull light from the window had made Meltor look much younger. The dancing shadows had made the High Priest's beard appear black and not grey. "I know you from somewhere... don't I?"

"Yes... we have met before - young Bradley" replied Meltor. "By the way... how is your Aunt Vera?"

"Old Mac!" exclaimed Musgrove. "You look just like Old Mac... the fisherman from Sandmouth!"

"So he does... I thought I knew you from somewhere," said Bradley. "And your boat... it was called..."

"Galetis!" interrupted Musgrove.

"Yes... of course - the Galetis Empire!" concluded Bradley.

"Keep your voices down," requested Meltor, as he smiled at the boy's enthusiasm. The three children became more excited, as the High Priest explained that he had acted as the Good Samaritan for King Luccese following the Freytorians visit to Pathylon. "The gold coins that you all found in Amley's Cove were actually placed there by me... and when Musgrove and Bradley here found the last coin - I deliberately kept Aunt Vera busy while you two went off to explore the rock pools."

"And what about my shoes and socks?" asked Musgrove. "Did you move them?"

Meltor nodded his head. He also explained that he had found the nine other coins together with some more grobite currency in the cask that was dropped by the Freytorian scouting party when they first visited the Mouth of Sand in their small landing craft. During one of his visits to Sandmouth on the outside world he delivered the cask and made it much easier for someone else to find the contents.

"This may sound obvious to the others, but I'm getting a little confused," said Musgrove. "Can you please tell me why you look so old and have a grey beard here in Pathylon... but when we met you in Sandmouth posing as Old Mac - you appeared much younger and had a black beard?"

"No it isn't that obvious and it's a very good question Muzzy..." replied Meltor. "And... there is a simple explanation, my dear friend." He continued. "Pathylon and your world are one and the same... separated only by time," explained the old Galetian. "The Mouth of Sand and Sandmouth are actually the same place."

"We did think that was the case," said Bradley.

"So what you're saying is... anyone who makes a journey out of Pathylon to the outside world through the Vortex of Souls - becomes considerably younger?" asked Sereny.

"That's correct," replied Meltor. "Now... those tremors we all felt in the tunnel earlier - they were caused by the vortex being used by someone travelling through it."

"So does that mean someone has escaped from Pathylon and into our world on the outside?" asked Musgrove.

"No... quite the opposite, the tremors were very strong," explained Meltor. "The tremors also felt strange... they could only represent one thing - for some reason the vortex had been reversed."

"How is that possible?" asked Bradley.

Meltor explained to Bradley and the others about the use of the sacred gold coins and that it was possible to reverse the direction of the vortex by entering into its spiral holding a grobite in the palm of your left hand.

Sereny looked puzzled. She was trying to work out how Meltor was able to travel in and out of Pathylon without a gold coin. The High Priest was growing much stronger and his telepathic powers were returning. He intercepted her thoughts and surmised out loud. "How does he travel in and out of Pathylon without a gold coin?"

"How did you know what I was thinking?" she asked.

Meltor laughed quietly. "I have telepathic powers... it comes as part of the High Priest package!"

"Huh?" replied Sereny, as she scrunched her shoulders.

"Sorry Sereny... I don't mean to make fun," he replied. "There is actually a thirteenth sacred coin... and I have it!"

"You said there was only twelve," said Bradley.

"I told a little *white lie* about that bit," admitted Meltor.

"Yeah... you've been telling us quite a few of those!" exclaimed Musgrove.

Meltor smiled and ignored Musgrove's comment, as he continued. "Only one other person knows about the thirteenth coin."

"Who is that?" asked Bradley.

"Pavsik!" replied Meltor. "He is a good friend and ally... Pavsik was the one that ensured my messages always reached King Luccese in the Shallock Tower - that is why it is important to me that we also ensure his safe release from the tower, as well as the King and Queen."

Musgrove was now getting the hang of all this and he asked Meltor who he thought might have travelled through the Vortex of Souls and into Pathylon. He explained that it must have been the other chosen ones, because they must have located the sacred grobites in order to reverse the vortex. The Galetian concluded. "It must also be someone who has great fighting ability to get past the Skeloyds that protect and maintain the vortex... it must also have been someone who was desperate to enter into Pathylon in order to help someone that they loved who was in trouble."

Musgrove looked at Bradley and they both felt warmed by Meltor's words. Both boys felt something inside reassuring them that their loved ones were doing everything they could to find them. Little did Bradley know that his mum, dad and aunt were working with Musgrove's uncle and brother together with Tank and a new found ally – Turpol the Gatekeeper.

Meltor had tried in vain to determine the identity of the other chosen ones by using his telepathic powers. He was feeling weary and his powers were still weakened, but there was one thing he was right about; Simon and the other chosen ones had indeed travelled through the Vortex of Souls. The tremors that they had all felt were caused by the seven brave members of the search party travelling into Pathylon.

22

Battle of the Krogons

The campaign to save Pathylon from the evil clutches of Varuna had taken on a new offensive. Whilst Varuna and his followers were preparing for the battle between Zule and Grog a new breed of vigilantes had entered into Pathylon. They were making their way up the River Klomus from the Satorc Estuary and were led by Turpol the Gatekeeper.

Patrick directed a question at his wife. "Have you noticed something different about everyone since we travelled through the vortex?"

"It's funny you should mention it – I can't help feeling that our Vera is looking remarkably older," replied Margaret.

Turpol overheard them and turned to explain about the affect the reversal of the vortex has on the age of its passengers. "It affects us all in different ways... take Simon and Tank for example - it has merely added months to them... yet five or six years to the age of your tubby lady friend over there," concluded the dwarf, as he pointed to Vera.

P.C. Sharp interrupted Turpol. The group had been travelling for some time up river and the police officer wanted to change the subject of conversation to a more serious note. "How do you expect us to find Musgrove and Bradley in a place as vast as this?" he asked. "This world of yours is so dark and gloomy - and this damn river seems to go on forever."

Turpol acknowledged the police officers concerns. "We should be coming up to a rope bridge quite soon... look - can you see it?"

"Ah yes... there it is - I see it in the distance," replied P.C. Sharp, as he squinted his eyes to focus on the bend in the river ahead.

The group quickened their steps and arrived at the bridge in no time. It did not take long for all seven group members to cross over the River Klomus, following in the footsteps of Meltor and his band of rebels.

"Where exactly are we going?" asked Patrick, as he helped Margaret step off the rope bridge onto the Devonian side of the river.

"We are heading for the Shallock Tower... on the outskirts of the City of Trad," replied Turpol. "If my instincts are correct... I believe Meltor will be heading there in an attempt to free King Luccese."

The way to the City of Trad was left clear by the departure of Varuna, who was well on his way to Krogonia. Turpol led the reinforcements and they made their way to within sight of the Shallock Tower without stopping to eat or drink. The mood within the group was very sombre and everyone was intent on finding Musgrove and Bradley alive and safe.

As well as his concerns for Musgrove, Simon was especially keen to avenge the death of Bomber. Both he and Tank were looking forward to helping the rebel alliance in their quest to free King Luccese.

Aunt Vera was feeling very weary. The long journey was taking its toll on the dumpy disciplinarian. She sat on a nearby cretyre tree stump to catch her breath and nursed her sore feet.

"How are you feeling, Vera?" asked Margaret. "Would you like to rest for a little while?"

"Just for a few minutes, our Margaret," replied Vera. "My legs aren't what they used to be you know… and the bunion on my right foot is playing me up again."

Patrick recognized that Vera was going into one of her crotchety moods and quickly rescued Margaret before she received the full force of her sister's vocabulary of complaint after complaint. "Maybe we should send your Vera in head to head with this King Varuna bloke," he uttered. "He would run a mile once he caught sight of the lumps on her feet… and he'd run even further if she started listing her body ailments to him."

"Please don't be like that… Patrick," requested Margaret. "Our Vera is very tired… I think we should all rest for a while."

Meltor opened the door that led from the torture chamber into the corridors beneath the Shallock Tower. He signalled to Sereny to follow him and told the boys to stay put until they had checked the coast was clear. As the Galetian made his way down the passageway with the timid girl in pursuit, Bradley put his head around the door and peered along the arched corridor to witness them disappear out of sight.

"Well Muzzy... I guess that means we've got to stay put for a little while," said Bradley. "I hope they will be okay."

"They shouldn't be too long... at least it gives us a chance to take in all this information," sighed Musgrove.

"Hey, Muzzy?" questioned Bradley. "I hope you don't think I'm being nosy or anything... but seeing as we've got a little time to talk – do you mind if I ask you about your Father?"

"What about my Father?" replied Musgrove, in a defensive tone.

"Well... what happened to him?" asked Bradley.

"Oh... I don't really like to talk about it much," replied Musgrove, trying to put aside his friend's inquisitiveness.

"I'm sorry... I didn't mean to offend you," said Bradley, as he picked up a small stone and threw it at the Wartpig skeleton hanging from the chamber wall.

The stone ricocheted off the Wartpig's skull, rebounded off the wall and hit Musgrove on his shin. "Ouch!" he yelled and rubbed his throbbing leg.

"Sorry mate... that was a bit unlucky," said Bradley.

"Yeah... story of my life," replied Musgrove. "I guess it runs in the family... it just about sums up my father's disappearance – you could say he was unlucky too."

"What do you mean?" asked Bradley in a surprised tone. "I didn't think you wanted to talk about him?"

"Well being cooped up in this damp room reminded me of the day he disappeared," explained Musgrove. "It happened about twelve years ago... I was only two years old."

"What happened?" asked Bradley.

"My father and my older brother Simon decided they were going to take me down to Amley's Cove to the rock pools... you know - to catch some crabs and tiddlers," said

236

Musgrove. "I don't really remember much about what happened... Simon stayed with me - whilst my father searched the caves at the far end of the cove."

"What happened next," asked Bradley, as he listened intently to his friend's story.

"I heard my Father scream... then nothing!' replied Musgrove, as tears started to well up in his eyes. "He sounded so scared... my Father was terrified."

"That's terrible, Muzzy... then what happened?" asked Bradley, as he reassured his friend.

"Don't know... I remember shouting for my dad then I slipped on the rocks – apparently I woke in hospital with a suspected concussion," said Musgrove. "I never saw my Dad again!"

"Oh Muzzy... I'm so sorry!" exclaimed Bradley. "Did the police try to find him?"

"Simon told me they searched for weeks... my uncle reckons he may have been swept out to sea," explained Musgrove. "My uncle was one of the police officers that found my Father's hat in the rock pools... he's been very protective of my mum ever since the disappearance – I hope he'll be searching for me now."

"We need all the help we can get," replied Bradley. "Anyhow... your Dad could still be alive – you should never give up hope," he encouraged. "Maybe Meltor knows something... after all - plenty of strange things are happening around here!"

"Thanks for your support and your kind words Brad... but my mum still has the newspaper cuttings with '*Thomas Chilcott Presumed Dead*' written across the headlines," said Musgrove. "I appreciate your concerns Brad... but believe me - it's much easier to accept that my Father is dead!"

Just then the two boys jumped and they were startled, as the door to the chamber flung open. It was Sereny and she was crying uncontrollably.

"What on earth is the matter?" asked Bradley. "Where's Meltor?"

Sereny sniffed and gasped, but managed to control her emotions to inform the boys of Meltor's capture by the tower guards. "I think they may have followed me too!" exclaimed the frightened girl.

As Bradley started to put his arms around Sereny to comfort her, he heard the clanking of chains and a loud voice emanated from the doorway. "You're coming with us!" instructed the guard.

The three children turned simultaneously and found to their horror, one of the tower guards standing in the doorway. Three other guards stood close behind and the order was given to escort Bradley and his friends into the tower.

The clouds hung heavy over the region of Krogonia. An occasional flash of lightening brightened the grey sky, as Harg made the necessary preparations for the battle between Grog and the newly elected High Priest of Devonia. Zule had made everyone aware that he was more than ready to face his old rival. Varuna was keen for the dual to end swiftly, but Harg had other ideas. The High Priest of Krogonia had insisted that all the ceremonial things, which associated itself with a dual of this importance was installed.

An impressive arena was quickly erected and an endless supply of flags and buntings adorned the circumference of the battleground. The temporary seating for the audience was in place and the stage was set. All that was missing was the two battling gladiators and the necessary spectators to cheer on the proceedings.

Grog sat with his head lowered between his legs. The paunch of his belly supported his large chin as he stared at the dusty floor of his temporary mobile prison cell. The door of the wagon cage opened and a gruesome looking Krogon guard threw a set of battle armour at Grog's feet. He ignored the pathetic gift and started to sway side-to-side as the wagon began to move slowly, the bumpy journey came to an end and the cage was lowered onto the ground. He sensed a loud noise all around him. He looked up and realized that the cage had been positioned at the centre of the arena and the crowds, that had now gathered, were jeering and booing. A slow handclap evolved and spread around the circle of spectators, as they waited for Grog to don the battle armour and vacate the portable cage.

Zule was already dressed in a magnificent suit of precious Krogon metal. His fearsome spear-like weapon stood erect in his right hand, as he held it out by his side. A shiny jewelled shield adorned his left arm and the colourful set of ceremonial feathers, which were attached to the top of his helmet, moved gently in the breeze.

Grog looked across at his opponent and then dropped his head once more. He was feeling very deflated and feared desperately for his life. The crowd was growing more restless and urged Harg to start the proceedings. Two Krogon warriors entered the cage and pulled Grog out and threw him onto the hard stony floor of the arena.

Harg stood in the royal enclosure high in the arena and looked down on Grog. The Krogon leader laughed sarcastically and then shouted. "I take it you don't want to wear your new battle armour?"

Grog gave no reply and Harg threw a dull looking shield and small dagger towards the disgraced amphibian. Again, he gave no response and refused to pick up the shield and pathetic antique weapon. He knew if he could prolong this event as much as possible it would give Meltor enough time to carry out the planned jailbreak of Luccese.

"What are you waiting for swamp scum... get to your feet and fight!" shouted Zule. "Get up Grog or your koezard will feel the coldness of my blade though its neck!"

Grog was being considerably calm and relaxed about the whole affair, but the mention of Zule's threat to Shatar stirred feelings of anger inside his belly. The thought of any harm being inflicted upon his childhood mount was enough to entice him into the inevitable challenge. He rose to his feet to the chant of *Krogon Coward* from the masses above. He then proceeded to bend down and pick up the mediocre dagger and shield. "Is this all you can afford me, Harg!" he shouted and tentatively held the small weapon in his trembling webbed hand.

"Think yourself lucky you have been awarded any weapon at all!" replied Harg, as he took his seating position on a makeshift throne inside the royal box.

A fanfare struck and the master of ceremonies announced to the crowd that the dual would begin at the third stroke of the ancient *Jastak Drum*.

There was a deafening sound of cheers around the arena as the crowds waved their banners and flags, which were emblazoned in colour with the name of their champion. Zule walked with his head aloft to the centre of the arena, as the crowd cheered and waved their hands in the air. Grog followed and the cheers turned to hisses and objects were thrown from the stands. Pieces of fruit landed near to where he was stood and then a loose crotharo berry smashed into Zule's face. The crowd fell silent as he wiped the red juice from his raging brow and the first beat of the Jastak Drum was struck. "Who threw this?" he roared, as he faced the crowds near to the royal box where Varuna sat amused.

The master of ceremonies held aloft his drumstick, which was made carved from flax bone with animal hide stretched around its knuckle. Another beat thundered around the arena, as the deep-based sound of the Jastak Drum was struck again.

Zule was still airing his anger at the spectators. "I demand to know who threw it!" roared the angry Krogon warrior, still unaware of the drum's second beat.

The tension around the arena was getting more intense and Zule received no reply, as the third beat of Jastak Drum was struck. Grog seized his opportunity whilst his opponent still seethed at being struck by the rotten piece of fruit. He launched all his weight at his rival's midriff with his dagger outstretched and aimed at the soft area beneath the ranting Krogon's armoured chest plate.

The crowd erupted at the sight of the assault, as the blade penetrated deep into the warrior's chest. The Krogon champion was caught off-guard, as he reeled backwards. He fell to the ground with a heavy thud and the crowd fell silent again. They could not believe the speed at which the dagger had been thrust into Zule. Harg stood out of his seat, as he looked down at the motionless Krogon and then turned to Grog. "You are truly a worthy victor and you have utilized your quick thinking against the shear brute strength of a proven champion... I now invite you to stand at my side!"

Varuna stood up out of his seat and vetted his disagreement at Harg. "You can't do that... this pathetic lizard is a member of the rebel alliance!"

Harg sensed the crowd's dissatisfaction and faced Varuna in the royal box. The wise old Krogon spoke quietly and explained what should happen at the end of such an important Krogon Ritual. "My King...in a fight to the death, the victor earns the right to stand at the side of the sitting High Priest - the victory also entitles the champion warrior to be the new heir to the High Priesthood of the Krogon region."

"Your rules are senseless and stupid!" roared Varuna, as he turned away from Harg to address the disgruntled crowd. "I am your King... the King of Pathylon – and I order you to send this pond creature to your dungeons to await execution!"

The crowd was even more incensed by Varuna's words, not even the King has the right to question an ancient Krogon ritual. The mass of onlookers became more and more angry and awaited Harg's response.

The Krogon leader was facing an impossible decision. Harg had the choice of either dishonouring his fellow Krogons or suffer the repercussions of an angry Hartopian King, should he decide to carry out the wishes of his forefathers. "Very well... my King!" he bellowed, as the crowd fell silent and shocked at his response. "Our great ruler must be obeyed on this occasion... Grog does indeed pose a threat to Krogonia and indeed to the world of Pathylon – it would be ludicrous to appoint a member of the rebel alliance onto my council!"

The unsettled spectators vented chants of treachery, as Harg retook his seat. The Krogon High Priest bowed his head to avoid eye contact with the crowd, as Varuna spoke. "Harg... I am glad to see you have taken control of your senses!"

Harg's wrinkled face reddened and he turned to face Varuna again. He grunted and paused for a moment then plucked up enough courage to stipulate. "Yes... but there is, however - one condition."

"You dare to impose conditions on your King?" replied Varuna, his red eyes narrowing and affording an evil stare.

Harg leant over to whisper in Varuna's ear. "My lord... I don't mean anything derogatory against your reign over our lands - should you wish to restrain Grog, may I suggest you imprison him in the Shallock Tower," advised Harg. "As you can see by the reaction of the Krogon crowd... I feel it would be more fitting that Grog is taken out of Krogonia to avoid a potential revolution against my authority as their High Priest."

Varuna sniggered and stood up to face the large hoards and shouted out his response. "Silence... do not feel betrayed by Harg – your leader has made a very wise decision!"

A fading silence spread around the arena as Varuna continued to speak. "We will take Grog to the Royal City of Trad where he will be imprisoned in the Shallock Tower until such time as I see fit to release him for trial before the Devonian Privy Council!" roared the Hartopian, as the dark clouds thundered above. "It is important to rid Pathylon of this rebel scum and I appeal to your allegiance to the crown and ask for your help to find Meltor and his band of rebels!"

The crowd reacted unfavourably to King Varuna's response and they all stood to vent their feelings by throwing seat cushions into the arena. The unruly audience fell silent again, as Zule's limp corpse was dragged unceremoniously from the arena.

Grog was approached and led away by two Krogon guards towards the edge of the arena. One of the guards bowed his head over towards Grog's ear to whisper encouragement to the brave warrior. "We are honoured by your presence and we admire your courage… we shall not let your victory go unrewarded - when you reach the Shallock Tower tell your friends they now have new allies in Krogonia."

Grog afforded one of the guards an appreciative look and then turned to the other. Both warriors gave him a coherent nod. This provided Grog with the reassurance he needed. He had been treated unfairly and Krogon rules of battle had been broken. He was now confident that the Krogon masses would turn against Harg and the evil rule of Varuna.

Grog's visit to his homeland had not just been a time wasting exercise after all. His life expectancy had taken a swift improvement for the better and the battle of good against evil to determine the future of Pathylon had just taken another positive turn in favour of the rebel alliance.

23

A Tail in the Plughole

Frannie was feeling very tired, so Jules helped Bradley's little sister up the stairs of Aunt Vera's cottage. Jules could sense that Frannie was getting worried about the whereabouts of her mum and dad and older brother.

The caring teenager suggested a quick wash and brush up before bed and led the weary red head into the bathroom. "Do I have to go to bed, Jules?" asked Frannie, as she positioned her chin over the hand basin to begin the arduous task of cleaning her teeth.

"I think it's best Frannie... anyhow - you look very tired," replied Jules. "And it looks as though your Mum and Bradley have decided to stay out with your Aunt Vera for the evening and your Dad must still be out looking for Muzzy," she explained. "Don't worry... I've no doubt they will all be back soon - I will get them all to come up to give you a goodnight kiss when they all get back."

"Do you think my Daddy will find your boyfriend's little brother?" enquired Frannie, as toothpaste dribbled down the side of her mouth.

Frannie displayed all the confidence of a young adult in her understanding of the present situation. Jules wiped the child's reddened face and reassured her that Musgrove would be found safe and sound.

At that moment, the telephone rang downstairs. "Wait here Frannie while I go and answer that," said Jules, as she clambered out of the bathroom and headed downstairs at a hares pace.

K2 was curled up asleep against the bottom stair and Jules had to change footing to avoid stepping on the great mountain dog with her size sevens. The noise of the tall teenager thudding onto the lower landing made K2 jump up and the brown and white bundle of fluff clambered up the stairs to escape the danger of the clumsy girl's footsteps.

Jules picked up the receiver and began to listen to the caller; it was Simon's mother. "Hi... Mrs. Chilcott - have you heard anything yet?" She enquired and listened hopefully for any good news about Musgrove's whereabouts.

Simon's mother proceeded to inform Jules that she had received a radio message from Chris, who was still waiting in the police van at the foot of the cliffs at Amley's Cove.

Chris had informed Mrs. Chilcott that the rescue party had found a cliffside cave down in Amley's Cove earlier. Tank had made his way back through the winding passageways from the Vortex of Souls to report back to Chris.

"Tank was very upset," said Mrs. Chilcott, as her voice trembled at the other end of the phone.

"So what did he have to say?" asked Jules, as she waited for a reply from Simon's mum.

"Well, my dear… some of the news is not very good at all," replied Mrs. Chilcott. "Chris has relayed to me a message from Tank… he has informed me that Bomber has been tragically killed!"

The stress was finally getting to Mrs. Chilcott, as she broke down and started to weep. Jules tried to calm the sobbing that flowed at the other end of the phone and the woman finally controlled her tears. The distressed woman continued to inform her son's girlfriend of the events leading up to Bombers death. She told Jules about the little Gatekeeper and the vortex, but nothing made any sense especially when Mrs. Chilcott spoke of Frannie's mum and aunt turning up from some far off world called Pathylon.

"What on earth are you going on about, Mrs. Chilcott?" said Jules. "You are obviously still upset about Muzzy's disappearance… now just take a deep breath and calm down."

Mrs. Chilcott repeated the details that Chris had reported to her. She informed Jules that all the necessary arrangements had been made to retrieve Bombers body from the cliffside caves. She had also been informed that Simon, Tank and the others had decided to enter the so-called vortex and travel into Pathylon to find Musgrove and Bradley who were stranded in the strange and mystical world.

"I find all this very difficult to comprehend," said Jules, as she sat down on the stool adjacent the telephone table in the hallway. "So how did Muzzy and Bradley get into this mess… and come to mention it how did Bradley's Mum and Aunt Vera get into this - Pathylon World?"

"Well… that's the other reason why I have phoned you my dear," said Mrs. Chilcott.

"You must stay out of the bathroom in Vera Penworthy's cottage."

"The bathroom?" questioned Jules. "But Bradley's little sister is up there cleaning her teeth as we speak."

"Then go and get her out of there!" shouted Musgrove's mum. "Tell her to stay away from the plughole!"

"What's wrong with the plughole?" replied the startled teenager, as she scrunched her pretty face.

"The plughole has a magic coin in it!" screamed Mrs. Chilcott. "Apparently... that's the way into Pathylon!"

Jules dropped the telephone handset and rushed up the stairs. As she reached the top flight, she witnessed a green ray of light and flashes of sparkling lasers blasting out of the entrance to the bathroom. Jules shouted out Frannie's name and hurled herself through the bright light and into the steam filled room. Jules turned to look down into the bathtub and as she focused on the plughole she could see the gold coin glowing. K2's fluffy tail was disappearing down the centre of the coin. "Oh my goodness!" shouted the shocked girl. "Simon's Mum was right!"

Jules quickly ran out of the bathroom before she too was sucked down the plughole. The trembling girl made her way back down the stairs to retrieve the telephone handset. "Mrs. Chilcott... you were right about the bathroom – and I was too late!" admitted the distraught teenager, as she choked from her excited exhaustion. The girl's voice then started to wither. "What shall I do?" she said quietly. "Frannie and the dog have disappeared down the plughole!"

It was now Mrs. Chilcott's turn to calm the situation. She told Jules to hang up and she would be straight round to Vera's cottage. Jules reset the receiver on top of the telephone and slumped to the floor. The confused seventeen-year-old burst into tears, as she hung her head forward in total disbelief and cupped her face in her hands.

Frannie and K2 had embarked upon an incredible journey down the drainpipe. The magical grobite in Aunt Vera's bathtub had claimed another two victims and had launched them down the swirling drains which would eventually led them to the strange new world.

Following their decision to journey into Pathylon, the rescue party led by Turpol had severely weakened the Vortex of Souls. During their transportation, the portal roof around the opening to the vortex had collapsed and it was only a matter of time before the swirling spiral at the centre of the vortex would burn out.

"Musgrove and Bradley must be found," reiterated P.C. Sharp. "We will have to move pretty fast if we are to return to our own world in time before the vortex self-destructs."

The odds were stacked heavily against them, especially as they had promised to help save Pathylon from the grip of the evil Varuna. Margaret was comforting Vera and reassuring her that their nightmare would soon be over and they could all get back to the reality of clotted cream and strawberry jam very soon.

The Gatekeeper had heard of the egg-shaped rock that marked the spot for a secret tunnel that led to the Shallock Tower, but he was unsure of its exact location. The busy dwarf made his way towards Patrick and P.C. Sharp. "It must be around here somewhere!" exclaimed the dwarf, as he scanned the vast area of land that surrounded the tower. "Meltor explained to me that the rock was near a very tall cretyre tree with a large hollow trunk."

"See those guards over there… who are they?" asked P.C. Sharp, as he pointed to the base of the tower in the distance.

"They look like Devonian Death Troops," replied Turpol, as he continued to search for the hollow tree. "That doesn't bode well for us… they are *the* elite soldiers of Pathylon - not to be messed with!"

"A bit like our SAS, back home," said Simon, who was closely followed by Tank. Both marines were still in shock following their colleague's untimely death.

"So how do you suppose we are going to get past them?" asked Patrick.

"We aren't," said Turpol. "We need to find the secret tunnel to avoid them," confirmed the Gatekeeper.

Simon and Tank moved away from the group and assessed the immediate area for any sign of a boulder that resembled an egg. Musgrove's brother moved sideways and noticed the long grass moving over to the right. He nudged Tank and the two marines moved slowly towards the area where the movement had come from. "Who goes there?" enquired Simon. "Show yourself!"

"Please don't hurt me," pleaded the girl, as she looked up at the tall soldiers.

Simon held out his hand to the pretty girl and she accepted his offer by pulling herself upwards out of the long grass. Patrick summoned Margaret, Vera and the others and they all rushed over to Simon and Tank to see what all the fuss was about.

Margaret pushed her way to the front of the group and approached the frightened girl. "What is your name, young lady?" She asked and placed her hand on the girl's shoulder.

"My name is Sereny Ugbrooke… but I haven't got time to explain - have you seen Grog?"

"Who is Grog?" asked Patrick.

Sereny briefly explained to the adults about orange-skinned lizard man and that he was supposed to be guarding the entrance to the secret tunnel. She told them that she had made her way back out to get his help. "The tower guards have captured Meltor and the two boys… and I too was taken - but I managed to wriggle free and was able to escape via the underground tunnel without being spotted."

"You mentioned Meltor," enquired Turpol. "You say he has been captured?"

"Yes," replied Sereny. "Along with Bradley and Muzzy," she added, as she picked at some grass seeds that had caught in her sleeve.

"Bradley!" exclaimed Margaret, as she grabbed her husband's arm. "He's alive!"

"Muzzy… he's alive too!" shouted Simon, as he turned to his uncle and clasped a tight-fist and punched the air.

It was such a relief to the group to know that Bradley and Musgrove were still alive, but they would have to move fast if they were to rescue them from the tower.

The commotion had now alerted the guards at the base of the tower and Tank moved swiftly. He ordered everyone to get down as two of the Death Troops were heading in their direction. The group heeded burly Scotsman's command and they all lay still and quiet in the long grass, as the guards neared their location.

Simon crawled over towards Tank and the two marines whispered instructions to each other. Simon then moved over to his uncle and informed him of their plan. Tank and Simon were going to flank the two Death Troops and they wanted someone to create some kind of distraction to allow them to carry out their maneuver.

The two marines crawled into position, one to the left and the other to the right just in front of the main group. The guards passed between Simon and Tank, as Aunt Vera stood up from the undergrowth. The Devonian Death Troops were startled and peered at the tubby old lady through their bright red battle helmets. When they spoke their voices appeared to amplify as if they were speaking through some kind of electronic device. "Stand still... don't move or you will be executed,'" said one of the troopers. "State your name... who are you?"

"Why, my dear... I'm Vera Penworthy," she said, very calmly. "...and if you would excuse me for a moment – I would like to make a suggestion?"

The Death Troops looked at each other and then back at the unusual female species. They waited impatiently for the strange woman to make her suggestion, but she never did. Aunt Vera's distraction was working perfectly, as Simon and Tank sprang from the grass so stealthily that the troopers did not have time to react. The marines pulled the helpless guards to the ground simultaneously, raising their right fists together and smacking them straight through their helmet visors. Both Death Troops reeled backwards in tandem and hit their heads on the ground.

"Elite troops... you're having a laugh!" boasted Tank. "Not a patch on our special forces back home... what do you think, Si?" he asked, turning to his fellow marine.

Simon smiled, as he raised the palm of his hand to slap against Tanks to commemorate their successful maneuver. The group then huddled together to plan out the next move.

"Right you lot... here's what we are going to do," said Simon. "Tank and I are going to put on these Death Troop suits and act as if we have taken two prisoners."

"What prisoners?" enquired Vera, as she adjusted the waistline of her pants to fit more comfortably around her huge bottom.

"The pretend prisoners will be my uncle here and you," ordered Simon and he pointed a confident finger at Patrick.

Tank added. "We will launch our attack from the outside, whilst the rest of you... headed by Turpol here, will counter a second attack from inside the tower - via the tunnel."

They all agreed the strategy and Sereny showed Turpol the location of the egg-shaped rock. Margaret, Vera, Sereny and the dwarf proceeded to make their way down the ladder and into the tunnel. They hurried along the winding passageway, as Sereny guided Turpol and the ladies to the base of the ladder that led up to the dungeon.

Now dressed in their newly acquired Death Troop uniforms, Simon and Tank led their prisoners towards the Shallock Tower. Musgrove's brother was fascinated with the metal implement that covered his mouth. "This must be the device that enables the Death Troops to speak with an alien voice."

Tank nodded then made Simon aware of the situation ahead. "Look Si... there's another eight of those death troops at the base of the tower."

As the two marines approached the tower, the armed guards gathered around the disguised soldiers and their prisoners. "We see you have captured some ugly mortals!" stated one of the troopers, as he inspected Patrick and P.C. Sharp.

"Let's have a closer look at them," demanded another one of the troops, as Tank stepped aside. The eight enemy fighters surrounded Simon and the prisoners. The two marines kcpt eye contact and readied themselves for arm-to-arm combat. All the intense training at Lympstone was about to be put to the test.

One of the guards reached out to prod Patrick's shoulder and started to tease him by calling him names. Bradley's father looked over at Tank and received the prompt he needed to start the combat. The heavily built Glaswegian clicked a button on the arm of his suit. Within seconds a panel opened on his right thigh and he drew out a laser gun. Tank aimed the gun at the guard who was still prodding Patrick.

'BLAAASSSSSSSTTT!'

A thin blue line of bright light pierced out of the laser gun, as it penetrated the guard's arm and severed the limb at the elbow joint.

More beams of bright lines blazed in parallel, as Simon drew his laser gun from its holder and shot three more of the Death Troops.

'BLAASSSSSTT!...BLAASSSSSTT!...BLAASSSSSTT!'

The lasers pierced the body armour of three more Death Troops in quick succession and their limp bodies fell to the ground like lead weights. They lay motionless on the ground and the molten metal on their chest plates smoked from the intense heat of the laser beams.

The four remaining Death Troops drew their weapons and started to fire at the intruders. Patrick and P.C. Sharp dived for cover whilst Tank and Simon continued to fill the air with blue streams of light. Two more of the Death Troops fell to Simon's accurate shooting, and then Tank hit the third with a shot to the leg. The remaining Death Trooper fired a multitude of shots at the two Marines before being sensationally felled by Simon's accurate laser blast, which penetrated the guard's battle helmet.

As the felled death trooper slumped sideways, he managed to fire a final shot at the two marines. A fatal beam of light struck Tank in his stomach and the burly marine jolted backwards. He landed heavily against the base of the tower with a massive thud. Tank ended up on his backside leant against the wall with blood oozing from his abdomen.

All eight Death Troops were finally destroyed; but at a price. The offensive unit had taken a casualty and Tank groaned, as he drifted in and out of consciousness. The lower front part of his battle helmet rested on his red armoured chest plate and blood leaked from the open wound in his ruptured stomach.

"Tank… Tank – are you okay?" shouted Simon.

Tank's head remained still as Patrick unclipped and removed the battle helmet that hid the Scotsman's whitened face.

P.C. Sharp knelt down next to Tank and tried to revive the heroic marine. "Come on old boy," said the police officer, as the blood continued to flow from the open wound. "Don't you dare die on us now!"

Tank opened his eyes briefly and gazed at the three onlookers. They appeared blurred as he tried to focus on his friend's worried faces.

"Och… it's no looking good, is it?" moaned Tank, in his usual broad Scottish accent. "I guess I'll be joining my mate Bomber pretty soooooooon……"

The final word slipped out of Tank's mouth and he gently passed away. He bowed his head for the last time, as his eyes gently closed. Simon took hold of his friend's hand and held it to his heart. The sadness in Simon's face gave Patrick and P.C. Sharp an immense feeling of loss. Both Tank and Bomber had fallen victim to the forces of evil that enshrouded this strange world. Simon quickly got to his feet and looked down at Tank. The trainee marine officer was very calm, totally the opposite to how he had reacted when Bomber lost his life at the hands of the Skeloyds.

"Let's get him away from the tower so we can lay his body somewhere safe," said P.C. Sharp.

The heroic rebels took hold of Tank and lifted their burly colleague over to some nearby bushes. Their timing could not have been more precise, as they hid out of sight, the sound of stamping hoofs approached and the royal entourage with Varuna perched arrogantly on the Royal Chariot paraded in front of them on its way to the Royal Palace.

Grog was still gagged and bound to Shatar's saddle. The koezard was being guided away from the royal party by two-foot soldiers towards the main entrance to the Shallock Tower. Simon and P.C. Sharp watched on with Patrick in amazement as the great orange amphibian was pulled from his mount and pushed hurriedly through the gothic arched doors and into the entrance hall of the tower. "Isn't that the orange amphibian that young Sereny had described?" suggested Patrick.

"Yes… that must be Grog," whispered P.C. Sharp.

"Yeah… and boy is he a *big un*!" replied Patrick.

Simon ignored them and knelt down over the dead frame of his fellow marine. He put his hand on Tanks gaping bloody wound and used the warm liquid that dripped from his fingers to smear two stripes on either side of his rugged face.

"What are you doing?" insisted the police officer.

"These marks will be my battle camouflage," said Simon proudly. "It's time to find our Muzzy and his young friend Bradley… it's also time to beat the living daylights out of that Varuna and his cronies!"

24

The Staff of Evil

The commotion between the Devonian Death Troops and the intruders at the base of the Shallock Tower had alerted the attention of the guards inside. One of them sent a message to Basjoo Ma-otz, who was located at the top of the tower. The High Priest from the Blacklands was conducting the interrogation of Meltor and the two boy humans who had been captured earlier.

Meltor was desperately trying to hide his hatred for Basjoo Ma-otz. The *Staff of Evil* that held the small skull from the sacrificial slaughter of his granddaughter was a painful memory that poured fuel on the flames that raged in Meltor's stomach. Basjoo Ma-otz wasn't making any attempt to hide the provoking staff and waved it in front of the rope-tied Galetian, as he carried out the interview.

"I have just been informed that more of your friends have been causing havoc at the base of the tower," stated Basjoo

Ma-otz, as he passed by and then moved behind Meltor. "It would seem that yet another futile attempt from your pathetic resistance movement is about to fail… still, I have no worries - my guards will find the remaining rebel scum and they will be crushed upon Varuna's return."

"You are a deluded fool Ma-Otz," stated Meltor, calmly.

"Silence you imbecile!" shouted Basjoo Ma-otz. "You are the fool… for I shall take all the credit and the glory for your demise – meanwhile, you will be left with nothing but your memories of a failed bid to overthrow our great King Varuna!"

Meltor shook his head and insisted. "Varuna will not be allowed to continue his masquerade… I shall make sure of that."

"I told you to be quiet… you Galetian piece of trash – be silent or I will strike you down in front of your little children!" threatened the angry Hartopian. "Then they will get what they deserve for helping you in your failed rebellion!"

"That's just about your style… Ma-otz – striking innocent children down when they are bound and gagged," replied Meltor. "I haven't forgiven you for killing my granddaughter and I shall torture you slowly for blatantly parading her skull in my face."

"Ha… ha - what utter gibberish," laughed Basjoo Ma-otz. "You are hardly in a position to defend yourself… are you?"

Meltor replied. "You are a Hartopian half-breed coward… it is not possible for you to beat me – especially as you were fathered by a primitive flax. You forget… a Galetian will never bow down to your kind - both you and Varuna will pay for your disloyalty to the true King Luccese!" Declared Meltor, as he looked over to where Bradley and Musgrove were sitting. The two boys were gagged and bound with rope to a wooden bench over by the large leaded window. The dull grey light from outside reflected on the window panes in a vain attempt add some brighter tones to large round stone clad room.

Suddenly, the main door to the room opened and in walked one of the tower guards. He handed over a scroll to Basjoo Ma-otz and stood to attention in anticipation of his master's response. The Hartopian pulled the ribbon and un-wrapped the paper, as he absorbed the contents of the message. He then looked at the guard and ordered him to un-gag the two boys. The scroll contained news of King Varuna's arrival in the Royal City of Trad and he had forwarded on a new prisoner to be restrained in the tower. "Ahhh... I see we have a new prisoner here to meet you!" announced Ma-otz, as he waved his arm at the guard. "Show him in!"

The guard left the room and returned with the prisoner. The eight-foot giant dipped his Krogon head under the doorway and pulled at the chains that secured his webbed hands.

Bradley spat out the loose remains of cotton thread from the gag and exclaimed. "Grog... you're safe!"

Meltor and the boys were unaware of Grog's recent dual with his rival Zule back in his native Krogonia and could not understand why the lizard man was smiling so much. "It's good to see you all again, my friends," stated the Krogon.

"Well... isn't this quaint," taunted Basjoo Ma-otz. "The helpless *band of outlaws* are having a quaint little reunion... now tell me - how many more of you are out there plotting your pathetic plans to overthrow Varuna?"

"I'll answer that," said Grog. "You've definitely got a problem Ma-otz... why don't you take a look out of the window."

The Hartopian walked over to the window and looked out towards the outer boundaries Trad. Ma-otz was taken aback by what he saw. Tens of thousands of lizard men were progressing in unified ranks towards the royal city. They were regimented into parallel lines of army battalions, as row upon row of Krogon warriors marched towards the capital under the dark grey skies that still enshrouded Pathylon.

"This can't be happening!" shouted Basjoo Ma-otz. "The Krogons are supposed to be Varuna's allies!"

Grog proceeded to tell everyone in the room about his victory over Zule on the Flaclom Straits. He also explained how Harg and Varuna had failed to adhere to the ancient Krogon rituals and instead they had decided to banish him to the Shallock Tower. This had incensed the Krogon masses and had resulted an uprising from the East.

"The Krogons appear to be unhappy with your evil King," said Meltor. "Release us now and we may spare your life once the true King... *Luccese* - is reinstated to the Pathylian throne!"

Basjoo Ma-otz was confused and did not know what to do for the best. He did not believe that Meltor would spare his life and so the Hartopian half-breed began to panic. He picked up his *Staff of Evil* and brushed past the guard, as he turned to face Meltor. "I promise you... old Galetian – I will have my revenge!" He retorted and then turned quickly to hurry out of the room, as Meltor rose to his feet.

Meltor chose not to pursue the coward but instead ordered the guard to unchain Grog and then release the two boys. He did not hesitate and obeyed the respected High Priest's request, as the temporary chains that bound the Krogon's wrists were unfastened.

The plan had worked and the heroic Krogon loosened the ropes that secured the Galetian High Priest. "I think that's the last we'll see of Ma-otz," laughed Grog sarcastically.

"I doubt it... I still have an old score to settle with that murderous coward," replied Meltor. "He is probably on his way back to the Blacklands... but it is a small region and I will hunt him down - I promise you that!"

"I'm sorry to hear about your granddaughter," said Bradley. "That was a terrible thing to have happened."

"Thank you Bradley," replied the High Priest. "Your words are comforting... but they do not take away the pain that I carry inside me – I can assure you my granddaughter's blood will not have been spilt in vain... Ma-otz *will* suffer for his unforgivable act!"

"I wouldn't like to be in his shoes!" declared Musgrove. "When are you going to go after him?"

Meltor made his way over to the window and looked out towards the Royal Palace. "Later... first we must release Luccese and confront Varuna – hunting down the coward Ma-otz can wait!"

The Gatekeeper guided Margaret, Vera and Sereny out of the dungeon and into the lower floors of the Shallock Tower. They made their way through the underground passages and into the great entrance hall, which was now deserted. At that moment the heavy oak studded doors that secured the tower from the outside were forced open. In scrambled an aggressive looking Simon closely followed by Patrick and P.C. Sharp.

The two groups of friends were glad to see each other. Patrick rushed over to Margaret and gave her a reassuring hug. She looked over Patrick's shoulder and gave a broad smile as if to award a look of comfort to everyone. Margaret surveyed the group and noticed the absence of Simon's fellow marine. "Where's Tank?" she asked and released herself from Patrick's protective embrace.

"I'm afraid it's bad news dear... Tank is dead," replied Patrick, as he looked over to Simon who was explaining to Turpol about the bloody fight with Devonian Death Troops. "We lost the poor lad during a bitter scrap with some guards at the base of the tower."

"Oh, that is so terrible," said Margaret, as she held either side of her face with the insides of her slender fingers. "Poor Tank... so young - that's such a tragedy!"

Aunt Vera made her way over to her sister and brother-in-law, as she put her arm around Margaret to comfort her. "Have you seen our Bradley yet, Patrick?"

"No, not yet Vera... but according young Sereny here, he must be with Musgrove and Meltor on the upper floors - let's get up there and find them," suggested Patrick, as he set off in the direction of the great winding staircase, which connected the entrance hall to the first floor of the tower.

Margaret, Vera, Sereny and Simon followed Patrick up the staircase whilst P.C. Sharp and Turpol stayed in the great hall to guard the entrance, just in case any of Varuna's supporters decided to make a last desperate attempt to storm the tower.

Meanwhile on the upper floors, Bradley and Musgrove followed closely behind Meltor and Grog, as they made their way along the corridors. They descended down the stone staircases that led to the lower floors within the Shallock Tower. The rebels were carrying out a systematic search of the tower, trying to locate the secured cells that housed King Luccese, Queen Vash and Pavsik.

Grog ran ahead of the others and made his way down the passageway that led to the cells on the fourth floor. Because of his great size, he was careful not catch his head on the underside of the corridor. As he reached the end of the passageway, a small figure moved out of a darkened alcove and stood in front of the giant amphibian. Grog focused his large reptile eyes in an attempt to determine who the small creature was that had startled him. As his eye's finally adjusted to the dim light and he recognized the intruder standing in the corridor. It was Varuna's cowardly lieutenant and the nervous looking Wartpig froze, as the Krogon approached.

Dergan stood his ground, shaking as he drew his sword. He held his outstretched weapon in front of him and warned Grog not to move any closer. Meltor, Bradley and Musgrove finally caught up with their Krogon friend and stopped about six feet behind the orange warrior. As Dergan threatened his position, Grog pulled out his sword in readiness for combat and the stand-off continued. The petrified Wartpig looked the giant lizard-like creature up and down and he stood in bewilderment because he knew his small frame did not stand a chance against the huge amphibian.

Meltor shouted out a controlled warning to Dergan. "Don't do anything stupid… you are out-numbered and the rule of your evil leader is about to end – now put down your weapon!"

Meltor guided Dergan's attention to the left, towards a narrow opening in the tower wall, used by archers to defend the tower against would-be attackers. "Look at the thousands of Krogon warriors and Devonian noblemen standing side by side… your time is up – now please be sensible and put down your weapon!"

Bradley stood forward and confirmed Meltor's demand. "They have surrounded the Royal Palace…Varuna is finished – lay down your sword!"

The Wartpig laughed at the boy's outburst and kept his sword outstretched, as he turned his head to look out of the opening in the outer wall. He could see the Krogon army and Devonian noblemen surrounding the Royal Palace, just as the young human had described. "I guess you have a point… the odds against me are pretty slim," he replied, sarcastically. "It looks as if your rebel alliance as gathered some overwhelming support!"

Just then, everyone's attention was taken by a loud scream of delight that emanated from behind the group at the far end of the passageway. A familiar voice shouted out to her son. "Bradley… you're alive and safe!"

Bradley turned around to see his mother running towards him, her arms outstretched ready to welcome him. He was literally crushed, as his mother's grip took a firm hold. He could just about make out his father's image through her scrunched-up clothing, which had enveloped his face. He felt a little embarrassed in front of his friends, by the affection he was receiving from his over protective parents.

Lieutenant Dergan watched in bemusement, as the family reunions continued and his sword was still raised in readiness for Grog's next move. Musgrove saw brother appear behind Patrick in hot pursuit and moved away from Meltor to meet him along the corridor. "Hello, mate!" said Simon, as he hugged his young brother and scuffed up his hair with his large military hand. "Am I glad to see you in one piece… our Mum is so worried back home."

"Eh... I like the suit, Bro!" exclaimed Musgrove and pressed the button on Simon's arm, which opened the thigh holster that contained the death troop laser pistol.

"Ah... it's a long story, Muzzy - I'll tell you all about it later," replied the marine.

The Wartpig bawled out his disapproval at being ignored. "Stop all this family reunion nonsense... I still have my sword and I am still willing to fight for Varuna!" yelled Dergan, as he lifted his weapon aloft and took up a pathetic fighting stance in front of Grog.

"You have proved your loyalty to Varuna, little Wartpig... now do what we asked and put down your weapon, before you get hurt," said Grog, calmly.

Dergan was still shaking and displayed signs of accepting the Krogons request by lowering his weapon. He thought back to when he had been ordered by Varuna to set up camp, whilst pursuing Meltor and the renegades. He recalled how the evil dictator had insulted him by calling him *an insolent, incompetent hoffen faced fool.* The resentment boiled in Dergan's stomach, he hated being insulted and the thought of his King's derogatory remarks made him lower his sword further. He looked into Grog's eyes and started to hand over his sword. "So be it... I surrender to you, Krogon!"

Grog lowered his guard and reached out for the weapon, as he walked slowly towards the Wartpig. Then Dergan suddenly had a flash back to the beheaded scout under his command that had been slaughtered by Meltor on the banks of the River Klomus. The thought of one of his soldiers being killed filled him with rage and with a sudden change of heart he raised his sword again and thrust his blade into the top of Grog's left thigh. He pulled back his weapon and witnessed green slime gush out of the injured Krogon. The giant amphibian dropped his sword and reached down to control the flow of emerald blood that oozed from the wound.

Meltor rushed forward with his sword aloft, but the High Priest could not prevent the next fatal blow. The Wartpig forced his weapon into Grog's neck, as the Galetian thrust his blade into Dergan's chest. Simon simultaneously drew his death troop laser pistol and pulled the trigger, as Meltor struck. He fired an electric blue light that pierced the Wartpig's face. The power of the laser penetrated his forehead and the contents of his skull splattered against the wall. Lieutenant Dergan let out a final squeal and then slumped to the stone floor like a heavy weight.

Sereny released a piercing scream that echoed down the passageway and she ran over to where Grog had fallen. His huge body lay motionless and the deep cut had severed the nerves around his spinal cord. His great frame slumped against the cold stone, as the distraught girl fell on top of the Krogon warrior. She tried desperately to revive him by smashing her clenched fists onto his heaving chest. She stopped pounding and threw her arms around his neck, as her tight blonde ringlets draped over his face. "Please don't die, Grog… please don't die!" she pleaded, as tears poured down her cheeks. "Remember, you are my true hero… you must not die!"

Grog struggled to breath and tried to move his large head, but the gash at the back of his neck was too deep. He looked into Sereny's eyes and smiled at his young human friend. "Don't be sad my sweet little angel… everything is going to be fine," he replied, in a soft croaky voice. "Always remember me as your *tangerine man!*" The giant lizard man tried to clear his throat and choked, as he slouched back then dropped his head for the last time.

Bradley and Musgrove aborted their family reunions and joined Sereny at Grog's side. All three children held onto the gentle Krogon giant. Musgrove and Sereny wept uncontrollably, as Bradley held back his tears in an attempt to retain control of the tragic situation. He stood up and turned to the others who were now gathered around helplessly. "We have lost a true friend... Grog will be a great loss to Pathylon - he was a true Champion and would have made a wonderful High Priest for Krogonia!" Bradley bent back down and leant over to whisper into the dead Krogons ear. "Do not worry, Grog... I will protect Sereny and no harm will come to her - I promise you my dear friend."

Margaret and Patrick approached their son to comfort him. Sereny let go of Grog and fell into Bradley's arms, as she continued to cry uncontrollably.

Musgrove was stunned. He could not come to terms with the fact that Grog was dead. The jealous teenager was also not happy at the sight of Sereny in Bradley Baker's embrace once again. It was an immature thought, after all he was three years his junior, but he felt threatened by his new friend's responsible signs of maturity in handling the girl's grief.

Musgrove shed the thought and quickly got to his feet. He walked over to join his brother and put his arms around the sibling marine, but Simon was unable to offer any comfort to his younger brother. Instead, Simon released his hold and addressed the group of mourners. He hoped to ease the pain in a more direct way... by making a statement of revenge in response to the Krogons death.

"Tank and Bomber have sacrificed their lives to this cause... now we have lost Grog too!" declared Simon. "We will avenge their deaths by bringing Varuna to justice – he is trapped inside the Royal Palace and we need to smoke him out!"

"Not so fast soldier," said Meltor, as he held onto Simon's arm. "There has been enough killing for one day... it's time to bring Varuna to justice – but it will be up to King Luccese to decide his fate."

"Then it's time to release King Luccese!" declared Musgrove, as he offered his vocal support to his brother.

Meltor released his gentle grip on Simon's arm and made his way over to the door, which was blocked by Dergan's dead body. The strong Galetian dragged the Wartpig to one side and prized open the door to reveal a row of cells, one of which must be imprisoning the King and Queen Vash.

Everyone followed Meltor into the chamber and the Galetian systematically forced open each of the cell doors by kicking them one by one. All the rooms appeared empty until they approached the last two.

The first door was forced open and out stumbled a weary Pavsik, who eventually fell into Meltor's arms from sheer exhaustion. "It's good to see you again, my old friend," he sighed, as Meltor lowered the weak Devonian nobleman to the floor.

Vera rushed over to pick up a nearby vase of water and placed the vessel against Pavsik's mouth. He began to drink the precious liquid and thanked the tubby female for her kindness. She acknowledged Pavsik's kind remarks and then looked over to where Meltor was standing. The grey rays of light that reflected from the window cast a silhouette against the wall portraying the image of Meltor's handsome facial features and Vera recognized them instantly. "Well I'll be damned... if it isn't my fisherman friend - Old Mac!"

Meltor turned his head for a moment and acknowledged her recognition of him. The Galetian quickly glanced his reddened face away from the woman's stare, as the last cell door was forced open from the inside. King Luccese appeared in the doorway followed by his beautiful Queen. They had finally emerged from the dark chamber that had been their home, whilst Varuna had been extending his evil tyranny over Pathylon. The couple still looked very regal and stood very tall. They had not lost any of their royal prestige and everyone bowed as the monarchs moved towards them.

Meltor knelt, as he took the right hand of his King into his and kissed the royal glove. King Luccese placed his left hand on the Galetian's head. "I knew I could rely on you, Meltor... you are a brave servant and you have proven not only to be a good – but a *great* Samaritan."

Meltor looked up and smiled. He rose to his feet and they both embraced each other. They patted each other's robes continuously, as they laughed with sheer relief and joy.

Queen Vash approached Margaret, Vera and Sereny. "A special thank you for your help... I am particularly proud that some females have taken part mine and my husband's release – I admire your bravery."

Margaret told the Queen that it was an honour to take part in the rescue and she explained how they had journeyed into Pathylon in search of her son. Vash was impressed with her story and then Sereny caught her eye. With the young girl also involved, the Queen felt it was a great honour to have the three females appointed as chosen ones.

It was not long before King Luccese summoned all the male members of the alliance to meet in the upper chamber of the Shallock Tower. From the top floor they could see the Royal Palace clearly and it would make an excellent control point, to oversee the joint Krogon-Devonian raid on the palace, in order to capture Varuna. "Do you know the whereabouts of Harg and Flaglan?" asked Luccese, as he turned to Meltor.

"We are not sure, your excellency," replied the High Priest. "It is possible that they may have taken refuge in the royal palace with Varuna."

"Then this could work to our advantage... I don't particularly want our armies to rush into the palace - I would prefer to take Varuna alive," said Luccese. "If Flaglan is in the palace... I would expect her to switch her allegiance and turn against Varuna as soon she realizes I have taken back control of Pathylon again - after all, we are all aware that her loyalty only lies with the person on the winning side... don't we Meltor?"

Meltor awarded his King a laugh of approval. It was good to see Luccese stepping back into his royal leadership with such panache and control. Luccese suggested that everyone in the Shallock Tower get some rest, for it was going to be a long night and he hoped the dawning of a new morning would also bring Flaglan to her senses.

25

Trapped in the Royal Palace

Meltor issued a message to the Krogon warriors and the Devonian noblemen, who were waiting patiently and still surrounding the Royal Palace. They were ordered to resist an attack without first receiving necessary the authority of the King. The angry masses reluctantly accepted the order and the skies transformed into another blackened night; as they settled down to make their camps around the perimeter of the palace.

Varuna's multiple organs were pounding beneath his ribcage, as he stared from behind a pair of velvet curtains that draped the tall leaded window at the far end of the palace ballroom. He witnessed the enormity of the revenge seeking crowds that now threatened his control over Pathylon.

The camp fires flickered below, as the Hartopian moved away from the window and he started to pace up and down the full length of the royal ballroom. He visualized General Eidar also pacing up and down the command bridge aboard the great iceberg ship. The thought of failing the Freytorian commander incensed Varuna and he spoke out loud. "I will be the laughing stock of Freytor... I must quickly think of a plan to overturn the rebellion and maintain the curse." He declared and continued to march with his paws clenched behind his back, as Harg and Flaglan sat at the far end of the elegantly decorated room. Varuna looked up at the ornate ceilings and displayed an evil snarl of razor sharp teeth. "Why did I listen to you, Harg?" He growled. "Why... why - why?"

Harg stayed silent. He knew if the battle between Grog and Zule had not taken place there would have been more than enough guards at the Shallock Tower to prevent the release of Luccese.

Varuna stared at Harg again and aimed a vile retribution at the cowering Krogon leader. "Look what you've done... why was I stupid enough to agree for you to hold your damn contest in Krogonia?" he snarled. "Your attempt to pacify your people by insisting on rituals and traditions has back-fired on you... the Krogon masses have risen against you Harg – and that has put us all in danger!"

"I am truly sorry, my lord," replied Harg.

"Silence you fool!" shouted Varuna. "Grog has become a hero and your simple lizard men have sided with him... we don't stand a chance of getting out of here – and it's all your fault!"

The evening was drawing to a close and Harg turned away from Varuna. He knew he had failed his leader and he made his way over to a nearby chair to rest his weary body. Earlier, he had heard from a Royal Palace guard that Grog had been killed and he knew full well that all this uprising could have been avoided in the first place. Should Varuna get to know about the lizard man's death, he would be in big trouble, for there was nowhere for him to run. It was bad enough that Grog was to become a Krogon hero; let alone a martyr. Harg was in a no win situation. He either suffered at the hands of his own Krogon army that surrounded the palace or face the wrath of Varuna when he found out about the death of Grog. It was going to be a long night for Harg and the night was certain to pass slowly.

As the dawn broke, the thick grey clouds hung even lower over the Royal City. The Krogon and Devonian armies started to stir outside the palace and the noise of metal against wood could be heard, as the united armies prepared their weapons in readiness for an order from Luccese.

Harg had been awake for some time and he had come to a decision on how to handle Varuna. The old Krogon leader felt he must confide with Flaglan about the fate of Grog. He moved over to where the sorceress lay and nudged her gently then whispered. "Wake up Flaglan."

The beautiful High Priestess opened her eyes and starred at the leathered snout of the heavy-breathing Krogon. She tried to focus her left eye by keeping the other shut and muttered. "Move away now or I will turn your fat wrinkled face into a block of stone," threatened the sorceress.

"I have a plan," declared Harg, as his stale breath turned Flaglan's face in the opposite direction.

"Go away Harg… you'll get us both killed" she insisted.

"I had hoped that you would side with me and together we can overpower Varuna," whispered Harg. "I believe Grog is dead… if Varuna finds out – he'll kill us both!"

"What are you two whispering about?" enquired Varuna, as he approached Harg and Flaglan.

"Nothing, my lord," quivered Harg. "Just talking about the weather… I wasn't aware that you were awake!"

"Do you honestly believe I could have slept, whilst thousands of your frog warriors sat at my doorstep…I haven't slept all night - you idiot!" snarled Varuna. "And I know what you are up to… you are plotting against me, aren't you?' he declared, as he drew his sword and placed the blade tip beneath Flaglan's delicate chin.

Flaglan was shaking and her chest heaved, as she breathed nervously. Varuna could not help but notice the movement of the slender curves of the beautiful sorceress and he reached out his hairy paw with sharp talons fully exposed.

Harg noticed that Varuna's aggressive attention span had lapsed for a moment and he seized his opportunity. The overweight Krogon pulled out his sword and brought it crashing down onto Varuna's outstretched wrist. The evil Hartopian reeled away in agony, clenching his dismembered limb. He frantically pulled the cape of his dark cloak around the severed stub to stem the flow of the bright yellow blood that gushed from the horrific injury. Harg dropped the blade, as the ailing Varuna roared. "Arghhhhhhhh… you Krogon traitor - I will kill you for this!"

At that moment the ballroom doors opened and in rushed six palace guardsmen. The sentries were still unsure of their allegiance and had heard the commotion so they had decided to enter the room without permission.

Varuna was quick to react. "Guards… arrest the Krogon – he has severed my hand!" he shouted, as they stared at the Hartopian's injury and noticed how weak the evil King had become. "Well… don't just stand there – arrest these vermin!"

The guardsmen looked over to Flaglan and Harg but took no action against the two nervous traitors. Instead they refocused their attention on the injured Hartopian. The opportunity had presented itself to seize the weakened creature and show allegiance to their true King. Two of the sentries linked arms with Varuna, whilst a third palace guardsman voiced the arrest. "In the name of our true King Luccese... I arrest you for high treason."

As the guards steered Varuna away Flaglan bent down to pick up his severed paw and shouted. "Hey... Varuna!"

The frustrated Hartopian struggled to release himself from the guardsmen's grip and turned around to face the beautiful sorceress. *"What do want now... witch?"* he snarled.

Flaglan threw the blood-soaked limb towards Varuna and offered some calm words of advice. "I thought you might need a hand!"

Harg and Flaglan burst into concurrent laughter, as Varuna kicked out his leg and sent the severed hand flying into the hanging crystal chandelier that adorned the ceiling of the great ballroom. The seething Hartopian was then led out of the room screaming abuse at the radiant sorceress and her bloated accomplice.

Harg and Flaglan's laughter was short lived, as more guards arrived and escorted them from the confines of the palace ballroom. They were led down the ornate staircase and ushered outside to join Varuna in the courtyard. A chorus of loud cheers of relief and anger were aimed at the Hartopian and the two disgraced High Priests. All the palace guards and servants crowded around the deposed evil King, as he was led towards the citadel gates.

The heavy chains that held the drawbridge were lowered and the Hartopian, with his head held low, was pushed out of the palace grounds and across the moat bridge to the cheers and waving of weapons by the waiting hoards of Krogons and noblemen.

Harg and Flaglan had their hands bound tightly behind their backs and sixteen sentries flanked them as they followed close behind the disgraced Varuna. Both feared for their futures, as they made their way towards a hay wagon harnessed by two hoffen. The primitive form of transport was ready and prepared to take them the few hundred yards towards the Shallock Tower where the decision of their fate awaited them.

Varuna was ushered separately into a waiting chariot and its snorting hoffen were immediately spurred on and followed closely by the hay wagon carrying Flaglan and Harg. Half a dozen Krogon warriors mounted on koezard formed an entourage and escorted the three traitors. The prisoners were now ready be transported to the base of the tower to answer to Luccese - their true King.

Queen Vash joined her husband and they both stepped out onto the balcony at the top of the Shallock Tower to acknowledge their jubilant public. Bolts of lightning sparked angrily between the clouds in the skies above that were still darkened by the evil curse. A role of thunder cast a solemn reminder of the Freytorian General's anger, but the crowds cheered and saluted the appearance of their true King and Queen.

The large gathering of Pathylian folk now focused their attention on Varuna, Harg and Flaglan, as their wagons approached the base of the tower. The cheers soon turned to jeers, as the three traitors were escorted towards the entrance. Varuna lowered his head to avoid the hostility of the crowd, which grew more incensed at the sight of their King's enemy cowering aboard the chariot. A small section of the crowd were showing signs of mischief and to avoid the chance of a fracas, the entrance doors to the tower were opened and a temporary sanctuary was offered to the nervous prisoners until their sentencing commenced.

Meltor joined Luccese on the upper balcony and they could be seen entering into a deep conversation. Two important and influential decisions needed to be made by Luccese. Firstly, the King had to decide on the level of punishment to be instilled upon Varuna, Flaglan and Harg. Secondly, as Meltor had reminded Luccese, he had to make a decision about the fate of the Freytorian Prisoners. Now that the true King had at last been reinstated, the curse over Pathylon still had to be lifted. The granite figures, which still adorned the hooded doors in the Forbidden Caves, would need to be released in order to dispel the evil that still enshrouded the land.

The royal party welcomed Bradley's family and friends onto the balcony. They were encouraged to wave at the crowds and were rewarded with rapturous applause from the grateful populous. The members of royal party then turned to go back inside the upper chamber. Luccese acknowledged Meltor's request to free the Freytorian Prisoners and suggested that the Galetian gather the *twelve* chosen ones together once he had dealt with Varuna, Flaglan and Harg.

"I trust I can leave this to you, Meltor?" asked Luccese.

"Yes, your highness," replied the humble Galetian.

"Excellent... then we will deal with the matter later," said Luccese. "I think the time has come to make our way down the tower to confront our treacherous enemies and inform them of their punishments."

"I'm all for that!" agreed Simon, as he patted Luccese on the royal shoulder. King Luccese smiled and gestured with a friendly nod at Simon, then looked away again.

Meltor walked over to the marine. "Can I suggest that patting the King of Pathylon on the shoulder is not a good way of showing respect?"

Simon agreed and with a very red face approached the King. "Your highness... please accept my sincere apologies – I can assure you I meant you no disrespect."

"My dear Simon your apology is not needed... you are a brave young man and I understand your enthusiasm and eagerness to see Varuna punished - especially after witnessing three of your good friends die during this arduous campaign to secure my release."

"Thank you, sir...it has been an honour!" replied Simon.

Luccese continued. "In fact, as a mark of respect... I have already given instructions to the tower guards to make all the necessary arrangements for Tank's body to lie in state until an opportunity arises to send him back to his own world."

Simon bowed his head, as the King and Queen marched out through the door of the upper chamber and into the passageway, which led to the staircase. Their entourage quickly followed them, as Bradley and Musgrove deliberated the grandioso of the event.

"It's all getting a bit exciting," whispered Musgrove, as he leant over to Bradley. "The suspense is killing me."

"Yeah... and I'm looking forward to the next bit," replied Bradley. "I can't wait to meet Varuna and see the look on his face when King Luccese imposes his sentence."

Word was sent to the tower guards that the royal entourage was making their way down the Shallock Tower. Varuna, Harg and Flaglan were taken back outside and re-introduced to the hostility of the waiting masses, which were becoming even more restless. At last the King and his royal party finally completed their descent of the tower and congregated inside the great entrance hall.

At that moment a fanfare sounded from the courtyard in front of the main entrance to the Shallock Tower. King Luccese, accompanied by Queen Vash, appeared at the entrance followed by Meltor, Bradley and the others. Everyone gathered round and they all stared at the disgraced Hartopian, as he continued to hold on to his severed wrist. Varuna's black robe was now well stained by the yellow sticky fluid that had oozed from the wound.

Luccese approached Varuna and officially stripped him of the Pathylian Crown by removing his skull-bearing headdress. The true King then bestowed upon him the same fate, as he had to endure whilst the Hartopian was in temporary control of Pathylon. Varuna was sentenced to spend the rest of his years in the Shallock Tower.

A great vocal harmony emanated from the crowd, as they cheered the Hartopian's demise. Varuna was not fazed by the sudden uproar and he stayed remarkably calm. He had not been searched properly and he still had a battle sabre hidden beneath his great black robes. The evil traitor was not prepared to spend the rest of his days in the tower and felt for his trusty sword. He could fight with either hand so the wound to his severed right wrist would not hinder his ability to wield his sharp blade.

Bradley had noticed the movement in Varuna's cloak and alerted Musgrove's attention to it. He carefully bent down and picked up a wooden batten that was acting as a temporary support for one of the tower entrance doors. Both boys watched in horror as the Hartopian pulled out the weapon and took his first swing at Luccese. He missed by a few inches and with wrath in his eyes pulled back his blade for a second time.

Bradley appeared from behind Meltor and the brave boy ran up the Galetian's frame like a gymnasium horse. He launched himself into the air and brought the wooden batten parallel above the King's head just as Varuna's sabre crashed downwards. The timber was severed in half like paper by the Hartopian's jagged weapon and Bradley's lightning reflexes ensured the sword deflected away from the King.

Still in mid-flight Bradley dropped one half of the timber and continued his path through the air, as he fell downwards. He then swung the other half of the baton around and hit Varuna on the snout. The Hartopian's head jolted backwards and he landed heavily on the ground.

Bradley fell awkwardly and Varuna quickly regained his balance then lifted his sword again with the cruel intent of penetrating the boy's chest. At that moment Meltor drew his weapon and forced the attacker to stumble back by twisting his trusty blade around his out-stretched sword. The Galetian then span around completely and lifted his leg high in the air, as his white cloak flowed in formation with his body. He kicked out the base of his foot under Varuna's chin and forced the Hartopian into a backwards somersault and sent him sprawling to the floor. His sword was released, as he hit the ground and Bradley rushed over to kick the weapon away from the reeling Hartopian's searching hand.

Several guards jumped on Varuna and dragged him away kicking and screaming. "You will all regret this… I promise you!" warned the Hartopian. "I will escape your wretched tower one day and I will find you all and kill you… Luccese, watch your back!" shouted Varuna, as he was finally led away by Pavsik and the guards, through the entrance doors and into the tower.

Luccese offered his thanks to Meltor. "Your heroic performance was incredible my Galetian friend!" he praised and held out his hand to the High Priest.

Meltor was out of breath following the incident but was quick to pass the King's kind words on to Bradley. "Don't thank me, my lord," he replied. "It was Bradley Baker's quick thinking that saved your life."

Luccese looked at the young hero and offered him his hand. "Your actions were admirable and I am forever in your debt... you displayed great courage - I am grateful to you!"

Bradley was also quite breathless after the ordeal and was still shaking nervously. He bowed his head and accepted the King's praise with great pride. "It is a pleasure to serve you, sire!"

Musgrove smiled at Bradley's stately pose and ran over to his friend to congratulate him. "Nice one, Brad!" he said, patting his friend on the back. "You're making a bit of a name for yourself in these parts... aren't you?"

"Yeah... so it seems – I don't know what came over me," replied Bradley calmly, as he reflected on his selfless act of bravery.

"Well... I guess you've probably been acting out most of those moves in the shower back home - from what you've told me about the imaginary *Emperor Thorag*!" laughed Musgrove. "Good to see you put some of them into practice at last!"

"Very funny!" replied Bradley, as his face turned a slight crimson colour and he simulated a light punch on his friend's upper arm. "You're very funny... not!"

26

The Missing Chosen Ones

It was not long before Pavsik reappeared from the Shallock Tower. He approached Luccese and assured the King that Varuna was now safely locked away and he handed him the key to the cell.

The King stared at the rusty key for a moment then offered it to Bradley. "Here my young friend... you hang on to this for me for a little while," said Luccese, as he recomposed himself.

"My pleasure, Sire!" replied Bradley, as the King turned his attention to Harg and Flaglan.

"Now what am I to do with you two?" teased Luccese, as he marched back and forth in front of them. "You haven't exactly set a great example to the High Priesthood... have you?"

Both Harg and Flaglan shook their heads from side to side and then looked at the ground in disgrace. The King had a dilemma for he needed to fill three vacancies within the High

Priesthood - t*he Blacklands, the Forest of Haldon and Krogonia*. He was still contemplating the reinstatement of Flaglan to the great forest across the River Klomus. Luccese felt in his heart that the beautiful temptress had been led astray by Varuna. The King believed she had learnt her lesson and that the sorceress would now stay loyal to him.

Everyone was waiting with baited breath as to the fate of the two traitors. Luccese was finally ready to make his decisions and he turned to the Flaglan. "My dear, you..." the King paused for a moment. "...*you* especially have disappointed me - however, I still retain an admiration for your leadership qualities." He paused again and then added. "Prior to your recent loss of direction... your record within the forest region has been exemplary and I am prepared to reinstate you as the High Priestess for the Forest of Haldon region."

There was a chorus of stunned gasps within the crowd and Flaglan looked shocked. "Thank you my lord... I welcome your decision and I will not let you down again – I promise!"

King Luccese smiled and placed his royal hand on the slender shoulder of the sorceress. "Just remember, Flaglan... you must always fight for the good of Pathylon and its people - there is no place in our world for those who promise rewards from their evil actions."

The High Priestess looked very relieved and there was a mixed response from the crowd in reaction to her release. The many thousands of Tree Elves, who had journeyed across the river to Trad from the Forest of Haldon to witness the proceedings, sounded out their appreciation by blowing a chorus of thanks from their handmade cretyre-horns. The tree dwellers continued their display of approval by cheering, as

Flaglan's ride was brought around to the front of the tower and she mounted the koezard.

Luccese uttered a parting comment. "Serve the forest region well sorceress... I shall be keeping a close eye on you - now don't let your people down for they deserve better!"

"You have my word, my lord," replied Flaglan. "Be assured, I will serve the great forest and its people well!" She concluded and pulled at the reigns, as the Koezard's head turned in the direction of the River Klomus. Flaglan kicked her heels into her mount and it reared up before galloping off, as her delicate clothing flowed in the wind. The sorceress disappeared into the distance, as the attending Tree Elves started to disperse in a controlled manner and made their way slowly from the Shallock Tower proceedings.

The rest of the crowd, made up of Devonians and Krogons, now focused their attention on the royal entourage as the King turned to Harg. The fat bloated Krogon wrestled with the chains that now bound his hands and feet. Pavsik had shackled the aging lizard man as a precaution, following Varuna's surprise attack on Luccese.

Bradley was intrigued with the way the King had handled Flaglan and he spoke quietly to his father. "What do you think the King will do to Harg?"

"I don't know, Son," replied Patrick, as Luccese paced in front of the embarrassed Krogon leader. "However, I can't see him letting Harg go free as well... that would surely give out the wrong message to everyone!"

"Shusssshhhh!" hushed Aunt Vera, as she elbowed her brother-in-law in the ribs. "King Luccese is about to speak... have some respect Patrick."

Musgrove moved closer to Bradley and whispered in his ear. "I think your Aunt Vera is taking this entire royalty lark a bit too seriously."

"Yeah, I think you're right there mate… you should see her back home during the Queen's speech on Christmas Day," replied Bradley.

The two boys started to giggle and were quickly reprimanded by Aunt Vera again, as Patrick nursed his rib cage. Their conversation was interrupted by the deathly silence of the crowd, as King Luccese had finally reached his decision about the Krogon's fate and he stood in front of Harg.

The populous mumbled in excited anticipation, as Luccese leant across and delivered a brief message in the Krogon's ear. The King then stood back and faced the crowd, as Harg's mane head of horns dropped and his eyes looked down at the ground. A sullen reply was emitted from his mouth. "Very well my lord!"

The deposed Krogon leader was led away and immediately ushered onto a Devonian patrol chariot, as Luccese informed Meltor of his decision.

A loud murmur started to spread through the gathering masses. The mumblings escalated into a full-scale debate, especially within the Krogon sections, as they surmised what fate had been cast upon their disgraced High Priest.

The unrest between the lizard men continued, as Patrick moved forward and touched Meltor on the arm. "Where are they sending Harg?"

Bradley interrupted. "Dad… don't put Meltor in a difficult position – I'm sure King Luccese will make the announcement in a bit."

Meltor admired to the young boy's boldness and turned to respond to his father question. "Your Son demonstrates great leadership, Patrick... you should be proud," he stated and continued. "I can tell you what the King whispered to Harg."

"What did he say?" asked Bradley.

"Unlike Varuna's fate, Harg has been spared a lifetime of solitude in the Shallock Tower... however, he has been banished to *The Unknown Land* - beyond the Peronto Alps in the far southern regions of Pathylon," replied Meltor, as he placed his clenched fists against his hips. "No one has ever returned from there... listen - Pavsik is about make the announcement."

The Kings aide relayed the fate of Harg to the crowd, as Luccese and Queen Vash turned away and walked towards the waiting royal chariot. They were very excited and pleased to be returning to the Royal Palace for the first time since their imprisonment. It had been a terrible ordeal for them during their time in the Shallock Tower and they were now looking forward to a peaceful reign over Pathylon.

Now that the fates of Varuna, Harg and Flaglan had been decided, the opportunity had come to proceed with the debate for the release of the Freytorian Prisoners and to discuss the whereabouts of the three missing chosen ones.

"King Luccese... please wait!" shouted Bradley, as he ran over to the royal couple. "What about the chosen ones?" he asked. "You said you would release the prisoners from Freytor once you had sorted out Varuna."

"Young Bradley... it isn't quite that simple," replied Luccese, as he aborted his boarding of the royal chariot. The King looked up at Vash. "Please go on ahead my Queen... I will join you back at the palace later." He then took hold of Bradley's hand and accompanied him back into the entrance hall of the tower. The others quickly followed and they all gathered around Luccese.

Margaret leant over to Patrick and gave him a gentle kiss on his cheek. Her motherly instincts were kicking in and she was thinking of Frannie. Margaret was anxious to get back to Aunt Vera's cottage in Sandmouth.

Luccese explained to Bradley that once the task of finding the missing chosen ones had been achieved; the twelve would then have to travel to the Island of Restak to form a circle around the ancient Kaikane Idol. "Once the chain is complete... and only then, would we be able to release the Freytorian prisoners from their infinite state of sleep - this should then allow us to lift the evil curse from Pathylon," explained the King.

Meltor approached Luccese. "If I may interrupt my lord... whilst you were dealing with Flaglan and Harg, I gave the situation a great deal of thought and I have to say - I'm very concerned, you're excellency!" exclaimed the wise Galetian. "The task of finding *all twelve* chosen ones has been severely overlooked... we were concentrating so much on fighting the main campaign, in order to free you from the clutches of Varuna's dictatorship - we never really paid too much attention as to how the evil curse would be lifted."

"What do you mean?" asked Luccese.

"Well... we seem to have only *nine* chosen ones, my lord!" exclaimed Meltor, as he introduced the brave heroes that were gathered in the entrance hall. "As you can see, we have young Bradley, Simon, P.C. Sharp, Patrick, Margaret, Aunt Vera, Musgrove, Sereny and Turpol... nine chosen ones!"

"I see your point, Meltor... so where are the other three?" demanded Luccese. "The prisoners from Freytor can't be

released without a full assembly of the twelve chosen ones…
it clearly states this inside the ancient scrolls of Restak."

"Surely… Tank would have been the tenth," interrupted
Simon.

"That's correct" said Turpol, as the little Gatekeeper
moved forward to explain the situation to Luccese.
"However, because poor Tank died for the good cause… it's
obvious he's not be able to make the journey to Restak –
however, I am sure he may be represented by Meltor."

Patrick decided to enter the conversation, which had
rapidly now become a serious debate. "But Meltor is a High
Priest… I thought the chosen ones were supposed to be from
our world - not from the land of Pathylon."

Turpol re-entered the debate. "Not necessarily… that
would mean that I could not be a chosen one – remember I
am also from Pathylon," stated the dwarf. "Like me, Meltor
can pose as a chosen one because he has passed through at
least one of the two vortex's that lead in or out of Pathylon…
after all - we have both used a grobite which bears the sacred
inscription," concluded the Gatekeeper.

Bradley moved forward and spoke clearly. "Okay, let's say
Meltor can act as the tenth… who will represent the other
two chosen ones?"

At that point, Aunt Vera stuck her nose in. "Excuse me…
can I make a suggestion?" she asked. "It's obvious… Grog
and Bomber must have been the other two chosen ones - so
that scuppers any chance of us getting out of here!"

Bradley gave his aunt a disapproving glare. "Grog didn't
even pass through a time portal… so even if he had been
alive - he couldn't have been a chosen one!" He then looked
over to Musgrove, just as his friend stepped forward to add
his input to the debate.

The teenager declared. "Mrs. Penworthy may have been right about Bomber... like Tank – he could have been a chosen one and he also died to save your world from the evil Varuna." Bradley agreed and nodded, as Musgrove continued. "Anyhow, they are both no longer with us... so all arguing aside - the situation doesn't look too good!"

All this talk of death made Sereny cry and reminded her of Grog's unceremonious end. She missed her Krogon friend dearly and had to be consoled by Margaret again. Bradley made his way over to offer her additional support and summarized. "Well, we have now been informed that Meltor can be a chosen one... so if it's not Grog, Tank or Bomber - who are the remaining two individuals?" he asked and turned to the wise old Galetian.

Meltor did not know what to say, he had not given any thought to who would make up the final twelve to be chosen to release the Freytorian prisoners. As far as he was concerned, by re-positioning the cask containing the sacred grobites in the rock pools of Amley's Cove, he felt that he had done enough to ensure the successful recruitment of the twelve chosen ones. The High Priest of the Galetis Empire had not taken into consideration that any of the grobite holders would be killed and felt he had completed his mission to attract the necessary personnel to help dispel the evil curse. He turned to Turpol for moral support. "Can you shed any more light on this, Turpol?"

The Gatekeeper clasped his hands behind his back and started to stride from one side of the great entrance hall to the other. "All I can say is... the two replacement chosen one's must be present in Pathylon – and they must be capable of making the journey to Restak in order to complete the link around the Kaikane Idol!" replied the dwarf. "The reason I believe they are present in our world is because there must have been twelve individuals who passed through at least one of the two vortexes that lead into our mysterious world... if this were not the case, the release of King Luccese would not have been possible – if that makes sense!"

Pavsik had been standing next to P.C. Sharp watching over the debate patiently and acknowledged the Gatekeeper's explanation. The King's closest confidant approached Meltor and placed his hand on the Galetian's shoulder, as he whispered in his ear. Meltor nodded and stood to one side and raised his arms above his head and closed his eyes, as his great cloak sleeves layered backwards to reveal his muscular forearms.

"What is he doing?" asked P.C. Sharp.

"Meltor is using the Galetian powers of telepathy bestowed upon him by the High Priesthood," replied Pavsik. "Hopefully he will be able to receive images in his mind, in relation to the whereabouts of the missing chosen ones."

Everyone looked over to witness Meltor concentrating very hard, as he leant backwards to rest the weight of his huge cloak on his broad shoulders. He held his fingertips to his forehead and lifted his head upwards. It was not long before he fell to his knees exhausted and then opened his eyes. The Galetian looked both concerned and unhappy at what he had visualized.

Meltor was now in receipt of information, which was unbeknown to Bradley and everyone else involved in the debate.

"What is it Meltor?" asked Margaret, as the Galetian positioned his hands against his temples. "What did you see?"

Meltor dropped his hands and got to his feet, as he readjusted his cloak. He focused his attention on Margaret, then looked at Patrick and finally rested his eyes on Bradley's innocent face. "I am very concerned about your sister, Frannie," he said, calmly. "She has travelled through the vortex that leads to the Forbidden Caves inside the Forest of Haldon."

"Oh my gosh... not Frannie!" screamed Margaret. "I knew my instincts were right... oh no – not our little girl too!" she cried, as she turned to Patrick.

"Are you trying to tell me that my little sister has followed me down Aunt Vera's Plughole..?" asked Bradley. "...and Frannie is one of the missing chosen ones?"

"Yes... I'm afraid so," replied Meltor, as he approached Margaret and Patrick and gave them a gentle touch of support.

King Luccese called over to Bradley. "Do not worry... we will find your sister."

"If Frannie is the eleventh... who is the twelfth?" asked Musgrove.

"Frannie is not travelling alone... she has a large furry creature with her," said Meltor, as he recollected the thoughts from his mind.

"That must be K2... my dog - he wouldn't have let Frannie out of his sight!" shouted Bradley. "He follows her everywhere... he must have jumped in the bath in an attempt to save her – I don't believe this!" He despaired as he had to come to terms with the fact that a certain little redhead along with his burly brown and white dog had travelled through the centre of the gold coin lodged in the plughole of Aunt Vera's bathtub. Bradley's little sister and the family's loyal hound *were* the two chosen ones missing from the line-up.

P.C. Sharp intervened again. "I suggest we arrange another search party immediately... the safe return of Frannie and the dog is now our priority – heaven knows what they are going through right now."

The police officer started to reorganize the group in readiness for the search but his efforts were interrupted by the muffled sound of barking that could be heard in the distance.

"Listen!" said Aunt Vera. "Did you hear that?"

The entrance hall below the Shallock Tower fell silent as everyone strained their ears to listen for the distant sound. The familiar barking of a dog drew nearer and nearer and it was not long before the large canine frame of K2 came bounding through the main doors of the tower and jumped up at Bradley.

Amongst the excitement of the over-friendly dog's greeting, everyone focused their attention at the doors in a desperate hope to see the young Baker girl. A scream of delight erupted from Margaret's mouth, as a very tired and filthy-looking little girl appeared at the entrance to the tower. Frannie shrugged her shoulders and ran across the entrance hall towards her relieved mother, as she met her open arms.

Frannie flung her arms around Margaret's neck and nestled her face into Margaret's warm neck. The girl hugged her tightly and released her grip temporarily to kiss the tip of her mother's nose. "Hello Mummy... you'll never guess what happened to us?" she said cheekily. "And I've missed you so much, Mummy!"

"Oh, I've missed you too, *pumpkin*," replied Margaret, as she was joined by Patrick and Aunt Vera. "You are such a brave little girl. Frannie then released the grip and jumped into Patrick's lap, as the girl proceeded to plant a multitude of kisses over his relieved looking face.

Luccese led the applause, as the family reunion reached its pinnacle with Bradley picking up his sister and squeezing her tightly. The King announced that the whole campaign had been a complete success. "All we need to do now… is set off for the Island of Restak at first light tomorrow," he declared. "Then once the Freytorian prisoners are released we can think about getting all you guys back home."

Meltor stepped forward with a solemn look on his face. Turpol had stayed quiet again but now narrowed his eyes for he knew what was wrong. Before the Gatekeeper could speak Margaret asked a question. "What's the matter, Meltor… why are you looking so serious?"

Turpol interpreted the old Galetian's thoughts. "It's the Vortex of Souls… there is something wrong with the vortex - isn't there?" asked the Gatekeeper.

"Yes, my wise little friend," replied Meltor. "You are right... the Vortex of Souls has indeed died – I felt it whilst searching my mind for the missing chosen ones!"

Bradley released his embrace and ushered Frannie over to his mother. He walked across the entrance hall and stood in front of Meltor. "Are we ever going to get back home… Old Mac?" he asked, as he took hold of the great Galetian's hand. His eyes started to well up with tears and Meltor brushed his cloak sleeve across the young boy's cheek to soak up a stray teardrop. The old man did not answer the boy's question and the atmosphere within the great entrance hall was filled with an empty silence.

27

Hatchers Rock

Jules opened the front door to find Mrs. Chilcott stood next to her friend Mrs. Montgomery, under the rosemary-tiled canopy that fronted Aunt Vera's cottage. The distraught teenager welcomed the two ladies into the hallway and then closed the door. Musgrove's mother led the way into the lounge and everyone sat down on the three piece suite.

Mrs. Montgomery owned the local newsagents and had been staying with Mrs. Chilcott whilst the search party had embarked on their mission to find her youngest son. Musgrove's mother had never recovered from her husband's disappearance some twelve years earlier. The painful memories of Thomas had now re-surfaced due to the strange disappearance of Musgrove and she was grateful for the support from her childhood friend.

Jules stared down at the flowered pattern in the carpet, continuing to sob in disbelief; she was still in deep shock after hearing of Bombers death and losing Frannie and K2. Mrs. Chilcott put her own grief aside, got up out of her chair and went over to comfort the girl. She sat down beside Jules and put her arm around the girl to pull her in close.

"There... there, my girl - don't you get all upset," reassured Mrs. Chilcott. "Everything is going to be alright."

Mrs. Montgomery explained to Jules that the police had brought Bomber's body back up from Amley's Cove and had taken all the necessary steps to inform his parents back in London about the tragedy.

"Have you heard any more news from Chris about Simon and Muzzy?" asked Jules, as she wiped away some of the tears that ran down her swollen face.

Mrs. Chilcott shook her head. "Nothing since I last spoke to you on the phone... but I've brought the walkie-talkie with me in case he tries to contact us."

"Whilst we wait to hear from him again... let me show you what happened upstairs," said Jules, as she released herself from Mrs. Chilcott's embrace and got to her feet. The girl walked across the lounge and over towards the hall, indicating to the two ladies to follow her upstairs to Aunt Vera's bathroom. "I'll show you the coin I was telling you about... the one that's stuck in the plughole!"

Mrs. Montgomery and Mrs. Chilcott were both intrigued and followed Jules upstairs and into the bathroom. It was a bit of a tight squeeze, but they all managed to lean over simultaneously to peer into the bathtub. Jules could not believe her eyes, the coin had gone.

"Well... where is it?" asked Mrs. Montgomery, as she straightened her back.

"I swear it was in the plughole earlier," replied Jules. "The dog's tail disappeared through the centre of it – I saw it with my own eyes!" she added, as she held her hand up to her head and began to scrunch her hair.

All three inquisitive females scanned the bathroom in search of the gold coin. Just then, as Mrs. Chilcott looked up and she noticed the edge of a round disc lying flat on top of the mirrored cabinet above the wash hand basin, as she pointed it out to Jules. "Is that it?" asked Musgrove's mother, as she attempted to reach up to retrieve the object.

"I'm not sure," replied Jules. "Here let me get it... I'm taller than you." Mrs. Chilcott moved to one side to allow the skinny girl access to the washbasin. Jules collected the disc from the cabinet and held it in the palm of her hand for the two ladies to see. "Yes... this is the same coin I saw stuck in the plughole - but I don't understand how it got up *there!*"

As the three women examined the coin, the bathroom floor started to shudder. The light on the ceiling dimmed as though there had been some kind of power surge and the whole room started to fill with a mysterious green-coloured steam.

The bathroom door slammed shut and Mrs. Montgomery screamed. Jules turned towards the closed door and noticed a haze of light around the mirror on the wall cabinet. "Look!" she shouted. "The mirror!"

The two ladies turned around to view the amazing bright red glow that had appeared around the edge of the mirror. It was as if an electric element had been powered up and placed as a picture frame around the condensation on the mirrored glass. The steam filled bathroom had caused the water vapour to cover the mirror and then, to their amazement, the coin lifted of its own accord out of Jules's hand. All three watched in disbelief as the coin hovered back towards the mirrored cabinet and began to move with the action of a writing implement. A message began to appear in the condensation, as the coin glided across the surface of the glass. The message read;

'Go to Hatcher's Rock and wait for the fortune!'

The three bemused women could not comprehend the magical moment that they were now experiencing. They watched the coin conclude the message with an exclamation mark, as the grobite lifted itself off the surface and hovered in front of the mirror. After a few seconds it plummeted into the wash hand basin and the coin clattered against the porcelain round.

Jules quickly picked up the glowing object again before it could settle into the plughole; she wasn't taking any more chances. Mrs. Chilcott suggested that she put the coin somewhere safe, so the girl unzipped the pouch on her hipsters and placed the coin inside. She re-zipped it immediately. "There… it should be quite safe now!" exclaimed Jules, as the door swung open and the steam started to clear from the small bathroom.

The hot mist wafted out onto the landing and down the staircase and Jules made her way out of the claustrophobic environment, hastily followed by to two ladies. "That was amazing!" exclaimed Mrs. Montgomery. "I can't believe what I just experienced!"

The two women stared at Jules who was leaning against the flock-papered walls on Vera's landing. Her pocket was still glowing, but Jules covered the zipper with her hand and assured the ladies that she would not release the coin again.

Mrs. Chilcott sat down on the top stair and put her head in her hands. She was totally overwhelmed by the events to date; the stories relayed by Chris about ancient wall painted caves and his description of the flesh covered skeletons… magic spirals… the drainpipe shenanigans… and now to top it all - she had witnessed with her own eyes, a flying coin that could write a strange message on a steam covered mirror.

"What do you think the message meant?" asked Jules, as she sat down beside Mrs. Chilcott and returned the earlier compliment, in the lounge, by putting her arm around the transfixed lady.

"I think she's in shock," said Mrs. Montgomery. "Let's get her downstairs and I'll make her a nice cup of Devon's finest."

Jules and Mrs. Montgomery helped Mrs. Chilcott downstairs and sat her down in front of the kitchen table. Mrs. Montgomery fulfilled her promise and made everyone a nice brew accompanied with some of Aunt Vera's *Royal Edinburgh Shortbread*, which was hidden behind the cereal packets and sealed in a tartan coloured tin.

"I'm sure Vera won't mind us helping ourselves to these lovely biscuits," said Mrs. Montgomery, as she un-wrapped the plastic cover from the all-butter petticoat tails and emptied the contents of the tin onto a china plate.

Jules stood in the kitchen doorway completely gob-smacked at the way Mrs. Chilcott's friend was able to help herself to Vera's secret stash and make a pot of tea after what they had just experienced. The teenager thought to herself that maybe it was just the old lady's way of coping with such a bizarre situation. "I must find out what the message means," she declared and started to pace the kitchen floor frustratingly. "Can I borrow your car, Mrs. Chilcott?" she asked, as she approached the kitchen table.

"What do you want it for my dear?" asked Musgrove's mother, as she showed a distinct sign of re-joining reality.

"I want to drive up to the north end of the bay... Hatchers Rock can be seen from there," replied Jules. "If you remember... the message read - *Go to Hatchers Rock and wait for the fortune!*"

Mrs. Chilcott reached into her jacket pocket and pulled out a bunch of keys. She was not prepared to deny Jules the opportunity to use her car, the message on the mirror was quite clear and neither she nor her friend were in any fit state to travel. She tossed the keys over to her son's girlfriend. "The car is in my garage... it's not locked, but you will need the key with the black plastic cover to start the car - and don't forget to turn off the alarm first!" she shouted, as Jules disappeared out of the front door.

Within minutes a loud high-pitched siren could be heard emanating from Mrs. Chilcott's nearby garage. The two ladies looked at each other and smiled, as Jules finally managed to silence the deafening tones and climbed into the driver's seat.

The teenager sped out of the driveway and headed up the coast road towards Torr Point - from there she would be able to get a clear view of Hatchers Rock. It did not take Jules long to arrive at the car park which neighboured the beach below Torr Point. She turned off the engine, got out of the car and made her way over to the sea wall to get a better view of the great rock. Hatchers Rock was all that remained of a small island that once stood proud in the waters off the Devon coastline many thousands of years ago.

As Jules looked out towards the rock she recalled a school history lesson that had informed her of the ancient rituals that were carried out on the island. She also remembered how her teacher always used to write the whole history lesson on the classroom blackboard and all the pupils just had to copy what he was writing straight into their schoolbooks. Jules could only recall Dr. Illingworth ever saying two sentences throughout each lesson; *'hello class four, sit down'* and *'goodbye class four, dismissed'.*

During one particular writing marathon, she remembered that the teacher had written about an ancient populous, which had settled in the bay many thousands of years ago. She recalled that the settlers had renamed the island Hatchers Rock after part of it had mysteriously fallen into the sea. Prior to this the island had taken its name from some ancient god called Restak.

Jules attention was averted from Hatchers Rock for a brief moment. She looked to her right and noticed a sea mist working its way towards her. As the thick fog started to envelope the rock, she jumped over the wall and ran down to the beach. In the distance she could hear a faint foghorn sounding and she tried in vain to focus through the mist.

The eerie warning sound was getting much louder and Jules could not believe her eyes, as a gigantic slab of ice pierced through the dense fog. History was repeating itself as the impressive iceberg vessel negotiated its way into the bay and laid its anchor again. Just as before, in the *Mouth of Sand*, its honed sail towered upwards and its breath-taking giant hull stretched across the bay. The vessel had now created an icy barrier between Hatchers Rock and the cliffs.

Jules stared at the front of the great vessel in amazement and her eyes were transfixed by the giant chain links that had plunged the huge anchor into the salty water, as they creaked under the tension created by the ship's colossal weight. She moved her eyes upwards and followed the chain to where it entered the ships icy hull.

The excited teenager tried to make out the name of the vessel but the mist that surrounded the nameplate was still too thick. She decided to take a closer look and ran over to a small upturned rowing boat that had been leant against a disused fisherman's hut. She noticed a wooden plaque hanging from the door with the words *'Old Mac's Place – Keep Out'* carved into it.

Jules was totally unaware of the significance of the homemade sign. The teenager continued to address the upturned boat and with absolutely no fear whatsoever, she pulled it to the edge of the water. She jumped in with oars in hand and started to row the boat towards the vessel.

The confident girl guided the small boat nearer to the iceberg and she could now feel the coldness that emanated from it. When she got to within ten metres of the sparkling hull Jules looked up at the nameplate again. This time she could make out the name of the vessel, as the letters stood in bold capitals. "Fortune!" she gasped. "The message in the mirror…"

The message now made sense to Jules, but she wasn't sure what she should do next. She heard a creaking sound and an opening appeared in the side of the ship, just above where her small boat was floating on the water. Two bear-like figures emerged from the ship and they both stood at the entrance to the porthole. The two Freytorian crewmembers lowered a platform down to Jules and one of the figures directed the nervous teenager off the rowing boat by pointing at a metal ledge that suspended below the opening. Jules reluctantly obliged and the platform began to move slowly upwards towards the porthole.

Back in the City of Trad, Bradley paced up and down his bedchamber inside the Royal Palace. He waited impatiently for his father to finish fastening the buttons that secured the back of Margaret's ceremonial dress. At last, all the Baker family members were ready and they made their way out of the master suite that had been privileged to them by King Luccese.

Aunt Vera had been afforded her own private suite, much to the annoyance of Margaret. However, K2 had managed to sneak his way in to Vera's room earlier, where he had made a nuisance of himself on the tubby little lady's face cloth. Aunt Vera was not impressed and the smell still lingered following several facial scrubs.

Bradley Baker was proud to lead his family down the great sweeping staircase that led to the elegantly decorated reception area of the palace. All the other chosen ones were waiting below and looked up towards Bradley. They had been preparing themselves for the ritual ceremony that would secure the release of the Freytorian Prisoners and they were now all together again in readiness for their journey to the small Island of Restak.

Meltor summoned the palace guards and the main doors to the reception area were opened. King Luccese entered the room with Queen Vash at his side and everyone kneeled and bowed their heads as the royal couple approached.

"It is time to cement your efforts," declared Luccese. "We will head for Restak... and offer our thanks to the Kaikane Idol – where we will offer our services to enable the ancient gods to lift the evil curse laid down by the intruders from Freytor."

Bradley, Musgrove and Sereny had regrouped and were listening intently to what King Luccese was saying. They were not quite sure what he was trying to cement but they got the just of what was about to happen. As far as Bradley was concerned, this adventure of his was getting a little bit too intense and too many adults and younger sisters were getting involved. He thought the sooner this ritual was over the better. He and his two friends could then get on with finding a way out of Pathylon and back to their own world. "Eh... Muzzy," whispered Bradley, as he nudged his friend.

"Yeah... what's up Brad," replied Musgrove.

"You said that you had visited Pathylon previously on three separate occasions... and you said that you couldn't remember how you got back to Sandmouth," stated Bradley. "So why didn't Turpol recognize you when we met in the Shallock Tower?"

"How do you mean?" replied Musgrove.

Bradley went on to explain to his friend that his father had told him that no outsiders had passed by the Gatekeeper whilst he had been guarding the exit from Pathylon. "You see... if you had left this strange world via the Vortex of Souls, you would have had to get passed the exit door that Turpol was guarding – therefore, you must have left Pathylon by another means."

"Oh... I see what you mean," replied Musgrove. "Even though the Vortex of Souls is dead... you're saying that there must be another way out of Pathylon."

"Exactly... you did not pass Turpol - so there must be another way out of here," confirmed Bradley, feeling very pleased with his astute analysis.

The boys continued their discussion as the royal entourage gathered outside the palace in readiness for the journey to the Island of Restak.

Meltor and the twelve chosen ones were escorted by an entourage, which included Pavsik and the royal couple. Twenty Devonian Death Troops flanked the trail of carriages and chariots, as they set off on their short trip to the edge of the Red Ocean. During the journey Bradley told Meltor about the conversation he had just had with Musgrove and the old Galetian listened intently.

"Let us complete the ritual my friend and then you will find that everything will fall into place," assured Meltor, as he squeezed Bradley's shoulder.

Bradley was intrigued by Meltor's words. He felt the High Priest was holding back on something, but he had a good feeling about it. The young boy's attention was then taken by the sound of waves crashing against rocks, he looked over to his left and as the chariot cleared the trees he saw the great expanse of water.

The Red Ocean looked magnificent, and there, sticking proudly out of the water, stood the Island of Restak with its Kaikane Idol central and prominent. Part of the island looked familiar to Bradley. He felt he recognized the silhouette of the large peaked rock standing to the right-centre of the idol.

The journey from the Royal Palace to the water's edge was over and everyone dismounted from their carriages and chariots. They proceeded to board the waiting canoes, which would take them across the small expanse of water that separated Restak from Devonia. A rumbling of thunder bellowed from the dark clouds above, as the small sailing crafts set off for the small island.

Bradley glanced over to Musgrove in the canoe adjacent. He gave his friend a wink and held on tightly to K2 as the boat chopped over the small waves that lapped the sides. He secured his hand around K2's collar to prevent the restless hound from jumping out of the boat too soon. The Burnese Mountain Dog barked excitedly as they neared the shores that edged the Island of Restak.

At last they had reached the shores of the ancient rock. Bradley and the others clambered out of their canoes and headed off up the shallow beach towards the Kaikane Idol. It would not be long now to the start of the ceremonial activities, which would affect some of the intrepid adventurers more than others. One thing was for sure - this group of intrepid chosen one's were about to take part in the most amazing event of their lives and it promised to be an experience they would never forget.

28

Friends Reunited

The ceremony was planned for midafternoon when the sun would normally be at its strongest. If there was the faintest chance of the Pathylian sun piercing through the grey clouds that engulfed the skies, then this would be it. The rays would be required to cast the appropriate light needed to ignite the ancient spirits, which currently lay dormant inside the Kaikane Idol. The strong light would create the necessary shadow strong that was dark enough to shield the opening at the base of the statue.

It was written in the ancient scrolls that the souls of any prisoners could only be released from the opening upon the formation of a full circle. The natural chain, created by the chosen ones around the sacred idol, had to remain solid to guarantee success. A faultless orchestration by King Luccese should result in the release of the souls and hopefully lift the dark curse bestowed upon Pathylon by the angry Freytorians.

The sun was trying hard to pierce the blackness above and a faint shadow appeared on the ground. As Bradley and the others waited patiently for the shadow to make its way slowly across the opening, a request was made by Simon for Tanks body to be transported from Trad to the ritual site on the island. The marine felt that his dead colleague should be present for the ceremony; after all he was supposed to be one of the original chosen ones and Simon felt Tank would have wished to be there with the rest of them.

Meltor and Pavsik listened intently to the marine and agreed to approach King Luccese to convey Simon's request. The King was more than happy to approve the idea and instructed Pavsik to make the necessary arrangements to collect Tank's body, which was currently lying in state inside the chapel at the Royal Palace.

Earlier, Bradley had requested that Grog's body be present too but the Krogons had already made arrangements for him to be collected and returned to his homeland for a hero's welcome.

The shadow from the sun was growing darker and was now half way over the opening below the Kaikane Idol. The royal entourage prepared the garlands that would be placed around the necks of the chosen ones and a fanfare sounded from a quartet of horn blowers. Bradley followed the other eleven worshipers into position around the great statue and the fanfare of cretyre-horns sounded again, as the shadow completely covered the opening.

A great feeling of relief spread around the group; the shadow appeared to be dark enough to protect the opening. The King and Queen made their way up a set of stone steps and sat on the makeshift boulders that represented the inaugural thrones for the ritual. Luccese stood to address the audience. "It is time my friends for us to join together so we can release the souls of the Freytorian prisoners... for they have spent far too long entombed within the granite doorways of the forbidden caves!" bellowed the King, as he held his left arm aloft and clutched his robes with the other. "The chosen ones have completed their task by ridding our land of the evil Varuna... they must now help us to discharge the curse that hangs over our darkened world!"

They all stood to attention around the idol, in order of age and creed. Bradley looked down at K2, who was sitting up on his hind legs, as his slobbering pink tongue hung out to the side of his mouth. The poor canine was dehydrating and Bradley gave him a pat on his head, as a sign of encouragement.

Pavsik walked over to Meltor and handed him the end of a silk rope, the Galetian accepted it and proceeded to pass the rope to Aunt Vera. This continued until the silk rope connected all twelve chosen ones together. Pavsik then tied a knot in the rope to complete the full circle. All that was left to do now was for King Luccese to utter the ceremonial words that were written on the ancient scrolls of Restak.

A canoe had berthed on the islands shoreline and four pole bearers were carrying Tanks body on a wicker stretcher over towards the ritual site The King afforded respect to the fallen marine and waited for a moment before he opened the first scroll. Simon looked at Meltor and smiled, he nodded his head as if to thank the Galetian High Priest for persuading Luccese to allow his friend's body to be present at the ceremony.

The four pole bearers lowered the dead marine's body to the ground and everything was now in place for Luccese to continue with the sermon. He unraveled the scroll and started to preach from its ancient vocabulary. As he shouted out the words a cloud of dust started to swirl around the statue, spinning faster and faster. Luccese launched himself further into the spiritual readings;

"Dartum fas carjum dey grastothay vum hestartom!" chanted Luccese, as the Kaikane Idol started to vibrate and the tremors created by its movement shuddered beneath the feet of the chosen ones.

Frannie let out a loud piercing scream and Margaret shouted over to her daughter, telling her not to be afraid. Sereny secured a tighter grip on the silk rope as the ground rumbled beneath her feet. The red lights in the soles of her sports shoes were flashing constantly and this made her think of Grog, when they had first met in the great forest.

P.C. Sharp was shaking so much, his helmet toppled off his head and Aunt Vera screwed up her face as she fought with her spectacles as they slipped down on to the edge of her turned-up nose. Patrick was staying very calm and gave his wife a raw smile as he maintained his hold on the rope.

King Luccese uttered more immortal readings from the scrolls; *"Hertad mantu das cofertium… pertonigos dey mowtonifez!"*

Sereny closed her eyes to avoid the disheveled strands of her hair lashing against her face, as the gusts of magical winds twisted like a tornado around her slim frame. Turpol looked over and shouted to the terrified girl. "Be strong young maiden… you must hold onto the rope tightly to maintain the continuity of the circle!"

She opened her eyes slightly and peered over to where the Gatekeeper stood. "I'll try my best!" replied Sereny, as the dust swirled higher and the dwarf fought intently to stay upright.

With the wind still lifting her hair in all directions above and around her head, Sereny then directed her attention towards Bradley, as the brave young boy battled ferociously with the rough gravel beneath his sandals. He felt his feet lifting off the ground and looked around the full circle. He witnessed everyone starting to raise about three metres off the ground, as the rope continued to hold them all together around the circumference.

All the chosen ones began to travel in the direction of the swirling dust and everyone closed their eyes as a great white light shot out of the opening at the base of the statue. The blast from the light beam caused everyone in the circle to jolt backwards. Disorientated legs drifted behind outstretched bodies and everyone clung helplessly to the silk cord that extended to almost breaking point under the strain of the sudden shockwaves that had emanated from the opening below the statue.

King Luccese became more animated as his voice grew louder to overcome the noise from the rushing winds. The attempts to drown his recital were futile and the ancient scriptures continued to orate from the King's royal mouth. *"Yark dun grotenik pourtenot vas derutareb sertyged dun urdinsek!"*

Frannie managed to crook her neck and face towards the family pet. She was growing very concerned about K2. The dog was secured to the rope by his neck collar, and the great heap of fur was swinging around violently as the torrents of unkind gusts ripped through the dust filled air that created a cruel turbulence around the pitiful canines' distressed frame. "Hang on K2!" she shouted, as her soft cheeks warped under the pressure.

Faster and faster they travelled as Luccese continued to shout out the ancient words written in the transcripts.

Bradley opened his eyes slightly and stared at the bright light as it soared up into the Pathylian sky, creating a large split in the dark clouds. He could make out some ghost-like figures twisting and turning within the light and he thought to himself that they must be the souls of the Freytorian prisoners.

Bradley was partially right, the ghost-like shapes weren't just the souls; they were actually the Freytorian prisoners themselves transforming back into bear-like creatures.

Deep within the Forbidden caves the hooded doorways began to disintegrate, as the ghostly figures regained their form from the granite in which they had been imprisoned. Eight bear-shaped bodies finally parted from the white light and floated effortlessly to the ground and finally came to rest next to the Kaikane Idol. Then to everyone's astonishment a ninth figure appeared from the bright light. It transformed into a faceless hooded being and then joined the other eight figures, which were now standing upright and very still.

The twelve chosen ones gradually landed safely back on the ground and the swirling finally stopped. The dust around the Kaikane Idol settled again and everyone stared at the nine figures, as their heads remained facing the ground.

"Wow… that was awesome!" shouted Musgrove, as he let go of the silk rope.

All the others let go of the rope too, just as Luccese had instructed from his lofty position up on the rocks.

"Yeah… wicked!" replied Bradley, as he rubbed his hands up and down his arms.

There was a sudden cold chill in the air and everyone looked up at the skies as the dark black clouds started to disperse. This was quickly followed by a dense mist that engulfed the ceremonial proceedings, as the Kaikane Idol stopped vibrating and settled back into its pre-historic position.

"Quick everyone... head for the canoes!" shouted Meltor, as the island began to move. "We don't have much time... let's move!"

"The island is breaking up!" exclaimed Margaret, as she grabbed the back of Frannie's T-shirt. "Let's get out of here children!"

King Luccese and Queen Vash appeared at the base of the stone steps and were quickly ushered away through the choking mist, assisted by Pavsik as he guided them towards the boats. Meltor called out to P.C. Sharp to round up the rest of the chosen ones and meet him at the water's edge.

The Island of Restak continued to shake violently and the clouds turned into dense fog making it virtually impossible for the ceremonial party to find the boats. At last Bradley had located the berthed canoes and shouted out to Musgrove. "Over here Muzzy!"

Luccese and his Queen were already making their way across the choppy water to Devonia and three more canoes followed, carrying the King's royal entourage.

The tremors underfoot were becoming unbearable as Bradley and Musgrove freed one of the boats from the shingle beach. They pushed it into the water, as Simon shouted to his brother for some assistance. He had recovered Tank's body from the stretcher and was carrying the lifeless marine over his shoulder. "Help me get Tanks body into the canoe!" he demanded and lowered him onto the beach, as the two boys rushed over to assist. "I can't leave his body here... not after what he's been through!"

Bradley helped Musgrove and Simon lift the burly marine off the sand into the canoe. "Where's Sereny and Turpol?" asked Bradley.

Patrick overheard his son. "Meltor and P.C. Sharp have gone to search for them!" he shouted and summoned Margaret, Frannie and Vera to join them.

"What about K2?" declared Bradley, as he looked around. "I've got to find Sereny and K2!"

Bradley was incensed at the thought of losing Sereny and his beloved dog. He was determined to find them and he jumped out of the canoe and splashed into the shallow water. Patrick took hold of his son's arm and ordered him to get back in the boat.

"It's too dangerous!" cried Bradley's father. "Meltor and the police officer will find them... don't worry!"

"Come on Brad... stop being stupid," said Musgrove calmly, as he pleaded with his best friend to climb back aboard the canoe.

Just then a dog's bark could be heard above the crashing noise of the waves. K2 appeared in the distance, followed in hot pursuit by Sereny and Turpol, with P.C. Sharp struggling to keep up. Bradley was relieved to see them all safe and they all proceeded to board the remaining canoes and started to set out across the choppy water.

"What about Meltor?" declared Musgrove. "We can't go without Meltor!"

"There he is!" yelled Patrick. "He's coming towards us... but look – he's carrying someone across his shoulders!"

Meltor calmly approached the waiting canoes and called ahead for assistance. "Someone help me... please – this one is quite heavy!"

P.C Sharp and Simon jumped out of their canoe and ran over to assist the exhausted Galetian. They lifted the limp figure from his shoulder and lay it on the sand. Simon helped Meltor to the canoes whilst P.C. Sharp started to remove the cloak hood that covered the face of the strange figure.

"It looks like the ninth body that appeared from the bright light… along with the Freytorians!" exclaimed Bradley.

"Holy brother-in-laws… that's not just any old body - it's only Thomas Chilcott!" shouted the police officer. "Simon… Musgrove – it's your father!"

Simon and Musgrove jumped back out of the canoe and ran over to their uncle. Simon could not believe his eyes as he stared down at his aging father. Musgrove didn't recognize the bearded figure and held on to his brother's arm for support. "It's okay Muzzy… I don't blame you for not recognizing him - you were so young when he disappeared."

All Musgrove had back home were photographs to remind him of his father, however he appeared much younger and clean-shaven. The nervous boy leant down to touch his long lost parent and was startled as Thomas opened his eyes. "Muzzy, is that really you?" he croaked. "My goodness… you're all grown up!"

"Are you really my father?" quizzed Musgrove. "I can't believe this is happening… my dad is alive!"

"Calm down bro!" said Simon, as he patted Musgrove's shoulder.

"But Simon… how can this be happening – after all these years?" insisted Musgrove, as he shook his head in disbelief.

Simon was too over-whelmed and confused to provide an answer for his younger brother. Then   Patrick made his way over to join P.C. Sharp and his nephews. Bradley's father congratulated police officer on his family's wonderful find, but stressed that they needed to get off the island before they were all killed. The excited policeman acknowledged his concern and helped his nephews lift their long lost father into one of the canoes.

As the fleet of small boats neared the Devonian shoreline, a large explosion occurred which was followed by a loud cracking noise that emanated from the island. Everyone turned their heads to witness the amazing sight of flying debris and rocks that filled the misty air. The spectacular disruption to the atmosphere had cleared the fog slightly and the onlookers watched in amazement as the Kaikane Idol toppled over and disappeared into the ground. The quake caused a large crack to appear in the island and the ancient statue was swallowed up like a light snack.

A brief storm followed, then the tremors finally stopped and the sea calmed as the tired party of worshipers maneuvered their canoes to safety onto the wave swept sand. Pavsik immediately gathered each of them together for a roll call to make sure everyone was accounted for. Simon and Musgrove comforted their father; both still in disbelief. Meltor assisted his fellow High Priest and his efforts were interrupted by a strange distant noise. The old Galetian also noticed that the sea mist around the island took a turn for the worst and the dense fog had reappeared again and was beginning to encroach on the Devonian shoreline.

"What's happening, Margaret?" asked Aunt Vera, as she shivered and huddled up to her drenched sister. "Why has the fog reappeared?"

Meltor appeared next to Vera and offered an explanation. "I think they are coming back for their lost ones... the mother ship is returning to collect the Freytorian prisoners."

As Meltor spoke the great iceberg sounded its foghorn again and reappeared through the sea mist. K2 barked and Frannie held onto her mother, as Margaret tried to mute the dog's excitement and calm her daughter. It was a magnificent site for all to see, as the enormous vessel laid anchor and nine figures appeared on the deck above the ships nameplate.

"Simon!" shouted a voice from the ship. "Simon... up here!"

The handsome marine looked up and saw a tall slim figure jumping around on the icy deck. Simon could not believe his eyes, as Jules waved and pointed to the eight strange figures standing next to her. They were the re-moralized Freytorian prisoners; now back on board their vessel thanks to the efforts of the chosen ones.

The fog quickly cleared and Bradley looked beyond the great white ice-ship at what remained of the island. A single rock jutted out of the water and he turned to Musgrove to ask for his opinion. "Do you think the Island of Restak reminds you of anything back in Sandmouth?"

Musgrove looked puzzled. "What do you mean Brad?"

"Look at the remains of the island... see the shape of it – does it remind you of a landmark in our world?" asked Bradley. "Imagine you're in Amley's Cove looking out to sea!"

"Come to think of it Brad...yes it does!" exclaimed an overjoyed Musgrove, as he held his father close. "Look father... it looks like Hatchers Rock back home – you know the little island just off Torr Point!"

"Ah... yes - so it does my boy," replied Thomas, as the warm sun shone down from the blue skies that now enshrouded Pathylon. "It's been a while... but I do remember it and I can't wait to see home again - your mother will be in for a bit of a shock though!"

"I've missed you so much Father... and mum is going to be so pleased to see you," insisted Musgrove, in an excited tone. "I don't think she'll be too shocked about seeing you again... once she hears about all the other things that have happened."

Bradley smiled and held out his right hand to congratulate his friend, as the two boys shook hands. "I'm so pleased for you Muzzy... it's great to see you reunited with your dad again."

Musgrove released his grip and turned to his father. "I'd like to introduce you to my best friend... and a real hero - this is Bradley Baker!"

29

The Journey Home

Arrangements were made for King Luccese and Meltor to board the Freytorian ice-vessel. The High Priest insisted that Bradley came with them and the King agreed. A meeting was set up with General Eidar, who had been watching proceedings from the command bridge and speaking with his brother Admiral Norsk back in Freytor. The intense conversation with his brother about the delayed progress of the Navy's new underwater craft was interrupted by the group's arrival.

The muscular Freytorian General cut short his communication and returned the handset to the ice cradle on the command desk, as he cast a frozen stare at Bradley. "Why do you bring this *young human* with you?" demanded Eidar. "I cannot take this meeting seriously…with a boy present!"

"*This boy…* is Bradley Baker!" announced King Luccese. "*This boy…* risked his young life to save the souls of your fellow Freytorians!"

"This is all a bit too much for me… Mr. Eidar," said Bradley in a very nervous tone. "It has been quite an adventure… I can assure you – General, Sir!"

The General admired the boy's confidence. "Well… I don't quite know what to say – I suppose you have earned the right to be here," he replied and turned to a member of the crew. "Quartermaster… bring us some fresh *jerga*!"

"Yes Sir!" replied the Freytorian crewmember.

General Eidar addressed King Luccese. "Will you partake in sampling some of our finest traditional beverage your Highness?"

"That would be splendid General… err; may we sit down now?" requested Luccese.

"Oh, of course your Majesty… please be seated," replied the commander, as he looked over to the old Galetian. "…and you must be Meltor!"

"Yes… General Eidar – I am Meltor," he replied. "I have to say… I was not looking forward to this meeting, however I feel we must put our differences aside and look to the future prosperity of both our lands."

The great white bear sat down beside the three peace brokers. "The actions of your people are unforgiveable… the eight Freytorians you imprisoned have been through an unnecessary ordeal," he explained. "We came to your world in peace and you treat us with contempt!"

King Luccese explained to the General that the Royal Congress was not responsible for the capture of the eight crewmembers. He apologized for the actions of the renegade Death Troops and the stress this had caused his people. The

King also promised Eidar that he was prepared to reopen negotiations for a possible trade agreement between the two worlds.

It took some time to convince the ship's commander and the meeting lasted a few hours. Bradley, Meltor and the King finally appeased the General and then disembarked from the ship to re-join the waiting crowds that had gathered on the shores of Devonia.

Meltor took a step forward. "Everyone... please may I have your attention!" The mumblings of the crowd diminished and the Galetian High Priest continued. "Our King wishes to address you!"

King Luccese thanked Meltor and began to speak to the crowd. He informed the masses what the ships arrival meant to everyone. The proud King explained that the population of Pathylon could now feel secure in the knowledge that all the conditions had been met regarding the release of the prisoners and that the evil curse had finally been eradicated. He finished by thanking Bradley, his family and his friends for their help in securing peace to the regions and pointed towards the colossal iceberg.

"It's now time for you all to go back to your own world... to go back to the safety of your own homes!" shouted Luccese, as he turned to Meltor for confirmation.

"The King is right," assured Meltor. "The ice-ship will transport you back... but hurry - board it quickly before it disappears into the mist again."

Simon wasted little time, as he picked up Frannie and whistled to K2. They raced over to the wedge-shaped landing craft that had been deployed by order of General Eidar from the command bridge. Patrick and P.C. Sharp said their goodbyes to the royal party and proceeded to carry Tank's body onto the landing craft. A hooded Freytorian figure took control of the craft and guided it back to the mother ship. Once the passengers had disembarked, the craft was steered back to the Devonian shoreline to pick up the remaining members of the party.

Margaret and Aunt Vera had already said their goodbyes to Queen Vash and were making their way over to the where the small craft had re-docked. Meltor approached the ladies and asked Vera to wait a second. "I will not be making any more journeys into your world," he said, as he took hold of Vera's hand. "My work is now done... I have managed to entice the chosen ones and my work as the Good Samaritan has ensured Pathylon is safe again thanks to you and your brave family and friends."

"I shall miss you, Old Mac... I mean, err - Meltor," replied Vera, as the old Galetian kissed the back of her hand. "Why don't you come with us?"

"I am afraid I cannot leave my King... he still has many enemies - including Basjoo Ma-otz," replied Meltor. "I have unfinished business with the Hartopian half-breed... and I have to stay here to protect Luccese and Queen Vash against any potential rebellions – it is my duty."

Aunt Vera bowed her head and accepted Meltor's explanation with some sadness but fully understood his reasons for staying in Pathylon. "I guess I will have to buy my Halibut from the resident fishmonger... in *Sainsbury's* from now on!"

Meltor smiled and stepped back to allow the two ladies to board the landing craft. Bradley, Sereny, Musgrove and Thomas took the opportunity to approach Meltor and both boys simultaneously embraced the Galetian's midriff.

Bradley broke away first and looked up at the High Priest. "Thank you for protecting us... it really has been a great adventure."

Musgrove and Sereny attracted Meltor's attention by tugging at his cloak. "Were you ever uncertain that we might not make it back to our own world... at some point during our adventure?" asked Sereny.

"It was never guaranteed that the ice-ship would return for its own people," replied Meltor. "I was certainly relieved, when I heard the fog-horn in the distance," he added and smiled at the three children.

Thomas was now well enough to walk and he moved forward to offer his hand to Meltor. Musgrove put his arm round his father's waist, as he spoke with the High Priest. "I want to thank you for bringing me back from obscurity inside the Forbidden Caves... I never thought I would ever see my two sons again."

"I can't say it was done intentionally... I guess the words spoken by King Luccese were strong enough to release you from the granite as well," replied Meltor. "Now go on... all of you - get on the ship!"

There was one last task for Meltor to convey to Bradley. He instructed the Freytorian onboard the landing craft to hand a sacred grobite to new boy hero. It was the same gold coin that Jules had put in her belt purse back in Aunt Vera's bathroom. "I believe this belongs to you... please keep this coin Bradley - I have a strong feeling that you are indeed *the eternal chosen one* and we may need to call for your help again."

"Thank you Meltor... I will definitely look after it – but how will I know when you want me?" asked Bradley, as he looked down at the gleaming disc in his hand.

"Oh… the coin will let you know!" laughed Meltor, as he brushed back his cloak and placed his large hand on the handle of his sword. "And remember... you are the eternal chosen one, Bradley Baker - never misuse your powers and always put them to good use!"

Bradley nodded and stared at the jeweled handle at the top of the Galetian's trusty blade. It reminded him of the weapon carried by Grog. "Thank you again for entrusting me with this sacred grobite and don't worry I would never put my powers to misuse… but I have one last question - what will happen to Grog's body now that the curse has been lifted?"

"That's a good point and I know you all cared for Grog deeply… it is such a great shame that the Krogon fell to such a cowardly act by the Wartpig Lieutenant Dergan - but do not worry, our dear friend will be taken care of by his own people," assured Meltor. "Grog will be honoured as a Krogon Champion," continued the old Galetian. "And his body will be taken to the Flaclom Straits… in his homeland of Krogonia - and there his death will be celebrated by his fellow lizard men during a very special ritual."

"What kind of ritual?" asked Bradley.

Meltor replied. "The Krogons believe in life after death for their champions and they will place Grogs body in an eternal tomb inside one of their sacred temples so that the God of the Red Ocean can watch over him till the time comes for him to rejoin his people."

"Rejoin his people… but he's dead!" exclaimed Bradley, as Meltor encouraged him to join his family.

"Do not worry yourself anymore about Grog my young chosen one… it's time for you to go to your family - I bid you all a fond farewell my friends," said Meltor and he waved to Bradley, as he moved away to join the others in the landing craft.

The Freytorian oarsman guided the small boat gently away from the Devonian shoreline and back towards the giant iceberg. Turpol appeared at the side of the Galetian High Priest and offered his goodbyes by waving at the three brave children.

"Goodbye Meltor!" shouted Bradley, as the boat drifted away from the shore. "I will never forget you!"

It did not take long for the landing craft to dock onto the mother ship. All seven boarded the frozen vessel and made their way to the upper deck to join the others.

Bradley's mind wandered for a while as he stood at the icy railings and looked out over towards the Pathylian horizon. The thoughtful boy began to picture his friend Grog. The fine view resurrected memories of the giant frog-like creature around the campfire and he remembered how the orange-skinned Krogon warrior had prepared the evening meal in his little lodge by the River Klomus.

Bradley's brief recollections of Grog were interrupted by the great sailing vessel's icy foghorn, as it bellowed out its eerie sound. The grey sea mist fell upon the ship once more and Bradley felt a tightening in his stomach, as he clenched his fingers around the handrail. Within a few seconds the fog had dispersed and the horizon had taken on a more familiar look. It was the Devon coastline of Sandmouth and he could just make out Aunt Vera's cottage at the top of the cliffs. "Look Mum, we're back in Amley's Cove!" shouted Bradley, as he stretched out his arm and pointed at the delightful landmark.

Margaret smiled at Bradley and put her arm around her precious son, as if to protect him, she was so relieved to see the familiar sights of Sandmouth again. At last her family and friends were safe and although some of their experiences had resulted in tragic consequences, Margaret was keen to put the events behind her so they could all get back to enjoying the rest of their holiday at Aunt Vera's.

"Here you might want this," said Margaret, as she handed Bradley the plastic toy soldier that she had found outside the Forbidden Caves.

"Ah, one of my soldiers... thanks Mum - and it's the captain... see - the one with the binoculars!" exclaimed Bradley, as he held on tightly to the little green figure that had journeyed through the plughole with him.

Bradley thought back to the frightening experience he had endured in Aunt Vera's bath tub and his mother interrupted. "Are you okay... Bradley?"

"Ermmmm... yeah Mum – I'm fine," he replied and stared out towards the great cliffs. "I was just thinking about a few things..." He then started to wonder how they were all going to explain the mystical world of Pathylon to the Devon County Authorities. The deaths of Bomber and Tank would take some serious explaining and no court in the land would ever believe such a fantasy; especially the reappearance of Musgrove's father.

Bradley's concentration was broken again by a second chilling sound of the ice-ship's foghorn and the huge vessel came to a gradual halt. The giant anchor was lowered once more and the wedged-shape landing craft was deployed again. He was now starting to feel insecure as he made his way down to the lower decks. He looked over to the others, who were getting ready to board the small boat that would take them back to the safety of Amley's Cove.

It did not take long for the Freytorian landing craft to complete its final leg of transportation to the Sandmouth shoreline. The boat berthed against the jetty that had proudly moored Old Mac's fishing boat on previous occasions and all the passengers were now safely ashore.

Musgrove was eventually detached from his father's arm by Bradley and Sereny, who then stood to one side as they witnessed the removal of Tanks lifeless body from the landing craft. Thomas then joined Simon and Jules, as Patrick and P.C. Sharp carried the dead marine recruit along the jetty. The task was made awkward by the interference of K2, who was intent on biting at the police officer's trouser leg and he struggled to maintain his balance.

Margaret and Aunt Vera guided Frannie along the jetty and joined the deceased marine and the others on the rock-laden shoreline. Bradley had managed to prize open K2's jaws and the over-friendly hound was reluctantly removed from P.C. Sharps dark blue uniform. The dog continued to growl as Bradley removed the remains of the navy material from his teeth and he handed over the torn piece of cloth to Musgrove's uncle. Bradley lowered K2's front paws onto the wet sand and the big hound scampered off and proceeded to sniff frantically around the rocks, leaving numerous markings as he cocked his hind leg at every opportunity.

Chris arrived in the police van and drove over to the waiting entourage. The rear doors of the van flew open and he climbed down carrying a stretcher under his arm. He dropped the stretcher and greeted Simon with open arms.

P.C. Sharp and Patrick lifted Tank onto the stretcher and slid his body into the back of the police van. Jules and Frannie also climbed into the back of the vehicle and they were soon joined by a very wet K2, as Bradley's mum pushed the sand-soddened pooch up the onto the rear step of the van. Simon held out his hand to his father and he pulled him up into the van. Thomas waved to Musgrove, as Chris climbed back into the driver's seat. Bradley, Patrick, Margaret and Aunt Vera stood on the jetty, as the van sped off and made its way back up the cliffside track.

Bradley asked permission to rejoin his friends and left his parents and aunt on the jetty. He made his way over to the water's edge to join his two chums who had been stood for a little while looking out to sea. The gentle breaks of the ocean waves, caused by the landing craft returning to the mother ship, washed over their feet. Sereny and Musgrove were reluctant to leave the beach and flanked Bradley as he stared out to the ice-ship that was still anchored about a thousand metres out at sea.

"Great result for you… eh Muzzy – seeing your dad alive after all these years," said Sereny.

"Thanks… but I still haven't yet come to terms with it," replied Musgrove.

"It's bound to be a big shock to the system," said Bradley. "Anyhow… I thought you would have gone back with your father in the police van."

"I wanted to… but, I thought it best for mum to see him first – I don't think she would have been able to handle both of us turning up at the same time," said Musgrove. "Anyway…I'll see them both in a little while - when the police van comes back to pick us up."

The friends had only been chatting for a short time, when Margaret shouted over to join them beside the jetty, in readiness for the police van's return. Bradley hesitated and explained his fears to Musgrove and Sereny. "What about Tank and Bombers families disbelieving our story."

"How do you mean?" replied Musgrove.

"What if no-one takes us seriously... who is going to believe our amazing adventure in Pathylon?" exclaimed Bradley, as he stamped his foot into the wet sand. "What if we all go to prison for man-slaughter... or even - murder!" he continued, as more soggy sand was carved out of the wave swept beach and tossed into the air with his Pathylian footwear.

"Well I guess convincing the Sandmouth folk about the existence of creepy Skeloyds and macho Devonian Death Troops will take some persuading," said Musgrove calmly. "But don't worry Brad...my uncle will explain everything, after all - he is a police officer."

"I guess you're right... Muzzy!" said Bradley.

Musgrove offered further evidence. "And don't forget... my father *has* returned - he will be able to back up our story."

Sereny re-joined the discussion in order to quash Bradley's concerns. "P.C. Sharp is a greatly respected policeman and the people of Sandmouth are sure to believe his explanation of what went on in Pathylon ... and Musgrove is right - the fact that is father has turned up will add further proof that we are telling the truth."

They continued to reassure Bradley that he should not be so worried, as he stepped back and looked down towards the leather pouch that was strapped to his ceremonial costume. The grobite started to vibrate violently and the familiar green glow appeared at the lip of the pouch.

"Look at that Sereny!" exclaimed Musgrove, as he pointed at the emerald glow.

The three children stood back in amazement with their mouths wide open, as the spinning coin lifted itself out of the

328

pouch. The grobite shot into the air and made its way over to where the adults were waiting patiently for the police van. Patrick, Margaret and Aunt Vera were unaware of the gold disc that was now hovering about ten or more metres above their heads.

The coin grew in size to about twenty metres in diameter and it took on a more sinister appearance, as it increased its speed. All of a sudden the bay darkened and a flash of green bright lightning pierced the cloudy skies above Amley's Cove and struck the giant disc. A haze of brightly coloured lights showered out from the centre of the grobite like a giant firework and surrounded the stunned onlookers.

A display of multi-coloured streams of light continued to illuminate beneath the black skies of the bay. The children cowered away and covered their eyes to protect them from the sparkling bright lights that shot out from the centre of the sacred coin. The kaleidoscope of coloured laser beams finally stopped discharging from the grobite and the last few sparks of light gradually faded away into the black clouds above.

A silent darkness fell upon Sandmouth's rocky cove. The ebony clouds gradually dispersed and the mist lifted. There was an eerie feel to the air and Bradley gasped, as he stared at the empty shoreline adjacent the jetty – both his parents and Aunt Vera had disappeared.

30

The Secret is Safe

The three children were still focusing their attention on the spinning coin, which hovered above the jetty. Sereny broke her concentration for a moment to scan the immediate vicinity for Bradley's parents and his aunt.

"That thing is amazing!" exclaimed Musgrove. "Look at the size of it!"

Bradley noticed Sereny looking around. "Where have my parents and aunt gone?" he asked, as he held on to Sereny's arm.

"Whilst you were concentrating on the grobite... I had a quick look around – but I can't see them," replied Sereny. "Do *you* know what happened to them Muzzy?"

"No, sorry... I was watching the coin as well - it's as if they've disappeared into thin air!" said Musgrove.

As the children discussed the whereabouts of Bradley's family, the enormous airborne coin began to spin even faster and faster and following another series of bright green flashes of light, the grobite disappeared.

"Hey... look down there!" shouted Musgrove, as he pointed at the floor. There was a message written in the damp sand at the base of their feet. Bradley looked down and to his amazement the grobite had shrunk back to its normal size and it was lodged edgeways into the moist sand. The coin was simulating a full stop at the base of an exclamation mark, which ended a written message;

'*THE SECRET IS SAFE!*'

Bradley bent down and picked up the grobite and then began to examine the coin thoroughly. "It's definitely my coin," he declared. "Look ... here's the mark where the lightning struck it - but it's not seriously damaged."

"What do you suppose the message means?" asked Sereny.

Bradley hunched his shoulders and returned the grobite to the pouch. "I'm not sure... but never mind about that - let's find my parents and my aunt!"

Following a quick search for the missing adults around the jetty area, the three children agreed to make their way back up the dirt track, which led up the cliffside. The steep incline took its toll on the trio's primitive sandals and they were relieved to rest their blister-shod feet at the summit. They walked tentatively along the roadside and arrived back at Aunt Vera's cottage to see the police van parked outside the front gate.

Bradley quickened his pace with his two friends in hot pursuit. He then made his way through the gateway and down the cobbled path that led to Aunt Vera's front door. He quickly depressed the doorbell and without any hesitation the door opened and there stood his aunt. Her face was like thunder and she stared daggers at her astonished nephew.

"Where on earth have you been young Bradley... and why are you wearing those ridiculous looking clothes?" shrieked Aunt Vera, as she pulled the stunned boy into the porch by his crimson robe. "Now get yourself inside and go and explain yourself to your mother and father," added the cynical woman, as she reluctantly invited Musgrove and Sereny to follow Bradley into the front lounge.

The lounge was full of people, all looking very relieved to see the three children and they joined Aunt Vera in their appraisal of the young adventurer's brightly coloured medieval attire. Bradley walked over to his mother who stood next to Sereny's father. He looked back at his friends and shrugged his shoulders as Margaret pulled her son towards her and clutched him into a tight embrace.

Musgrove joined his parents and Simon, as Jules hung onto the marine recruit's arm like a love-struck puppy. Sereny hugged her father and they all waited for someone to explain what was going on. At last, Thomas Chilcott broke the silence. "We've been worried sick about you three children... P.C. Sharp here and our Simon have been scouring the bay for you three all day – Simon even asked three of his marine friends to give up their leave to help find you."

Musgrove stared at his father in disbelief and looked even more puzzled regarding his comments. "Are you feeling okay now, Dad?" he asked. "Have you recovered from your ordeal – how did mum react when she saw you after all these years?"

"What on earth are you talking about, Musgrove?" asked Mrs. Chilcott. "Your father's fine – he's been fine for years... it's you we've been worried about."

Musgrove looked over to his friend for support and Bradley quickly changed the subject of conversation, as he turned to his mother. "Where's Frannie and K2?"

"They're both upstairs… Frannie has been getting herself upset - not knowing where you were and all," replied Margaret

Musgrove stepped away from his parents and rejoined Bradley who was now staring at the kitchen doorway with an open-mouthed expression on his face. He followed the course of his friend's stare and replicated his shocked look, as they caught sight of three royal marines. Chris was making a brew, ably assisted by Tank and Bomber. The two burly soldiers were very much alive and they both winked simultaneously at the boys, as the clinking of spoons concluded the tea making process.

The three marines entered the lounge with trays of hot steaming tea and a tin of shortbread biscuits. Sereny could not believe her eyes and she began to feel very insecure about the whole situation. She leant over and whispered in Bradley's ear. "I feel a few words in private might not go a miss right now… tell Muzzy we need to get out of here."

Bradley nodded and he nudged Musgrove, who was now completely transfixed on the mugs of tea that Tank and Bomber held in their hands. Sereny acted quickly to avert a possible crisis. "Would you all excuse us for a moment?"

"Is everything alright my dear?" asked Aunt Vera. "Musgrove looks like he's seen a ghost!"

Bradley answered. "He's okay Aunt Vera… a bit tired – that's all." He echoed Sereny's request. "We're just going to pop out the back to get some fresh air!"

The adults agreed that it might be best for the three children to take a moment or two for themselves. They all appreciated that it must have come as great shock for the three youngsters to see so many people in one room affording so much concern for their safe return. So the children made their way out through the kitchen and into Aunt Vera's back garden, leaving the grown-ups in the overcrowded lounge to help themselves to the cups of freshly brewed tea that had been prepared by the three marine recruits.

Musgrove orchestrated a metallic scraping sound as he sat down on one of the wrought iron patio chairs. Bradley stood and leant his bottom against the matching olive green table beneath the out-spanned parasol that shielded them all from the hot rays of the Devon sun. Sereny occupied one of the other patio seats and proceeded to chair the meeting. "Well I think we can all agree... something very special and most unusual has just happened."

"That's the understatement of the century!" replied Musgrove. "Just look at us... dressed in these ridiculous costumes - there's no wonder they were all looking at us funny!"

"Yeah... it does look a bit suspicious – we'll have to make up some story about how we found them or something," said Sereny, as she crossed her arms and sank back into the chair next to where Bradley was still standing.

Musgrove stood out of his seat and paced the patio slabs back and forth. "It's not just about Tank and Bomber being alive and well... it's also about Bradley's parents and his Aunt Vera disappearing from the jetty and then us finding them safe and sound in the Cottage - and everyone in the room being totally oblivious to where we have been for the past who knows how long!" he exclaimed. "Not to mention the fact that my father looked like he been around for the past twelve years... I'm beginning to doubt whether or not anything we experienced - actually happened or not!"

Bradley was still leaning very casually against the patio table and he was being remarkably cool about the whole situation. The young hero had certainly matured well beyond his eleven years during the Pathylon adventure and he was showing positive signs of assured leadership.

Bradley listened intently to his two peers, in readiness for an annalistic response to their questions. He waited for Sereny and Musgrove to finish their debate and then finally broke his silence. "Well I think we can safely say... that we have definitely experienced a great adventure," he said calmly, as he cast Musgrove an assuring look. "Don't forget I still have the magic coin to prove it and the message carved out in the sand suggests that the grobite must have cast its mystical powers in order to help protect the identity of Pathylon." he surmised. "It would have been disastrous if everyone in my aunt's front lounge were allowed to retain their knowledge of the other world...the security of Pathylon would have been seriously threatened if too many witnesses were left to spread idle gossip - as the message in the sand suggested... *the secret is safe*!"

Bradley was right, the grobite had indeed performed its final act in relation to this particular adventure and it had entrusted only the three children with the opportunity to retain the memories of their experience and hold the secrets of Pathylon in case they should be needed by its inhabitants again. Musgrove acknowledged Bradley's summing-up, but was still unconvinced about his father's reappearance and that he was stood the lounge. "How can you explain away the fact... before I travelled down the plughole - he had been missing for the past twelve years?"

"I'm afraid there's no logic about that... Muzzy – I guess you'll have to accept the fact that your father is here and count it as a gift from Pathylon!" replied Bradley.

"Eh... I'm not complaining - but it's going to take some getting used to!" said Musgrove. "But it's going to be weird catching up with him when he's not even aware there's any catching up to be done!" Musgrove then made reference to the other grobites that had helped Sereny and himself to enter the depths of the drains beneath his hometown. "If you have been entrusted with the powers that are contained within your coin... then our sacred coins must still be lodged in the plugholes in our bathtubs," he declared. "Don't forget... both Sereny and I used the same type of coin when we made our initial journeys - at the start of this adventure."

Sereny displayed a look of doubt, as she made her way across the patio towards the fence at the bottom of the garden. "I've got a funny feeling they won't be there anymore... come on Muzzy - let's find out."

The three friends decided to risk a further scolding from their respective parents and elected to leave the confines of Aunt Vera's garden and proceeded to scale the picket fence that bordered the footpath at the top of the cliff above Amley's Cove. They ran along the cliffside path, two doors down and clambered into Musgrove's back garden.

They made their way up to the rear entrance door to his house. Musgrove lifted the doormat and retrieved the rusty key that would successfully open the back door. They could not contain their excitement and it reached a crescendo when they finally entered the house. Musgrove led the way, as they scampered up the staircase and onto the landing that guided them to the bathroom. All three children looked tentatively into the bathtub, but there was no sign of Musgrove's grobite.

"It must have gone down the plughole and back into the world of Pathylon," assumed Musgrove, as he looked on disappointedly.

Bradley felt some kind of relief inside. He thought it was a very selfish feeling and his guilt was further fueled when it was found that Sereny's grobite was no longer in the bathtub at the Ugbrooke household. Bradley was the only one that had been entrusted to hold a sacred grobite.

Musgrove and Sereny were obviously envious of Bradley Baker's good fortune but drew some satisfaction from the fact that they would not have to live a constant vigil, by having to wait for the gold coin to call on them at any time.

Bradley was indeed the *eternal chosen one* and he would be solely responsible for the safety of the coin. The two friends congratulated their younger peer on his accolade, as they quickly made their way back to Aunt Vera's cottage in the knowledge that they must keep the promise made to each other that the mystical powers of the coin must never be told to any non-believer.

The children made their way back to Aunt Vera's cottage and re-entered the lounge to face the adults. The predictable inquisition followed and they covered their disappearance with a story about wandering off to explore the rock pools in Amley's Cove. They concluded by explaining that they had found their weird looking clothes in a skip outside the charity shop next to the village hall. Their far-fetched explanations were accepted with some trepidation by their parents, but more importantly it was enough to satisfy the curiosity of P.C. Sharp.

Bradley still found it hard to believe that his parents, the police officer, Aunt Vera, Simon, Jules, Frannie and K2 together with the marines, Musgrove's parents and even Mrs. Montgomery from the newsagents, had no idea of the important part they had played in the arduous task to free the true King of Pathylon and release the Freytorian prisoners. Bradley whispered in Sereny's ear. "If only they all knew that they had just taken part in a fabulous adventure... they would be kicking themselves right now."

Sereny giggled and placed an affectionate kiss on his cheek. "Aren't we the lucky ones?"

The atmosphere in the lounge was much more relaxed and Bradley was feeling extremely important. He felt the weight of the sacred gold coin against his thigh, as he stood in the centre of the room. He knew that Meltor's parting gift from Pathylon would offer him the opportunity to encounter more great adventures down the plughole and the he was looking forward to every single one of them. He slipped his hand into the leather pouch and clung on tightly to the magical grobite.

The week that followed passed very quickly, but it afforded Bradley the opportunity to share many more enjoyable moments with Musgrove and Sereny.

The three children had managed to persuade their parents that it would be a great idea for the three friends to be reunited during the half term holidays at the end of October. It was decided that Bradley's home village of Ravenswood would be the perfect place for a reunion, as Mr. Ugbrooke had arranged a business meeting in Sheffield. Sereny's father was more than happy to take his daughter and Musgrove with him on his trip.

It was now time for Bradley to leave his Aunt Vera's cottage and the picturesque town of Sandmouth. The Bakers ushered their children into the car and loaded the luggage before carrying out their customary goodbyes.

K2 jumped into the back and found a space between two suitcases. He turned on the spot several times before slumping into a snug position. The burly hound then slapped his jowls together a few times and let out a huge sigh.

Aunt Vera made her way over to the vehicle and decided not to attempt to kiss Bradley goodbye. She was keen to avoid a repeat of the coke cup and straw incident that had left a small scar at the opening of her left nostril. She settled for a begrudged hug from her nephew and then proceeded to slobber over Frannie, much to his delight.

Musgrove and Sereny had just arrived to say their farewells. They had brought three plastic stacking cups together with a bottle of cold dandelion and burdock. Sereny passed one of the cups to Bradley, who was now sitting comfortably in the back of the car, as she began to pour them all a small tipple of the brown fizzy refreshment. "Do you think Grog came back to life as well?" she asked. "Just like Bomber and Tank did!"

"I really do hope so," replied Bradley. "But I guess we'll never know!"

"Well let's imagine he did... anyhow, I would like to propose a toast," said Sereny, as all three friends lifted their plastic cups. "To Grog!" she shouted.

"To Grog!" replied Bradley and Musgrove in chorus, as the children thrust their plastic cups together.

Margaret, Patrick and Aunt Vera afforded a curious look towards the three children, as the young adventurers continued to laugh and complete their cup-clashing tribute to the Krogon warrior. The adults were still none the wiser that they had actually met the strange creature from Krogonia.

"See you in the October school holidays... Brad," said Musgrove, as he patted his best friend on the shoulder.

The amicable gesture from Musgrove caused a small drop of dandelion and burdock to spill from Bradley's cup onto the car's upholstery. He gently wiped it away and then focused his attention on Sereny as his cheeks glowed crimson. "Well... I guess it's goodbye for now."

Sereny replied in a kind and sweet voice. "It has been a pleasure meeting you... Bradley Baker."

Musgrove interrupted. "Oh... by the way - we must have a Halloween party when we come up to your house."

"I hadn't thought about Halloween... that should be fun - especially if the gold coin starts playing up again," replied Bradley.

"That would be so brilliant!" exclaimed Musgrove.

All three children started to giggle and Sereny leant over to kiss Bradley on the cheek. "You're making a habit of doing that!" he declared.

"Are you complaining?" replied Sereny, as Bradley's complexion turned an even deeper shade of scarlet upon receipt of the girl's affections.

Margaret interrupted the romantic interlude and ensured Bradley and Frannie's seat belts were securely fastened and then she proceeded to shut the rear passenger doors. Bradley quickly lowered the rear window and looked out towards Musgrove and Sereny. The car started to move off and the three chums waved frantically at each other.

"Goodbye Brad... take care of yourself!" shouted Musgrove. "See you in a couple of months!"

"Have a safe journey home - Bradley Baker!" added Sereny, as she blew him a kiss.

"Bye!" replied Bradley, as he settled into his seat and looked down the drinks stain beside his leg. He lifted his head and glanced at the dashboard, as his father reset the odometer. He then focused his attention on the chewed straw and drinks carton that still lay where it had fallen following the encounter with Aunt Vera. He smiled and closed his eyes, then thought out loud. "Only two hundred and seventy eight miles to go... and plenty to think about."

"What did you say?" asked Frannie. "What was that?"

There was a brief silence. Bradley kept his eyes closed and then replied. "Oh nothing Frannie - just thinking about..."

Frannie waited for her brother to finish but Bradley's mind drifted deeper and his thoughts were soon filled with a wonderful image.

King Luccese and Meltor were standing in front of the Royal Palace, as a colourful array of medieval flags and banners blew in the warm breeze. Queen Vash and the royal entourage stood close by and they were surrounded by all the strange creatures that Bradley had encountered during his visit to the mysterious land.

The evocative scene was clearly represented in his thoughts, as sunny skies cast a gentle shadow from the Shallock Tower over the assembly of happy faces. The magnificent cretyre trees in the Forest of Haldon stood tall behind the palace and they swayed proudly in a gentle current of air.

Then a white cloud wisped into view and a familiar image appeared within its soft swirls. It was the face of Grog and a convenient gap in the cloud appeared to produce a broad

Krogon smile. The sun shone through and emanated an array of dancing beams across the Pathylian landscape.

The wonderful image in Bradley's head panned out like the zoom lens of a movie camera during the final shot of a Hollywood blockbuster. The breathtaking picture became a wonderful panoramic view of Pathylon, as the magical land was revealed from up high!

…………..

Look out for the second book in the

Pathylon Trilogy...

BRADLEY BAKER

and the Amulet of Silvermoor

Sneak preview of the first chapter...

1

The Mauled Miner

The year is 1975 and the coldest Halloween eve you could imagine has been bestowed upon the small mining village of Ravenswood. A young Patrick Baker has not yet met his beautiful wife Margaret and he is currently working as a colliery electrician maintaining the surface plant at Silvermoor in Yorkshire. Many more years will follow before his son Bradley is born, who at the tender age of eleven will become the eternal chosen one. At this point in time the boy hero apparent is just a twinkle in his father's eye.

Silvermoor is a record breaking pit and is producing a million tonnes of coal per year, which feeds the local power station situated on the outskirts of Sheffield. It is a time of camaraderie, as the union of miners worked together in dirty and treacherous conditions. Coal offers the workforce job security within the local community and it forms the back bone to support local industry.

The black crystalized fossil fuel is being mined with great precision deep beneath Silvermoor's landmark winding wheels. The odourless methane from the freshly cut coal mixed with the sulphur dioxide emitted from the fault lines fill the underground workings with a deadly cocktail of gas, as the constant droning of heavy machinery simulates the sound of the industrial grind. The main colliery fan on the surface circulates the bitter October air through the inter-linking manmade passageways. This helps to disperse the heat that emanates from the heavy operating plant, which requires minute-by-minute maintenance from the perspiring mineworkers. There is constant a hive of activity within the parallel headings, which lead to each coal face. Both the inlet and the outlet headings carry an airbourne mixture of stone and coal dust, as the steel toe caps of the miners boots rake up a haze of trodden ground.

Row upon row of razor-sharp tungsten teeth from one of the coal producing cutters tear into the jet-black strata of the Ravenswood seam. The huge drum turns progressively slow, as it moves along the *Number 5* coal face. Hydraulic jets of cooling fluid smash against the grinding picks and the creamy white liquid turns to black slush, as it mixes with the fine airborne dust. Not all the coolant hits its mark and the resulting over-spray covers the machine operator from head to foot with an ebony coat of black sludge.

Patrick Baker's older brother carries the huge responsibility of controlling the main coal-cutter on the *Number 5* district. Henley is guiding the heavy machine and it moves steadily along the metal-linked panzer chain that carries the coal away from the face. The experienced machinist wipes the dust filled coolant from his brow and he watches in amazement, as the spliced chunks of coal tumble onto the steel conveyor unit.

An elite team of chock men operate the hydraulic supports, as the entire coal face setup moves forward in a unified tandem. A series of loud explosions emanate from the cavities behind the supports, as solid rock collapses to fill the void left by the rich vein of black glistening coal. The miners work relentlessly and move around like a warren of burrowers, as the underground activities near the end of the afternoon shift. The dancing rays of light from their cap lamps cross like laser beams, as they ferry back and forth along the hundred metre long coal face.

Barney Huddlestone tapped his work colleague on the shoulder and raised his voice to conquer the noise of the heavy machinery. "Hey… Baker, it's nearly time to finish the cutting – it'll be shift end in five minutes so make sure this is the last run mate!"

Henley turned his head and shouted out his response. "You've got no chance me old cocker… there's still time for this beast to make another run along this line of black firewood!"

"Come on… enough is enough!" pleaded the tired face worker. "The lads have done their bit… it's time to go home!"

Henley laughed and maintained is stubborn authority. "We all need to earn some extra bonus and I'm sure Silvermoor's top brass will appreciate an extra ton of coal in their hopper tonight!"

Barney shook his head and his cap-lamp flickered, as he shouted. "We'll miss the paddy train back to the pit bottom if you don't make this the last one… my missus will kill me if I don't get home in time to mend her washing line – she's been going on at me for three weeks and I promised her I'd fix it ready for the morning!"

"What you going on about Barney... forget the washing line – I'm taking this baby down that face again!" replied Henley, as he pushed the reverse button on the control panel. "Anyhow, your missus won't need a washing line... it's probably still snowing on top - now get back on those chocks and follow me down!"

Barney's request had fallen on deaf ears and he had no choice but to reluctantly agree to Henley's instructions. He shook his head and followed his team leader's order then crouched to return to his chock support position.

Barney turned and gave a thumbs-up, as Henley pushed the metal lever and the coal cutting machine droned into life again. The large drum began to turn with an effortless motion and the grating of metal against coal echoed down the face, as the picks started to embed themselves into the prehistoric strata.

The operation had only moved about twenty metres along the return face when there was a loud bang. "What on earth was that!" shouted Henley, as he instinctively held up his arm to shield his eyes from the stray slithers of coal that flew from the cutter.

"The drum is stuck... I think we've hit some hard rock – there must be a fault line in the coal seam!" replied Barney.

"I'll see if I can release it... here hold this!" shouted Henley, as he pointed to the operating lever.

"What are you doing, Henley?" demanded Barney. "You can't go over the panzer when it's not isolated... it's too dangerous mate!" he warned and took hold of the lever.

"Don't be daft man... I've done it before – I just need to hammer this wooden block under the base and it'll cut free!" replied Henley, as the machine groaned under the pressure of the trapped drum.

"I'm not at all happy about you going behind that machine while it's still running!" insisted Barney, as he pulled at the sweaty grey vest that clung to Henley's back. "Don't be an idiot man... you'll injure yourself – now stop being stupid!"

The machine began to smoke under the immense pressure and Henley grabbed his work colleague's hand to pull it away from his clothing, just as the coal face deputy approached. "Let go of my shirt, Barney... the machine is overheating and the sooner I get in there to release the drum – the sooner you can go home to mend that blooming washing line of yours!"

Barney released his grip and turned to acknowledge the deputy. "Hello Ralph, before you ask... don't worry - Henley says he knows what he's doing and he has things under control!"

The deputy ignored Barney and asked. "What on earth is going on... why has the drum stopped?"

Barney explained that the cutters had bitten into a fault line of solid rock. He then insisted that the deputy tell Henley to turn off the machine.

"You're a bit late Barney... he's gone over the metal conveyor – he's disappeared behind the drum!" declared the deputy. "He's in big trouble... he could get the sack for that!"

"Henley Baker... get back here - Ralph says you'll be in the dog house if you don't get yourself out of there!" shouted Barney, as the colossal coal face machine began to vibrate.

There was no answer from his colleague and the machine let out a huge crunching noise, as the drum began to turn again slowly. Barney pulled the control lever back to stop the cutters from eating further into the coal and shouted out to his friend. "Well I'll be damned… you've done it – well done, Henley!"

Still no answer came from behind the drum and the deputy hit the emergency stop button. The whole coal face operation came to a standstill as machine after machine stopped humming and the metal-sheathed lights beneath the chocks went out one by one. "Let's get over there!" he insisted.

Barney did not hesitate and he followed the deputy over the panzer conveyor belt and witnessed their colleague lying motionless with his face down in the freshly cut coal. "Henley… are you okay mate?"

There was still no movement and Barney knelt down next to Henley. He took hold of his arm and gently turned him over onto his side, as he put his friend into the recovery position. "Henley… please talk to me!"

The deputy knelt down beside Barney and reached out to remove Henley's hard hat. "Turn your cap-lamp down… it's too bright – I can't see anything because you keep shining it in my eyes!" he ordered. "Is he alive?"

Barney reached up to his helmet and turned his lamp down to the dim position. He then focused the light on the back of Henley's head and placed two fingers on his neck. "I don't like this boss… I can't feel a pulse – I think we need to turn him on his back!"

"Okay… after three!" agreed the deputy, as they both took hold of Henley's clothing. "One…two…three - lift!"

"Arrrrrrrrgh!" shouted Barney, as he jolted backwards and landed hard against the panzer side.

"Oh my God!" exclaimed the deputy. "His face…it's gone!"

Barney regained his balance, as he lifted himself away from the metal conveyor belt and re-approached the horrific scene. The two men stared in disbelief at their dead mineworker friend. Henley lay still and his facial features had been removed by the sudden movement of the drum. The sharp cutters that he had so meticulously maintained each and every arduous shift had now gouged out the front of his skull. His featureless face glistened, as the black coal dust clung to the open wounds like iron filings to a magnet.

A chilling rush of air gusted from behind the hydraulic chocks and at that moment every light along the coal face flickered then extinguished again. The rays of light beams that emanated from every miners cap lamp along the chock line were snuffed out too, as the coalface fell in to complete darkness.

Barney reached up to his helmet and attempted to turn on his lamp but to no avail. "What's happening... my cap lamp isn't working?"

"I don't know!" shouted the deputy, as he too tried to turn on his light and tucked up his collar to shield his neck. "That wind... it feels so icy and it sounds so eerie!"

"Yeah and it smells disgusting... like decayed flesh!" exclaimed Barney, as he covered his nose to smoother the stench. "It reeks of death!"

There was a sense of confusion and the noise of frightened voices echoed along the coal face, as all the mineworkers panicked in the still of the clammy darkness. Then suddenly the coal face was illuminated again and all the cap lamps re-lit simultaneously, as the commotion stopped.

There was an empty feeling amongst the ranks and the men stared at each other in amazement, as the deputy let out a shocking cry. "He's gone... his body – it's disappeared!"

A search of the district ensued but Henley Baker's body was never found. The cutting of coal at the *number 5* face was halted prematurely and the area where he perished was shut down soon after his disappearance. Up until the colliery's closure in 1992 the haunting sounds of the *Mauled Miner* could be heard along the old underground passageways following the horrific accident.

Many miners refused to work along the Ravenswood seam and most fled the scene when the cold mid-winter winds blew along the district and the eerie hallowing sounds echoed out from behind the old mine workings.

Barney Huddlestone has since retired and still spends most of his afternoons in a drunken state at the bar of Silvermoor Working Men's Club where he continues to recite his tale to any interested listener. The legend of Henley's ghost has passed the test of time long after the unfortunate event.

Patrick Baker swore never to speak of the incident again and he has hidden the truth about his brother from both his children. Bradley and Frannie have never been told about the way their uncle died on that fateful day back in 1975.

....

Follow the Author

DAVID LAWRENCE JONES

http://www.facebook.com/davlawjones

twitter: @DavLawJones

"Like" Bradley's Facebook Page and follow his adventures;

http://www.facebook.com/thebradleybaker

Discover more about Turpol the Gatekeeper (pictured) and all the other characters in the Amazing Adventures series;

http://www.bradley-baker.com